The Regency *Season*

PASSIONATE PROMISES

ANN LETHBRIDGE

Published in Great Britain 2018
By Mills & Boon, an imprint of HarperCollins*Publishers*
1 London Bridge Street, London, SE1 9GF

THE REGENCY SEASON: PASSIONATE PROMISES © 2018
Harlequin Books S.A.

The Duke's Daring Debutante © 2015 Michèle Ann Young
Return of the Prodigal Gilvry © 2014 Michèle Ann Young

ISBN: 978-0-263-93151-8

52-0118

Our policy is to use papers that are natural, renewable and recyclable products and made from wood grown in sustainable forests.
The logging and manufacturing processes conform to the legal environmental regulations of the country of origin.

Printed and bound by
CPI Group (UK) Ltd, Croydon, CR0 4YY

THE DUKE'S
DARING
DEBUTANTE

The *Regency* Season

DANGEROUS DUKES

August 2017

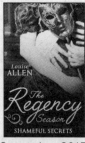

SHAMEFUL SECRETS

September 2017

BLACKMAILED BRIDES

October 2017

RUINED REPUTATIONS

November 2017

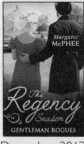

GENTLEMAN ROGUES

December 2017

PASSIONATE PROMISES

January 2018

SCANDALOUS AWAKENING

February 2018

CONVENIENT MARRIAGES

March 2018

WICKED RAKES

April 2018

HIDDEN DESIRES

May 2018

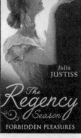

FORBIDDEN PLEASURES

June 2018

DECADENT DUKES

July 2018

Each book has a life of its own and is influenced by many people but I would like to dedicate this book to those who serve their country in whatever capacity they choose as my Dad did in the army. I believe he would have liked my foray into authorship, since he was a dedicated Georgette Heyer fan and loved reading about history.

In her youth, award-winning author, **Ann Lethbridge**, reimagined the Regency romances she read, and now loves writing her own. Now living in Canada, Ann visits Britain every year, where family members understand, so they say, her need to poke around every antiquity within a hundred miles. Learn more about Ann or contact her at www.annlethbridge.com. She loves hearing from readers.

Chapter One

The foul stench coated Minette Rideau's throat. With her skirts held high in one hand and the other clutching Granby's arm, she focussed on taking only tiny sips of air as she picked her way over Bridge Alley's slimy cobbles. One of many narrow passages in the reviled district of St Giles, it led to London's most infamous hell. The only one owned by a duke. Falconwood. The man she now risked her reputation to track down in his lair.

Ancient tenements crowded in on both sides, the glimmer of lanterns behind oilpaper giving them menacing aspects. All around, noises of a seething mass of humanity pierced the darkness. Shouts and curses, music from the tavern on the corner. A child crying. A woman coughing.

So very different from the elegance of Mayfair, but not the worst she'd seen.

Granby halted before a low wooden door bound with iron and set with studs. The lantern above the door cast an oily gleam in the slime oozing along the alley's central runnel.

'This is it?' she asked. 'The Fools' Paradise?'

'It is,' Granby croaked as if his throat was parched.

It had required all of Minette's powers of persuasion to convince Lieutenant, the Honourable Laurence Granby, to be her escort when she'd named her destination. Now he was peering over his shoulder with the expression of one who had regained his sense of self-preservation and feared for his life. Finally he had realised that if this little adventure ever came to light, he was destined for a wagonload of trouble.

He cleared his throat. 'You can't want me to take you in there.' Begging her to change her mind.

An unpleasant sensation squirmed behind her breastbone. A guilty conscience was an uncomfortable companion, but not unfamiliar. Guilt lay behind this expedition to London's worst slums. Even as the idea had germinated, she'd known her escort hadn't deserved to be placed in such an awkward position. Honour balanced against gentlemanly conduct and no way to reconcile either. He was a nice young man. Open. Honest. And too terribly susceptible to female manipulation. For all that her conscience pricked her, in the end she'd been unable to come up with a better alternative.

Worse, it might all be for naught. The man she'd come to for help had been going out of his way to avoid her for years, hence this charade. For all her careful scheming, he could easily turn her away and report her to Gabe, her sister's husband.

If so, she'd have to think of another way to achieve her ends and avert disaster.

A disaster she'd set in motion years before. When she'd been young and exceedingly reckless. Not to mention in love.

She patted Granby's arm. 'Surely you aren't going back on your word?' She put a full measure of disappointment at his lack of courage into her voice.

The young man straightened his shoulders. 'Certainly not. Gentleman, you know. But really—'

'*Courage, mon ami*. Knock. It will be *très amusant, n'est-ce pas*? No one will ever know.' She cast him a blinding smile.

Predictably dazzled, Granby rapped on the door with the head of his walking cane.

A square peephole opened. A glimmer of light quickly blocked by an eye peering out. Pah. Men and their dramatics.

'Ah, 'tis you, sir,' a gruff voice said from behind the door. The peephole snapped shut, and the door swung inwards. The porter's glance slid over her without interest. Unlike proper gentlemen's clubs, here there was no ban on admitting females. It was part of the hell's attraction, along with wickedly deep play. Hopefully there would be others of her gender present tonight. Creating a stir was not her aim. A simple word with the club's owner, His Grace, the Duke of Falconwood, was all she wanted.

Granby tucked her arm under his in a rather sweet gesture of protection and escorted her along a short, dimly lit passage to a red velvet curtain drawn to cover a wide doorway. A liveried lad of about fifteen pulled the curtain aside, and they entered the low-ceilinged subscription room. The smell and haze of cigar smoke hung so thick in the air that Minette struggled not to cough as she gazed at men of every age and social class seated at green baize tables. Games of chance occupied their full attention. Pharo, deep basset, dice, to name but a few. Sovereigns and scraps of paper littered the tabletops. The bowstring-taut atmosphere reeked of both triumph and despair.

No sign of her quarry. The elusive Duke of Falconwood, Freddy to his friends, though she did not rank among their number. Anticipation tensed her shoulders, her stomach fluttering with the hope he wouldn't turn her away mingled with the expectation he would. The unpleasant churning brought bile rising in her throat.

A stocky, pugnacious-looking young man in his thirties, neatly dressed in the style of a butler, his light brown hair fashionably dressed, stepped forward to greet them. 'Lieutenant Granby. What is your pleasure tonight?' The maître d'hotel, then. His gaze focussed on Minette, and she read surprise in his narrowed blue gaze.

She held her breath, waiting for him to turn her away. Instead, he gave her escort a look of enquiry and she let her breath out.

'*Vingt-et-un*, if you don't mind, Barker,' Granby said, as agreed earlier in the evening.

The maître d' settled them at a table and snapped his fingers for a waiter to take their orders while Minette casually glanced around, trying to spot her man. The back of her neck prickled. Awareness. Someone watching.

The suave-looking gentleman seated at the next table leaned back in his seat. His heated gaze took in her face and the low cut of her gown. 'Welcome, lovely lady,' he said, eyeing her escort in the way of a male prepared to compete.

She merely inclined her head and leaned closer to Granby. The gentleman shrugged and turned back to his game.

After an hour of play in which Granby lost a great deal of money to her and there was still no sign of the Duke, she decided her quest was hopeless. So disappointing. And irritating. She'd been certain she would find him here tonight after trying for days to catch him at his lodgings. Now she'd have to think of a different way to meet him. She was running out of ideas.

'Why am I not surprised?' The familiar deep male voice struck a chord low in her stomach. He'd always had that effect on her, though she'd tried to ignore it. As she did now.

Slowly, she put her cards face down and glanced up to meet a pair of dark, insolent eyes set in a lean, saturnine face.

A face of pure male beauty, his eyes of the darkest blue ringed by grey. He'd changed since she'd last seen him. His expression had grown colder, harder, more remote. More darkly fascinating. And while his form remained elegantly slender, he'd broadened across the shoulders to match his six-foot frame, which he now used with great effect to loom over her with all the menace of a greater physical force.

Not that she was surprised by the anger smouldering in his dark eyes. She'd invaded his very masculine sanctum.

'Good evening, Your Grace,' she said coolly, the daringly low cut of her gown seeming far more outrageous than when she'd left home. *Nom d'un nom*, she would not give him the satisfaction of feeling embarrassed. She lifted her chin. *'Quelle surprise.'*

His intense dark gaze shifted to her companion. The cold, hard scrutiny of an offended aristocrat.

'Your servant, Your Grace,' Granby said, rising to bow, colour flooding his face.

A dark eyebrow lifted in question. 'Hardly the place to bring a lady, Lieutenant.'

Granby tugged at his neckcloth. Perspiration popped out on his brow. 'A wager,' he choked out. 'Lady wanted to see the inside of a hell. Debt of honour and all that.'

'Naturally you are not one to argue with a lady.' The Duke's narrowed gaze flicked down to the cards and the guineas on her side of the table. 'Your companion has the devil's own luck, I see.'

He was being careful not to use her name. She couldn't help but be grateful for the courtesy. She offered him a sweet smile. 'Don't you mean skill, Your Grace?'

'A newly won skill, then.'

As she had hoped beyond hope, he hadn't forgotten her

or their card games aboard ship some two years before. While she had played off her feminine wiles to get his attention, he'd treated her as little more than an annoying child. Brat, he had called her on the last occasion he had visited Meak, or any other of her brother-in-law's residences.

'Unfair, sir,' she said, keeping her expression flirtatious. 'I learned from the best.'

His lips quirked at the corners, his eyes glinted, the brief smile making him appear less austere. And more devastatingly handsome. An unwelcome pang pierced her heart. As if she had missed his smiles, which back then had been wickedly teasing. Oh, of a certainty she had missed him. The way one missed a stone in one's shoe.

The maitre d', standing at a little behind him, gave an impatient cough.

The flash of amusement on Freddy's face vanished as quickly as it had appeared. He turned his chilly gaze on her escort. 'Lieutenant, may I offer you a parlour where you can continue your game in private?'

The commanding tone of his voice was something she certainly didn't miss. His attempts to act like her older brother. To take charge, as if he had some authority over her actions. She damped down the instant raising of her hackles. After all, this was the reaction she had set out to achieve. His wanting to protect her from her own folly. Not that she would let him know the full extent of her error.

Granby's expression collapsed into something like relief. He gulped. 'Very civil, Your Grace. Perhaps...' He gave Minette a pleading look. 'Perhaps we should leave?'

Several nearby patrons, including the man who had inspected her when she'd first arrived, had paused in their game to watch the unfolding drama.

'Oh, no,' she said, rising to her feet. 'We should accept His Grace's kind offer.'

Granby's face crumpled. 'Really?'

'Naturellement.'

Freddy bowed, his expression mocking. 'Be so good as to follow me.'

He led them through a door in the back wall of the subscription room. As she passed him in the doorway, Freddy leaned close and murmured in her ear, 'I wonder what Gabe is going to think of this piece of mischief?'

She cast him a glance from beneath her lashes. 'I didn't take you for a tattletale, Your Grace.'

Granby gasped.

His Grace glowered.

Minette gave him her brightest, most innocent smile and breezed past him. Her gamble had paid off. She had his full attention.

Now came the most difficult part of her plan.

Following in the wake of the shamefaced Granby and the clearly recalcitrant Miss Rideau, Freddy curbed his ire. The attraction he'd always felt towards the stunningly beautiful French girl, with her velvety brown eyes flecked with gold and her deliciously creamy skin, of which he and everyone else in the club had seen far too much this evening, had nothing to do with his anger.

He was a normal, red-blooded male, and she was a lovely young woman.

No, it was Minette's lack of respect for the feelings of his friends, Gabe, the Marquess of Mooreshead, and his wife, Nicky, that had him clenching his jaw to the point of cracking his back teeth. How could she be such a little idiot as to come to a place like this? 'Heaven', as his customers like to call his establishment when in the throes of their disillusion. For he had no doubt this was all her doing.

Fortunately for her, Barker, his maître d', knew a member of the Quality when he saw one. The moment Freddy had come in by way of his private entrance, his man had brought him the news that the wrong sort of woman had strayed onto the premises. She wasn't the first lady to wander through his portals. Usually they were older, married, matrons looking for a bit of excitement after doing their marital duty. As long as they were discreet, no one paid them any mind. However, never did freshly minted debutantes like Minette Rideau darken his disreputable door. Neither did he want them to. He liked his women as dissolute as he was, when he bothered with them at all.

She was lucky no one had recognised her. If they had, not even Gabe could save her reputation.

Minette was trouble. Reckless. Heedless. Things the male predator within him had recognised at their very first encounter on board ship. Apparently, she had no more idea than a baby about the harsh truths of the world in which he resided. The need to beat a little sense into the baby-faced Granby pulsed in his blood. How could the man have let her inveigle him this way?

He escorted the pair along a carpeted passageway, the salacious pictures on the walls advertising the purpose of the rooms at the back of the house. Some of his customers preferred their amusements out of the public eye. Such as those who held political positions, where deep play would cause a raised eyebrow or two. Others demanded more carnal forms of entertainment.

Minette carefully kept her eyes lowered, but he knew she saw them.

He opened the door to a room set up for gentlemen who took their cards seriously to the point of utter ruin.

Windowless, panelled in dark wood, the only ornament a marble fireplace and mantel.

Once the pair were inside, Freddy closed the door and turned the key. Granby started.

Freddy put up a hand. 'To ensure we are not interrupted.'

The lieutenant nodded and looked relieved.

Freddy fixed him with a look designed to freeze. 'Are there maggots in your brain, Lieutenant? What do you mean by bringing a gently bred girl to a hell?'

'Pardonnez-moi,' Minette said, her voice equally icy, 'I do not believe what I do is your concern.'

'Well, you believe wrongly,' Freddy said. 'Well, Granby? Are you indeed so bacon-brained you did not realise that any one of your friends might have walked in and recognised Miss Rideau?'

The poor tongue-tied lad gulped and shifted on his feet. 'Told you. Debt of honour.'

Freddy leaned against the doorjamb and crossed his arms over his chest. 'Tell me about this wager of yours.'

'Lady Cargyle's *al fresco* breakfast,' he blurted in a rush.

Freddy waited for the next burst of words. If memory served, the young man had a bit of a stutter, which he manfully controlled by these staccato deliveries.

'Croquet,' Granby choked out. 'Wager. Ball through three hoops with only one knock of the mallet.' He blushed. 'Not possible.'

'So did she?'

'Kicked it through the last one.' He looked at Minette with a wan grin. 'Fair. No rule about kicking.'

Minette lifted a defiant chin.

Unwanted laughter bubbled in Freddy's throat. With great effort he managed to hide it. The girl was a minx.

As smart as paint and always got what she wanted—by fair means or foul, according to a harassed Gabe.

Too bad she wouldn't want— He cut the thought off before it fully formed. He wasn't interested in respectable young females and if he had been, she had certainly never masked her dislike of him from the very first. Intelligent woman.

Now she was staring at him in that direct way she had, as if daring him to criticise.

He focussed on Granby. 'What on earth made you agree to such a hen-witted wager?' He waved a hand to encompass the club.

Minette bridled, her brown eyes flashing sparks of gold. Saints, in a temper she wasn't just beautiful, she looked like a goddess of war. Gabe really needed to take a firmer hand on her bridle or the girl would find herself dished before she had time to make an eligible marriage.

The thought of her married painfully pierced the wall of ice he'd built around his emotions. Really? Mentally, he shook his head. It wasn't possible. He didn't care what she did, as long as it didn't ruin his friendship with Gabe. One of the very few people he valued. He focussed his attention on her young idiot of an escort.

The boy looked as if he wanted the floor to open beneath his feet. 'I didn't know. Secret wager. Written on paper. Held by the judge.'

'I can imagine what you wrote on yours.'

The blush turned fiery. That was the trouble with fair hair and skin—there was no hiding your embarrassment. Freddy felt a grim sense of satisfaction as the discomforted young man swallowed hard. 'Nothing terrible. I swear.'

The fact that Freddy had sympathy for Minette's victim didn't mean he would be let off the hook. 'What? Are you a sheep to be led by the nose?' Some other part of his anatomy more like. 'You are fortunate I do not intend to report you to your colonel for conduct unbefitting.'

Resentment flared in the boy's eyes at the slur. No doubt he was thinking his tormenter was a pot calling the kettle black, but Freddy held his gaze and knew he'd made his point when the lad's shoulders slumped. 'Yes, sir.'

'You can go. As a family friend, I will see Miss Rideau home.'

Granby looked at Minette in question.

An expression flickered over Minette's face. If he had to guess at the meaning of that brief flash in her eyes, he would have said it was triumph. It didn't make sense. Chagrin more likely. Annoyance at being stuck with him as an escort. She knew very well he'd not put up with her nonsense.

She gave Granby the nod of acceptance. He felt as much relief as Granby clearly did that she'd decided not to refuse or make a fuss.

He really ought to tell Gabe about this little escapade, but he wouldn't, as long as she was reasonable. It would only worry Nicky, who he had heard was in a delicate condition. No, Miss Rideau would have to endure a lecture from him instead.

Freddy unlocked the door and opened it wide. 'Lieutenant?' he said softly, making sure the other man heard the authority in his voice. 'Not a word of this evening to anyone. Do I make myself clear?'

The young man snapped a quick salute in reply. 'Wouldn't dream…' he blurted. 'Mum's the word.' He scuttled out.

Freddy closed the door and turned to face the real villain of the piece.

Taking in her false expression of innocence, something inside him snapped. Fear for what might have happened had she chosen some other club in which to exercise her need for adventure. 'What the devil did you think you were doing? Did you want to marry the fellow, or simply ruin his career?'

She recoiled, the colour draining from her face, but, pluck to the backbone, she recovered in a second, squaring her shoulders. 'I wanted to see inside a hell.'

He narrowed his eyes, instinctively sensing dissembling. 'Why?'

The defiant gaze met his square on and, like the first time they had met, he was struck by her fragile beauty and the shadows in those beautiful doelike eyes. Secrets and pain. Once more, he was aware of a very real desire to shield her from a harsh world, even knowing she'd seen far more of it that any gently bred girl should have to witness during the years she'd wandered revolutionary France.

He gestured for her to take a seat. When she did so, he strode to the decanter of brandy and the two glasses on a side table. As was usual in the presence of a beautiful woman, he was aware of his awkward gait. He carried the glasses back to the table, taking care not to spill the contents yet not showing he was in any way conscious of making an effort. He'd had years to practise what other men took for granted. And while the slight halt in his left leg was so much a part of him it rarely discommoded him, it did demand more care in some of the simplest actions of life.

She looked at the glass he set in front of her with an expression of surprise.

'You will find it to be the finest cognac,' he said.

'Smuggled, no doubt.'

He shrugged and sat down in the seat on the other side of the table. 'Naturally. How else is one to obtain French brandy?'

Her shoulders relaxed. She sipped and nodded her approval. 'Excellent.'

'I am glad you approve.'

Her gaze shot to his face as if she suspected him of sarcasm. He was careful to show nothing of what he was feeling. Anger that she'd risked her reputation on a whim. The wish that she'd chosen some other club in which to play her games. No. He was glad she had come to Heaven. At least here she was safe. He took a mental inventory of those present in the subscription room who might know who she was and spread gossip. None sprang to mind.

'What do you think Gabe will say?' he asked. 'Or your sister?'

His jab clearly hit home. Though she disguised her reaction well, the winding of the strings of her reticule around her fingers gave away her nervousness. She had small hands, neat and quick as they knotted and unknotted the delicate cord. Hands that would feel wonderful on his body, stroking and caressing— He cut the thought off, dragged his gaze from their restless twisting. He hated it that he'd made her nervous, but it was as he had intended.

'Does Gabe know you own such a wicked place?' she asked.

Wicked. His body tightened at the image of the sort of wickedness he'd like to engage in with this girl who had become a woman since they'd last met. A beautiful desirable woman he had no right to be near. But, of course, it was the gambling she was talking about, not the other vices rampant beneath his roof. He considered the other import of her words. 'What makes you think I own it?'

'Bah. I'm not a fool. The pugilist dressed as a maître d' went to fetch you and stood back as if you were in charge.'

No, she wasn't a fool. 'I own a part share.' He wondered

what she'd think if she knew who owned the other share. Sceptre had thought it a grand joke.

Her head tilted. 'An odd enterprise for a duke.'

He'd inherited his title a little over a year ago, six or seven months after he had invested in the Fools' Paradise. He still had a nasty feeling in his gut it had been the last straw for his father. The last straw in a long line of them that had caused the apoplexy that had taken his life. He took a long pull at the warming liquid in his glass. 'Why are you here, Minette? If you think I am fooled by that tale of a wager, you can think again.'

Women never did anything without an ulterior motive. Not the intelligent ones. And he had no illusions about the sharpness of her mind.

A crease formed between her straight brows as if she was trying to make up her mind about something. Probably whether she could trust him with the truth. She couldn't, of course, but that was something he didn't intend to point out.

'Tell me,' he said. 'Or explain it to Gabe later. Your choice.'

Looking down at her hands, she slowly unravelled the twisted strings.

Not going to trust him. The hollow ache of disappointment in his gut was a surprise. Perhaps it was merely because he was left with no recourse but to force the issue. He tossed back the balance of his brandy and went to pull the bell.

'Wait,' she said. 'I need to locate someone. I thought you might help me.'

Yet another surprise. His breath caught in his throat. She'd come to him for assistance. The cold inside him seemed to melt a little. As if he liked the idea she'd turned to him for aid. Not good. Not good at all. He was the wrong man to be offering his help to a woman with a reputation to protect. He strode back to the table and looked down at her. 'Who?'

A defiant lift of her chin. 'You must swear to say nothing of this to Gabe or Nicky.'

'Not tell them verbally, or in writing, or both?' Two could play at the game of cheating. She needed to understand that, unlike Granby, he was nobody's fool.

She glared at him. 'Not to tell them in any manner, shape or form through your own actions or that of any other person.'

Another bubble of laughter fought for escape. It was so long since he'd wanted to laugh, no wonder it hurt. But this was no laughing matter. 'You would have made a good lawyer, I think.'

'Women aren't allowed to be lawyers. They are not allowed to do anything useful.'

Oh, was that was she thought? 'Oh, believe me, they have lots of uses.' He let the wicked ideas in his head show in his eyes, echo in his tone of voice.

Undisturbed by the innuendo, she lifted one shoulder in a very Gallic gesture of disdain. 'Men.'

Not a blush in sight. His blood heated. Was it her boldness that attracted him, when most debutantes had him running for the hills? 'So jaded?'

A flash of pain in her eyes, followed by an acceptance he didn't understand, robbed him of amusement. He should not have resorted to idle teasing. They weren't on those kinds of terms. 'I beg your pardon, but that is the sort of male jocularity you exposed yourself to by coming here.'

'Thank you for your concern, but I am perfectly able to take care of myself.'

'Are you?' He pulled her to her feet, tilting her chin with one hand to look down into a stormy gaze that reminded him of trees in autumn lashed by the wind, pulling her hard against his body with the other. Her sweet curves were an aphrodisiac in his blood. His body hardened as he took her mouth in a punishing kiss. *Show me, sweetheart*, he willed. *Resist me*. His heart thundered and blood roared in his ears.

For a satisfying moment he felt her tense, but even as he prepared to force himself to let her go, she melted sweetly, kissing him back with a passion that would have seared his soul. If he'd had one.

His mind blanked of everything except the sensations scorching through his body, the feel of her softness melding into him, the taste of brandy on her silken tongue sliding against his, the scent of her, jasmine and hot summer nights. Delicious. Tempting.

Luscious and...not for him. He pushed her away before he forgot himself entirely.

Twin spots of colour blazed on her cheekbones. Embarrassment. Shame.

Self-loathing burned like acid in his throat. 'See how vulnerable you are?' he said harshly, all too aware of his raging desire and uneven breathing. 'No woman has the strength to prevent a determined man from taking what he wants. Dressed as you are, you told every man in the establishment that you are available and willing.'

Her eyes widened as if he'd wounded her feelings. Good. Perhaps she had learned her lesson. He'd certainly learned his. Keep his distance. 'Give me your word you won't try anything like this again and I'll take you home.'

He reached out to take her arm.

She jerked away. 'If you promise not to tell Gabe about this evening, I will not tell him of your insult to my person.'

Though he showed nothing on his face, he was surprised to discover her words hurt more than a slap would have done. Yet she was right. It had been an insult. Deliberately so. Outcast by the more respectable members of the *ton*, his attentions should be unwelcome. He'd used his reputation for vice to gain the trust of the dregs of society, the informants, the spies, and earned the scorn of his peers. He raised a brow. 'Blackmail. How unworthy. And what do you think Gabe would do? Call me out? He'd be more likely to insist we marry.'

A strange look came to her face. Yet another one he couldn't read. She shook her head. 'No, thank you.'

He did not bother to keep the bitter edge from his tone. 'My sentiments exactly.' He intended never to marry, and certainly wasn't going to let a little chit like her change his mind.

'I wouldn't have had to come here,' she shot back, 'had you responded to my notes.'

Notes he should have returned unopened, instead of stuffing them in his desk drawer. 'A young lady doesn't demand a gentlemen wait on her. It is not good *ton*.'

'Oh, and I suppose you are good *ton*,' she muttered, then lifted her gaze to meet his face. 'You avoided me on purpose.'

He'd been avoiding her like a man avoided the hangman's noose. She was too damnably attractive. 'Well, here I am now.' He poured chill into his voice. No easy task when his body burned with lust. 'Tell me who it is you want found and then I'll take you home.'

'You've no doubt heard that Moreau is back in England.' Clear, velvet-brown eyes met his in challenge.

A spy placed in England by Fouché, Moreau had very nearly succeeded in a plan to assassinate King George. He had used Minette to lure her sister Nicky, now Gabe's wife, into helping him. He'd almost captured Gabe into the bargain. It had been a near-run thing, but ultimately Nicky and Gabe had outwitted him. Moreau's spectacular failure had resulted in him being relocated to Madrid, where he must have helped Napoleon's brother gain the throne of Spain. No doubt back in favour, he was once more assigned to help in the downfall of the only country stopping Napoleon from ruling the whole of Europe. Britain.

'Nothing I didn't already know,' Freddy said. 'And not your concern.'

Her eyes darkened. 'Is it not?' She took a deep breath. 'What if he goes after Nicky? After the way she tricked him…' The slight gesture of her hands encompassed the enormity of what a man like Moreau could do to an enemy.

Admiration caused something in his chest to expand. She looked like such a fragile creature, with her glowing skin and fine bones, while the blood of a Valkyrie ran in her veins. The understanding shook him to the core. He forced himself to focus on the very real danger within her words.

'He will be found and dealt with.'

'Like you dealt with him before? You don't even know what he looks like. I do. And if you won't help me, I will find him by myself.'

The challenge in her voice, her manner, raised his hackles. The Frenchman had a network of informants all over England. One hint that he was at risk of discovery and he wouldn't hesitate to kill.

Anger at her bravado chilled him to the bone. He kept his voice was calm. 'What have you heard?'

'You have to let me help in his capture.'

He almost laughed. But that would have hurt her feelings. And, besides, it wasn't the least bit humorous. 'Do not be ridiculous.'

Her chin went up. 'Someone I know has seen him. I

thought you would want to know. If you won't let me be part of it, I will seek his aid.'

His blood ran cold. Moreau was a dangerous man. A killer when cornered.

'Why this renewed interest in Moreau?' he asked.

Shadows skittered across her face. 'He tried to use me to harm Nicky. I need to know first-hand he is no longer a threat.'

Sincerity shone in her gaze. She'd given him the truth, but only part of it. He'd spent too long working for Sceptre not to recognise a half-truth. 'Trust me to do my job and I will let you know when he is taken care of. Come, I will take you home.' And in the meantime he'd have to discover what she was hiding.

When she hesitated, he gave her a glare that would have turned Granby to a pillar of salt. On Minette, it had no effect.

She glared right back. 'You always did treat me like a child.'

To stop himself from treating her like a desirable woman. Not something she needed to know. 'My carriage awaits us at the back.'

'Would you mind dropping me off in the mews?' she said airily. 'I left the gate open before I left, since no one knew I went out this evening.'

Thus embroiling him deeper in her scheme. He bit back a curse.

Chapter Two

Seated in his curricle, Minette watched Freddy leap nimbly aboard to take the reins. He showed no sign of discomfort or awkwardness. She'd noticed that, although he limped, he did not seem to find whatever ailed his leg an impediment. Except when people offered him a seat as if he were some sort of invalid. Then he looked ready for murder.

The horses' hooves ringing on the cobbles, they turned onto Broad Street. The roads were quiet at this time of night and, in this quarter of Town, ill lit. Ruffians lurked in shadows, watching their passing with keen eyes. It said something about the dangerous air of the man beside her that their carriage suffered no interference and they soon reached the well-kept streets of Mayfair.

'Why do you never come to see Gabe and Nicky?' Minette asked. 'Are you too good for us now you are a duke?'

The streetlight caught his grim expression in stark relief. 'Gabe has moved on. It is better if no one knows of our prior…association.'

Gabe had once worked as a spy, too. 'He saved the King's life.' The attempted assassination had never been mentioned in the newspapers, and Moreau remained at large. The sound of his name in her head left a bitter taste on her tongue. A vile concoction of betrayal, regret and guilt.

'If you would accept my help, I am sure we could find him more quickly,' she said.

'You need someone to put you over a knee and give you a spanking,' he muttered.

She swivelled in her seat to face him and traced a fingertip along the length of his thigh. 'Is that your idea of fun with a woman?'

He turned a choke into a cough, and she smiled innocently up at him as the next streetlamp caught her full in the face.

'You little minx,' he said, when he finally caught his breath. 'You should know better.'

Since Gabe had first warned her and Nicky that Moreau had been recalled to France, she'd been expecting him to show up in England. He wasn't one to leave unfinished business. She'd had her French maid, Christine, ask discreetly among the *émigrés*. Moreau, as he'd called himself in England, had destroyed more lives than the English could even guess at. The families of those people had long memories. 'I have a contact who will give us the name of someone who has seen him.'

'Us.'

He made a sound of scorn, the kind one's elders made when one said something stupid. Apparently her kiss— she resisted the urge to touch her lips where the heat of his mouth on hers still lingered—hadn't convinced him he was dealing with a woman grown. If he knew, if any of them knew what she'd done...

She should never have allowed Nicky to bring her out, as they called it here in London. They all thought her so sweet and innocent. How could she reveal the truth when Nicky had given up her own dreams to protect her little sister? Nicky had married the brutal Count Vilandry to keep Minette safe and she had thrown that sacrifice away. So now she faced the prospect of refusing any and all perfectly acceptable offers of marriage. And there would be offers. She wasn't an antidote, as Gabe called ladies lacking in charms, and the dowry Gabe had so generously bestowed on her made her a very eligible *parti*.

But that was mostly her problem. Worse was the weapon she had given Moreau. He could, whenever he wished, destroy her and Gabe and Nicky with the gift she had given him. He would have no hesitation to use it against them. It did not bear thinking about. 'I won't get in your way. I would help identify him and ask him one question. Nothing more.'

'No.'

Men. They never listened. 'As you please.' She folded her hands in her lap in a parody of innocence.

Freddy shot her an exasperated glance mingled with something she could not quite read. 'If there was any possibility at all of you being able to accomplish the matter alone, you would not have come to me for help.'

The man had a brain. Gabe had said he'd been brilliant at university. Too clever by half, she'd always thought, when she'd tried to cheat him at cards. And he knew it, which was worse. 'It needs money to get my informant to give up what they know.'

He pulled the carriage into the alley behind the mews in Grosvenor Square. Relief shot through her. Until that moment she'd half expected he would give her away to Gabe. At least he wasn't going to give her up tonight. Perhaps she was making some headway.

'You want money.' He sounded aggrieved, as if she should have wanted something different. 'Who is this contact you speak of?'

'Why would I tell you when you won't help me?' Her maid, an *émigrée*, had been given only a titbit of information. 'Please, Freddy.'

'You picked the wrong man for your games. Tomorrow I will have the truth. Or I will reveal the whole to Gabe.'

He tied off the horses' reins, jumped clear and helped her down. He gazed at the garden gate she'd left ajar. 'Bolt that behind you.'

She stepped inside and then turned to look up at him, put her hand on his arm and felt him tense. 'I don't care how much you and Gabe badger me, I will tell you nothing unless you involve me in the plan for Moreau's capture. It is of the utmost importance.' It was the most she dared say and she was surprised she was trusting him this much. Except that he had never made her feel unsafe. Irritated, yes. Annoyed, yes. But never in any danger.

He put his hand on the brick wall and loomed over her. 'Why?'

'I told you. I was his victim. I need to know he can never harm me or Nicky again, even if it means killing him.' She held her breath.

His eyes widened. 'You will not approach him.'

'Not if you agree to my involvement.'

A frustrated growl issued from his throat.

'Don't call in the morning,' she said. 'I will know more tomorrow night. Meet me at Gosport's ball and we can talk again.' She whisked inside and shut and bolted the gate behind her.

A fist slammed against the wood.

'Hush,' she whispered. 'You'll wake someone.'

She fled down the garden path in case he should decide to break his way in, but as she slid through the French doors into the breakfast room she heard the sound of his carriage moving off.

Everything depended on the slim chance she'd told him enough to stop him from exposing her visit to Gabe in the morning.

Nicky's future depended on it.

She touched a finger to her lips, remembering their kiss. How quickly she had responded, how good it had felt. The intensity, almost as if he, too, had felt something deeper between them than passing lust.

Ridiculous. It was his attempt to scare her, that was all. There had never been any doubt in her mind that he disliked her. Probably because she was French. His whole purpose in life was to defeat her countrymen.

'Now, don't you look as fine as fivepence? Bang up to the knocker, you might say.'

Freddy met Barker's gaze in the mirror and grinned. '*Sartorial elegance* are the words you are seeking.'

Barker liked to pretend he came from the stews rather than a respectable merchant family. 'Unlikely.' He narrowed his eyes. 'Pity you can't do something about your expression. You look like a man walking up the steps to the nubbin' cheat.'

The gallows would be preferable to what he had planned for tonight. 'Are you sure no one has seen him?'

'Nary a peep, but we'll find him, given time.'

Freddy cursed. With Minette on the rampage, he didn't have time. Neither did he want to play foolish games with manipulating little baggages like Minette Rideau. He should have gone to see Gabe this morning, but that would have finished any hope he'd have of getting her to talk. He'd recognised the signs. He certainly didn't want her going off half-cocked and ruining any chance they had of finding Moreau before he did any damage. She was as stubborn as she was beautiful. He closed his eyes briefly as the recollection of their kiss flooded his mind. The feel of her soft body pressed against his own. His blood heated. Damn it all, that was the last thing he needed.

He gave one more twitch to his neckcloth and turned from the mirror.

Barker held up his coat, fingering the cloth. 'As fine a bit of yardage as I've ever seen. Weston, did you say?'

'Yes.' He slid his arms into the sleeves, and Barker eased the coat over his shoulders.

It was like slipping into a disguise. The persona of aristocrat, rather than that of owner of a hell-cum-brothel. It was the latter part that stuck in the craw of the *ton*. A gentleman might not mind enjoying its offerings but they didn't want their wives near the owner of a bawdy house. Not that a truly ambitious mama would care if she thought she had a chance at the title.

The main reason he never went to balls and such.

Hopefully, the Gosports wouldn't throw their uninvited guest out on his ear. While the ducal title trumped a mere baron any day of the week, likely his host wouldn't be pleased at such a disgraceful duke darkening his doors.

Freddy grinned at the alliteration. It would make a good title for one of the romances the ladies like to read.

'Is the carriage ready?' he asked.

He'd had his mother's town carriage dragged out and dusted off. Lord, his father must be turning in his grave right now, given the path his heir had decided to follow. As if he wasn't disappointing enough as it was.

'Ready and waiting, guv. Er…I mean, Your Grace.'

'No need to stand on ceremony, Barker. You know me too well for that.' Barker had dragged him home half-seas over too many times after long nights of talking to his eyes and ears in London's lowest taverns to scrape and bow to his title.

Barker grinned. 'Right you are, then, guv. Time we were off.'

Freddy grinned back. Whatever happened, tonight was going to be unpleasant, but at least it wouldn't be boring. Minette Rideau was never dull.

When he arrived at Gosports' house he saw that he had timed his arrival to perfection. The receiving line had already abandoned its post at the head of the stairs, his host and hostess off enjoying their party. He slipped the butler a coach wheel. The man closed his fist over the silver coin and agreed there was no need to announce a latecomer, particularly since he'd come at the behest of another guest.

Following the sound of music, Freddy ascended the stairs to the first floor and located the ballroom. A large drawing room with the furniture removed and a three-man orchestra at one end.

Minette, in proper debutante white, looked glorious, her face flushed, her eyes sparkling as she pirouetted beneath the arm of a fresh-faced youth. This was what a girl like her should be doing. Dancing. Flirting. Establishing herself in society. It would be a shame to spoil all that, but if he had to he would tell Gabe what she'd been up to and have her sent to rusticate at his country house until they had Moreau firmly in their grasp.

Her glance met his across the room. He stilled. Caught by the laughing brightness of her face. His chest tightened. She wouldn't be smiling at him by the end of the evening. Most likely she'd hate him. The thought made him feel colder than usual. He scanned the room, found Gabe and Nicky standing with a group of friends. He took a deep breath and straightened his shoulders.

'Freddy. I didn't know you would be here tonight.' Arthur Stone's cheerful greeting at his back had him spinning around.

Arthur, his cousin, put out a hand to steady him. Freddy gritted his teeth, avoided the clutching hand and smiled. 'A surprise to me, too.'

The slow-top frowned his puzzlement. 'It is good to see you, Freddy.' He winced. 'I suppose I should be calling you Duke now or Falconwood.'

'Freddy will do, cuz. Falconwood sounds too much like Father to me.'

His cousin's open countenance cleared of worry. He had a naturally cheerful disposition and a dullness of intellect Freddy found hard work, but he was a nice enough chap. 'It's hard to believe the old fellow's been gone more than a year, isn't it?' His cousin glanced about him, pity in his eyes. 'There are some chairs over there by the wall if you need to sit down. I'd be more than happy sit and keep you company.'

Pity for Freddy's lame leg. Along with the unease people generally felt around someone less than whole. Not to mention a man whose mother had accused him of making a play for the dukedom. A charge levelled behind his back but never laid to his face. Fratricide. The unspoken word lingered in the air like the smell of rotten eggs.

Rather than offering to plant the man a facer, Freddy ignored the suggestion that he sit, along with those other unspoken sentiments. 'How is the family?'

'The boys are just like me at their age, full of pluck.' His face beamed with pride.

Freddy liked that most about his cousin, his love of his boys. 'I imagine they have grown a great deal since I saw them last.'

'You really ought to pay us a visit. I'll have Liz send you an invitation.'

He couldn't think of anything worse. If Arthur was oversolicitous, his wife vacillated between offers to help the poor benighted invalid and the secret worry that he might yet marry, beget a family of his own and cut out her sons. He had the feeling she agreed with the old duke, his father, that if his older brother had to die in the accident, when they had been little more than boys on the cusp of manhood, it would have been better if Freddy had found the decency to accompany his brother to the pearly gates.

The old man was likely right. And if Freddy had been a kinder man, he would set Liz's mind at rest. He had no intention of passing on what his father had called, on good days, the taint in his blood.

He watched Minette chattering to the woman beside her in the set and found the tension in his shoulders easing. 'Perhaps I'll come down during hunting season.'

'Hunting?' Anxiety creased Arthur's brow. 'It's rough country, you know.' His brow smoothed out. 'Shooting, you mean. The very thing. We can carry a chair out with us in case...' He seemed to realise his words were not going down all that well. 'See how you feel on the day, what?'

Such a dolt, his heir who would one day inherit the dukedom. Biting back the words, he bowed. 'If you will excuse me, I need a drink.'

He found his way to the refreshment table and had the lackey pour him a brandy. A few minutes with Arthur always left him ready for murder. Guilt pushing to the forefront, no doubt. Glass in hand, he watched Gabe and Nicky chat with friends, but could not bring himself to join them. He hated to break up what looked like a merry party. Such a handsome couple and the darlings of the *ton*.

Three years ago he would have wagered his best horse that Gabe would never marry. What must it be like? Marriage? And now incipient fatherhood. The emptiness inside him seemed to expand at the reminder of his vow. He downed the brandy as the group around his friends dispersed and walked over to join them.

'*Quelle surprise,*' Nicky said, greeting him with obvious pleasure. 'I thought you must be hibernating somewhere in the country it is so long since we saw you.'

Gabe rolled his eyes. 'Stop prying.' He gave Freddy an intense look. 'Everything all right?'

'Perfect.'

They both knew it for a lie, but there were too many ears in such a public place to say more. Gabe was no longer involved in espionage. He was part of the establishment now. It was certainly not the right place to reveal what his ward had been up to. Indeed, Freddy hoped that tonight's conversation with Minette would put a halt to any need to do so. The set came to an end and Minette tripped back to her sister, her lovely face radiant. She dipped a curtsey to Freddy. 'Your Grace. How unexpected.'

Minx. She knew he'd have no choice but to gather the information she'd promised. He forced himself to ignore the way his blood stirred at the saucy look she cast up at him from beneath thick russet lashes. Somehow she managed to convey all manner of wickedness with a glance beyond any demure English miss. The French called it *je ne sais quoi*. Whatever it was, it exuded from her skin like sensual perfume.

But he was not completely lacking in the charm department, as more than one woman had told him. Though he suspected it was his title they found alluring. 'Miss Rideau. May I compliment you on your appearance? The other ladies present are no doubt gnashing their teeth.'

Her amber eyes danced with laughter, while her expression remained innocent. 'Or perhaps they are jealous because I am the only unmarried lady such a great personage has deigned to speak with this evening. You only have to dance with me to completely ruin their night.'

Beside him, Nicky shifted. She knew he could not dance and was tender-hearted enough not to want him embarrassed. Strangely, though, Minette's words warmed him deep inside. It was as if she had not noticed his halting gait. Or thought nothing of it. The girl certainly had a way, like no other, of catching him off guard. He kept his face impassive. 'I do not dance, but let us take a stroll about the room, unless you have another partner waiting for this next set?'

'Oh, pooh. 'Tis only Granby and he is nowhere to be seen.' She placed her hand on his arm. 'He must have forgotten.'

The young idiot was probably somewhere hiding behind one of the potted palms strategically placed around the room, in case Freddy was inclined to tell Gabe about his lapse in judgement.

'Run along,' Gabe said, smiling, but with puzzlement clear in his eyes. Not surprising when he and Minette usually traded nothing but barbs.

Gabe turned to Nicky. '*Madame*, may I have this next dance?' His voice was a caress, and Nicky blushed like a girl.

'*Certainement.*'

They strolled out onto dance floor.

Their happiness filled Freddy with gladness for his friend but, damn it, he missed Gabe. They had worked well together.

He guided Minette in a gentle stroll around the dance floor, not bothering to smooth out his gait. When he'd been younger he had spent a great deal of time in front of the mirror, trying to appear normal. It had been a complete waste of time.

'So,' she said, sotto voce, 'you have considered my proposition?'

'The answer remains the same. And in case you have forgotten, it is no.'

Her chin went up.

'Also,' he continued, 'if you even think about going after Moreau yourself, I'll have you arrested for treason.'

Her eyes widened a fraction, something dark skated across their gold-flecked depths that had him tensing. What the hell wasn't she telling him?

Her smile turned mischievous, a feminine sideways glance that had his blood running hot. 'You'd have to catch me first,' she murmured in velvet tones.

God, it sounded salacious, a challenge of a very different sort.

'Stop it,' he said, keeping his voice cold with some effort. 'Keep your tricks for the likes of Granby.'

She laughed. 'If I didn't know better, I might think you were jealous.'

Something like a growl rose in his throat. He stopped it dead.

'My informant discovered someone who has seen Moreau. Knows the name he is using,' she said, as lightly as if she'd passed a comment on the weather.

He only just stopped himself from grabbing her arm and spinning her around to face him. It was the information he and his men had been seeking for weeks. 'Who is this informant?'

She dipped a curtsey at a passing matron of obvious consequence. 'I won't tell, unless you agree to let me speak to Moreau before you arrest him. I have a plan. Bother, here comes Granby. We can't talk here. I'll make an excuse and meet you in the library in a few minutes.'

'Minette—'

But she was already moving towards the lieutenant, who had halted a few feet away, his expression wary.

Damn it. He should leave. See her tomorrow in Gabe's presence. But he had the feeling that if he did not talk to her tonight, she might not be at Gabe's house in the morning. Why the hell did she want to speak with a man who had held her prisoner for several weeks? There was something she had not told them when she had been rescued. Something he had the feeling he needed to know before he went after the man.

He strode out of the ballroom, heading for the library.

Men, Minette thought darkly as she moved down the set with a smile pinned to her lips. They always thought a woman needed protection from the least little thing. She glanced around and didn't see Freddy. Either he would meet her in the library or she would find him on Gabe's doorstep in the morning.

Then how would she get her property back before Moreau was taken?

She should have known Moreau would find a way to get back in favour with Napoleon's spymaster, Fouché. But what was his purpose here in England? If she'd learned one thing about him, it was that he did not like to be crossed. People paid for it, in blood. A shudder ran down her spine.

If only Freddy trusted her enough to know she would never ask for such a concession if it wasn't vital. And trusted her enough not to ask why. Then again, she didn't trust him, either. Men like Moreau and Freddy used people to get what they wanted.

She glanced around. If she was going to meet him before he got impatient and left, it would be best to go before Nicky and Gabe left the dance floor. She smiled at

Granby, took his hand for a backward pass across the set and deliberately stepped on her gown's train. The hem tore beautifully.

'Bother,' she said.

Granby stared at her blankly.

'I tore my lace,' she explained. 'I'll have to pin it. Excuse me.' She dived through the other dancers, making for the door, in her haste brushing the arm of a tall girl in regulation white.

The young woman gave her a hesitant smile. 'Is something wrong?'

Nom d'un nom, now she'd have to be polite or risk causing a stir. 'Someone stepped on my gown.' She pulled at her skirt. 'I can't see, but I think the lace is torn.'

The girl stepped closer, peering down. 'Yes. There is a long strip hanging by a thread.'

Minette gave a theatrical sigh. 'I thought so. I was on my way to pin it.'

'Would you like help?'

Oh, now one of these snooty English *mademoiselles* decided to be kind. They usually ignored her as an upstart *émigrée* trying to steal all the best men on the marriage mart. This one looked a nice young woman, like someone she might have liked to know better. Too bad circumstances demanded she turn her offer down. '*Merci*, but I think I can manage.' She hurried on her way.

The library was only a few doors down from the ballroom, according to a footman, and it wasn't long before she was slipping inside a room lit by one candelabrum on the round central table.

Standing beside it, Freddy's lean, almost saturnine face looked thoroughly devilish. A very handsome if austere devil. Her heart gave a little kick. Most unnerving, when he always seemed so utterly indifferent. Except when they'd kissed. Heat rushed upward, engulfing her face. Thank goodness for the gloom.

She closed the door.

'Well?' he said, his voice low and menacing. 'Who is this person who knows of Moreau's new identity?'

The demand in his voice brought a hot rush of temper to the surface. 'I will tell you when you agree to let me question him.'

'You can do so and welcome, once we have him in chains.'

She folded her arms over her chest. 'If you capture him, you mean. You let him get away once. And without my help you will lose him this time, too.'

His face became even more haughty. 'Are you proposing that I drive you around London chasing shadows? Gabe may be my friend but he isn't a fool. He won't allow his ward to be seen alone in my company.'

'We could pretend to be engaged.' It was an idea she'd had in the night when she'd recalled his words at the hell about Gabe insisting they marry. It had seemed like the perfect answer. Then. Now, from the look of horror on his face, she wished she hadn't mentioned it.

'Have you lost your reason?' His expression changed, became harder. 'Or is it a title you are after?'

Hot anger raced through her veins. As if she would do anything so dishonourable. She struck out at those dark, mocking eyes, her fingers curled into claws, and found her wrist caught in long, strong fingers. Slowly, inexorably he forced her arm behind her back and loomed over her, forcing her to bend back. His breath was a harsh sound in his throat. Her heart raced wildly as she gazed at his beautiful, cruelly smiling mouth inches from hers. 'No?' he murmured with soft menace. 'Then perhaps it is another kiss you seek.'

She froze. Lord help her, but she did want him to kiss her. And more. She swallowed against the dryness in her throat. As if sensing her weakness, her racing pulse, he brushed his mouth across her lips. Recklessly, she kissed him back, twining her free hand around his neck, though she had no need for balance he held her so firmly, so powerfully within one arm. She could not resist the hard, strong feel of his chest against her breasts or the pressure of his thigh between her legs. Such a sweet, painful ache.

She parted her lips to the flick of his tongue and revelled in the way he stroked the inside of her mouth. So stirring, so exciting. So achingly perfect.

He released her wrist and held her close while his mouth and tongue worked their magic. His hand went to her breast, his thumb seeking the hardened peak. A groan rumbled up from his chest.

She made a small sound of longing, knowing the pleasures he could bring with his touch. Her head spun with the sensation of the kiss, the sensation of his hand languorously learning the shape of her breast and teasing at her nipple through the thin layers of fabric. Her insides became all liquid fire and exquisite tension.

She wanted…him. His hardness, inside her. She wanted the vast pleasure a man could bring to a woman, not the pale imitation she achieved in her lonely bed.

As if he knew her inner thoughts and needs, he backed her up until she was pressed against the book shelves. The hand at her back slipped down over her buttocks, his fingers rucking up her skirts, while his other hand continued to caress her breasts, attending to each in turn.

She trembled at the promise of delight. Shook with need as the cool air in the room hit her naked flesh above her stockings. The gown now bunched high behind her back, his fingers, those long clever fingers dipped into the crevasse between her buttocks, tickling and teasing and promising. He withdrew his tongue from her mouth, and she followed it, licking and tasting, tangling with his tongue. And then he sucked.

Her knees gave way at the salacious sensation rippling through her body. Her inner muscles clenched, squeezing and begging for the bliss his body could bring.

She wanted all he could give her and he knew it.

He widened his stance. Unable to resist, she reached between them, cupped him between the legs, found the hard ridge of his arousal and the softness beneath. She caressed him with all her skill, squeezing and rubbing until he groaned into her mouth.

Heady triumph shot through her as he broke free, his breathing as loud and uneven as hers.

He pushed one hand deep into the neckline of her low gown, his warm palm meeting bare, hot flesh, grazing across her thrusting nipple.

His other hand brushed her questing fingers away and cupped the hot flesh between her thighs. She rocked into his palm, increasing the pleasure of his touch tenfold.

So delicious. So unutterably, exquisitely pleasurable. Yet not nearly enough. She wanted him as she hadn't wanted any other man since Pierre's betrayal, perhaps even more. *'S'il vous plaît,'* she whispered in his ear, and felt him shudder at the whisper of her breath across his skin. And the words. The words had such meaning. They spoke of mutual pleasure. Of pleasing. Of wanting.

And how she did want. It had been so long.

His hand left her body to tear at the buttons on his falls. 'I want your breasts,' he said thickly, as if he, too, warred with a hunger so great it could not be denied.

'Ties at the back,' she gasped, longing to feel his mouth and tongue hot and wet on her nipples.

He spun her around, his arousal now pressed against the dip in her buttocks, rocking into her, making her moan with each forward push of his hips, while his hands dealt with the laces of her bodice and then her stays. She reached behind her and cupped him, making him draw in a hiss of breath that caused her insides to quiver with blissful anticipation.

Bodice undone, he brought her around to face him, stepping aside to let the subdued light of the candle play over her breasts. Full and proud, the nipples, dark rose and hard with excitement, jutted towards him, seeking his touch. His gaze travelled to the juncture of her thighs. She knew he must see the evidence of her desire, even as she gazed in longing at his own readiness.

'Lovely,' he said, hoarsely.

She licked her lips.

He covered her with his body and kissed her full and hard, while he took himself in hand in preparation for entry.

'Oh,' a female voice cried.

Freddy cursed, froze, looking down into her face. His eyes widened as if with realisation. He shook his head in disbelief and horror. 'You little fool,' he whispered. 'What in the devil's name have you done?'

Chapter Three

Why the hell hadn't he locked the door? He should have guessed she'd do something to force his hand. A typical female trick. Freddy fastened his buttons and turned to face the intruder, shielding Minette from view as much as was possible. Behind him, he heard the rustle of the adjustment of clothing.

He glared at the young woman in white hovering on the threshold, light spilling in a wide arc into the room. A woman he didn't know, of pale complexion and mousy brown hair. Fortunately the light from the corridor did not reach fully across the room, though the candle gave enough light to reveal their embrace, if not the details. 'You required something?'

The girl, whose pallid face was clearly visible, gulped, her eyes round. 'Oh, no. I was looking for someone. Miss Rideau. She had torn her gown and I thought to offer my pins. Someone said they saw her enter the library. Please, excuse me.'

She started to close the door. God. They were going to get away with it. He moved towards the door to lock it.

'What are you doing here, Priscilla?' A male voice. 'The ballroom is at the other end of this corridor.'

The young woman turned to look at whoever had spoken. 'I was looking for the withdrawing room, Papa. I missed my way.'

'Not meeting someone, are you, my girl?' The door swung back.

Freddy swallowed a curse as he faced an irate-faced gentleman. Lord Sparshott, if he recalled correctly.

'Good God,' the other man said, his face turning turkey red. 'Priscilla—' He halted, and Freddy knew the man had no illusions about what he was seeing.

Sparshott grabbed his daughter's hand. 'Come away. This is no place for a decent gel.'

'I don't see why not,' Freddy said, hoping like hell Minette had herself decently covered. 'I am sure you and your daughter would like to be the first to congratulate Mademoiselle Rideau and me on our betrothal.'

The other man snorted and bowed stiffly. 'My commiserations, *mademoiselle*. Come, child.' He stalked off with his daughter in tow. Just before she disappeared she glanced back over her shoulder. Freddy had the distinct impression there was regret in her eyes.

He closed the door. Hell and damnation, there was no key. Had she planned that, too? He swung around to face her, to assess the full extent of the damage. Thank God she was decently covered, if a bit dishevelled. At a quick glance one could assume it was no more than a kiss they had been sharing in the dark. The dull throb of an arousal denied served to increase his fury.

'You did it on purpose.' He kept his expression cool, his emotions under guard. Now was not the time to express his anger.

'I did not,' she snapped back, her eyes flashing fire.

A fire he would like to have put to better use than an

argument, but it was far too late. He was dished. Done up. Betrothed, when he had planned never to marry.

'Turn around.'

Her jaw dropped. 'Are you going to—?'

'No, I'm bloody well not. I'm going to see you properly laced and back into the ballroom. We have to break the good news to Gabe and Nicky before the gossip gets out of hand.'

'Oh.'

Damn it, had that been disappointment he'd heard in her voice? That they wouldn't finish what they'd started? His body twitched appreciatively at the very idea as she turned around and let him fix what he had undone. Hell and damnation, the girl had made him lose all sense of civility and reason. He should never have met her alone. It had been far too long since he'd taken a woman to his bed. Surrounded by women in the brothel had given him a distaste of coldly commercial transactions. And, if he was honest, seeing Gabe's marital happiness had made him want more. No wonder the first brush of Minette's skin against his palm had sent all his good intentions going up in the flames of lust. Because she was the one woman he had always wanted and could never have for the flick of a finger.

And now he was trapped. After years of him denying his unwanted attraction out of respect for Gabe, who knew of his vow never to marry. Who knew dalliance was all he ever wanted or needed. As Gabe's ward, Minette deserved far better than he would ever be. And a far better life than he could offer. Finished with the buttons and lacings, he spun her round to face him. 'You and your little friend have properly put us in the basket. There's no backing out of this, you know. We are shackled for life.'

She lifted her chin, her eyes huge and roiling with emotion. 'I didn't plan it, you idiot. You kissed me, remember? And, besides, it will be forgotten in a week.'

'It won't. Of all people, you had to pick Sparshott's daughter to help in your schemes. He's one of the biggest sticklers I know. You can be sure he won't let people forget, even after we tie the knot.'

'*Mon Dieu.* You will stop saying I planned this. She saw my hem was torn and offered to help. I said no. She followed me of her own accord.'

'A happy coincidence, then,' he said, trying to bury his frustration. There was no sense in being angry. What was done was done.

She eyed him speculatively, as if she didn't believe his resignation to his fate, and dug in her reticule. 'You had better pin up my hem before we go back.' She handed him some pins.

Grimacing, Freddy fell to one knee and worked on re-attaching the delicate flounce.

The door opened to admit a grim-looking Gabe.

'How very touching,' he drawled, his expression as hard as granite.

'Don't be an ass,' Freddy said, placing the last pin. He leaped to his feet, grabbed Minette's hand and gave his friend a smile he did not feel. Although there was something satisfying in the feel of that small gloved hand within his palm, as if it belonged there. 'We were about to come and find you and share our good news. You can be the first to congratulate us on our betrothal.'

The grimness around Gabe's mouth did not ease. 'I gather, then, that Sparshott did not offer his felicitations.'

Sarcasm. From his friend. They'd often disagreed, but they'd always had mutual respect. 'It was a rather awkward moment.'

Minette's hand quivered in his. His spine stiffened, the

tension growing second by second as he prayed her temper wasn't such that she would deny their engagement and send Gabe's anger over the edge. He was a good friend, but when it came to his women he was very protective. Renewed anger simmered in his own veins. At her role in driving a wedge between him and a man he'd come to think of as a brother. He held Gabe's gaze without flinching. 'Well, aren't you going to wish us happiness?'

Gabe blew out a breath and stuck out a reluctant hand. 'Congratulations.'

The tension in his neck eased as he shook it. He glanced down at Minette and realised she wasn't looking any happier than he felt. He pulled her close and kissed her cheek. 'I'm sorry, Gabe. Our passion got the better of us when we realised we both wanted this. We should have come to speak to you and Nicky right away.'

'We will talk more in the morning. You will both come with me now.' Gabe shot a glance at Minette. 'We need to look like a family with joyous news.'

A bright smile appeared on Minette's lips. *'Bien sûr,'* she said gaily. *'Très heureux.* Is it not so, my dearest Freddy?'

'Without question,' he replied, with an equally false smile.

God help him, what a mess.

To Minette's acutely sensitive emotions, it seemed as if the buzz of conversation ceased when she and Freddy entered the ballroom. But it resumed too quickly to be sure. She held her head high, showing not a scrap of shame on her face. The heat she felt on her cheeks was caused by her anger at Freddy's assumption that she had intended to trick him into marriage.

Why she would care so deeply about what he thought

she didn't know. This engagement was the perfect answer to her conundrum, so why did she feel so uncomfortable inside? The answer struck her in one of those odd flashes of realisation. Freddy's reaction. His horror. Pain stabbed behind her breastbone. The pain of betrayal.

Nonsense. The whole thing was a horrible accident. One she'd find a way to put right.

Shackled for life, he'd said with such cold remoteness. Hardly. She would cry off after a time and that would be that. Not even a duke could force a woman into a marriage she didn't want. This wasn't the Middle Ages. And certainly she wouldn't marry a man who thought he'd been tricked. A girl had her pride.

Sweet smiles and blushes were to be expected from a newly betrothed debutante, so all she needed to do at this moment was curve her lips and fool the world. The anxious look from her sister said it wasn't working, so she surged forward and took both of Nicky's hands in hers. 'Wish me well, sister. His Grace has done me the honour of asking for my hand.'

If anything, Nicky looked even more concerned, but a warning glance from Gabe had her lips curving in the well-practised smile of a politician's wife. 'Dearest,' she said, leaning forward to kiss each of her cheeks. 'Are you sure?' she whispered.

Always Nicky offered her support. And always Minette felt as if she'd let her sister down. She threw her arms around Nicky's neck. 'Positive.' Later would come the recriminations and even later the disappointment of an ended engagement, but right now they would show a united front.

She stepped back and received Gabe's blessing, a formal kiss on each cheek.

Her brother-in-law then shook hands with Freddy.

Nicky also held out her hand, and Freddy bowed over it with the manly elegance that always stole Minette's breath.

'You will be good to her,' Nicky warned.

He nodded and looked perfectly content, as if he really did want this marriage. The man was an excellent actor, easily able to hide his true feelings. He wasn't the only one. She kept her smile bright.

The musicians struck up the opening bars of the next set and everyone's attention drifted slowly away. A quick scan of those about her assured her no one really cared. Her gaze met that of the girl who had accidentally given her and Freddy away. Priscilla.

Seeing that Minette had noticed her regard, the girl offered a tentative smile and mouthed, 'I'm sorry.'

Minette waved an airy hand of forgiveness. Not that she had anything to forgive. This was the outcome she'd wanted. Almost. Freddy's agreement to her plan without all the scandal would have been a hundred times better than what had occurred. She'd seen Lord Sparshott's face as she'd peered around Freddy. He'd definitely realised things had gone quite a bit further than a peck on the cheek or even a passionate kiss. He'd be quick to express shock when she cried off.

A pretend engagement agreed to by both parties in private, as she'd suggested, would have been a much better idea.

Tiens. It was far too late for remorse. What was done was done. But Freddy was wrong about one thing. The situation was not irretrievable.

Freddy left Gabe's study reasonably satisfied with the settlement he had reached with his future wife's outraged brother-in-law. At first, Gabe's attitude had bordered on starchy, but once he realised Freddy had no intention of being anything but generous, and that he intended to observe all the courtesies with regard to his prospective bride, he'd mellowed. They'd even managed a cordial glass of brandy and a toast to the future. Indeed, Freddy had the very real hope he might one day regain the trust of his once best friend.

One thing he had not done had been to relay his suspicions about Minette's entrapment of him or her reasons. That concerned no one but the two of them.

Good God, he was actually going to be married. To a little spitfire who heated his blood beyond reason. Heaven help him. The thought of having her in his bed almost made up for how she'd got him to the sticking point. And the thought of Liz's anger when she heard the news of his engagement was almost worth the price. Not that he intended to do his nephews out of their inheritance. He didn't want children any more than he had wanted a wife.

And that was going to be a problem, based on what he'd learned in Gosport's library. He found Minette's boldness practically irresistible. Before coming to England, she'd not led the innocent, protected life of her peers. And if during that time she'd used her feminine wiles as a means of defence he would not blame her one bit. The fact that she also used them as a weapon, against him, gave him pause. And sent blood racing south.

There were ways to prevent the arrival of children that did not require forgoing mutual pleasure. He certainly wasn't going to let her cry off, as she had suggested.

He would not permit another scandal in his family. Particularly one easily avoided.

And now he would have yet another responsibility he had never wanted. A wife.

No doubt this one would be troublesome. Demanding. Wily. Untrustworthy. Utterly, deliciously sensual. Hell, his mind was wandering again. Theirs was going to be a marriage of convenience. With added benefits. The coldness inside him prevented any deeper feelings. As long as children didn't ensue, everything would be fine.

He headed for the drawing room, where Gabe said Minette was waiting, knocked on the door and entered. She was standing at the window, looking down into the street, standing to one side so she would not be seen.

As always, her feminine allure called to his baser urges.

But it wasn't that alone, it was her audacity, her passion, the energy she exuded. Dangerous attributes to a man in his line of work.

Slowly, she turned to face him. 'Is it done?'

The calmness in her face troubled him. Their dealings had never been calm. No doubt she was trying to hide her triumph at the success of her little plot. He would do well to remember how she had tricked him.

'The terms are agreed upon,' he said.

She nodded.

For some reason, he wanted more than cool looks and calm acceptance. He crossed the room and took her hands in his. They were cold. As icy as her expression. Was she suffering qualms? Too bad. It was too late for second thoughts. He lifted first one hand to his lips and then the other. A formal acknowledgement of their future. 'I will inform my mother of the good news and arrange for an engagement ball at my estate in Kent at the end of next week. That will be time enough to send out invitations. The wedding will take place in three months. After the banns are called.'

She lowered her lashes as if to hide her thoughts, but her gaze was clear when she finally looked at him. 'Engagement ball? Is it really necessary?'

'Gabe insists. And I agree. A ball will confirm our assertion that what Sparshott saw was a congratulatory kiss, as well as uphold your virtue and put paid to some of the gossip. An event attended by all the right people showing their approval will do the trick.'

She looked far from happy. 'What about our other plans? Won't it interfere?'

'I thought this was what you wanted. An engagement, so we can go about together without engendering comment.'

'It was, but is it necessary to involve so many others?'

Could it be that while she wanted the title, she was ashamed of the owner? Or had she been truthful all along and it had been nothing but a dreadful coincidence? None of it mattered. 'We have no choice but to go through with it in proper style.'

'You are right. We will deal with the engagement part later.'

Deal with it? He eyed her narrowly as with quick, short steps she headed for a chair by the hearth and perched on its edge. She gestured for him to sit on the sofa. 'We need to arrange our meeting with the person who can help us find Moreau.'

The reason for this whole fiasco. 'So it was not some Banbury tale?'

A slight shake of her head, a puzzled frown. 'Banbury? I do not understand.'

'It means lies.'

Her face cleared. '*Mon cher* Freddy, you misjudge me but then, you always have. There is a woman who lives in Southwark who can tell us what we need to know. For a consideration, as I mentioned.'

'Us? I wouldn't take a dog of mine to Southwark, let alone a young lady.'

The determined chin came up. 'If you go alone, she

will tell you nothing. Women talk to other women. And she is French.'

'There are other women I can use.'

She shrugged. 'But you do not know her name. Come tomorrow at nine in the morning. I will guide you to her door.'

With a glare, he rose to his feet. 'I will take you driving tomorrow. In Hyde Park. It is important that we be seen together. But we will not be going to Southwark, *je vous assure*.'

'How prettily you speak French,' she said with a catlike smile. 'So perfect. So very English.'

He cursed under his breath. God preserve him from stubborn women. As he saw it, he had two choices. Refuse her request and risk her going off half-cocked without him, or give in.

'Nine tomorrow morning,' he said through gritted teeth.

Surely by then Barker could find this woman, now he knew where to look.

Minette tried to sit still while her maid finished dressing her hair. Anxiety gnawed at her belly. What if Madame Vitesse was lying about her knowledge of Moreau? What if it was a trap? Freddy would be so angry. He would certainly never give her a second chance. No. She had been so very careful. Things had to go according to plan. They must.

'All done, *mademoiselle*,' the maid said, eyeing the effect of her handiwork in the mirror. Curls framing her face. Her hair piled on her crown, ready to receive the straw bonnet whose plumes matched her form-fitting carriage dress of pale blue sarsenet.

Minette rose from the rosewood dressing table and took the bonnet from her maid's hand, placing it on her head, just so. The maid tied the blue velvet ribbon under her left ear. 'You look beautiful, *mademoiselle*. The Duke is sure to be pleased.'

Unlikely, but that was no reason not to look the part.

'Christine, you must promise not to breathe a word of our intention to visit Southwark today to anyone.'

'*Mais, non, mademoiselle*. Your secrets are safe with me. Always.'

Minette believed her. The maid, too, had lost innocent family in France's grand experiment and had been embarrassingly grateful when offered this position. She would not lie to Minette about anything.

Nicky breezed in looking very matronly in a pale green morning gown that clearly showed her expanding waistline. 'Freddy's phaeton is outside the house. He sent his tiger to the door, since he won't leave the horses. Are you ready?'

'Oh, yes.' Ready for battle. She kissed her sister on the cheek and hurried down the stairs. If there was anything to put a man in a temper, she'd learned since coming out, it was keeping his horses fretting at their bits. And an irritated Freddy would only compound the difficulty of her task.

The butler bowed her out of the door with a warm smile. At the kerb stood a shiny black vehicle with wheels picked out in navy and gold, drawn by a pair of matched black horses with white stars on their foreheads. The phaeton had attracted the rapt attention of the street sweeper, who had left his customary post on the corner to stand mouth agape.

Helped up by the waiting footman, Minette bestowed a smile on Freddy. 'Good morning, Your Grace.'

The dark look he gave her did not augur a better mood than yesterday. Fa-la. No more than she'd expected.

He gave the horses the off and the tiger jumped up behind.

When they entered Hyde Park she glowered. 'We were to go to Southwark.'

He reined in the horses. 'Jimmy,' he threw over his shoulder, 'go and find some violets for the lady.'

'Wot, at this time of year, guv?'

'Violets,' Freddy said firmly. 'Take them to Barker. He will arrange for their delivery upon my return.'

The tiger muttered something under his breath and jumped down.

'If you wanted us to be alone, you could have sent him home, instead of on a wild-goose chase,' she said.

'I could. But then I wouldn't have had a reason why we were driving alone.'

'Ah.'

He set the horses in motion. 'Now I'll have the whole of it.'

'I do not understand your meaning.'

A brow shot up. His lips pressed together as if he was seeking to contain words he did not think he should say. After several long seconds he spoke. 'Who is this woman in Southwark and how do you know of her?'

She gave him a glance full of sympathy. 'Your men didn't find her, did they? When we get there you will learn all you need to know.'

He muttered something under his breath. A curse, no doubt. 'I hope you don't live to regret this, Mademoiselle Rideau.'

'Should we not be on a first-name basis now we are betrothed?'

He glanced over at her, his lips eased very slightly, and was that a twinkle in his eyes? 'Minette.'

Yes, indeed, his voice had laughter at the edges.

She smiled at him. 'Come, it will not be so bad, Freddy. We will work together to put Moreau in the ground.'

He gave a slight shake of his head. 'I do not like this game you are playing and, believe me, I'll not be giving you a free hand, my sweet.'

My sweet. Her heart gave an odd little flutter. Too bad he did not mean it. She smiled coolly. 'Naturally not. But there are some things I must insist upon at the outset.'

'We'll deal with those later. Right now I need to know where I am going.'

'We cross the river at London Bridge.'

His expression darkened. 'So I am to follow your directions street by street. You do know Southwark is a hotbed of unsavoury types, do you not?'

'*Naturellement.* But, then, I have you to protect me.'

His jaw flexed, his expression became thoughtful. 'So you do.'

Chapter Four

The drive to London Bridge remained starkly silent, with Freddy apparently too engrossed in managing his team in the press of traffic for conversation. Or too annoyed with her prevarication. Not that the streets were quiet. Indeed, they bustled with people and carriages, assaulting hearing, sight and each indrawn breath. The cacophony of colour, noise and smells became more intense as they drove east. A stench of manure, rotting vegetables and overcrowding battled with the noise of street vendors and vehicles of every kind.

It took more than an hour to reach London Bridge and make their way to Southwark.

'Now where?' he asked, with his usual chilly reserve and an expression she was sure was designed to keep her at a distance. Her and the rest of the world.

'Aren't you going to ask for the address?'

'I have no doubt you will tell me when you are ready. I have no doubt that it will be located among the worst of the slums. You have a penchant for going where no lady should tread.'

A jibe at her presence at his club. So there was to be no quarter given between them. Not that she had really expected it. Not when he still thought she had trapped him on purpose. She almost wished she had, then she wouldn't feel quite so aggrieved, since she could not deny that this engagement suited her purpose admirably. But his anger and distrust gave her a miserable feeling. They had never been friends, but now they were going to have to spend a great deal of time in each other's company, and it would be better if they could at least be cordial.

'The house we seek lies behind St George's Church,' she said.

His mouth tightened but he continued along Borough High Street. As they proceeded, the buildings on either side of the street became meaner and the road muddy and ill maintained.

'When we arrive, let me do the talking,' she said.

'So I am to remain silent and pay the bill.' He sounded less than pleased.

She turned in her seat the better to see his face. 'This family has not been well treated since their arrival in England. They are bourgeoisie. They gave up much to follow the king and feel they have been abandoned.' There were a goodly number of French families living in Southwark who were scratching out the most meagre of livings in the worst of circumstances. 'They no longer trust the English to treat them right.'

'And you think they will trust you?'

She gripped her hands in her lap. 'I don't know. I do know they want their king back in France so they can return home. If they believe this will help, then perhaps, yes.'

'Very well, I'll remain silent. As long as you don't promise them the moon.'

It was a warning he would not let her make promises he could not keep. Fair enough.

'Turn onto Mint Street.'

'You may as well give me the address,' he said, throwing her a glance of suppressed anger.

He was right to be angry. She could not continue to treat him as if she didn't trust him, even if good sense advised caution. She needed his help. 'Well's Court. They are expecting us.'

'How do you know people living in Well's Court?'

She winced at his harsh tone. 'Through my maid, who I found by talking to the parish priest. We *émigrés* help our own whenever possible.'

He halted at the entrance to a small alley. He glanced up at the surrounding buildings and around at the loiterers in the street. He gestured at one of them who lounged over to them. *'M'sieur?'*

He tossed the man a silver coin. 'Mind the horses. There's another for you when we return.'

The man's eyes brightened. He touched his forelock and went to the horses' heads.

'Will they be safe?' she asked.

'It's a little late to be thinking of that.'

Freddy guided Minette through the narrow entrance to the court, surreptitiously checking the small pistol he had tucked into his waistband at the small of his back. He also had a dagger in his boot. Barker, who had been instructed to follow them, would be somewhere nearby. He doubted all these precautions would be needed—it was, after all, broad daylight—but it didn't pay to take chances. Not if he wanted to survive. The contrast between the wealth of Mayfair and the poverty of this area was a stark reminder of the desperation of some of London's people. He placed his hand in the small of her back, ensuring that anyone watching would know he took her safety seriously.

A pang of guilt twisted in his gut. Minette thought

she was in control. In the not-too-distant future she was going to discover he had no intention of involving her in the capture of Moreau. If Gabe knew he'd gone this far, bringing her to such a dangerous part of town, he'd be stringing Freddy up by his thumbs. No, after today, she would discover herself on the sidelines. He would not let her put herself in danger.

A small, ragged boy sitting on a step in front of one of the tenements leapt to his feet the moment they set foot in the courtyard at the end of the alley. He approached warily.

'You are here for Madame Vitesse?' His English was carefully spoken. Not the accent of the local people, but that of a well-tutored boy.

'We are,' Minette replied.

'Follow me, if you please.' The boy led them into the building and up a set of rickety stairs to the third floor. On the landing he opened one of several doors. He reverted to his mother tongue as he spoke to the occupant. 'Maman, they are here.'

A woman of about thirty with hard eyes and a careworn face appeared in the doorway. The look she gave Freddy reminded him of an animal preparing to defend its young, then she turned her attention to Minette. 'You are Christine's mistress?'

'I am.'

'This is your fiancé? The Duke?'

'I am,' Freddy said.

'Come in. We will discuss the matter between us.'

They sat down on a pair of rickety wooden chairs, while their hostess took a stool. She glanced up at the boy. 'See we are not disturbed.'

The boy closed the door, shutting himself outside.

'Christine said you might be able to help us in our search for a certain man,' Minette said.

'For a price,' the woman said.

'How much?' Freddy asked. 'And how can we be sure you have the information we need?'

Minette glared at him. He ignored it. If she thought he was going to sit here like a bump on the proverbial log, she should have known better.

The woman rolled her shoulders. 'You cannot be sure, but this man you seek is as much my enemy as he is yours. If not for him and his like, my husband would be alive and I would be living in Paris.'

'We understand, *madame*,' Minette said gently. 'You have lost much. I would like to help you as well as find the man we seek. We will pay what is reasonable for the information.'

The woman's expression contained resentment. 'I am not asking for charity, *mademoiselle*. The chance to make a decent living, to bring up my son in a good home, not this…' she shuddered, glancing around her '…this rat-infested room, surrounded by criminals who are allowed to wander the streets.'

Many of the criminals were debtors, allowed the freedom of Borough as long as they did not step outside set boundaries, but there were other sorts of criminals here, too, as there were in all the poorer neighbourhoods of London.

'Name your price,' Freddy said. 'And we will see if the information you have is worth it.'

'I personally do not have the information you seek,' the woman said.

Freddy looked up at the ceiling, a plea for divine intervention. None came. 'Why am I not surprised?'

'Freddy,' Minette said in a warning. 'Who does, *madame*?'

'My brother. He hides where you will not find him until our demands are met.'

'Your brother,' Freddy said. 'His name is Vitesse?'

'No.'

Of course not. The woman was a widow, using her married name. To find her brother he'd need her maiden name. No doubt the Alien Office would have collected that when they had permitted her to take up residence in England.

Minette also looked unhappy with the woman's reply. 'You told Christine you had information about Moreau.'

The woman tensed. 'Henri is afraid. He wants to help, but if this man finds out…' She pressed her lips together. 'He needs to know, if anything happens to him, that I will be cared for. It is his duty as the head of our household. It is a small thing to ask.'

'What is it you want?' Minette asked with a very practical tone to her voice.

'Christine says you are to be married. To this Duke.' She nodded at Freddy. 'You will need a trousseau of the finest.'

Freddy frowned, but Minette was smiling. 'You are a seamstress.'

The other woman nodded. 'I do fine work. You will see.' She raised her voice. 'Lilly!'

A girl of around eight peered around the open door. *'Oui, Maman?'*

'Bring them,' the woman commanded.

The child disappeared and returned a moment later, struggling to carry in her arms what looked like three dolls. Madame Vitesse took them from the girl and stood them up on the table. 'This is my work.'

Dolls?

'Oh,' Minette breathed, fingering the fabric of the doll's gown. 'This is beautiful. I have seen nothing like it in London. Look, Freddy, isn't it exquisite?'

Really? He narrowed his eyes at the doll. The dress was some fancy silky stuff, and it revealed quite a bit of the doll's shape above the neckline. Revelation came like a flash. He'd seen something like it in his mother's drawing room as a boy. 'They are dressmaker's dolls.'

Both women looked at him as if he was a dolt.

'You see, *mademoiselle*,' the woman said, 'I was just beginning my business in Paris. I had left my old mistress to start on my own. I had one very important client, a woman at Court. She would have made my name but—' She made a chopping motion with her hand. 'There was nothing. No work. No food. Everything we had we left behind.' Tears welled in her brown eyes. 'Family. Money. Everything. Henri was positive we could start again. But for that I need a patron. I have no contacts here in England. No money for a shop. For fabric.'

'So if we give you money to open a shop, you will tell us what we want to know.'

The woman's face hardened. She shook her head. 'That is only part of it. You will wear the gowns. Go to parties. Talk of my work. Then I will give you the information you seek.'

She was using them. Imposing on Minette in the worst possible way. Anger surged in Freddy's veins. He rose to his feet and glared at the woman, who seemed to shrink in her chair. 'That will take weeks. I am sorry, *madame*, but there are other ways to obtain this information.'

'Freddy is right,' Minette said also rising. 'We do not have time—'

'Two weeks,' the woman said, her face white, her voice weak, scared. 'I can do it all in two weeks.' She glanced over at her daughter. 'Please. For the sake of my children.'

'Not a day over two weeks,' Minette said.

'No,' Freddy said. 'That is too long to have him running freely around England.'

The woman's eyes became crafty, as if she sensed she could drive a wedge between them and come out a winner. 'The man you seek, he has much to do before he is ready. You will not want him alone. You will want his web.' She nodded. 'Web. That is what Henri called it. Move too soon and you will cut off the head, but you will not have the body.'

'If she's right...' Minette said, looking at him.

He clenched his jaw so hard he felt his back teeth give. 'If she's lying, her children will be orphans.'

A satisfied smile crossed the Frenchwoman's face. Clearly she did not believe the threat any more than Minette did, because she was shaking the woman's hand. 'It is a bargain.'

Freddy reached into the pocket in his coat. 'How much do you need to get you started?'

The woman's eyes gleamed. 'A hundred pounds. It will rent the shop and the accommodation above and buy enough fabric for the first gown.' She narrowed her eyes, her gaze running over Minette. 'A carriage gown like this one,' she said, picking up the doll dressed in green velvet with fancy decoration down the front. 'Are you to attend a ball soon?'

'My engagement ball is in a couple of weeks,' Minette said. 'Many important people will attend. It is to be held at my fiancé's estate in Kent.'

The woman beamed. 'You shall wear my gown.'

'Understand this, *madame*,' Freddy said. 'If this delay causes me to fail in my task to find this man, you will not like the consequences.'

The woman's gaze flew to Minette and back to him. 'I assure you all will be well.' She picked up a small cloth bag at her feet and pulled out a bunch of string. 'I will measure now and send a note to say when I will come to you for a fitting. Then we will choose the fabric for the rest of the gowns. Please, stand and I will help you unclothe.'

Minette rose and turned her back to the woman. 'Freddy, please. Madame Vitesse will help us.'

Madame Vitesse was helping her all right. Helping her to be naked.

Freddy's body tightened at the thought of seeing her wearing nothing but little bits of string. Inwardly cursing, he turned his back. 'Hurry up. I don't want to keep my horses waiting any longer than is needed.'

A low laugh from Minette said she didn't believe his impatience for a moment.

It must have been the hoarseness in his voice.

'That went excellently well,' Freddy said, once they were back on the road. 'The woman gulled you. Gowns.' He snorted.

The derisive edge in his voice brought Minette straighter in her seat. 'It could have been worse.'

'I suppose it could. She could have asked me to dress every lady in the *ton*.'

'You are being a bear. This way you will get both him and his men.'

He grunted. 'If I didn't know better, I might think she knew about this betrothal of ours before we did.'

She winced. 'About that. As soon as we have dealt with Moreau, we will announce our engagement is at an end.'

He sent her a look full of disgust. 'And how do you propose to do that?'

'I'll cry off.'

'Wonderful. Tell me what other schemes there are floating around in that lovely head of yours.'

'There is no need for sarcasm.'

'I'm not being sarcastic. I simply want to know what I am in for next.'

Why was he arguing about this? He had made it quite clear he didn't want to wed her any more than she did him. Contrary man. No matter what she said, he would argue. And yet... She frowned. 'Are you saying you actually want this marriage?'

The glance he gave her was full of exasperation and something else. Bleakness? Loneliness? 'I'm saying we don't have a choice. What about Gabe and your sister? If you don't care about anyone else, what about their sensibilities?'

'I will simply inform them we discovered we did not suit after all.'

His chest rose and fell with a huge sigh. A man tried to the limit of his patience. She braced for his next assault. It wasn't long in coming. 'After what Sparshott and his daughter saw, your reputation will be ruined, Minette. Those things don't go away. There will be no decent men throwing their hats in the ring. Not after that. You need the protection of my name.'

For a man who had been so set against marrying, his insistence was odd. Something inside her twisted painfully. Longing. Surely not. The man was marrying her to preserve his honour. Using her for his own purposes, as Pierre had used her. She wasn't fool enough to think it could possibly be more. 'I don't want to get married. To you or anyone else. You don't even like me.' Dash it, why had she given voice to that little bit of resentment?

'I don't dislike you.' His voice was arctic.

'In truth? When you think I planned to trap you into marrying me?'

He winced. 'I beg your pardon. I am as much to blame as you for what happened.'

She gasped theatrically. 'Are you actually apologising?'

'Now who is being sarcastic?'

She laughed. '*Touché*, Your Grace.'

He smiled, albeit a little unwillingly and fleetingly. Still, it made her heart feel a little lighter to see his expression ease. He looked much younger, more approachable. Perhaps... But no. She was right. When this was over they would part company. Because when this was over, even his honour wouldn't be enough to make him want her as his wife.

A pang twisted in her chest. 'Let us see how we feel about it once Moreau is caught.'

He looked unconvinced but resigned, and that was the best she could hope for.

Chapter Five

The next three days were a whirl of activity for Minette. First Madame Vitesse had involved her and Nicky in the selection of a site for her new shop. Nicky had been more than willing to help the woman after Minette had told her that their countrywoman had provided her with assistance, though she did not correct Nicky's misunderstanding that the help had come while Minette had been alone and struggling to survive in France.

If guilt was a pain in her chest, she consoled herself with the knowledge that the seamstress was helping them both, or she would be, once she retrieved her property from Moreau.

Then there had been the fittings—first the promised carriage dress then this evening gown. Not the one for the engagement ball—that would come later in the week. This one was for a rout they'd been invited to at the last moment. She smoothed her hands down her skirts as she sat at the dressing table while her maid put the final touches to her toilette. Madame Vitesse was undoubtedly talented. The gown was extraordinarily beautiful with a floor-length slip of white satin and a white gauze overdress draped in the style of the ancients. Fastened at the side, the overskirt fell to an inch below the knee and was edged with Greek keys. White satin sandals and gloves finished the ensemble.

No one would doubt it was an original or very French.

Tonight would be her and Freddy's first appearance in public since the betrothal announcement. The *ton* would be watching, waiting to see how he reacted to her. Waiting to condemn if he gave the slightest hint he wasn't pleased with the match. After all, he was a duke and she was nothing but an upstart *émigrée*, even if her sister was married to a nobleman who had the support of the royal family.

More importantly, tonight would give her an opportunity to speak to him alone. Madame Vitesse had been none too happy when she'd arrived with this gown. And with good reason.

Christine settled a tiara of carnations, in a colour Madame Vitesse had called maiden's first blush, low on her brow, careful not to disturb the ringlets framing her face and clustered on her crown. She slipped her hands into the elbow-length gloves her maid held out and stood before the pier glass to judge the effect.

Christine sighed. 'Perfect, *mademoiselle*.'

Yes, Madame Vitesse knew her business. It would not be her appearance that put the Duke of Falconwood to shame this evening. She turned away from her reflection at the same moment Nicky entered.

'Oh, my,' Nicky said, her eyes alight with joy and admiration. 'You will outshine them all.' Her hands went to her stomach.

A self-conscious laugh left her lips when she realised Minette's gaze had followed the movement. 'The baby has quickened,' she said a little breathlessly. 'Little flutters deep inside. The doctor said it is quite normal, but honestly they are quite startling.'

An ache pierced Minette's chest. By falling for the

wrong man she had given away the chance to know such joy herself. She shook off the feeling of loss. She would revel in her sister's happiness and be the best aunt any child could have. She crossed the room and hugged Nicky. For several years she had thought she might never see her sister again. The joy of their reunion had been tempered by the knowledge that she had thrown away all that her sister had sacrificed. But she would make amends.

They broke their embrace. 'Turn around,' Nicky said. 'Let me look at you.'

Minette spun around and her skirt gently swayed with her movement.

Christine discreetly withdrew.

'Freddy will be dazzled,' Nicky said. 'I can't believe you two…' Her words trailed off and she cast Minette an enquiring look. A look of concern as well as love.

'I know,' Minette said, putting all the joy and lightness in her words and expression she did not feel deep inside. 'It came as quite a shock to us, too. Who would have guessed that what we thought was dislike was something else entirely?'

She could not bring herself to say the word 'love'. It would be too much of a lie. Even for her. She let her gaze take in her sister, who was dressed in the high fashion of a married woman. The deep turquoise suited her and disguised the coming of a child. 'You look lovely.'

Nicky smiled. 'Gabe loves this colour.' She gave Minette a sly smile. 'And when you are married you won't be stuck with boring old white.' She tipped her head. 'Though I must say you are one of the fortunate few who has the colouring to carry it off.'

They linked arms and headed downstairs.

At the foot of the staircase, two men looked up at the sound of their steps. Both men were dark. Both men were undeniably handsome in their own way. Gabe an absolute charmer with a smile that could melt the hardest of hearts. Naturally he had eyes for no one but Nicky.

Freddy was a very different story. Although his gaze showed approval as he took Minette in from her head to her feet, there was little warmth in him. He used to smile when they had first met years ago. Not at her, but at things Gabe had said. Male humour at things unspoken but understood. He'd even smiled at Nicky from time to time, like a brother at a sister. But where she was concerned, for the most part she'd felt only cool distance.

A layer of ice like a wall to keep her out that seemed to have grown thicker over time.

She wanted to take a hammer to it. Shatter it. Find the man beneath. She'd prefer active dislike to this chilly indifference.

As they reached the bottom step, both men stepped forward, Gabe to take Nicky's arm, his eyes awash with his love as he gazed at his wife, and Freddy to present her with a small posy in a silver holder. The flowers matched those in her hair, but these were real. She took the offering with a curtsey. 'Thank you. How clever of you to find exactly the right shade.'

An expression flashed across his face and if it hadn't been impossible she might have thought he was pleased. 'Lady Mooreshead offered her aid.'

Disappointment flickered to life. No doubt Nicky had arranged the whole thing. 'Thank you, Nicky.'

Her sister gave her an odd look. 'I merely informed His Grace of the colour. No more.'

Gabe was frowning at them as if he sensed something wrong. Minette brought the posy to her nose. 'They are perfect.'

Freddy leaned forward and kissed her cheek, a brief

hot brush of his lips across her skin. 'You are welcome,' he said silkily.

As she met his blue-black gaze she had the impression of heat flaring in their depths. An act for the benefit of others? Or something more?

Coolly, deliberately, he set her away. 'I believe it is time we left.'

As the carriage rocked through the night, Freddy relaxed against the squabs and contemplated the woman he was to marry. Lovely. Beautiful. The words didn't do justice to the vision he'd witnessed walking down the stairs of Gabe's townhouse. Freddy didn't have the words to express what he had felt inside him. She was, of course, both of those things, but she was so much more. Warmth. Light. Joy. And there was also darkness. A shadow that lingered around her as if waiting to blanket her inner glow.

If only she would trust him enough to tell him what caused those shadows. To let him help overcome her dragons. But then again, he didn't have the right to her trust. They might be getting married, but they would never be a husband and a wife in the truest sense.

It was his cross to bear.

How he had managed to hide the jolt of lightning that had coursed through his blood the moment his lips had touched her silky skin, he wasn't sure. He was still reeling from the effects of their other physical contacts. His body wanted her. Hungered for her. And now she was his. Or would be soon.

He didn't deserve her. In the years since he had been Gabe's apprentice, he'd washed his hands in so much blood he'd become insensitive to death and destruction. He'd become a tool for the use of his country. Of Sceptre in particular. Weeding out spies and traitors without fear or favour. It was his role. His purpose. He needed it or he'd be nothing.

And now he was to be a husband to a young woman who, while stubborn and reckless, had always seemed to embody what was right and good with the world. The world of youthful hope for the future. A world in which he'd never belonged. She'd always looked at him in a way that made him think she could see right into his darkness. His unworthiness. No wonder she talked of crying off as soon as the dust settled. A kiss in the dark with a dangerous man in the hope of bending him to her will was one thing, but marriage to such a man was a very different matter.

It was too late for second thoughts.

Honour required that he offer marriage. Honour required that he see it through no matter what. At least he had that much honour left.

The glow of the streetlights flickered across her face, her expression changing with each pass of the light so that it was like watching a disjointed progression of thoughts. Thoughts he could only guess at.

His task was clear. He had to make her want to marry him. Use her passionate nature against her reason. Woo her. Blind her to his faults. Once they were wed, she could do as she pleased.

He realised his hands had curled into tight fists. Anger. Frustration. Regret. So much emotion, when he usually experienced none. Minette made him feel too much. And feelings hurt. He relaxed his hands, glad of the deep shadows inside the carriage.

'How on earth did you manage to extract an invitation from Lady Craddock?' Nicky asked her husband. 'I know she didn't plan to invite us, because the invitations went out weeks ago and we didn't receive one.'

'Craddock belongs to my club,' Gabe said. His teeth

flashed white with a smile. 'I put him in the way of a good investment.'

'I wager Lady Craddock was none too pleased,' Freddy said. The Craddocks, like Sparshott, were part of his mother's clique. They and their high-stickler friends saw themselves as the most important in the land because their roots went far back in the annals of England. Above even the royal house of Hanover, which had thrown its full support behind Mooreshead on the occasion of his marriage to a woman who could have been considered an enemy.

'Let us hope she is too well bred to show her displeasure,' Gabe said, and there was something dangerously protective in his tone. He'd proved before he wouldn't tolerate any insult to his wife. A word in the right quarters could be very damaging to even the wealthiest family, when power was their preferred form of currency.

'Dommage,' Minette said. 'We will dance and talk with our friends. No one will care what the stuffy Craddocks think. Indeed, they will wish they were part of our circle, if they have any sense at all.'

Nicky laughed.

Amused despite his better judgement, Freddy mentally shook his head. Spirit. That was the indefinable quality of Minette. The spirit of a goddess of war.

And that was what made her so damned dangerous.

Freddy didn't dance. Ever. And everyone knew it.

Minette wasn't sure if he didn't because of his lameness, or because he didn't want to. His leg, whatever was wrong with it, didn't stop him from doing anything else, even if he did have a bit of a limp. She'd seen him walk across the deck of a pitching ship without losing his balance or stumbling. She'd seen him play cricket on the lawns at

Meak the first summer she'd arrived in England. Then he'd stopped visiting.

He worked for Sceptre, a secret organisation that carried on the war with Napoleon in the dark world of espionage. She wasn't supposed to know about it, but she'd been there the day Nicky and Gabe had been carted off to appear before the head of the organisation. To Nicky's everlasting gratitude, Gabe had been relieved from active duty. Freddy continued to serve. No one said he did, but there could be no other explanation for why he had disappeared from their lives.

And neither Nicky nor Gabe had ever commented on his absence. It had been as if they had forgotten he existed. Until she'd gone to find him and they'd ended up engaged to be married. She still didn't quite believe she was betrothed. In some ways it was a dream come true. He was a handsome, if aloof, man to whom she had been instantly attracted. Had he shown interest all those years before, she would have been tempted.

Tonight, he had encouraged her to dance every dance with any young man who asked, including Granby, who seemed to have recovered from his funk. She was dancing with him now, while her gaze sought out a very different man. A man so cold that sometimes she thought he would chill her to the bone with a look.

The music came to a close, and Granby walked her back to Nicky, seated among the matrons and chaperones, no doubt having grown tired of standing.

'May I fetch you some refreshment, Miss Rideau? Or you, Lady Mooreshead?' Granby asked.

'I would love some lemonade,' Minette answered.

'Not for me,' Nicky said.

When the young man was out of hearing, Minette scanned the room. 'Where is Freddy?'

'He and Gabe went to the card room.'

Minette frowned. 'Do you think he gambles as much as everyone says?'

Nicky sighed. 'I don't know. His fortune is vast. I would hate to see him lose at the tables the way so many others have done.' She glance around and lowered her voice. 'It may be a front for other activities.'

Surprise that Nicky would mention such a thing must have shown in her face.

'I don't want you to think the worst of him,' Nicky said.

She didn't know *what* to make of him. So often she had felt as if he didn't like her. At other times she thought he also felt the same wild spark of attraction she did, especially when they kissed. Until he looked at her with that chilly expression. Clearly he was set on this marriage. Except tonight he seemed to be avoiding her. Perhaps he had changed his mind.

The disappointment that hollowed out a painful space in her chest didn't make any sense. His changing his mind would make it so much easier to cry off once they found Moreau.

As if her thoughts had conjured him up, Freddy appeared across the other side of the room, listening to something Gabe was saying, his expression austere, his eyes intense. He looked up and his gaze caught hers. She froze in the intensity of that look, so dark, so cold, until a hint of a smile quirked the corners of his mouth and caused flutters low in her belly.

'There they are,' Nicky said, and the connection was gone as if it had never existed. Remoteness fell over his expression like a shutter as he and Gabe sauntered over.

Gabe smiled down at his wife. 'Are you too tired to dance?'

'Never.'

He walked her into the set.

'I am surprised to find you not up on the dance floor,' Freddy said, clearly not caring one way or the other.

'I sat out because I want to know how Nicky was faring.'

'You care for your sister.'

'Of course. She is my family.'

He looked less than convinced.

'You care for your family, surely?' Wasn't that why he undertook deeds society would frown on? To save his country and his family from being crushed beneath the boot of a tyrant?

'It is my duty to care for them.'

Cold duty. As it was his duty to marry her after they'd been caught in the library. The man seemed to have no heart, no passion. Yet his kisses had been more than passionate. They had been searing.

'Would you care to stroll in the gardens?' he asked. 'I am told they are something to see.'

'Someone mentioned they were lit up like Vauxhall Gardens.'

'Worse.' He gave her an odd sort of look. 'There isn't a shadow or a dark walk to be found and a footman at every corner.'

She chuckled. 'No chance for mischief.' She grinned up at him. 'Probably as well in our case. Who knows where temptation would lead?'

His eyes widened a fraction and again the small flash of the smile she adored made an appearance, much to the consternation of her insides. He held out his arm. 'Shall we go and see? After all, given the purpose of our attendance tonight, it wouldn't do for us not to spend any time together.'

A pang pierced her heart at the coldness in his words. A foolish pang that it wasn't his desire to spend time with her but his need to make it appear as if he did. 'Why not?' She placed her arm on his sleeve and they left the ballroom by way of the French doors.

'Is it too cool out here for you?' he asked, as if he really cared. 'Shall I fetch a shawl?'

It was a beautiful June evening. The scent of lilacs and early roses carried on the warm breeze, the walks sparkling with lights strung from trees.

'No, thank you. It is a relief to get out of the heat.'

They walked in a square around the formal garden. 'I am glad for a private moment,' she said. 'I have been wanting to speak with you alone. I thought you might have had some news of our quarry.'

He gave her a considering look. 'Why would you think that?'

'Because Madame Vitesse says someone has been walking around her neighbourhood, asking questions about her brother. She threatens to refuse to help us.'

He frowned, and she had the feeling he had caught him by surprise. 'Not my men. I am keeping to our agreement and so must she or find herself in dire straits.'

His frown deepened, and he paused to pick a rose. He broke the thorns off the stem and handed it to her in what, under other circumstances, might be seen as a very romantic gesture. She inhaled the delicate fragrance.

Once more he offered his arm, and they continued strolling. 'It is not only us looking for Moreau.'

Her breath caught in her throat. 'Who else?'

'The Home Office boys would very much to get their hands on him.'

She understood from the small things Gabe had let fall from time to time that the Home Office and the organisation Freddy worked for were on the same side, working to save England, they were also in competition and their goals did not always align.

'You think it might be them asking questions?'

'Rumours of our man's imminent arrival in Britain have been circulating for weeks. They might be overly bureaucratic at the Home Office but they are not completely without ability.'

'I should let Madame Vitesse know this. Warn her to be careful.' She clutched at his sleeve. 'What if they find him first?'

'It doesn't matter who finds him as long as he is out of action.'

Not true. Not true. She had to be first. Everything depended on it. 'I will see her tomorrow. I have a fitting for the gown I am to wear for the ball at Falconwood. I will impress on her the urgency.'

He stopped and turned her to face him. 'Why is it so important that you speak to him?'

'There is unfinished business between us.' It was all she dared say.

His mouth tightened. 'Very well. Keep your secrets. For now.'

For now. That sounded very much like a threat.

They had almost arrived back where they had started when he led her down a path leading to a walled garden with a display of fountains, each one in its own pool. He didn't linger, but he opened a gate hidden behind some creeper. The scent of lavender and thyme and other herbs filled her nostrils.

And not a lantern in sight.

'I don't think we are supposed to be in here,' she said.

'No.' He closed the gate and shot the bolt. Light from the moon was enough to see by. The party had been deliberately planned to take advantage of the moon for those travelling back to town. They were in a kitchen garden, the house, ablaze with light, only yards away, its top floors visible above the stretch of the wall. But no one inside the house would be able to see them among the shadows.

Her heart gave a loud thump. Not a warning exactly but definitely excitement tinged with a touch of wariness.

'Why did you bring me here?' she asked.

He tucked a hand beneath her chin, tipping her face up and looking down at her. One side of his face was in shadow, the other carved by moonbeams into hard, masculine beauty.

'A chance to talk without interruption.' He cast her a wicked glance that made her toes curl. Wicked and charming both. She had never seen him look quite so handsome or so devilish. 'And besides, you look so lovely, so tempting, I couldn't resist a few minutes on our own.'

The lovely words took her breath away.

It would be so easy to let herself believe he'd meant what he'd said. And so utterly foolish.

But that didn't mean she couldn't enjoy him while it lasted.

Chapter Six

'How did you know about this particular garden?' she asked, the hint of breathlessness in her voice calling to his desires.

'I took a walk when I first arrived.' He always made sure he knew the layout of any place he went. A man never knew when he might need to leave in a hurry. It had also seemed like the perfect spot to begin his campaign of seduction. Passion was the one thing that seemed to go well between them, as evidenced by his simmering lust since their kiss.

With any other woman, all he needed to do was wave the dukedom about a bit. Not with Minette. While her physical desire battered at him, she kept herself, who she was, at a distance. Intriguing and worrying. He did not intend to let her end this betrothal. Thus, he must woo her. Ceaselessly. Until she gave up any thought of crying off.

He caged her face within his fingertips, feeling an overwhelming sense of tenderness. Something that was not part of his plan. The urge to taste her again was like the beat of his heart. Unstoppable.

He lowered his head, slowly, hesitantly, silently asking permission.

Her hands slid up over his shoulders to rest there. She nipped at his lower lip.

A hiss of breath left his lips as lust hardened his body. He took her mouth in a wild and ravening kiss. She responded with a hunger that left him close to mindless.

Her sweet, luscious curves melded with his. A banquet waiting for him to savour it. He couldn't remember the last time he had wanted a woman as badly as he wanted this one. No other woman but she could slake his need. He pressed his thigh between hers, and she gave a sweet little moan of longing. Heat seared his veins as his blood rushed south. He deepened the kiss, tangling his tongue with hers, feeling her lips so soft and sweet moving against his, while her fingers combed the hair at his nape.

Desire shuddered through him.

The urge to lift her skirts and take her against the wall pounded in his blood. She deserved so much more. And, besides, a kiss in the dark between a betrothed couple was acceptable, even expected, but to take her back to the ballroom dishevelled and used hard would be too dishonourable even for him.

He broke their kiss and pulled her close. Breathing rapidly, she rested her cheek on his chest and he bent to kiss her crown, his own breathing none too steady.

'It wouldn't do to be caught out again,' he said gently.

'No,' she agreed, to his body's painful disappointment. She placed a hand on his lapel and stroked the fabric.

Delight with her response to his touch was a wild beat in his blood, despite knowing women were good at pretending things they didn't feel when it suited. This attraction was a positive sign for their marriage. There was much pleasure to be had between them. As long as he made sure not to let things go too far. Not get too out of control.

Hope blossomed in his chest, a strangely warm and

painful feeling that they might indeed have a future. He didn't want to leave the shelter of this garden. He wanted to run his fingers through her glorious mane of glossy brown hair, rip her gown from her luscious curves. He could barely keep himself leashed. Which showed just how little honour he had left. There would be plenty of time for exploration and enjoyment when she was his wife.

'We really should go, before someone misses us,' she said, not moving an inch. She sighed. 'We don't want to set tongues wagging again.'

Wagging tongues were the story of his life. He had told himself a long time ago that he didn't care. But he didn't want her hurt by their vicious gossip. Neither did he want to break his vow by making the mistake of not being fully prepared. 'Yes, we should.' He kissed her forehead and linked his arm through hers, feeling for the first time in a long time a sense of hope.

They strolled back through the moonlight in comfortable silence, until they reached the dazzle of lights strung through trees.

Other couples were also walking around the fountains and along the gravel paths amid the shrubs. The air was redolent with the scent of roses. But all he could smell was her fragrance. Jasmine and summer sun. He wanted to pull her close, press his nose to her skin and inhale.

'Shall we return to the ballroom?' he asked.

'A good idea.' So matter-of-fact. So calm. Certainly she didn't feel as he did. The formal touch of her hand on his sleeve was so light he could barely feel the weight of it, though it burnt him like a brand. Whereas another woman might be blushing and fluttering after that kiss, she seemed unaffected by what had happened between them.

He liked it that she wasn't missish or prone to giggles. He guided her up the terrace steps and into the ballroom, greeting those they passed. There were no suspicious stares but there was curiosity. It wouldn't take much for the old gossip about him to surface. To send them over the edge of propriety and out onto the fringes of society for evermore. He didn't want that for her, he realised with a protective surge.

He would be more careful in future. More in control. More like himself.

The hope inside him died. He wanted her too much. Once they were married, the wooing would have to come to an end.

A swirl of colour and glitter surrounded them. A girl in white stared at them. A tall girl. Rather thin. Right. Sparshott's daughter, Priscilla. When she realised she'd been seen, she hurried forward and dipped a curtsey.

'Your Grace,' she said, so softly he could barely hear her above the noise of the orchestra and the chatter. She raised her gaze to his and it quickly skittered away. Guilt. She should feel guilty.

He bowed. 'Lady Priscilla.'

She offered Minette a smile. 'I did not get a chance to offer you my congratulations the other night. May I do so now?'

Freddy was surprised when Minette smiled back, a gentle sort of forgiving smile. 'You may.' She glanced up at Freddy. 'Lady Priscilla and I have quite a bit to catch up on. Would you mind fetching me a glass of lemonade?'

The girl looked intensely pleased, and her face turned a bright raspberry shade. Good heavens, the girl was painfully shy. And he'd been sent off on an errand. 'It will be my pleasure.'

Each woman dipped a small curtsey and immediately put their heads together as if trading secrets. Now what was his bride-to-be plotting? He hoped like hell it didn't involve him. He had plots of his own.

* * *

'I don't think His Grace likes me very much,' Priscilla said, watching Freddy walk away.

'Don't worry about Falconwood,' Minette said. 'He's like that with everyone.'

'Everyone except you.' Priscilla blushed. 'I am truly am sorry for my gaffe the other evening. I hope I haven't ruined your life. Father says I am the stupidest girl imaginable for always putting my foot in my mouth.'

'Oh, no.' Minette couldn't believe a father would be so cruel. 'If he and I hadn't been so stupid as to meet privately, nothing would have happened.'

'I should not have followed, but you looked so worried I really thought you might need help. It was the worst possible luck, my father coming along right then.'

Priscilla was clearly bent on blaming herself. 'It is water down the river.' Minette patted her arm.

'Under the bridge, I think you mean.'

'Do I? These English sayings are very obscure.'

Priscilla laughed. 'What is done is done, but you know if there is anything I can ever do to make amends, you will let me know, won't you?'

How surprising. It seemed she had indeed made a friend. 'Thank you. I will remember.'

Priscilla cringed a little. 'His Grace is returning. I should go.' The girl pressed her hand and scurried away.

She wasn't surprised at the other woman's cowardice. The expression on Freddy's face wasn't the friendliest. 'Do you have to look quite so, quite so…?'

'Quite so what?' He handed her the lemonade.

'Quite so sternly aristocratic. Looks of that sort would get your head cut off in France.'

He recoiled. Then his mouth quirked in a tiny smile for the second time that evening. Again her heart gave an odd unwelcome lurch. Hopefully he wasn't planning on doing it too often, because she wasn't sure she would be able to resist him.

'Is that what you were plotting?'

'We haven't been plotting anything, either before or now. This is the first time we have really spoken.'

'You seemed on pretty friendly terms.'

He was teasing. She narrowed her eyes at him, but he had already schooled his face into its normal stern aloofness.

He hadn't been aloof outside in the kitchen garden in the dark. Her body heated, as did her face. Blushing. How strange. She hadn't felt the slightest bit embarrassed under the moonlight. What on earth was wrong with her?

Freddy's expression darkened. 'Here comes that idiot Granby.'

Nom d'un nom. If she didn't know better she really might have thought he was jealous. No doubt it was all part of the act to assure the *ton* they were really a couple. She turned in the direction he was looking. It was indeed Granby sidling up to them, his expression hot and bothered. He cleared his throat. 'Good evening, Your Grace, Miss Rideau.'

'Granby,' Freddy said repressively.

'Lieutenant.' Minette gave him a bright smile and dipped her knees.

'I wanted to beg His Grace's pardon. Thought it over. No excuse.'

Freddy's expression didn't ease, but his voice was not unkind when he replied, 'I think the whole incident is better forgotten, don't you?'

More fiery blushes. 'Very good of you, Your Grace.' He tugged at the edge of his jacket. 'Wondered if you'd care to dance this next set, Miss Rideau?'

She glanced up at Freddy. His face remained impassive, no indication that he cared if she danced with Granby.

'Thank you, Lieutenant, I would like that.' She put her hand on his arm.

'I am for the card room,' Freddy said with a slight bow.

It was not disappointment she felt at his display of indifference. Not at all. She had to be glad.

Freddy kept his face expressionless as he left the ballroom. Dancing. She should be dancing with Granby. They were of an age. Whereas he felt ancient. Weighed down by the responsibilities of a dukedom he'd never wanted in the first place and by the mess he now found himself in with regard to Minette. He'd been a fool out there in the garden. Thinking there might be something good in this marriage. He wasn't the right man for her. Never would be.

She'd be better off with a young innocent like Granby. His hands clenched into fists. His inability to retain control had robbed her of choices. When they were married, he would give her all the freedom she needed. The ice inside him grew colder and darker.

He strode into the card room and took an empty seat with men he knew would play hard and drink deep. 'Gentlemen,' he said.

The dealer dealt him his cards.

He didn't emerge from the card room until a footman came to tell him his party was ready to leave. He gathered up his winnings to groans from the other men, who had been hopeful of winning some of their money back.

'Duty calls.' He said the words carefully. It would not do to be seen to have imbibed too much when one was escorting ladies home. Besides, even though he had drunk more than his fair share, he didn't feel more than slightly up in the world. He was accustomed to hours spent quaffing blue ruin in taverns and cognac at his club while keeping his wits about him.

He met Gabe, Nicky and Minette in the foyer.

Gabe frowned at him. 'Ready to leave?'

'Absolutely.'

He held out his arm to Minette, and they walked out the front door and climbed into the carriage. He eyed Gabe warily. 'Something wrong?'

'Tonight was supposed to be damage control,' Gabe said, his tone just a little savage. 'You spent all night in the card room.'

'I did not. Minette and I spent a good long time together.'

'In the gardens, out of sight.'

The implied criticism flicked like a whip across his skin. 'Are you saying you expect us to live in each other's pockets? You know I don't dance. Am I to stand and watch my fiancée flit around the ballroom in the arms of other men, looking sullen? If so, you need Byron, not me.'

'Byron didn't put her reputation at risk.' Gabe's tone was implacable.

'Really, Gabe,' Minette said. 'Am I not supposed to dance at all?'

Freddy clenched his back teeth before he said something stupid like 'No'. And then realised she had actually come to his defence. He frowned at her, puzzled.

'I don't see why you are being so stuffy, Gabe,' she said. 'If we are happy with the way we spent our evening, then you should be, too.'

'They spent enough time together to stem the worst of the gossip,' Nicky said. 'As long as they continue in this way, I think all will be well.'

'Do you? You don't understand our English *ton*, *madame*. They are willing to forgive a romance but they are not willing to forgive indiscretion. You need to give them the romance. Spending half an hour in each other's company doesn't cut it. You might have taken her in for supper at the very least.'

'I am sorry, *mon beau-frère*,' Minette said soothingly. 'I am sure we shall do better next time, *n'est-ce pas*, Freddy?'

There was something in her voice that said she was pleased with the way things had worked out. And that she had not the slightest intention of doing better. No one would be in the least surprised if their passion died a natural death and the engagement ended. But there would be consequences.

Was that what she had been plotting with her friend? No wonder she hadn't been concerned when he'd gone off to pursue his own pleasure while she'd danced with whomsoever she pleased.

He leaned his head back against the squabs and watched her face from beneath half lowered lids. Now he saw the game she played. Well, he would not be foxed. Not by a chit barely out of the schoolroom.

'I will call for you at four tomorrow afternoon. We will drive in Hyde Park.'

'Good,' Gabe said.

Minette looked less than pleased.

Freddy showed his teeth. 'After all, I am sure you have another new gown from Madame Vitesse to show off.'

He could almost hear the grinding of her teeth.

Chapter Seven

Minette liked driving with Freddy. His skill meant she could relax and take in all that Hyde Park had to offer on a June late afternoon. Driving was slow at the fashionable hour, but driving wasn't the point. The afternoon was bright and warm. And despite the odd lazily drifting cloud she felt no need for a wrap or shawl. The perfect climate to show off Madame Vitesse's latest creation in a way that would make the seamstress rub her hands together.

They greeted and were acknowledged by gentlemen on horseback and couples in carriages, but not all the nods they received were warm and friendly. One elderly woman turned her head in a manner that made it clear she disapproved of them.

Freddy pretended not to notice.

'What did you do to her?' Minette asked.

His lips tightened a fraction. 'Lady Ransome is my mother's friend.'

She frowned. 'Then why would she cut you? That is what it is called when one presents you with their back, *ne'st-ce pas*?'

'It was more of a cold shoulder.' His face remained expressionless.

'Why, Freddy?'

He shrugged. 'They do not care for my rackety person any more than my mother does. Owning a gambling hell is hardly the thing for a gentleman.'

She was aware that it was considered *de trop* for a gentleman to be engaged in trade of any kind. But the bleakness in his eyes suggested there was more to it.

'It is not unusual for a mother to publicly disapprove of her son and heir?'

He grimaced. 'She sees me as a usurper of my brother's birthright.'

'You had an older brother?'

His jaw flickered, his shoulders tensed. 'I am surprised you haven't heard. He was killed in a driving accident.'

Pain coloured his voice, followed swiftly by such a coldness of expression it discouraged further enquiries. 'I'm sorry. Were you close?'

'Yes.'

She nodded. 'It would be hard for your mother, losing a child, but she cannot blame you because the law requires you to inherit.'

He took a deep breath and let it go. 'I prefer not to discuss my mother's motives.'

The look on his face was so frozen, so icily cold a shiver slid down her spine. Clearly, he did not want her sympathy. She searched her mind for something to say.

A young lady walking with a woman who looked like a governess caught Minette's eye and waved madly. A welcome distraction. She waved back. 'Freddy, stop. It is Lady Priscilla.'

When the young woman realised she'd been seen, she drew closer to the carriage, her face a little pink, no doubt having received a scold for her enthusiastic greeting.

Freddy drew his phaeton onto the verge so others could pass, and bowed. 'Good day, my lady.'

Lady Priscilla gave him a wary glance but beamed at Minette. 'I wasn't sure you'd see me from all the way up there.'

Freddy's phaeton was indeed fashionably high. Minette leaned over. 'How do you do?'

'Oh, very well. This is my companion, Miss Bernice, who used to be my governess. When I left the schoolroom we could not let her go she is so much a part of the family.'

The companion, a short, thin young lady in a drab coloured walking gown and a pair of spectacles on the tip of a pointy nose, dipped a curtsey.

'I am so glad I saw you,' Lady Priscilla said. 'I wanted to ask if you would care to go shopping tomorrow afternoon with Mama and me? We are going to the warehouse in Houndsditch to choose fabric for new curtains.'

Minette glanced at Freddy. 'We don't have any plans for tomorrow afternoon, do we?'

'None. I did have it in mind to ask you to attend an event with me the day after.'

Minette smiled at Priscilla. 'I would love to go.'

'Good. We always go to Gunter's afterwards for ices. We will call for you at two.'

Freddy bowed again and moved back into the traffic on the drive.

'I thought you said you hadn't known Lady Priscilla long?'

She winced at his frigid tone. He was still suspicious. 'Believe it or not, I met her for the very first time at Gosport's ball. It is strange. I feel as if we have known each other for years. It is nice to find a friend.'

'A fortunate first meeting, then.'

'Oh, for goodness' sake, do not tease. You know what happened was an accident.'

His lips twitched a fraction. 'Very well. We will never mention it again.'

'And I will tell Madame Vitesse that whoever was making enquiries about her brother was not you.'

A brow shot up. She'd clearly surprised him. 'You do believe me, then.'

'Gabe wouldn't have you for a friend if you were without honour. And lying is dishonourable, *n'est pas*?'

He bowed. 'You are as intelligent as you are beautiful, sweetheart.'

Sweetheart. A casual endearment that warmed her through and through. She felt the heat of it rise in her cheeks. 'A compliment?' she shot back, with a glance askance to hide her confusion. 'Now, that is something new.'

'Well, you are my fiancée.'

Something inside her delighted at the teasing note in his voice.

She batted her lashes in pretended flirtatiousness. 'So that is the reason. I suppose it makes sense when we have to keep up appearances. What is this invitation you mentioned to Lady Priscilla?'

'A cricket match at Lord's Ground.'

She wrinkled her nose. 'Cricket is a game I do not understand very well.'

'Mr Brummell is to play for Hampshire.'

For a moment she didn't quite believe she'd heard him correctly. 'Beau Brummell?'

'Indeed.' The teasing twinkle was back in the depths of his blue eyes. 'That Mr Brummell.'

She cast him an arch look. 'It would be important to attend, then.'

'Exceedingly.'

'Do you think we could ask Lady Priscilla to go with us?'

He frowned.

'She feels very badly about what happened. It would go some way to relieve her mind that you do not hold her to blame.'

'Not altogether to blame.'

The mock severity in his voice made her chuckle. 'Then you agree. And it would save Nicky the bother of having to act as chaperone. She becomes very tired in the afternoons.'

'Very well. If your friend will bring her antidote of a companion with her to give the whole event a veritable aura of respectability.'

'Then it is settled. I will ask Lady Priscilla tomorrow.'

This new feeling of harmony between them was very welcome. Indeed, the day seemed brighter than it had before. She glanced up. How strange, the sun was covered by cloud, but she was definitely feeling warm. Apparently, it was nothing to do with the sun, it was a glow inside her at their newfound accord.

They reached the end of the carriage road. 'Do you want to take another turn?' he asked.

She cast him a sideways glance. 'Would you let me drive? I hear lots of ladies own their own carriages and drive themselves.'

'They do.'

'And they have races,' she said, recalling a conversation.

'If that is your plan you can ask someone else to teach you.'

She recoiled from the harsh tone in his voice. 'It is all right for a man to race but not for a woman?'

'It is reckless for anyone.'

Her spine stiffened. Always this man had to be in control. 'Then certainly I will ask someone else. If you would be so good as to drive me home? I must dress for a ball this evening. It would not do to rush my toilette.'

He headed out of the gate.

'Are you also going to Lady Cowper's ball tonight?' she asked, breaking the chilly silence.

'I was not invited. She is another of my mother's friends.'

Did his mother really wield so much influence? 'Then I will look forward to seeing you at the cricket match.'

'I'll send a note to Gabe, just to make sure he approves before you invite your friend.'

'Perfect,' she said.

It was anything but perfect. Once more they were at odds. But one thing was certain, she was going to ask Gabe about Freddy's mother and her friends.

After properly messing up their budding friendship during the drive in the park, Freddy hoped today's outing would regain the ground he'd lost. He'd been a fool to react so strongly to her casual remark about racing. Clearly she had not heard the rumours about what had happened to his brother and he should not allow guilt to ride him so hard.

The past was over and done with, and if his mother could not let it go, he could do no more.

She would not be pleased about his engagement. Not one bit. He'd written to her, of course, given her the news and set things in motion for the betrothal ball. The people on the estate would be delighted. An engagement promised a wedding and a bride promised an heir and all the security of a continuing dynasty. Unfortunately, Mother hadn't replied to his missive. Not one word. No surprise there.

She would do her duty to the dukedom, as she always had done her duty. But no force on earth could make her show anything but martyrdom as she did it. A problem looming on the horizon. The woman's negativity would lend the perfect excuse to Minette's diffidence about the wedding. Something he would have to work hard to counter, when he hadn't yet managed to overcome his fiancée's objections.

Meanwhile, he needed to find out who else was clumsily trying to put a hand on Moreau's collar. He didn't want the Home Office or anyone else queering his pitch.

He had been surprised by Minette's acceptance of his word that it was not him or his men stomping around and poking their noses into finding Madame Vitesse's brother. He had discovered the man's last name. Every foreigner who entered the country had to register with the Department of Aliens and one Henri Latour was no different. But that was all they had done or would do—unless Madame Vitesse did not provide the information she'd promised.

To his relief, the ladies were ready and waiting in the drawing room at Gabe's town house.

'You recall Lady Priscilla and Miss Bernice,' Minette said, the light of mischief in her eyes.

'How could I ever forget you, Lady Priscilla?' he said, bowing, 'or you, Miss Bernice.'

'Too kind,' the companion murmured with a quick nervous glance at his face.

'I am grateful you were able to indulge us this afternoon and become one of our party or we would have had to cancel,' Freddy continued. 'Since I understand Lady Mooreshead had another engagement.'

'One of long standing,' Minette said.

Long-standing as of the day before yesterday. It mattered not one whit who accompanied Minette, provided he had an opportunity to spend time in her company and convince her that she desired to be wed. As long as those occasions were in places where he wouldn't be led any further astray by his lust for the woman. Uncontrolled desire came with unfortunate consequences, like children.

'Are we ready?'

'Nicky wondered if we should put up a picnic basket,' Minette said.

'All looked after.'

Minette gave him a brilliant smile, and he found himself wanting to nip at her full bottom lip as a reminder to keep that smile only for him. Damn it all, when had he ever been possessive about a woman?

Not with any other woman. The thought echoed in his mind. He decided to ignore it. Their engagement wasn't about possession or about passion and it would be wrong to let her think it was anything more. It would be not only dishonourable but cruel. He'd been acquainted with the cruelty of false hope all his life.

He helped the ladies into his carriage, seating the Sparshott party facing forward and Minette next to him on the opposite side.

'Oh,' said Miss Bernice, clearly dismayed. 'I should change places with Miss Rideau. It is not right for me to face forward.'

'Nonsense,' Minette said. 'I understand you do not travel well.'

'You are too kind,' the governess said, 'but I feel I really should insist.'

Freddy looked down his nose at the young woman in his best imitation of duke bored to death. 'I can assure you I have no ungentlemanly intentions towards my fiancée, Miss Bernice.'

The poor woman gasped.

'Freddy,' Minette said admonishingly. 'Take no notice, Miss Bernice. He is putting you to the blush because he is trying to be nice to you.' She gazed up at him. 'Isn't that so?'

'When did you become an expert on my intentions?' Then he smiled at the governess. 'Miss Rideau is correct. But you can blame her for my consideration. When she wrote to tell me of your acceptance of my invitation, she mentioned your affliction. And while it may be more proper for you to sit beside me in the polite world, I prefer you not be made unwell, with all its attendant difficulties.'

'Enough, Freddy,' Minette said. She smiled at Miss Bernice. 'Please, make yourself comfortable, ma'am. It is only a very short journey and I will not speak of our unusual arrangement if you will not.'

Lady Priscilla beamed. 'Poor, dear Bernie. She really is the worst of travellers. And she is very grateful for your kindness.'

The woman gave up with good grace. 'You are very kind, Your Grace. Thank you.'

'Have you ever attended a cricket match, Miss Rideau?' Lady Priscilla asked.

'I played once,' Minette said. 'On the lawn at Meak one summer. I have to admit I had trouble understanding the rules.'

'I expect His Grace will instruct you,' Miss Bernice said.

'Will you, Freddy?' Minette asked, her eyes full of laughter.

'I think between us, Lady Priscilla, who has three brothers, and myself, we should be able to make things clear.'

'Three brothers?' Minette said.

'I know,' Lady Priscilla said with a sigh. 'Such a trial. They are so overprotective.'

'Were they concerned about you coming with me today?' Freddy asked, the darkness inside him rising up.

'Oh, no. They trust Bernie to keep me in line, don't they, dearest?'

The little woman shoved her glasses up her nose, looking terribly unsure.

If they thought a timid companion could handle him, Freddy thought grimly, they were idiots. Which they weren't. He'd met the Sparshott twins and their older brother. He had no doubt at all that he'd find them at Lord's Cricket Ground, glowering at him in case he put a foot wrong with their sister.

The carriage pulled up, and he jumped down. 'This way, ladies. I have bespoken chairs for us.'

Being a duke carried responsibility, but it also had advantages he had, up to now, not utilised. Partly because the opportunity had not arisen, given his current line of work, and partly because he always felt like an impostor. A fraud. No matter what his mother thought, he hated having inherited his brother's title. He'd been set for a career in the army but once he had become heir to the title, his father had made sure no colonel would accept him. Losing one son was enough. If it had been because he'd been worried about Freddy, it might have mollified him, but it had only been out of concern for the succession. Mother, on the other hand, would have been very happy to send him off to war, never to return.

Knowing that, if not for Gabe's offer of employment he might have enlisted as a common soldier, he'd hated the ducal duties so much. The paperwork. The political manoeuvring. The criticism when he failed to live up to his brother's memory.

He shut the door on those useless thoughts. On the past. As time had progressed he'd come to understand that he would never be forgiven for being the one left alive. He'd learned to enclose his pain and guilt in a layer of ice.

He was Falconwood. For as long as he lived. And awaiting him and his guests were tables and chairs set beneath
a shady tree with attendant footmen. 'You should have
a good view from here,' he said as he seated the ladies.
'Champagne?'

'Yes, please,' Minette and Lady Priscilla said together.

'Oh, dear,' Miss Bernice said. 'I really don't think—'

'How about tea for you?' He gave her a gentle smile.

Her frown turned into an expression of heartfelt gratitude. 'Thank you.'

He signalled to the footman, who smartly went about
the business of catering to the ladies' wishes.

'I don't see The Beau,' Minette said, scanning the field.

'No,' Freddy said. 'Hampshire is at bat.'

She wrinkled her nose, staring at the two men at the
crease in what he was becoming to think of as a kittenish expression. It made him want to kiss her every time
she did it.

'He is playing for Hampshire county cricket team and
he is in the clubhouse,' Lady Priscilla elaborated further.
'Only two people are at bat at any one time.'

Minette seemed satisfied with the explanation and sat
back to watch, with the occasional explanation from either Lady Priscilla or himself when terms like 'bowled'
and 'stumped' came up.

The buzz of insects, the crack of the bat, the shouts of
'Huzzah' and polite applause of the ladies washed over
him in a wave of nostalgia. It was such a familiar scene.
He and Reggie had played on the local village team that
last year. Happy memories he hadn't recalled for years.

And if it hadn't been for his engagement, he might
never have experienced them again, so focussed had he
become on the darkness of what he did. He glanced at his
betrothed, at her lively, beautiful face as she listened to

something Lady Priscilla was explaining, and felt wonder at the feeling of the rightness of the day. Perhaps he could have this for the rest of his life.

Deserved or not.

Once he had served the ladies, the footman handed Freddy a glass of champagne. He lowered himself to the ground, his back to the tree, and settled in to enjoy watching his fiancée try to understand the rules of play.

'Oh, well caught, sir,' he called out, along with several others at a particularly good catch.

Minette glanced over at him with a smile. 'You like this game.'

It wasn't really a question, but he answered anyway. 'I do.'

'Do you also belong to a team?'

It was an innocent enough question, but it meant more than she might have guessed because she didn't see any reason why he might not belong to a team. The villagers hadn't minded his lameness, either. He may not have been a fast runner but he could hit, and had a good eye when it came to catching. He grinned at her. Yes, he was actually grinning. 'Dukes have their dignity to maintain, you know.'

She laughed. 'Lazybones.'

Out of the corner of his eye he noticed the companion twitching anxiously. Looking as if she felt the need to set the record straight, to defend him from the accusation of laziness and attribute it to his lame leg. His grin died.

'Oh, look!' Minette said. 'That is Monsieur Brummell. I really thought it was a tease to get me to come with you today.'

Brummell strode out onto the pitch to a round of applause and a few catcalls. As usual he looked cool and elegant.

'How on earth did they convince him to take part?' Lady Priscilla asked. 'I heard he hates any form of violent exercise.'

They watched in silent awe as the arbiter of fashion made run after run, reaching a grand total of twenty-three before he was finally caught. The man was good. He bowed to the applause that broke out as he left.

During the interval, the servants served delicacies designed to please the ladies—cucumber sandwiches and little cakes, along with more champagne and a fresh pot of tea.

'It is all so very English,' Minette said, glancing over at him with a challenging look.

'Is that good or bad?'

'Très bon,' she said in a decided way that gave him a sense of great contentment he found unexpected. She frowned. 'There is a man over there, he keeps looking this way.'

He kept his voice low, for her ears only. 'He's probably wishing he was here instead of me, given my lovely companions.'

She sat up a little straighter. 'Are you flirting with me, Freddy?'

'Is it not the duty of a fiancé to flirt with his intended?'

The kittenish look reappeared. 'Now you really are teasing.' She smiled at him, and something inside him contracted.

It wasn't lust, though there was always an undercurrent of that whenever she was nearby, it was about liking. Not something he had ever expected. On a day like today, it was too easy to imagine living this sort of life of easy companionship, mutual respect perhaps even— No. That was too much to ask. This marriage was all about maintaining the proprieties and keeping Gabe's friendship. It would only ever be one small facet of his life, of necessity.

'He's coming over,' Minette said.

Arthur. A cold fist settled in his gut. He rose to his feet. 'Cousin,' he said as the man reached them.

'I hear congratulations are in order,' Arthur said, his expression sour.

'Thank you, cuz. I did not expect to see you here today.'

'Liz's idea,' his cousin said, kicking at a tuft of grass.

Ah, yes. Liz would have been shocked to her toes at the news. Freddy couldn't help feeling a little twinge of satisfaction. Not that his impending marriage would alter the line of inheritance at all, but it might shake Liz out of her complacency.

'May I introduce you to my betrothed, Mademoiselle Rideau, her friend, Lady Priscilla, and her companion, Miss Bernice? Authur Stone. My cousin.'

Arthur bowed low over the two young ladies' hands and gave Miss Bernice a brief nod. It was without question the appropriate greeting, but Minette bristled. Once she knew Arthur, she would understand that his cousin had little or no self-esteem and, therefore, establishing the order of precedence was of prime importance.

'It is delightful to meet a member of Freddy's family,' Minette said, dipping a curtsey. 'You are the first.'

'I was at Gosport's ball,' Arthur said with a disapproving frown, 'though it did not seem quite the right time for introductions.'

Minette raised a questioning brow.

Arthur rocked on his heels, his ears turning pink. 'I had another engagement.'

No doubt he had scuttled off to confer with his wife. Minette smiled and said nothing.

'Are the boys here?' Freddy asked, looking around. 'And Liz?'

'No. I am here with a friend.' He winced. 'Didn't expect to see you here, old chap, cricket not being your sort of thing.' More foot-shuffling. 'Do you think we can have a word in private?'

'It looks as if the match is about to start again,' Lady Priscilla said.

The players were striding onto the field, talking and laughing, with Beau Brummell in their midst. They separated to take up their various positions. With the attention now focussed on play, Arthur leaned closer. 'About this engagement of yours. Do you think it is such a good idea?'

'I don't think it is any of your business, actually,' Freddy said, smiling.

Arthur flinched. 'There is the business of the *accident*.' He glanced around and lowered his voice still further. 'New information might come to light at any time. No statute of limitations, and that sort of thing.'

Freddy turned to face him square on, his anger icy in his veins. Arthur had always sworn he'd seen nothing of the accident. 'Have you regained your memory, then?'

The other man turned back to the game. 'I was a boy. I panicked. But in hindsight there are things I remember. Perhaps.'

Freddy's hand curled into fists. This was Liz's work, no doubt. 'Go to hell, Arthur. Whatever scandal arises will taint you, too, you know.'

Arthur shrivelled in on himself. 'You should think about it, though,' he said. 'That's all. Think about it.'

Freddy wanted to strangle him. Or Liz. Or both of them together. But they were his family. And he'd already been the death of one member of it. 'Tell Liz she has nothing to fear with regard to the succession.'

A shout went up and he turned his head to see a ball heading straight at his party. An excellent hit over the boundary. He stretched out a hand and caught it to a burst of applause.

'Well caught, sir,' someone yelled.

He threw it back to the bowler, who bowed his thanks. Meanwhile, the batsman was awarded six runs.

He glanced around. Arthur, the sniveller, had taken the opportunity to scuttle off and was now talking to a group a little distance away, but he must have felt Freddy's gaze on him because he half turned and gave a terse nod of understanding. It seemed he was content to accept Freddy's word, for now.

'Freddy,' Minette said, smiling at him over her shoulder. 'I cannot believe you caught that ball. They will surely ask you to join their team.'

The bitterness inside him escaped his control. 'No. They won't. I can't run.' And everyone knew it. Half of them had been at school with him.

Her expression of shock at his harsh words followed quickly by the look of pity in her lovely brown eyes only made him feel worse.

Damn it all. He never whined about his foot. 'And as I told you, dukes are far too important to be playing silly games. I invited you because you need to know about one of England's most important institutions.'

The ice coating his voice must have reached her as her back straightened. The smile disappeared. 'You are right.' She turned away from him and addressed a remark to Lady Priscilla.

He didn't hear what she said for the angry rush of blood in his ears.

Curse Arthur. If he really knew something, why had

he never mentioned it before? He was bluffing. Applying pressure.

And with that sort of thing in the wind, the thought of Minette meeting Mother made him feel physically ill.

Chapter Eight

While Freddy had maintained an outward calm and the rest of the afternoon had been enjoyable, it was perfectly clear to Minette he had withdrawn inside himself. Leaving only a walking, talking, icy shell.

The guilt of her careless words weighed her down, but it wasn't until after they had deposited Priscilla and her companion on the Sparshott doorstep and the carriage had moved off again that she dared to broach the subject. 'I beg your pardon. When I said about you joining the team, I forgot about your leg. I did not mean to cause you embarrassment.'

'You didn't.' His voice was shards of ice grating down her spine.

Oh, the man was too infuriating. 'Then why are you being so distant?'

He blinked. And something more humane appeared in his dark blue gaze. 'I apologise. I was thinking about something someone said.'

A flash of light went off in her brain. 'Your cousin. He said something that upset you, didn't he?' She pressed a hand to her stomach to still the sense of unease she felt.

His expression shuttered.

'I see.' She folded her hands in her lap. 'You do not trust me.'

'It isn't that.'

'Then what?'

'It is old family business. I'm sorry, I should not have let it affect me that way. But there is something else I need to tell you. We have the name of Madame Vitesse's *brother*. He is Henri Latour and he has black hair and brown eyes and a scar at the base of his right thumb.'

She gasped at the detail. 'How do you know this?'

'If I know it, the Home Office knows it, too. You need to trust me in this, Minette. Convince Madame Vitesse to put us in touch with the man right away and give me the information, or they will make a mess of the whole business.'

He had not answered her question, but it was no longer of importance.

'I apologise for not trusting you, Freddy. And I will persuade her to tell us everything. If you will promise to trust me.'

If he didn't Nicky's life would be ruined.

He regarded her for a long moment. 'I trust you.'

Her foolish heart gave a little skip. But her foolish heart did not always listen to reason. She only dared trust Freddy in this. After that she was on her own, as she had always been.

Minette called on Madame Vitesse the next morning. The interview proved uncomfortable, to say the least, once the woman realised what she was asking.

The woman folded her arms across her chest. 'You have not yet kept your side of our bargain.'

Minette lifted her chin. 'Why should I, if someone else obtains the information before I do?'

Madame Vitesse blinked. 'No one but me knows where my brother is.'

'You know that is not true. Someone knows. A street sweeper. An innkeeper. A landlady. There is always someone. And those seeking him are not all as honourable as Falconwood. He *will* keep his word to you. I *will* wear your gowns.' She reached out and grasped the other woman's hand in her own. 'Why would I not? They are beautiful. Unique. I have had more compliments this past week than ever before.' She gestured around the upstairs workshop at the women plying their needles. 'You already have more work than you can handle alone.'

Madame Vitesse swallowed. 'He is the only family I have left, apart from the children.'

'We both know what it is to try to protect our families,' she said softly. 'If I don't find this man we seek, if others reach him before me, those I care about will be in danger.'

The woman took a deep breath and leaned close. 'You will find Henri in the evenings at the The Town of Ramsgate in Wapping. He has work at the docks. There he goes by the name Henry Tower. It is what the English call him.'

Minette squeezed her hand. 'Thank you. I promise you will not regret it. Now, let me try on the ballgown.' She had to hurry. Freddy would want to hear this news.

'*Merci, Mademoiselle*. You are very kind.'

'Not at all. We Frenchwomen must stick together.'

Freddy left his phaeton with his tiger. She had apologised for not trusting him. Twice. Freddy didn't believe it. The lady doth protest too much. Shakespeare might be every schoolboy's worst nightmare, but he was also an insightful man. If Freddy had to make a wager on it, he'd bet his estate that Minette didn't trust him one little bit. And he couldn't help but wonder who had abused the trust of such a very young woman.

He glanced down at the note he had received at his lodgings.

I have what we need. Call for me in your phaeton.
I will tell Nicky we have arranged to go for a drive,
but come late, after six.

Given his visceral understanding, how was he to convince her to trust him to visit the seamstress's brother without her? Appeal to her sense? The risk? Danger came in a variety of guises. If the Home Office boys followed them, who the hell knew what they would do with the information that his French fiancée was involved in Sceptre business?

The butler bowed him into the Mooreshead town house. 'The ladies are in the drawing room, Your Grace.'

'Thank you. No need to show me up, I am expected.' He climbed the stairs to the first floor and found Nicky working on some embroidery while Minette read aloud. A picture of domesticity that tugged at a chord in his chest. Longing. Good God, since when had he found such dullness appealing? He didn't.

Minette put the book down the moment he entered. 'Freddy, what took you so long? I thought you were to come earlier.'

'One of my horses threw a shoe.' He bowed to Nicky. 'Good day, Lady Mooreshead. I hope I find you well?'

'Very well indeed,' Nicky said with a warm smile. She looked radiant. 'I am glad you are finally here to take this fidget out for a drive.'

Minette laughed. 'She made me read to stop me from pacing. It won't take me a minute or two to get my hat.'

She dashed from the room.

Nicky shook her head. 'So much vivacity. I am glad you are able to take her out. Gabe is so busy with the estate and Parliament he scarcely has a moment to spare.' She touched a hand to her stomach then blushed. 'The very thought of getting into a carriage makes me feel unwell at the moment.'

A child. What would it be like to bring another being into the world? One to care for and who would follow in your footsteps? Bile rose in his throat. Not his footsteps. He forced a smile. 'Then I am glad to relieve you of the duty and make it my pleasure. It is the only chance we have to converse alone.'

Nicky's eyes shadowed. 'You are sure about this, Freddy? I would hate her to marry for such a reason and be made unhappy.'

Frank words indeed. His shoulders tensed. The ice inside him spread outwards. 'I will do nothing to make her regret our union.' She would be a duchess, and have everything any woman could ever want. As long as she didn't want children. Thankfully she need never know it was by design rather than accident.

Minette appeared in the doorway, bonnet on her head and sunshade in hand.

'We are lucky it is not raining,' she said, once they were settled in his phaeton.

'Don't count your chickens,' he said, looking up at the fluffy clouds floating above their heads. Some of them had the darkness of rain in their hearts.

'Your tiger doesn't come with us?'

'He will wait for our return. I assumed we needed a bit of privacy. What did Madame Vitesse have to say?'

'I know where to find her brother. He is using the name Henry Tower and working at the docks. We can find him at an inn, The Town of Ramsgate, in Wapping, at the end of the workday.'

'The reason you asked me to delay our drive until later.'

She nodded. 'I am hoping we will find him there this evening.'

'Devil take it, Minette, gently bred girls do not visit dockyard taverns. I will tell you everything when I return.'

She folded her arms across her chest and glared at him. 'Nonsense. It's an inn. A public place.' She leaned closer. 'What could happen with you there to protect me?' She glared when she realised he was not going to change his mind. 'Now I wish I had kept this information to myself.'

'Wasn't it bad enough that you came to the Paradise, without exposing yourself to the sort of men who frequent a place like the Ramsgate?'

'There you go again, treating me like a child. Well, I'm not a child. And the taverns in France are far more dangerous than anything here England.'

She'd been a child when Nicky had left. He could well imagine what a girl left to fend for herself might have encountered. Or seen. The idea of it made his hands curl into fists. He forced himself to ease off on the ribbons before his horses did more than toss their heads in objection. 'You are not in France now. I will meet Henry and relay what he says upon my return.'

'Then I won't know anything for two days. We are invited to visit some friends of Gabe's and will leave early in the morning. We won't be back until the day after tomorrow.'

'It can wait a day or two.'

She huffed out a breath. 'I hate waiting.'

The urge to laugh surprised him. In some ways she was older than her years and in others she seemed so much younger than him. Not that he would dare show his amusement. He could certainly see from the determined look on her face that she wouldn't accept not knowing what he learned right away, and that was something he could arrange.

'I'll report back the moment I have spoken to him.'

Suspicion filled her gaze. 'You promise?'

'I swear it. Where will you be this evening?'

'At home. Because we leave Town tomorrow, we dine there with friends.'

'I will come when they have left.'

She frowned. 'I don't think Gabe will be pleased.'

'He isn't going to know. Leave your window open when you retire for the night.'

Her eyes sparkled. 'You are going to enter my room through the window?'

'Try not to give me away, would you? I don't want Gabe calling me out.'

She shuddered. 'Neither do I.'

He breathed a sigh of relief. Then why did the back of his nape prickle? Damn it all, why did he have the sense her capitulation had been far too easy?

Crammed between Oliver's Warf and the alley leading to Wapping Old Stairs, the Town of Ramsgate was indeed not the sort of place a young woman of good breeding should think about entering. On the opposite side of Wapping High Street, Minette hugged the shadows of St John's Church. Freddy was going to be furious.

And not just because she had gone against his express wishes that she wait for him at home.

She'd meant to, she really had. She'd been truly charmed by the idea that he intended to protect her, until her doubts had bubbled up. Hadn't she also been charmed by the way Pierre had sought to keep her safe? Hadn't she adored him and his protectiveness? Until she'd discovered it had all been a front. Freddy had never even pretended he wanted her participation in his plans. Once he had the information she had discovered, what was to stop him going off to find Moreau without her?

He could tell her anything when he visited her after his meeting.

No, she had been finely tricked by Pierre. She wouldn't give Freddy the chance to do the same.

Two men in rough clothing wandered down the street, shoulders slumped, feet dragging. They stopped at the door of the tavern, where the light over the door lit the profile of the taller man. Her heart picked up speed. Freddy. And from his brawny build, the other man was Barker from the Fools' Paradise. Their disguises were perfect. What would they think of hers?

They disappeared inside.

Squaring her shoulders, she pulled her ragged shawl up over her head and around her shoulders. She and Pierre had played this game often enough to make it second nature, but as always her heart beat faster and her breathing quickened, bringing to her nostrils the stink of the clothes she'd acquired, along with the dank smell of river, fish and the smoke from river coal. She forced herself to take ten deep, slow breaths to let the air become part of who she was, let poverty and hunger wash over her and then she shuffled across the street.

Inside, the Ramsgate smelled and tasted like so many other taverns she had lingered in, listening for information. For Pierre. Never guessing the use to which he had put it. The noise of men's voices, the acrid smoke of pipes, the stench of beer and unwashed bodies were the same. Only the language was different.

Behind the bar, a grubby innkeeper thumped a pair of

pewter pots in front of his most recent customers. The men took their ales to a table in the corner, Barker lighting a pipe, Freddy burying his nose in his tankard while he discreetly scanned the room.

Keeping her shoulders hunched and her face lowered, she shuffled around the room. 'Spare a copper for a poor auld wider lady?' she begged in quavering tones, and leaning heavily on her cane so people would see little but the top of her head. She had been practising her accent on the street sweeper on the corner since her arrival in London. A game she'd played for entertainment mostly. She had an ear for accents and she had amused Nicky and Gabe with her imitations, and shocked them, too.

One docker shoved her away fiercely. Another pressed a ha'penny in her mittened hand.

'She'll only spend it on gin,' his companion observed, and turned his back.

A glance from Freddy, who sported a scar on his cheek and nose reddened by drink, flickered over her. Without recognition.

Hah! She'd spotted him right away. To be fair, she had known to expect him. Still…

She sidled up to their table, clawed hand shoved under his nose. 'Spare a copper.'

'Clear off.' Barker tossed her a coin. It glinted silver as it spun on its edge on the scarred and stained tabletop. A 'thruppny bit', as the street sweeper called it. Threepence. She reached for it.

Strong fingers clenched around her wrist as she caught up the coin.

'What in hell's name are you doing here?' Freddy rasped in her ear.

She tittered. Let the shawl slip down to her shoulders, revealing the tangle of her hair and red-painted lips, changing from hunched old crone to ravaged prostitute. 'Want company out in the alley?' She danced the coin between her fingers. 'Sailor's choice.'

Freddy cursed.

Barker buried his face in his tankard, his shoulders shaking. Was he laughing?

The man who had given her the coin started towards them. 'You cheating baggage.'

Freddy's lowered brows halted him in midstride. He took the coin and tossed it back to the man. 'Sit.' He jerked down by her arm to perch on his knee.

She batted her eyelashes. 'Changed yer mind, guv? Wot's yer fancy?'

Barker choked back laughter. 'Does yer want me to leave yer to it?'

Freddy grinned. An evil leer. 'You can leave us to it, mate, when we get outside.' His accent was also of the lower orders and spoken with the ease of long practice.

A shiver went down her spine at the lecherous promise. Not fear. Anticipation. Damn him. Because she had no doubt he intended it as a threat of retribution, not a promise.

Freddy gestured to a waiter passing with a tray. 'Gin.'

Barker nudged Freddy with his elbow, and Minette caught the jerk of the innkeeper's unshaven chin at a man entering the taproom.

Minette gave Freddy a winsome smile, careful not to reveal her teeth. 'That our mark?'

Freddy lifted his pot of ale to his lip. 'It is.'

He nodded, and the innkeeper handed the new customer a bumper of gin and gestured in their direction.

The man, Henri, narrowed his eyes at her and then at Freddy, then shouldered his way to their table. 'You ask for me?'

''Ave a seat, mate,' Freddy said, lifting his tankard in salute.

The man glanced around him, grabbed a stool and subsided with a sigh. He took a long pull at his gin. 'So, *messieurs*?'

Freddy lowered his voice. 'You sister says you have news of a certain party.'

'Name begins with M,' Barker added.

'This man, he arrives six week ago. Here.' He made a vague gesture, encompassing them, the river, London.

'Where does he stay?' Freddy leaned back and swigged at his beer.

Henri shook his head and leaned forward, his voice little more than a whisper. 'He recently travels north. Urgent business.'

How vague could the man get? 'Not helpful, *mon ami*,' Minette muttered under her breath.

He looked startled.

'Ignore her,' Freddy ground out. 'Tell us what you do know.'

Minette bristled but contented herself with a scrape of her nail across the table, knowing it would irritate Freddy and, more importantly, not allow him to forget her presence.

'Un homme.' Henri grimaced. 'My friend. He says he returns.'

'He's coming back to London,' Freddy rephrased.

Henri nodded. 'He is expected. Soon.'

'What is he doing in the north?' Barker asked.

Henri shrugged. 'Gathering information?'

'Is there anything else you can tell us?' Minette asked, ignoring Freddy's glare. 'His appearance. The name he is using?'

Freddy kicked her under the table.

'Beard. Spectacles.' He touched his cheek. 'Dark of skin. He goes by Smith.'

Smith sounded nothing like Moreau. But, then, none of them looked like themselves tonight. Moreau was a master of disguises. He'd certainly fooled her for years.

'You will let your sister know the moment he returns,' Barker said. 'Warn him and you are a dead man.' He issued his threat in a dangerously conversational tone of voice.

Henri ignored him and kept his gaze fixed on Freddy's face. ''E is a bad man. I speak truth.'

Freddy nodded. 'Then we will get along famously.'

The Frenchman got up and went back to the bar. Minette leaned against Freddy's shoulder and started playing with his hair and stroking his cheek. He looked at her. She raised a brow in the age-old question.

'I'll see you back at the club,' Freddy said to Barker, and drew her closer to his side, bit the point of her shoulder, hard enough to make her twitch away. 'This mort owes me thruppence-worth.'

Barker stretched, got up and left. When he was clear, Freddy grabbed her arm and staggered out into the night air. While his steps were sloppy, his eyes slightly unfocussed, his grip was steely. He didn't lighten it until they were well clear of the inn and he was sure, as she was, that they had not been followed.

He put his arm around her shoulders. Slowly, inexorably, he backed her into the shadows of the nearest alley. He took her chin between her fingers and tipped her face up so she was forced to meet a gaze glinting from a nearby streetlight. Oh, my, he was angry.

'So, tell me, my dear Minette, what the hell did you think you were doing?' He spoke in a voice so calm as to be terrifying.

Intimidation. Her own anger rose. 'I wanted to hear what he had to say for myself and well you know it.'

His gaze dropped to her bosom. 'Dressed like that, you could have got a lot more than information.'

She pulled her knife from the pocket hidden in her ragged skirts, the pocket she'd sewn into the seam when Christine had come back with the dress, and held it to his Adam's apple. 'I think not.'

He cursed softly and fluently. At least she guessed he was cursing. They were English words and not familiar.

'Now, do you want the value of your thruppence,' she said softly, 'or do you take me home?'

He took her wrist and forced the blade away, taking it from her now nerveless fingers and stuffing it into a pocket. 'A man can get a lot for three pennies, my dear.'

He meant to frighten her. She knew those tactics.

He bent his head and took her mouth in a scalding kiss. Well-remembered sensations struck her low in her belly. She found she could not recall why they were standing in an alley late at night. She was too busy returning his kiss, tangling her tongue with his, plastering herself tight to his body while his fingers cradled her head and held her still to receive his punishing kiss.

Punishing, ravishing and utterly delicious.

Enough to make a girl lose her mind for want of more. Especially a girl who'd been celibate for years and had been tempted for days and days by this virile man.

As if he sensed her thoughts, he backed her up against the wall, while he kept her head angled just right. She felt his lovely weight all down her length and the ridge of his arousal against her belly. Her hands explored the musculature of his shoulders and the bones of his spine. She burrowed beneath his coat to feel the warmth of him, to shape the narrowing of his waist and the firmness of his buttocks.

A lean, beautiful male body she wanted on top of her, all around her, inside her.

He tasted of ale and smoke and of Freddy in the faint whiff of his soap.

He groaned softly and dragged his mouth away. 'Where on God's sweet earth did you learn to kiss like that?'

The words were like a dash of cold water. Like a wanton, he'd meant. A woman no better than she should be. As he'd soon find out, if they didn't stop now.

She pushed him away, breathing hard. 'You kiss pretty well yourself.' She flicked her skirts straight. 'For an Englishman.' Let him make of that what he would.

He gave a shake of his head as if to clear it. Then struck the wall behind her with the side of his fist. 'There is no need for you to take such risks. You are not in France any longer. You are not friendless and alone. When will you learn I am not your enemy?'

'Never.'

'Then we have a problem.'

'We have a worse one. We have lost Moreau.'

'We know he will return to London in due course. In the meantime, I will have men searching the north for him.' He took her arm. 'Come, time to see you home. We will be able to pick up a hackney in the next street.' He glanced down at her. 'I presume you left the garden gate open?'

'*Naturellement.*' She kept her voice calm. It wouldn't do to let him see how much Moreau's disappearance had her worried.

Chapter Nine

Minette climbed down from Gabe's carriage at Falcon-wood Hall. Dear man that he was, he'd insisted that his coachman drive her, along with a footman and her maid, while Freddy went on ahead, to be there to greet her along with his mother. Gabe was still angry at the incident that had brought them to this pass and hadn't been about to trust her to Freddy's tender care when he'd realised that he and Nicky would not be able to accompany her to Kent. Gabe's parliamentary business could not be abandoned on a whim.

She stared up at the house while she waited for her maid to gather up their belongings and alight. She had expected something on a grand scale—after all, Freddy was a Duke—but she had not expected anything quite so old and rambling. Freddy had called it a pile. It was a sprawling, warm red-brick place with stone towers above the arched front entrance.

The drive from the gatehouse, where she was sure there had been a portcullis at some point in time, had been extraordinarily beautiful, spreading oaks scattered across a rolling green park filled with deer. She could almost imagine Freddy riding hell for leather around the grounds as a boy. It would have been a wonderful place to bring up children.

A pang caused a hitch in her breathing. A sense of loss. The knowledge that it would not be her children who would grow up in this lovely old house. The footman climbed down from the box and hurried to ring the doorbell, but a butler with a prim mouth and small stature was already walking sedately down the steps. A groom appeared around the side of the house and led the carriage away, along with her maid and luggage.

'If you would care to follow me, miss, Their Graces are waiting in the drawing room.'

At that moment Freddy stepped out onto the drive. 'It is all right, Patterson,' he said. 'I will show Miss Rideau the way.'

The tension in her shoulders flowed away, though she hadn't realised quite how nervous she'd been about this meeting until it dissipated. After their last encounter, when it had been obvious she didn't trust him, she hadn't been sure he wouldn't withdraw from her completely. Every time she thought of the way she'd dressed and played her part, she flushed hot then went cold. If he didn't know the extent of her carnal knowledge, he must now guess she knew far more than a gently bred girl ought.

Pierre had been bad for her in so many ways, and not just because of his betrayal.

With the utmost courtesy, Freddy held out his arm and walked her beneath the stone arch, through an ancient door and into a rectangular medieval great hall. A beautifully carved screen occupied one end and a huge fireplace dominated the centre of one long wall. Faded banners and painted shields hung on stone above the dark panelling, along with ancient weaponry. The only items of furniture were an enormously long trestle table and some horribly uncomfortable-looking carved wooden armchairs.

'*Mon Dieu,*' she said in a low voice. 'It is positively antiquated.'

Freddy patted her hand. 'Don't worry, most of the house is quite modern. We only use the Great Hall for large events and when the Duke needs to make an impression.'

She breathed a sigh of relief. 'I can just imagine the three of us dining here in state, you at one end and your mother at the other and me in the middle, unable to speak without shouting.'

'If Mother had her way, your imagination might not be far from the truth.'

Another wry remark about his mother. The woman must be a veritable dragon. But then, she was a duchess.

He led them through yet another arch into a paved corridor and from there into an elegantly appointed room full of light, with pale green walls and cornices of white and gilt. It was, she realised, a perfect cube in the Palladian style.

The woman seated where the light from the window fell on her embroidery looked up at their entry. She was lovely. Dainty, with gold-blonde hair shot through with threads of silver and skin that made one think of peaches and cream. She was dressed in lavender. Half-mourning? Blue eyes arctic enough to freeze one's blood remained fixed on Minette's face while Freddy made the introductions. Now she knew from where Freddy inherited his cold expression.

Minette dipped a curtsey.

The eyes assessed her performance with chilly intensity, while the face showed no expression at all. The perfect aristocrat.

'Miss Rideau.' The duchess gestured for her to take a seat. 'Welcome to Falconwood. My son has told me much about you.' There was a fragility to her air, in the lightness of her voice. As if it was almost too great an effort for her to speak.

Oh, dear. This was likely to be a lot worse than she had hoped. She sat down in the seat set at a right angle to the Duchess.

'Was your journey bearable?' the dowager asked. '*I* would have sent our carriage for you. It was built for me by my husband, who took every care of my person, but Freddy said it was not necessary.' The blue eyes turned to her son. 'Not worth the bother of getting it cleaned and polished, I think you said.'

The barb apparently sailed over Freddy's head. 'Lord, no. You haven't had it on the road in years. The last time you went in it to Town you said it was the most dreadfully uncomfortable trip you had ever undertaken.'

'You misremember,' his mother said. 'It certainly was not the fault of the carriage. The roads are much improved since then.'

The atmosphere in the room was frosty. Minette smiled. 'It was a very pleasant journey, thank you. Mooreshead made sure I had all the necessary comforts.'

The duchess frowned. 'You accent is quite noticeable.'

'Miss Rideau is half-French, Mother, and lived in France until quite recently. I informed you of that fact both in my letter and when I arrived yesterday.'

Defending her, when he had not defended himself. Warmth spread in her chest.

His mother's shoulders stiffened. 'You said nothing about her speech. I am sure I had no intention to criticise, I just didn't expect...' Her voice trailed off in a weak gesture of her hand.

Freddy's lips flattened to a thin straight line as if he was doing all in his power not to say something harsh.

Minette kept her expression pleasant. 'My mother was

English, but she died when I was very young. I am sure, in time, I will become less noticeably French.'

'I like the way you speak,' Freddy said stiffly.

She gave him a grateful smile.

His mother gazed at him thoughtfully, her glance holding such coldness Minette stifled the urge to shiver. 'Ring for tea, Falconwood. Miss Rideau must be parched after her journey.'

Stone-faced, he strode across to the bell-pull beside a hearth of brilliant white plaster carved with vegetation and ferocious-looking animals.

'Your leg is dragging more than usual,' his mother said with a grimace. 'I told you not to hack out on that animal of yours this morning. It tires you.'

Freddy glared at her as he returned to his seat. 'What would you have me do, take up embroidery?'

His mother laughed, a tinkle of sound laced with malice. 'Do not tease so, Freddy. No, you would be better off spending time with the accounts, seeing to the business of running the estate. A gentle walk in the park…'

Fury heated Minette's blood. How could the woman be so stupid as to treat Freddy with so little regard for his pride? She wanted to take the woman by the shoulders and give her a good shake.

Fortunately for them all the butler entered at that moment, followed by a line of footmen carrying ludicrously enormous silver trays. The butler set a side table in front of the Duchess, and the footmen carefully set out a tea urn, sandwiches cut so fine it looked as if they would blow away if one breathed too hard, and small fancy cakes along with sweetmeats.

'Will there be anything else, Your Grace?'

'No, thank you,' Freddy said.

His mother stiffened as if he'd offered her some insult.

Freddy winced. 'Mother, did you require anything?'

'No, thank you, Patterson,' the Duchess said, her face a frozen mask. 'I will ring if I need you.'

What was going on here? It was horrid. Mother and son were at loggerheads in the politest of ways. Minette felt as if there were sharp daggers flying about her head. If she moved incautiously she might lose an arm, or worse.

The duchess commenced the ritual of tea.

'I assume you drink tea, Miss Rideau?' The Dowager Duchess's mouth turned down. 'I have heard the French prefer coffee.'

'I like tea,' Minette said, wishing her smile didn't feel so stiff and awkward.

Were mother and son always so tense? Was it the presence of a stranger in their midst making them so uncomfortable with each other? Hopefully, when they were used to her company, things would become more relaxed. She had a feeling she might be wishing for the moon.

Freddy glowered across the tea tray. If Mother made one more unpleasant remark to or about Minette, he would take her to task and to hell with propriety. She could carp at him all she liked. He didn't care. Neither did he any longer give a fig that the sight of him walking across the room made her queasy. He was hardened to her verbal attacks.

It did matter if she hurt Minette's feelings, though he couldn't help the surge of pride at the way Minette had stood up for herself against Mother's claws. Perfectly polite and yet showing the steel in her spine.

'From which part of France does your family come?' Mother asked, after a silence that had lasted a fraction too long. Deliberately so.

'The Vendée.' Minette smiled. 'Our château was like

your house, very old. Dating to the fourteenth century in parts.'

'Older than Falconwood, then,' Freddy said, glancing at his mother, who always bragged about the antiquity of their line.

'Our ancestors came over with William, Duke of Normandy,' Mother said. 'It was later in the family history that we settled here at Falconwood.'

Minette sipped at her tea. 'Perhaps we have some ancestors in common. I know that at least one chevalier from my father's family joined the Duke.' She put down her cup and saucer. 'I always feel sorry for the Saxon King, Harold. William's was the flimsiest excuse on which to base a claim to the throne.'

Mother pursed her lips. 'I am sure I have no idea what you are talking about. I am no bluestocking, Miss Rideau. Such topics are best left in the schoolroom.'

Freddy felt a growl form in his throat.

'Mais oui,' Minette said calmly, agreeably. 'I notice Englishwomen have a horror of being thought educated. In France the gentlemen admire a woman with whom they can converse.' She lowered her lashes a fraction. 'Among other things.'

An incautious mouthful of tea caused Freddy to choke. He carefully set his cup down on the table at his elbow. 'If you have finished your tea, Miss Rideau, perhaps I may give you a tour of the house before you retire to change for dinner?'

His mother gave him an assessing glance. A small smile touched her lips, and he steeled himself to parry her next thrust. 'Make sure you show Miss Rideau the Long Gallery, Falconwood.'

Oh, very clever, Mother dear. The last place he would want to take his intended.

She continued without pause. 'Our most recent addition is a wonderful portrait by Lawrence. A fine example of his work, I am told.' The smile disappeared. 'Dinner is at six. I like to keep country hours when we are dining *en famille.*'

'Naturally,' Minette said, rising to her feet and dipping a respectful curtsey. 'We always do so at Meak, my brother-in-law's estate.'

Freddy held out his arm, and they strolled from the room.

The fingers on his sleeve trembled. Damn Mother's mean-spirited innuendoes. Only when they were a good distance from the drawing room did he let himself speak. 'I apologise for my mother's sharp tongue. I hope she did not give offence.'

Her short, sharp exhalation spoke of impatience. 'Why is she so awful to you?'

Cross. Not hurt. Good lord, was she angry on his behalf? 'I was more concerned for you.'

'She looks at you so coldly, as if…' She breathed in and when he glanced down at her face he was surprised to see twin spots of anger on her cheeks. 'It is as if she has not a scrap of maternal feeling towards you.'

'She doesn't. Her firstborn was the sun, moon and stars in her eyes. I am a poor replacement.' The moment he'd spoken he regretted the bitterness in his words, but it was the truth. Some of it.

The concern remained on her face. 'I thought your older brother died years ago.'

'Yes. But as yet she is not reconciled to her loss.' It was one way to couch his mother's antipathy.

'It is almost as if she blames you for his death.'

He was to blame. He'd tormented Reggie into taking up his challenge. Freddy had always known how to make his older brother rise to the bait. And then he'd watched him die. Something burned at the back of his throat. He stiffened against the surge of emotion. Took a deep, slow breath. Damn it all, he never talked about the accident. Surely reliving that day over and over in his dreams was punishment enough? He let the ice inside him surround his unwanted emotions and took a deep breath. 'She is angry.' Angry that he had been the one to survive.

'She hurts you.'

How could she imagine she knew what he felt, when he felt nothing? His back teeth ground against each other. Forcibly, he relaxed his jaw. 'I don't let it trouble me, but I will speak to her.' He would not have Mother making Minette's life miserable. 'Would you like to see his portrait?'

She looked sad. 'Only if you would like to show me.'

For some reason he couldn't fathom, he did want her to see Reggie and he didn't. His brother would have liked her. They would have competed for her attention. And Reggie's innate easy charm would no doubt have won the day. It was a hard truth to swallow.

He walked her up to the second floor and along to the east wing. The long gallery was one of the most beautiful parts of the house and also one of the most ancient. He and Reggie had spent endless hours here on rainy days when not tied to their books. As they had grown older, Reggie had spent more time with their father, learning the duties he would one day inherit, spending less and less time with Freddy. He'd been envious of his father's attention to his older brother. Of his father's pride in his elder son. It was partly why he'd tempted Reggie into playing truant on the day of the accident.

They walked past the family portraits, some large by famous artists of the time and some little more than miniatures, until they came to the portrait of his immediate family done by a local artist. They stood together in front of a view of one of the most beautiful parts of Falconwood's park. Dogs gambolled at his father's feet, his mother a radiant beauty, not the pinched, pale creature she was today. Reggie stood beside his father, so like his mother with his golden hair and bright blue eyes, already showing signs of the man. Both parents were looking with pride at their elder son. On the other side of his seated mother stood Freddy. The ugly duckling, dark-complexioned with a beak of a nose and overly large hands and feet for the size of his frame. At twelve, he'd been embarrassingly short and skinny. He certainly didn't look like the rest of his family, though his father's hair was brown, not golden.

Minette viewed the portrait, tilting her head first to one side then the other. 'He looks like your mother and you look more like your father.'

'My colouring mostly comes from my mother's grandmother, I'm told.' Along with other less desirable traits.

'It is easy to see they loved your brother.'

His throat closed, but he forced himself to speak. 'As did I. He was one of the best brothers a fellow could wish for.'

He moved on to the next portrait. This one was of his brother alone, a few years older than in the previous one, a shotgun over his shoulder, a brace of partridge at his feet and a look of pure mischief in his bright blue eyes. 'This is the Lawrence Mother spoke of. Reggie was going to be eighteen later that summer.' He'd never reached his eighteenth birthday. Freddy had been sixteen.

'He makes one think of an English Apollo. Where is your portrait by Lawrence?'

The question jolted his gut. His hands clenched. His shoulders tightened. He turned from the picture and went to look out of the window, coward that he was. 'There was no need of a portrait of the spare at that time.'

He'd been so damnably jealous.

'His loss must have been a dreadful shock to you, as well as your parents.'

Worse than she could possibly imagine. 'I was devastated. And then, God help me, I was expected to step into his shoes. It was years before I could bear to think about it, let alone apply myself to the matter.'

'The reason you do not come to Falconwood very often.'

That and the bitter recriminations from his mother. Recriminations that echoed loud and clear in his conscience. 'I hate coming here.'

Chapter Ten

His words were cold. Perhaps even calculated to shock. He stood looking out of the window, so alone, so remote. And beneath the coldness Minette sensed the pain of an old wound. Something he was not talking about. She strolled to stand beside him at the window, looking out at the view. 'Thank you for bringing me to see your brother's likeness,' she said softly. 'I am sure he would be proud of you.'

He looked startled then turned away as if he did not want her to see his reaction. Sadness filled her that he would not share his thoughts with her, but it was only to be expected. Theirs was a betrothal of convenience and they barely knew each other and trusted each other even less.

Giving him time to collect himself, she gazed silently at the vista, from the formal gardens near the house across the ha-ha and out over the large expanse of treed park. A gleam of white beside a lake caught her eye. 'Oh, what is that?' She pointed. 'At the edge of the lake.'

'The Pantheon. My family's version of a folly from the early part of the last century. There's a hermit's cave in the woods nearby, too. And a grotto. Would you like to see it?'

'As long as we are back in time for dinner,' she said,

smiling at the eagerness in his voice. Clearly this was something he would enjoy showing her.

With the day warm and sunny it was not a hardship to take the path that led from the house down to the lake and meander across the grassy arched bridge to arrive at the folly she had seen from the upstairs window. The view of the house was lovely from this vantage point, the red-brick fiery in the afternoon sun. But it was the folly that held her attention. A fully realised Roman temple of glowing white marble. 'It looks so real,' she said. 'As if we have stepped back in time and been transported to Rome itself.'

'One of my ancestors had it build after the Restoration. They were all the rage.'

'Can we go inside?'

'Of course.' He took her arm and walked her up the steps and through an enormous set of oak doors. Inside there were marble statues and reliefs around the circular chamber.

'Oh, my goodness,' she said. 'It is astonishing. One almost expects to meet Caesar in his toga.'

'My mother used to hold picnics here when my father was alive. Before…' He pressed his lips together. 'Their summer parties were famous. No one ever turned down an invitation. Come, let me show you the grotto and the hermit's cave.'

'Was there really a hermit?'

'Oh, yes. There were three of them over the years, when they were fashionable. Before my time. They were paid a handsome sum to stay in the cave all summer. When the last one retired, the duke at the time gave him and his wife a cottage on the estate. Reggie and I used the place as a fort when we were young.'

They strolled back out into the sunshine and wandered to the other end of the lake. There, rocks had been placed artfully to form a tunnel that led to a grotto complete with natural spring. A shaft in the roof brought in light from outside, but the effect was cool and damp and unpleasantly gloomy. The white marble statue of a water nymph tucked against the wall behind the bubbling spring gazed at them soulfully.

Minette shivered.

Freddy took her hand. 'You are cold. Let us go back outside.'

The sunshine was a welcome relief. They turned the end of the lake, and he showed her the ruined walls of the hermit's dwelling. 'A great place for boys to play,' she said.

His eyes seemed to look inside himself, and then he smiled. 'It was.'

They strolled arm in arm back to the house. The coldness that had settled over Freddy in the portrait gallery had thawed and there was a pleasant easiness between them. It was as if they were becoming friends.

'Your home is beautiful,' Minette said, standing in the dappled shade of a tree at the edge of the lawn leading up to the house. 'This tree is huge. Oak, *n'est pas*?'

'It is supposed to be three hundred years old. It is on one of the earliest drawings of the house.' He looked up into the branches. 'It is amazing to think this tree was right here at the time of Henry the Eighth.'

She stroked the bark. 'If trees could only talk, they would whisper a great many secrets.'

His hand came down beside hers. Large. Encased in black gloves as hers were in tan. He didn't move. Slowly she turned to face him, and he brought his other hand up to cage her against the tree.

The heat of his body washed up against her like a wave. She raised her face to meet his intent gaze. While she could make out nothing from his expression, the heat in his eyes said exactly where his thoughts had gone. Her body flushed with answering heat, as it always did when he looked at her that way.

What was it about this man that brought forth longings she'd thought she had long ago repressed? She knew too well the heartbreak of giving a man what he wanted. The pain of betrayal. Yet inside she trembled with familiar sensations. The bloom of desire.

'We shouldn't be doing this,' she whispered.

'No.'

'Someone might see us.'

'No one can see us here.'

He would know all the secret places where a man could be alone with a woman.

When his eyes searched her face and his head dipped slowly, giving her every chance to reject his advance, she rose up on her toes and claimed his lips with her own.

His sigh of satisfaction made her breasts tingle and long for his touch. She arched into him, pressing her body against the hard wall of his chest.

One strong arm pulled her into him, the other caressed the curve of her spine, and he nudged her backwards until she was supported by the tree. His thigh pressed into her and she widened her stance to accommodate the sweet pressure against her lower body, rocking against him, purring deep in her throat, the sweet ache throbbing low in her core. Slowly one hand skimmed her bottom, then up her side until it rested heavy on her breast. She pushed into his palm, longing to feel his touch against the aching fullness.

He broke the kiss. 'Every time. You drive me beyond reason,' he said, his voice harsh. 'Have you any idea of the consequences of this game you are playing with me?'

'I think you are the cat and I am the mouse,' she whispered. Of course he was. He tempted her unbearably. Made her want things she should not want. And if she let him have his way, he thought she would have no choice but to marry him, when in truth it might cause him to send her away. Something she could not allow until the threat of Moreau was vanquished.

She pushed at his shoulder.

He lifted his head, gazed around and groaned. 'You are right. This is not the right place.'

'Or the right time,' she said as calmly as her frustration would allow.

'We should not anticipate our vows.'

She gave him a tight smile. 'Precisely.'

He glanced at the ground and then at her face with a wicked smile she'd never seen before, wicked and boyish. 'If it hadn't rained yesterday, I might think about trying to change your mind.'

Loverlike teasing. Such a shock from this emotionless man. 'Thank heavens for the rain, then.'

The smile remained.

She wagged a finger at him. 'A kiss between those newly betrothed is perfectly acceptable. It fits with our story. But anything more is not a good idea.' Oh, what a dissembler she was. She would like nothing more than to romp with him in the grass, but she didn't dare give him a glimpse of how she was tempted. She had no doubt he would take advantage of any sign of her weakening under the onslaught of his charm.

'You are right,' he said, though he sounded grudging.

A tone that made her foolish heart lift.

Dinner over, Freddy forwent the glass of port in solitary state after the ladies withdrew. Instead, he took it with him to the drawing room. He would not leave Minette to the tender mercies of Mother, despite the fact that over dinner she had more than held her own.

Once the tea was poured, he leaned back in his chair and sipped his port. 'Thank you for attending to the arrangements for the ball, Mother.'

'Given how the little time I have been given to prepare, I hope you are not expecting anything extraordinary,' his mother said stiffly.

'It was too bad of us,' Minette said, clearly trying to soothe the other woman's ruffled feathers. Given Mother's penchant for slicing into one with her tongue while looking as if butter wouldn't melt in her mouth, he could only feel admiration. Minette was kind as well as lovely, no matter how much she tried to hide it. But kindness would not help her with Mother.

'Perhaps we should scale back on the guest list. Keep it to family only,' he said, stretching out his legs.

Mother pursed her lips. 'The betrothal of a duke is a matter of great importance. It cannot be skimped.'

As usual she took the contrary position to anything he suggested. Just as he'd hoped. He shrugged. 'The wedding celebration is usually the main event.'

'You would put us to shame?'

Minette winced. 'If it would not be too bold an offer, I would love to help.'

Mother stiffened. 'I am perfectly capable of arranging for the entertainment of a hundred people, Miss Rideau.'

'A hundred?' Minette put down her teacup with a shaking hand. Her gaze flew to Freddy's face. 'I had no idea so many had been invited.'

Freddy winced at the sight of her consternation. 'A hundred is small for us.'

'Oh, Your Grace,' she said to his mother, 'you must allow me to be of assistance.'

Not unexpectedly, Mother turned frosty. 'My steward, Carter, and Mr Patterson are all the help I require, thank you. However, I did not receive instructions with regard to those to be invited from your family, Miss Rideau. How many people am I to expect from that quarter?'

Clearly she did not like it that he had asked Nicky to send out invitations to her and Gabe's friends. 'I gave the list to Patterson when I spoke to him before dinner.'

'Should I not know who is invited to my house?' Mother said.

'My house,' he said with lethal quiet.

The frost turned to a wall of solid ice. 'I might have known you would have no notion of what it is to take responsibility.' She sniffed. 'I trust you found your accommodations suitable, Miss Rideau?'

'Thank you, they are lovely.'

A scratch at the door, and Patterson entered. 'A message for you, Your Grace,' the butler said with a stiff bow, and held out a salver.

Freddy reached out to take it at the same moment as his mother.

'It is addressed to Falconwood,' the butler said with an apologetic glance towards Mother.

Freddy took the note, and as the butler left the room he slit the seal with a thumbnail. The shock of the words he read held him rigid for a second. He tucked the note in his pocket.

'Who is it from?' his mother asked. 'One of the neighbours thinking to ingratiate themselves now that you have finally decided to come home?'

Freddy looked up. 'No. It is business. Mother, why not let Miss Rideau plan the supper menu?'

Mother looked horrified, but he could see the calculation going on in her mind, the realisation that if she wasn't careful he might wrest all control from her hands. 'I suppose someone needs to plan the arrangement of flowers for the ballroom,' she offered.

'I would love to help with that,' Minette said. 'I will begin first thing in the morning.'

'Don't forget our plan to drive out in the morning,' he said, 'so I can show you more of the estate and some of the surrounding countryside.' Show her the note.

Her eyes widened. 'Oh, yes. I had forgotten.'

He nodded his acknowledgement of her quick wit.

Minette turned to his mother. 'I can work on the floral arrangements after lunch, if that is all right with you. Is there a budget?'

'You can spend whatever you think is necessary,' Freddy said.

His mother let out a small sound of protest.

'You have some ideas, Your Grace?' Minette said, as if she had no idea that Mother wasn't happy. 'Shall I come to you for direction first? Before Freddy and I leave for our drive. Say around ten?'

Mother never left her chamber before noon.

'Certainly not, my dear,' Her Grace said with sugary sweetness. 'I will leave it all up to you. I will have one of the gardeners put at your disposal.'

'The head gardener, Mr Jevens,' Freddy said, knowing the way his mother's mind worked. 'Since Minette will shortly be taking over the running of the household, I think that is a very good idea, Mother. She should also be present when you speak to Chef.'

The longing to object writ large on his mother's face was a painful thing to observe. She had prided herself on the running of the household since her marriage and Freddy had done nothing to alter her role since his father had died. Now was the right time to make changes. The servants, all loyal to his mother, had served him some unpleasant meals when she had been annoyed with him, and once his bed linen had been damp. Punishment for arriving at his home unannounced. There would be none of that unpleasantness for Minette. He was determined.

'Of course, dear,' his mother replied, and he heard the little break in her voice without a shred of emotion. It was all an act designed to make Minette feel uncomfortable.

'I shall look forward to it,' Minette said with forced brightness.

'Then I suggest you speak to Jevens first thing, before we drive out,' he said. 'Mother will make herself available after lunch.'

Ready for bed, Minette had never felt less like sleeping in her life. What on earth had made Freddy so anxious to take her driving in the morning? She'd seen insistence in those dark eyes that could be so expressive—when they weren't keeping her at a distance.

She still couldn't believe his mother's coldness towards him. It was horrible to be in the same room with them. Couldn't the dowager duchess see how much she was hurting her son? Or how much she lost by keeping him at a distance? She had barely stopped herself from taking the woman to task. She picked up the book Nicky had given her to read on the journey and flicked through the pages to find her place. She stared at the words. Clearly there had been something important in the note Freddy had received. Although he'd hidden it quickly, he had been surprised by its contents. And then he'd talked about arrangements they hadn't made.

The door to her chamber opened. Expecting to see Christine returning on some forgotten errand, she gaped at the sight of Freddy in a silk dressing gown closing the door behind him.

His hot, dark gaze swept over her. Answering heat raced across her skin. 'Freddy?'

He inhaled a breath and his expression shuttered.

Control. The man had icy control.

Something inside her wanted to smash down the walls. Only if she did, her own walls might come tumbling down, too. Not a good thing. 'Why are you here?'

'The note. It is from Vitesse. Things have changed.'

Her heart stilled at the seriousness in his voice. 'What is it?'

'Moreau is not returning to London.'

'We have lost him?' Damnation. She should not have left Town.

'According to Latour, Maidstone is his destination.'

Her heart lurched as if the ground beneath her feet had shifted. 'Maidstone? Is it not nearby?'

'It is.'

'Why does he go there?'

'There are only two reasons I can think of. The first is the barracks located in the town. Information about troop movements and so forth.'

'The second?'

'The news of our sudden engagement was in all the papers, and the ball was announced at the same time.' His mouth flattened. 'As a sop to the sensibilities of those that care about such things. He would no doubt have seen the London papers, wherever he was. He might see it as a chance to get to Nicky. Or he could be plotting yet another assassination. Someone attending our ball.'

She hadn't yet seen the guest list. 'People of importance will attend?'

'I'm a duke. Invitations went out to the Prince Regent,

half the cabinet and a couple of royal princes.' He sounded defensive.

'Will they come?'

A shadow passed across his expression. 'They might. For Gabe's sake.'

'What on earth made you invite—? Oh.' Furious, she strode across the room, glaring up into his face. 'You think I won't cry off if doing so would be utterly embarrassing for Gabe later.'

A slow smile dawned on his face, his eyes gleamed. 'I have always liked that about you, Minette. Your mind is as quick as a whip.'

'Not quick enough, since I did not realise what was in your devious mind.'

He leaned forward, kissed the tip of her nose, then shrugged apologetically. 'A man has to do what he must to achieve the outcome he wants.'

His eyes gleamed. Mischievous. Wicked. And, oh, yes, with a hint of triumph. Not since they'd played and cheated each other at cards all those years ago had she seen that look on his face. Her heart tumbled over. The sensation stole her breath. Blinded and robbed of speech by his pure male appeal, she could only stare. Why had he become so bleak and cold in the intervening years? And what was thawing the ice?

If it wasn't impossible, she could almost—almost— believe he really wanted this marriage. As if honour and duty had not forced him into offering for her hand. Something inside her unfurled. A sweet kind of longing. A flicker of hope. She doused the flame with a cold dash of reality. He was a duke. A man who should expect his wife to come to him pure, unsullied. He would not be looking so pleased with himself if he knew the full extent of her past, though he might guess at some of it.

An Englishman of principle, of honour, could not possibly marry a woman who had done what she had done. Using their betrothal to get to Moreau was one thing. She didn't care what she had to do in that regard. But marriage was out of the question. And not at all necessary. Moreau must be caught and be behind bars before the banns were called.

She spun away. Went to the table beside the bed and poured a glass of water. Anything to keep her hands busy, to resist the temptation he presented. 'So the purpose for our drive tomorrow is to seek him out?'

'He could be anywhere in the district. We need to net him before he gets close to Falconwood.'

She turned back to face him and was glad to see the man of ice had returned. He was handsome, no matter what he did, but when the ice cracked, when he smiled, he was overwhelming.

'It is good of Madame Vitesse to warn us, and I am grateful you told me. You could have said nothing.'

'We have an agreement.' He leaned against the door frame. 'And, besides, she could have sent a similar note to you.' His gaze narrowed. 'Did she?'

'No.'

'Would you have told me if she had?'

Heat crept into her cheeks. 'I don't know.'

He cursed under his breath and moved slowly towards her, like a panther stalking prey. A dark creature of the night who would stop at nothing to get what he wanted. 'Not good enough.'

A shiver rippled through her body, heating places she should not be aware of. The man was positively dangerous.

The closer he got the stiffer her spine became. Every nerve in her body urged her to run. She refused to back away. Would not give him the satisfaction.

He caught her upper arms in a firm but painless grip, looking down into her eyes with such intensity, she wanted to look away, but knew she must not or he'd know how weak she was when it came to him.

'Don't think I will give you a chance to act alone,' he ground out. 'I am not going to let you out of my sight. And you will tell me the truth of this overwhelming need to speak to Moreau before I even consider allowing you near him.'

She swallowed the dryness in her throat. 'I shall do what I think best.' Her voice was far huskier than she thought possible. Her heart pounding hard behind her ribs. Her body tingling as if the air was caressing her skin. She could not stop looking at his mouth, so close to hers, so very beautiful, so very good at kissing.

It descended on hers, gentle, soft, sweet.

She sank into its tenderness with a moan of surrender. Sensations swept her away, the feel of his mouth, the liquid heat in her core, the ache in her breasts.

When he finally broke the kiss she shook her head at him. 'You should go.'

'A man can kiss his betrothed once in a while.' The wicked gleam was back in those dark blue eyes. His hand curved over her breast, firm, hot, gentle. His thumb brushed across the beaded tip of her nipple. 'I won't tell anyone. Will you?'

She couldn't think for the distraction of his touch.

Chapter Eleven

She looked like a goddess in her snowy gown with her chocolate-brown hair in a tumble down her back and over her breasts. Irresistible. Temptation incarnate. All soft curves and pillowy swells. He wanted to take her onto that bed and lick and bite and suck.

The heat of her desire shimmered on her skin. Glowed in her slumberous eyes. Echoed in the catch of her breath. She wanted him, too.

Now. At this moment. And if it was wrong, dishonourable to use it to force her to keep her promise to wed him, he did not care. He would not let her walk away once their quest was over. His pride would not allow it. She was his. His? Where had that come from? This was not about possession, it was about protecting her reputation.

He curled his fingers and tipped her chin with a knuckle. 'Will you?' he asked again.

'No.'

The word was a low, husky murmur that sent his blood careening through his veins, heightening his lust and piercing him with other sweeter emotions. He pulled her tight against his body, taking her mouth with his, plundering the sweet depths, sliding his tongue against the silk heat of hers. He pressed against her hip, thickened and hardened. Ached.

She tilted her pelvis, and he swore he could feel the heat of her centre through the fabric of his trousers. Her hands roamed his shoulders. One stroked down his spine and skimmed his buttocks.

He left the tender softness of her lips to kiss her jaw, the sensitive place beneath her right ear. The clean, fresh smell of her, the scent of jasmine and warm feminine flesh filled his nostrils and his lungs. He opened his mouth and took a bite. Not hard enough to leave a mark but enough to make her shudder.

She gasped. Not a sound of shock or outrage but a sigh of pleasure. Her long black lashes swept up. The gold in her eyes sparkled like treasure as she met his gaze with a sinful abandon he hadn't expected.

The sensual pout of her mouth drove any thoughts of honourable behaviour from his mind, sending pounding heat to his groin. Only an opportunist, a man who lived by his wits would take her momentary weakness to tie her to him irrevocably. He was such a man and the chance was too good to pass up. He gazed down into her face, running his hands through the silken mass of her hair, feeling it slide over his skin like a lover's touch. 'You are so beautiful to look at it hurts.'

Her eyes widened. Surprise. He liked it that he'd surprised her. Something bubbled up in his chest. An odd feeling that made him want to laugh. As if he were young and carefree. As if the lives of thousands did not rest in his hands, and there was only this moment, this woman. Joy. It was joy. He stared at her in wonder. Was it possible that this woman could bring him out of the dark?

A twinge of conscience. A knifing pain deep in his

chest. She couldn't. No one could. He was a man who had killed his brother.

Accident. His voice. *Jealousy.* His mother's.

How could he be sure he was right when he didn't remember? A clawing doubt he'd lived with for years. But there was no doubt in his mind that he wanted Minette as his wife. And, ruthless bastard that he was, he would make sure she had no way out.

He pulled her close. Their mouths melded. A perfect fit.

His eyes held the intensity of a predatory male, Minette thought, dizzy with sensation as he ran his fingers through her hair, watching his hand stroke and pet. The expression on his face curled her toes inside her slippers and caused her inner muscles to clench in sweet, painful little pulses. Shivers ran down her spine. Her breasts felt tight and needful of touch.

Her fingers fumbled at the tie of his robe. She wanted to feel the heat of his skin beneath her fingers. With a low murmur, he let the heavy silk fall from his shoulders to puddle on the floor in a whisper. She smoothed her palms over the fine linen of his shirt and felt the thud of his heart against her fingertips. A heart beating as hard as her own.

He was built on the lines of a stallion. Sleek and elegant yet powerfully male. The skin exposed at his throat was more Mediterranean in tone than that of most of his countrymen. Darkly exotic. She breathed him in, the scent of his cologne, bergamot and lemon and the musky scent of him, like dark spices in mulled wine on cold nights.

More. She wanted more. There was no need to deny herself the pleasure he could bring. Marriage was not required for that.

Breathless with desire, she rose on tiptoe and pressed

her mouth to his, wooing, seducing, teasing his tongue with hers, arching into his hard wall of chest. A satisfying rumble of pleasure rolled in his throat. A hot wildness inside her held her in thrall as their lower bodies came into contact and she rocked her hips, feeling the pleasure of his hard-muscled thigh against her pelvis, separated from her only by the thinnest of garments.

Delicious. Tempting. Not nearly enough to satisfy feminine needs driven wild by his kisses. In a swift movement that had her gasping, he swept her up in his arms and dropped her in the centre of the bed. He leaned over her, a lock of black hair falling onto his forehead. Unable to resist, she brushed it back and he smiled down at her with low-lidded sensual pleasure on his face.

A starkly beautiful man. And not the least bit cold.

She reached up for him and he lowered his head, brushing his mouth across hers, his tongue tracing the seam with delicious little flicks. In return, she nipped at his lower lip. His hiss of indrawn breath, a sound of pleasure-pain, jolted to her core. Her insides felt liquid, her breasts tingling in anticipation of the touch of a man who was clever with his lips and tongue.

He raised his head, looking down at her as if considering the effect of his actions, like a master craftsman checking his work.

'Freddy,' she demanded, pulling at his shoulders, wanting the weight of him against her hot, demanding skin.

His gaze searched her face as if seeking an answer to a question he had not posed.

Had she been too bold? Too demanding? Was he a man who preferred to take control?

Right at this moment she didn't care. She wanted, no, she needed, what his kisses promised. She raised herself up on her elbows, pressing small kisses to the line of his lightly stubbled jaw, the rasp against her lips an erotic reminder of his masculinity. Heat bloomed upwards from her belly. Her core ached.

She grazed her teeth against his throat.

One lithe spring and he landed on the mattress beside her, his weight rolling her towards him as he cupped her face in his large, warm hands, his gaze fixed on her face. 'There is no chance of going back after this. No possibility of crying off.'

Dark warning filled his voice. And triumph.

Her mind cleared of the sensual haze that had held her in thrall. The realisation that once again he was using the attraction between them, her weakness, to control her, as Pierre had. Using her for his own purposes. And when he had what he wanted, what then? Would he leave her in this house with his mother and continue with his life, honour and duty satisfied?

The very idea was a betrayal, yet without question all a convenient wife could hope for.

'That was not our agreement.' She pushed at his shoulder. 'I believe it is time you returned to your own chamber.'

Bleakness filled his eyes. 'Your idea of our agreement, you mean.'

'The betrothal lasts only until Moreau is in custody.'

In one swift move he left the bed and picked up his robe. 'Then you need to stop playing with fire.'

He unlocked the door and left her with her body humming with desire and her heart feeling as if it had been ripped in two.

Because what she had seen in his eyes had been frustration, but also, she thought, hurt. Was it possible, when all that was between them was the need to bring down a traitorous spy? It hardly seemed likely. And that meant she was allowing her own emotions to colour her judgement.

* * *

The next morning, Minette wasn't sure whether to expect Freddy to take her driving or not. She'd met with the gardener, discussed what was available from the flower-beds and greenhouses and prepared a list of what would have to be ordered from the nurseryman he had recommended. Then she'd gone upstairs and dressed for riding. Now ready and waiting in the drawing room, she could not help wondering if Freddy would, after her rejection of his advances, set out alone. Or she might have if she hadn't known deep in her heart that he was a man to whom his honour meant a great deal. He would keep his word.

When he entered the drawing room in breeches and top boots that set off his muscular legs, and a coat that skimmed wide shoulders she knew intimately, she was both relieved and saddened. Relieved that he had kept his promise and saddened that they could never be more than friends. If that. Likely he would want nothing at all to do with her after this was over.

A cool gaze swept her person. A nod of approval. 'The horses are saddled.'

So they were back to chilly distance. She felt the loss but had to be glad. It would be easier to keep her own longings in check. And yet from the way her pulse fluttered she was no closer to keeping her longings under control this morning than she had been the previous night.

He escorted her out to the stableyard, where the horses stood ready. A small chestnut mare with a white blaze on her forehead and three white stockings carried the lady's saddle. The mare tossed her head and sidled, pleasing Minette no end. She'd half expected him to order her a quiet horse. The other animal was a beautiful bay gelding with black points.

They mounted up and set off down the drive. Both

horses were fresh and ready to run, but well behaved enough to hold steady in the trot.

'What is your plan for this morning? Go to Maidstone and see if he is there?' she asked.

'Too obvious. I wrote to the commanding officer and warned him to keep an eye out for unusual activity. He's a man I knew at university.'

'And us?'

'We protect Falconwood. I thought about it last night. If the occupants of the house are his target, he will need a base of operations.'

The frost in his matter-of-fact tone, the lack of the warmth she'd begun to enjoy in his company was a painful reminder of her rejection of him the previous evening. It was exactly what she had wanted. Then why did it hurt?

'A local inn, perhaps? We could ask at those close by.'

He nodded. 'We could but I have a better idea. The vicar's wife, Mrs Farmer, knows everything and everyone in the district. She will know if any strangers have moved into the parish.' He shot her a hard look. 'She would also expect a visit from the future Duchess of Falconwood, given that it is a family tradition to be wed in the parish church.'

Minette tried not to wince. It was terrible how many people they were involving in their lie. Yet it made perfect sense. No one would question their reason for visiting this Mrs Farmer, thus they would not alert Moreau should he be nearby.

'Will she not be offended by my arriving in such a fashion?' Ladies did not call in their riding habits as a general rule.

'We will make a formal visit later in the week,' he said. 'Mrs Farmer is an old friend. She will be delighted to see us. News travels fast in the country and she would be disappointed if I did not land on her doorstep my first morning home.'

'Mrs Farmer holds a special place in your life?'

'The Reverend Farmer was tutor to me and my brother. He used to bring us home with him sometimes for tea and scones. They were kind.' His dark eyes shuttered. 'Especially kind during my convalescence.'

Minette could remember what it was like to have neighbours who cared for one. Without them she would have perished on the day of the fire. They had hidden her away from the soldiers for days, before they had passed her on to a group of nuns who were escaping the area.

In the end, it hadn't done her a bit of good because she had ended up in Moreau's hands. But they had tried to help and if she ever saw them again she would want to express her gratitude.

It was another perfect June day and the ride to the village church took a scant twenty minutes. A man working in the small front garden of the stone house beside the church came and took their horses. By the time they had walked up the path to the front door a maid was waiting to greet them. She showed them into a comfortably furnished parlour. A plump grey-haired woman in a lace cap and a plain chintz gown rose as they entered.

'Your Grace,' the woman said, dipping a curtsey. 'How good of you to call so soon after arrival at Falconwood.'

'I am glad we found you home, since we sent no warning. Is your husband around?'

'Called out to visit a parishioner, I'm afraid. The Widow Redfurn. She's been ill in her bed for days.' Her glance went to Minette, her grey eyes twinkling.

'May I introduce you to my betrothed, Miss Minette Rideau,' Freddy said.

The woman curtseyed again. If she had notice the strain

in Freddy's voice she didn't show it. But Minette had noticed. Clearly he did not like deceiving this woman. She held out a hand. 'I am very glad to meet you, *madame*. His Grace has informed me of your past kindness.'

Mrs Farmer blushed and beamed with pleasure. 'My husband and I have always been fond of Freddy, him and his brother. Pair of mischievous lads. Always up to something they were.'

Freddy's expression softened. 'And we knew where to come when we were in a scrape.'

Mrs Farmer smiled at Minette. 'My husband had a soft spot for those two lads. Not an ounce of malice in either of them, he always says. It was the worst of bad luck, that accident. And so I'll say to anyone who asks.'

Her voice held a bit of a challenge, for which Minette felt grateful on Freddy's behalf. Before she could ask about this rush to defend him, Mrs Farmer gestured for them to sit. 'You will take tea?'

'Absolutely.' Freddy deposited his hat on a side table and helped Minette to sit, before sprawling beside her on the sofa. 'Tell us all the news. It is an age since I was here. How fares everyone?'

Having rung the bell for tea, Mrs Farmer sat down and began to talk about what seemed like an endless list of people. The tea tray arrived. The tea was drunk and still the gossip continued. Minette did her best to look interested when she was dying for Freddy to ask the all-important question.

'Mrs Pearson's husband died last year, you know,' the woman said, leaning forward with a sad expression. 'She moved to Yorkshire to live with her daughter.'

'Did she sell the house?' Freddy asked.

Mrs Farmer shook her head. 'Leasing. She was at her

wits' end, with no one local interested. She had to leave a solicitor to handle the matter.'

'Really?' Freddy said.

'It will be a blessing if she can find a tenant. If not she'll have to let it go and her Sammy always swore it would go to his grandson. It would be a real blow if she can't honour his wishes.'

'Have her to send word to me,' Freddy said. 'I could likely make use of the land, if not the house.'

'Oh.' Mrs Farmer looked surprised.

'What is it?' Freddy asked.

She shook her head.

'You asked Mother,' Freddy said in a flat tone.

Her face coloured. 'I mentioned it, but she said that while she could see you purchasing the land, Mrs Pearson's pure foolishness in wanting to keep it was not to be encouraged.'

Freddy got to his feet. 'As I said, if she doesn't find a tenant have her write to me.' He turned to Minette. 'It is time we were going if I am to show you more of the estate, my dear.'

They made their farewells, and Minette promised she would call with Freddy later in the week and discuss arrangements for the wedding with the Reverend.

'You didn't ask her about strangers.'

She sounded worried, as if she feared he could not protect her from this Moreau. A stinging blow to his ego indeed. Or perhaps it was simply part of the game she was playing with him. A way to lull him into a false sense of security. 'Asking would only make her curious. She would have told me if anyone new had moved in or been asking questions.'

The furrow in her brow said she was not entirely satisfied. 'So what do we do now? Seek him in Maidstone?'

'Hardly. Not with the ball in the offing.'

'You would let Moreau go free for the sake of a stupid ball?'

He decided to be honest. Up to a point. 'It is not stupid. The coincidence of the ball and Moreau travelling to this district at the same time is too much to discount.'

'You think to let him come to you. It is a very dangerous ploy.'

So intelligent. Whatever she had been doing in France she had not been sitting in a nunnery, saying prayers. Her appearance at the Ramsgate and her responses to his far-from-respectable kisses meant she had been involved in something far less innocent, something dangerous. And Moreau was at the heart of it. And was she warning him? Or pushing him one way so he would go in the direction she preferred?

The way he did with Mother.

He would have to tread very carefully if he was going to find out exactly where she stood in regard to this Frenchman. He'd hoped to gain her trust, but since he hadn't he would have to treat her as an enemy, until proved otherwise. 'Do you have a better idea?'

'How can you stop him, if someone at the ball is his ultimate goal?'

'We will watch. I would like to take a look at this farm that is up for lease. If I recall it correctly, it is quite isolated.'

'Oh.' She nodded and brightened considerably. 'Yes. It is the sort of thing that would be very useful. A place to hide. Do we go there now?'

'That is where we are headed.'

'You don't think we will scare him off?'

'If a tenant had taken up residence, Mrs Farmer would have told us. There isn't an ant that moves in this parish without her knowing.'

To his surprise, Minette blushed. The realisation why hit him a second later. 'The servants at the manor are completely trustworthy. Mother wouldn't allow anything else. One word of gossip about the doings of Falconwood and they would be tossed out onto the street.'

'Your mother is a formidable woman.'

'True.' He grinned. Couldn't help it. 'Not looking forward to your interview later?'

'I think it is going to be difficult. The head gardener was astonished that I was meeting with him and kept saying he would have to check with the "missus".'

Anger scored his insides, which were already raw enough. 'I'll have a word with him.'

'I really don't think we should be upsetting your mother to no purpose.'

He repressed the urge to tell her that he didn't care what she thought was going to happen after they caught Moreau, they would be wed. One battle at a time. It was wisdom he'd learned early. And this particular battle wasn't going to be easily won.

Beyond the village he turned off the main road and up one of the lanes that wound its way from farm to farm. The Pearson place was one of the most remote. They rode side by side at an easy walk, each apparently busy with their own thoughts. A rabbit darted out in front of them. Her mare startled and tossed its head but she quickly brought it under control. Whereas with another woman he might have moved closer ready to grab the reins, he merely gave her room to manoeuvre. She gave him a small smile of triumph as the horse quickly settled.

He'd already seen that she had an excellent seat and managed the spirited mare with ease. It pleased him to watch her lithe body sink into her saddle, her competent hands guiding the mare. He pictured them riding around the estate together, visiting tenants, discussing plans. He stilled. He was thinking like the Duke of Falconwood. Not like the second son. It was a bit of a shock to realise he was coming to accept his role in life. Because she would be part of it.

This would be his last job for Sceptre.

It would have to be. A man with a wife, with the kind of responsibilities that went with the dukedom, could not continue to play ducks and drakes with the estate's future by letting Mother have a free hand as he had been doing these past several years. It needed a different hand on the reins, according to his steward. Mother had too many old-fashioned notions. He'd seen the evidence of that on their ride this morning. The idea of serving the place where he grew up no longer felt like a penance. Not if he had the help of a woman he cared about. Liked. Lusted after. None of those words seemed to cover exactly what he felt for Minette, although he certainly felt all of them. And he still wasn't sure she'd have him, not in the way he wanted, on terms he would have to make clear before the wedding, if he was going to be fair.

The hedgerows were full of dog roses and the air redolent with their scent. The likelihood of meeting traffic on such a remote lane was slight, but it would be better to be sure. At the first gate they came upon, he called a halt. 'We'll cut across country.' He lifted the latch with his crop and ushered her through.

The mare rolled her eyes but trotted through as nice as you please. Minette held her at a stand while he closed the gate behind them.

'Which way?' she asked.

'Straight across.'

She eyed the distance with a look of mischief. 'I wager I can be over the wall before you. I dare you.'

'No,' he said.

The mare needed little encouragement. *'En avant, Freddy,'* she cried over her shoulder over the thud of hoof-beats.

Freddy urged his horse to follow. Damnation, she was a fine horsewoman. There was no doubt he would win but... His heart rose in his throat as he recalled the nasty drop on the other side of the wall.

'Minette. Stop,' he yelled, encouraging his gelding to greater effort when she didn't appear to hear him.

His heart pounded in his chest. His vision narrowed to one horse, one rider and the looming wall. The image of a twisted, broken body careened through his mind. Not his brother's this time but hers. And then they were neck and neck. He threw himself off his mount and grabbed at her horse's headstall, using his weight to bring the animal to a bone-wrenching halt. The mare stood, chest heaving, three short yards from the low stone wall, while his own mount swerved, slowed and started cropping at the grass a short distance away.

Fury in her eyes, she raised her crop. *'Idiot. Qu'est-ce tu fais?'*

He grabbed the whip from her hand and threw it down. 'You are the idiot. Do you know what is on the other side of that wall? No. Of course you don't. You'd sooner get yourself killed than lose a race.' Nausea rolled through his gut as he heard his voice speak the words that had resided so long deep in his soul. He took a step back. Pain shot up his leg. Damn it. He'd twisted his ankle. Furious, he let go of the bridle and hobbled across the grass to collect his mount.

When he had himself mounted and his horse turned around she was at the wall, looking over. She glanced over at him with an expression of chagrin.

'*Mon Dieu*. One would never guess the ditch was there.' She gave a little shudder. 'I beg your pardon.'

His heart refused to settle. His blood was surging hot in his veins. His throat was still dry. 'Even a schoolboy knows better than to go at a hedge he has never seen before.'

A red flush spread upwards over her face. 'Perhaps an English schoolboy,' she shot back. 'In France our boys have more courage.'

A red haze blurred his vision. The picture of her broken and bleeding on the ground slithered across his mind. 'Courage? Crass stupidity, more like. Perhaps you need to be led.'

She glared at him. 'Try it, if you are in the mood to lose a hand.'

Dammit, she'd apologised. What that hell was wrong with him that he couldn't let it go when she'd come to no harm? But he couldn't. The past remained too close to the surface. An unhealed wound. 'The gate is over there.' He pointed with his whip.

They once more moved off in silence, but it was no longer friendly and comfortable.

'You were limping. Are you injured?' she asked stiffly. 'No.'

Her lovely mouth twisted. 'Perhaps I should look to make sure.'

His blood turned to ice. Just the thought of her seeing... 'I did no more than wrench my ankle.' An ankle that did not like rough treatment at the best of times.

She looked away but not before he caught the tremble of her lower lip. A sniff. Was she crying?

'Minette?' Something inside him twisted painfully.

She turned back to face him, her eyes suspiciously moist. 'Why does it seem that you bring out only the worst in me?'

It was like a blow to his gut, those words. His mother

had always said he brought out the worst in his brother, too. He closed himself off from the stab of pain. 'I beg your pardon if my presence troubles you. I shall be more than happy to return you to Falconwood.'

She stared at him. 'You will not be rid of me so easily, Your Grace.' She lifted her chin. 'Are we near the farm we seek?'

Damn it all, she was back to Your Gracing him. 'Beyond the next field.'

'Are their further dangers I should be aware of?'

A curse caught in his throat. Pain pierced his chest. She was making it sound as if her near accident had been his fault. His gut fell away. She was right. It would have been. He should have warned her about the lie of the land. Had he been with another male, he would have done so the moment they entered the field. 'Nothing I am aware of.' He sounded as stiff and cold as she did, when he should be feeling glad no mishap had occurred. After a small pause, as if she expected him to say more, she turned her horse and set off at a brisk trot.

It seemed their brief hours of truce were over.

Chapter Twelve

Why could he not have simply accepted her apology instead of scowling and looking grim?

Did he think she did not care that she could have badly injured his horse?

The blood in her veins seethed with her anger at his injustice, as well as her embarrassment at her temper.

When they reached the gate she waited in frigid silence while he let them both through and closed it behind them.

He came up alongside her. 'I apologise for my rudeness. I feared for your safety.'

While his face remained grim, his tone was sincere. The hurt inside her subsided. 'Apology accepted. I had no wish to cause you concern, but I can assure you I have survived more than one tumble.'

The muscle in his jaw flexed. 'Not every fall is survivable.'

It was then that she remembered his brother. The reason for his unreasonable fury was suddenly clear. Not that she was about to let him wrap her in cotton wool but she should not have been quite so angry.

'I beg your pardon for striking out at you.'

His lips twitched at the corners. 'Likely I would have done the same if someone took control of my horse.'

She smiled at him. 'It seems we are both endlessly sorry. Shall we put it out of our minds?'

He nodded. 'The Pearson farmhouse is over that hill. We will enter the lane up ahead and come at it from the road.'

'In case anyone is lurking about.'

A small smile curved his lips. 'Exactly.'

The distance to the farmhouse took no more than a few minutes to cover. It was a thatched house washed white and gleaming in the sun. Several outbuildings ranged behind the house. No animals. No sign of inhabitation.

And yet...the place did not feel deserted. 'Someone is here.'

A surprised glance shot her way. 'I was thinking the same thing.'

'*D'accord.* What do we do? Pretend to notice nothing amiss and knock on the door?'

'I'm not out to invite trouble.' He raised his arm and pointed to the buildings and the house as if telling her something about them. 'I wish we could get closer.'

'Moreau would know me in an instant.'

'And you could tell me if he actually had chosen this place in which to hide.'

'Damned if we do—'

'And if we don't,' he finished. At that moment the door to the house opened and a grey-haired man stepped out.

'Hello?' he called out. 'Can I help you?'

'Not Moreau,' Minette confirmed over the pounding of her heart. It was already slowing now that she knew he was not the man they sought.'

'Will you please leave the talking to me?' Freddy asked as they started closer.

How could she say no when he asked so nicely? 'As you wish.'

He cocked a brow, but there was definitely a hint of

a smile curving his lovely mouth. Perhaps she was truly forgiven.

The man strode into the courtyard and they brought their horses to a halt beside him.

'Good day,' Freddy said. 'Falconwood.'

He didn't introduce Minette. The man looked like some sort of well-to-do tradesman.

'Pocock,' he said.

'Ah,' Freddy replied. 'The solicitor.' He looked about him. 'I didn't realise you were here, since there is no visible transport. I heard the place was available for lease.'

'Yes,' Pocock said, squinting against the sun as he looked up. 'My man went off to the village in the gig to arrange for a cleaning woman to go in once a week, to make sure the place is clean and to check on the place.'

'No tenant in the offing?' Freddy said.

Pocock shook his head.

Minette wasn't sure whether to be pleased or sorry. The thought of Moreau taking residence so close to where she was living was nerve-racking, but it would have meant they knew where he was.

'I'm surprised you didn't take up the lease, Your Grace, it butting up on your land,' Pocock said. 'The house is barely habitable, but it might do for a labourer.'

Freddy looked thoughtful. 'I'll do it. Send the papers to my steward.'

Pocock's jaw dropped. 'I was told Falconwood didn't need more land.'

'I've changed my mind.' He touched his crop to his hat. 'Send the papers along to my steward at your earliest convenience.' He turned back. 'Oh, and if anyone else enquires about leasing the property, anyone at all, would you let me know?'

'Certainly, Your Grace.'

Freddy said nothing until they were well out of earshot. 'Old Pearson would have been pleased.'

'It is kind of you,' she said. 'But do you really need more land?'

'Need, no. But having a legitimate interest in the place will make it easier to make sure no one moves in that I haven't vetted personally.' He pointed to a nearby copse. 'From just beyond those trees there is a good view of Falconwood's park. I will have Barker set up a command post there so we are not taken by surprise.'

He was actually telling her his plan. She couldn't help it, she smiled at him and, while he didn't blink the way Granby did, his eyes widened a fraction, a response that warmed her in ways it should not. 'Unfortunately it brings us no closer to finding where Moreau is at this moment.'

His expression darkened. 'No. It seems we are going to have to let him come to us. But with my men here we should have advance notice of any strangers in the vicinity.'

'And there's always Mrs Farmer.'

A smile appeared on his face and he looked like the mischievous boy Mrs Farmer had spoken of. It was enchanting. It touched a place inside her that was far too vulnerable for her liking. But it did seem as if they were on friendly terms again and for that she could only be glad.

And that feeling of gladness was a worry.

Because, in the end, she was going to disappoint him terribly.

While Minette discussed flower arrangements with his mother, Freddy closeted himself in his steward's office. The man seemed overly grateful and a little fearful. It didn't take Freddy long to understand why. His mother had been assiduous in her duties. Running the estate the way his father had. Everything done logically but without an iota of humanity. An unpaid lease resulted in an immediate eviction. An innovation resulted in a reduction of farm labourers. The pattern that emerged was troubling. All of those gone from his land were people he'd thought of as friends. People who'd believed him when he'd said the death of his brother had been a terrible accident.

In particular, his old friend Jake, the under-gamekeeper's son, who had started them off. He looked up from the ledgers. 'Where did Jake's family go?'

The man looked uncomfortable. 'North. To look for work. The factories are always hiring.'

'Jake was in line for the position of head groom.' No one knew horses like Jake. Nausea pushed up into his throat. He should have known about this. Stopped it. 'Do you have a forwarding address?'

'No, Your Grace.'

'And the Biggses?'

Bill Biggs had been at the bridge, cheering them on like a madman. His father had been a labourer on Falconwood lands, as had his father before him.

'Her Grace decided to pull their cottage down. It was in sight of the folly. A bit of an eyesore, you understand.'

That was what had been missing from the view when he and Minette had walked around the lake. 'Locate them.'

'Yes, Your Grace.'

He leaned back in his chair with a sigh. 'How many more?'

'The Clappers and the Webbs. They missed a payment on their leases because of a bad harvest.'

'Try to find them also. Webb had a widowed sister.'

The steward shook his head. 'She died two years ago.'

He cursed softly. 'Not because of us?'

'No.' The man's tone of voice dismissed any such notion, to Freddy's relief. 'A bad cold. Went to her lungs.

Your mother did all that was proper. Fuel for her fire. The doctor.'

Thank God she'd had that much heart. Clearly, he could no longer leave the management of the estate to Mother. He hadn't worried about it because the income was always as expected. But money wasn't everything. A landowner looked after his people. And a man took care of his friends.

The butler rapped on the door and came in. 'Her Grace sends her compliments. The ladies are taking tea in the green drawing room.'

The drawing room wasn't the place to discuss these particular issues with his mother, so he would still his tongue for now and enjoy Minette's company. He looked at his steward. 'Let me know as soon as you have located any of our people.' He gave the man a sharp stare. 'Me, you understand. No one else.'

The steward touched his forelock. 'It will be my pleasure.'

The sincerity in the man's eyes was genuine. The steward was clearly glad Freddy was taking up his affairs in person. No doubt he thought he'd left it a bit late.

Damn him. He was right.

When he wandered into the green drawing room, one of the least friendly rooms in the house, he found the two ladies sitting in what he could only describe as a strained silence. If Mother would only unbend to Minette a little, make her feel welcome, he would be able to forgive her anything. The realisation came as a surprise he did not want to examine too closely.

'How are the plans for the ball coming along?' he asked, sitting beside Minette on the sofa opposite his mother, who was presiding over the most formal tea set they owned. Likely using it as a means of intimidation. Something she had off to a fine art.

'I had a long discussion with Mr Jevens.' Minette picked up a portfolio bound with a green ribbon and opened it. 'I made some sketches of the ballroom and the terrace with some ideas for how we might utilise the flowers from the greenhouses.'

His mother looked down her nose. 'As I said earlier, Miss Rideau, I will look at your proposals and discuss them with the staff when I have a moment.'

In other words, Minette's ideas were not worth her time. Freddy looked through the drawings. The sketches of the rooms were excellent, giving the proportions and proper perspectives, but the ideas for the arrangement of the veg-etation was extraordinary. 'You have brought the outdoors inside.' He looked closer. 'These are orange trees.'

'Jevens said that if he is careful he can have them all in full bloom. The room will be filled with their perfume. He believes the trellises will not be too difficult to construct with some help from some of the men from the estate, and they will be perfect for the roses.'

'What of the flower beds?' Mother said. 'They will take years to recover if you strip them of blooms.'

'Jevens assured me that would not be the case,' Minette said. 'Indeed, he was saying that so few of the roses have been picked these past many years that they will benefit from a little thinning.'

'The Duke did not like flowers inside the house,' Her Grace said. 'He said they made him sneeze. I do not want my guests walking about sniffling. And this idea of yours of setting up the dancing on the terrace will not work. What if it rains?'

'Then we will move the dancing indoors,' Freddy said. 'Why have it outdoors at all?'

'It will be a full moon,' Minette said. 'It will be romantic. According to my sister, our mother often arranged *al fresco* parties.'

'That is France,' Mother said in a quelling tone. 'This is England.'

He could see that Minette was frustrated by his mother's intractability, but he was proud of the way she had made her case so reasonably. She would make a good Duchess.

And he was going to make sure she did not slip through his fingers, even if he did have to play dirty to do it. Last night he'd let his honour get in the way of accomplishing his goal. It would not happen again.

'I think it is a fine idea,' Freddy said.

Mother's spine stiffened. 'Well, if you do not mind your guests going home chilled to the bone and blaming us for their subsequent illness, I shall have nothing more to say on the matter.'

'Good. Then the matter is settled.'

'I would still appreciate your views on the detail,' Minette said to Mother, attempting to act as peacemaker.

As if she had not heard, Mother poured the tea and handed each of them a cup. 'I understand you spent the past hour or so with Carter, Frederick.'

That was one way to change the subject.

'I did.'

'You should have come to me if you have questions. Carter is all very well in his way, but he has not had the benefit of working under your father. He has no concept of our history. Of what is important.'

The man had been his choice after their old steward had begged to be permitted to retire. He forced himself to remain outwardly calm. 'He understands modern farming methods.'

'Modern.' She tutted. 'What was good enough for your father and for his father should be good enough for you.'

For the son who had stolen the true heir's birthright. He could hear the meaning in the inflection in her voice. He quelled his anger. Swallowed the bitterness. 'If the estate doesn't change with the times, our fortunes will suffer.'

Her mouth tightened. Then she trilled a brittle laugh. 'The man is impossible. He actually suggested ploughing up the five-acre meadow and planting some sort of disgusting vegetable. And then he wanted to buy some infernal machine to sow seeds.'

'I know. I told him to do so.'

Her back stiffened. 'You overruled my decision?' She stirred her tea.

'Because it was wrong.'

She fairly vibrated with indignation. 'My decisions are those your father would have made.' The tea in her cup became a veritable storm. 'He must be turning in his grave. If your brother had lived, he would know the right way to go about things.'

Back to that. Of course. 'I am sure he would.'

Minette took his mother's cup and set it on the table. 'Please, Your Grace. Do not upset yourself.'

'I know what I am doing,' Freddy said. 'I have been reading up on modern methods.'

Mother gazed at him sorrowfully. 'I might be less concerned had you applied yourself while your father was alive. Night after night he bemoaned your lack of application. Your disinterest. All you thought about was raking around Town. You were a constant source of disappointment.'

Minette gasped.

Freddy closed his eyes briefly. The silent accusation in his father's eyes and the bitter condemnation of his mother out of his father's hearing, along with his own guilt, had driven him to the worst kind of excesses, until Gabe had come along and given him a purpose. And then his father had died and left him with the blasted dukedom.

'It is all water under the bridge. You have been carping at me for years to take up my responsibilities, so here I am.'

Mother bristled. 'You should have discussed these decisions with me before countermanding my instructions.'

His hand clenched on his saucer. A taut silence fell.

'Mr Jevens thinks the weather will be fine for the ball,' Minette said. 'Something to do with his rheumatism.'

The look of appeal for support she sent Freddy made him take a deep breath. He had fallen into Mother's trap of trading barbs. As usual she had goaded and goaded until he could stand it no longer.

'If you ladies will excuse me, I am going to visit the home farm this afternoon.' What he really needed to do was get away from his mother before he tossed her out on her ear.

Chapter Thirteen

'I suppose it is time I went down,' Minette said to Christine. 'Yes, *mademoiselle*.'

The thought of another meal caught between Freddy and his mother made Minette shiver. The way his mother battered him with her disdain explained a great deal about the man. Particularly his chilly distance.

Clearly, his mother held him responsible for her elder son's death. Shouldn't she be happy that one of her sons had survived?

Poor Freddy. She had no trouble imagining his feelings, the guilt laid on him by his mother. Every time she thought about Moreau and the damage he could do to her family, she felt ill. It was why she had to make sure he was stopped.

Christine placed a sprig of silk flowers in her hair. *'Tout finis.'*

'Thank you.' She moved away from the mirror and picked up her shawl. Her gown was modest enough but somehow the chilly gaze of the Duchess always made her feel as if she was flaunting her wares.

When Christine opened the door, Minette was surprised to see a young footman loitering outside. He bowed. 'His

Grace's compliments, Miss Rideau. Dinner will be served in the dining room in the ducal apartments this evening.'

She had never heard of the ducal apartments. There was something about the footman's expression, the twinkle in his eye perhaps that seemed a little conspiratorial. As if he was privy to some interesting information. Or was it just the novelty of dining *en famille*? She couldn't help but be glad if the Duchess had decided to be a little less formal. Or perhaps not. Perhaps the Duchess would give even more free rein to her sharp tongue. She winced.

'If you would follow me, miss,' he continued, 'His Grace asked me to show you the way.'

He led her down the stairs and along a corridor on the ground floor past the library and along a passage that ran at a right angle. This was one of the wings of the house she hadn't yet seen.

He opened a door and stood back to let her into a room that was very different from anything she had seen in the rest of the house. Not a dining room but a sort of parlour. A room with overstuffed chairs, dark-panelled walls and several rather battered tables. It looked comfortable. Welcoming. And very male.

Freddy strode towards her. 'I hope you don't mind. Mother decided not to join us this evening. She is taking dinner on a tray in her room. I thought we might allow ourselves to be a little more comfortable.'

'Where is here?'

'This is my suite of rooms. Where I entertain friends without disturbing Mother.'

'When the footman mentioned the ducal suite I envisaged something different. I like it.'

'May I offer you a glass of wine? Or sherry? Dinner will be in the room next door. Patterson will let us know when they are ready for us.'

'Sherry, please.'

While he went to the sideboard against one wall, containing several decanters and glasses, she walked over to the window, which, as she approached, she realised was, in fact, a door out into a shrubbery with a path leading through it to the stables.

'Have all the Dukes used these apartments?'

He came back with her glass. 'No. These were the rooms assigned to me once I left the schoolroom.'

The heir at the time no doubt had something far grander in the main part of the house. 'It all seems very comfortable.' Unlike the rest of the house, which seemed cold and oppressive.

His shoulders eased and she realised he'd been expecting some sort of criticism with regard to his choice. 'It is. I spend little time at Falconwood as a rule and these rooms suit me very well.' He flashed a grin. 'I like being able to come and go as I please.'

She sipped at her sherry. It was of the finest quality. 'Something a young man might see as an advantage.'

A smile curved his lips and mischief flashed in his eyes. She had never seen him look quite so approachable. 'Mmm…'

She laughed at the noncommittal sound.

'Dinner is served, Your Grace,' the footman said, entering through the internal door to the room next door.

Freddy held out his arm and led her into the small dining room, panelled to match the previous room with a dining table large enough to seat six comfortably but set for two, the places adjacent to each other and facing yet another French window overlooking the shrubbery. An array of dishes was set out on the table—a duck, asparagus, a meat pie of some sort and a fish in white sauce.

The butler pulled out a chair for her, while Freddy seated himself.

Patterson poured red wine into their glasses and stepped back. 'Will there be anything else, Your Grace?'

An enquiring glance from Freddy had her shaking her head. 'No, thank you,' he said.

He gestured for the man to leave and they were alone. Surprising. Unusual.

Freddy must have seen something in her face because he smiled all too fleetingly. 'I thought we would be better off serving ourselves, if you don't mind. There are things we need to discuss that I would prefer to keep between us, and opportunities for private conversation are rare in this house.'

True enough. There seemed to be a footman in every room and at every corner. They were unobtrusive and no doubt carefully screened for discretion, but there were some things to which no one should be privy. Conversations and other things. She felt her face warm. Blushing. At the thought of his visit to her last evening. Had any of those footmen seen him enter her room in *dishabille*? Would they report him to his mother? The morals of the *ton,* or rather their lack of them, created little stir, as long as those involved were not innocent misses with impeccable virtue. As she'd discovered at first hand.

'What is on your mind?'

'Barker will be *in situ* at the farm tonight and will scour the neighbourhood for any sign of our quarry.'

The thought of Moreau stole her appetite. She watched without pleasure while he carved the duck and put portions of some of the other dishes on a plate and passed it across. 'Is it your belief that it is Moreau's intention to target someone at our ball?'

He stared at the slice of duck on his fork. 'Our enqui-

ries have not located him in the north, though we know
he took a post chaise to York. After that, he disappeared.
I honestly don't see the connection but I believe we would
be taking a risk not to assume he will arrive here in Kent
during our celebration. If I am wrong and the garrison is
his goal, then they have been warned.'

'And if he does not show up at all?'

'Then we will know we have been gulled by your
Frenchman.'

Her stomach dipped and then she realised the Frenchman he referred to was not Moreau but Latour. 'I hope he
is wrong. The house is vulnerable to attack when we have
no idea what he wants.'

'Barker's men will set up observation posts around the
house and watch for anyone coming or going. My tiger will
liaise between Barker and me two or three times a day.'

'It sounds as if you have done this before.'

He met her gaze. His face was serious. He was worried
and trying to hide it. 'More than once.' He addressed himself to his dinner as if what they were discussing was the
most commonplace thing, like the weather or a horse race.

She took a sip of her wine. The knowledge that Moreau
might be trapped before she had a chance to speak to him
was troubling. She needed to recover her property without anyone knowing. And she couldn't do that unless they
discovered where he was staying. It seemed Freddy and
his men were focussing all their attention on catching him
on the move.

Nom d'un nom, could nothing go smoothly?

His betrothed looked enchanting tonight. Her glossy
brown hair, caught high on her head and falling in ringlets on one side, made his fingers itch to pull out the pins.
The secrets in her eyes were a constant source of temp-

tation to a mind as curious as his. While she did her best to hide her thoughts, it was clear to Freddy from the way she picked at the food on her plate that she was worried. The exact cause of her concern he had not as yet divined. And clearly she wasn't going to tell him.

The imparting of confidences required a high level of trust, and he didn't have hers. He hadn't even been able to convince her to marry him to save her reputation. A pretend betrothal was as far as she would go. While he didn't blame her for her lack of trust, since he didn't trust himself all that much, he was not going to let her escape her vows.

He was a patient man. If being shut up indoors for weeks on end because of his foot had taught him one thing, it had taught him endless patience.

'Is the duck not to your taste?' he asked. 'Shall I ask for something else to be sent?'

She startled. 'Oh, no. The duck is delicious. You must excuse me, my mind was wandering.'

'Wool-gathering.'

'Pardon?'

'When someone's mind is engaged elsewhere it is called wool-gathering.'

She laughed. A delightful sound. Full of merriment. 'I beg your pardon. It is rude to gather the wool, I think.'

'No. I like watching your face. You give little away, but you were clearly not pleased by the direction of your thoughts.'

'I was thinking about our plans, what we will do if things go awry.'

She pushed a carrot from one side of her plate to the other. The urge to take her on his lap and feed her one mouthful at a time until he was sure she was suitably nourished had him putting his hands flat on the table in preparation. He forced himself to remain seated. She was a woman of spirit and pride. She would not welcome him ordering her about. Yet.

'Moreau is a clever and devious man,' she mused, sending a potato to join the carrot. 'He might sense a trap.'

The pain in her voice, the way she hid her gaze made him look forward more than ever to catching up with the man. He wasn't sure what he had done to Minette but apparently it had affected her deeply. 'We will catch him, no doubt about it. Sooner or later he will make a mistake.' He took a swallow of wine. 'Eat. There is no sense in worrying about the future. Plan, yes, but worry, there's no sense to it. We can never know what is to come.' Like becoming a duke because of one stupid bragging statement he'd do anything to retract.

'You advocate patience.' She cast him a brief and considering glance before returning to the rearrangement of her vegetables. Peas were now making the journey, one at a time.

'Eat. If we are to chase French spies around the countryside you will need your strength.'

A small smile appeared and this time her glance did not flitter away. 'You are right. And, besides, I gather your fancy French chef is likely to take a pet if the dishes are sent back untasted.'

'He's as French as my elbow.'

She grinned. 'I know. I met him on my tour with the housekeeper. He was clearly terrified I would ferret out his secret.' She forked up some fish in white sauce. 'I pretended not to notice. French or not, his food is excellent.'

'I will be sure to pass along your approbation.'

For the next few minutes they applied themselves to the meal in front of them in silence, and it wasn't long before they were finished. He rang for the footman to clear away and bring the dessert course. He would have preferred to have done away with the servant's services, but even a duke could only go so far down the road of informality before his servants began to regard him with disfavour. These were things he'd assimilated without realising as a child. Other things he'd had to work harder to learn, like when his father had finally accepted he had a new successor to train.

'What is this?' Minette stared at one of the desserts after the footman had left the room.

'Bread and butter pudding.'

'Pudding.' She made a face. 'It is a very English thing, this pudding.'

'I suppose it is. I hadn't thought about it. However, it was one of my Reggie's favourites. Mother has it served at every meal.' He never touched it, though he had liked it as a boy.

'Another slap across the cheek?' she said.

He frowned. 'I do not understand.'

'Always, she throws the death of your brother in your face. It almost seems that it pleases her to hurt you.'

He stiffened. He wasn't surprised that she had picked up on the relationship between him and his mother—they were, after all, at war, but it was hardly her place to have an opinion. He gave her a quelling look and hoped she would drop the subject.

She raised a brow. 'One feels the chill in the room when you are together.'

'You don't really expect me to respond to that, do you?'

She sighed. '*Tiens.* I will say no more.' She stared at the pudding on her plate and put down her fork. '*Je suis finis.*'

'Hopefully with dessert and not with me. I beg your pardon. Things have been less than pleasant with my mother for a very long time. I have given up caring. Come, let us retire to the sitting room. They will bring tea there while they clear away the dishes.'

They strolled back into the other room. 'You call this a sitting room?'

'It seems more apropos than drawing room. It really isn't elegant enough for such a distinguished term.'

He guided her to the chair by the hearth.

She glanced around, her face carefully blank. A chilly distance had opened up between them, no doubt because he'd refused to let her commiserate with him over his mother's behaviour. He couldn't do it. It would open wounds older than his brother's death.

'I feel as if I should have brought some needlework or some sheets to hem,' she said brightly. Too brightly. 'It is the kind of room where a *maman* plies her needle while *papa* reads aloud.'

A crack of light appeared somewhere in the darkness inside him. The idea of something as warm as domestic bliss. A far-off dream now dangling before him like a bauble he had only to reach out to grasp. A lie, though. Even when they married, it would never be true for them.

The footman arrived with the tea tray and put it in front of her.

'Everything like clockwork,' she commented.

Glad of a neutral topic to redirect the darkness of his thoughts, he took the seat opposite her and stretched out his legs. 'An establishment of this size cannot run on a whim.'

'But it could be less regimented.'

The implied criticism made him bristle. He wanted to defend, but forced himself to be more rational. 'You see improvements that are needed?'

She pursed her lips. 'The grandeur is impressive.' She gave a sad smile. 'But I would not be the right person to uphold such consequence, I fear. It is a house, not a home. It is cold.'

Like its occupants. The thought lingered, silent, accusing.

He left his chair and sat beside her on the sofa. Her perfume drifted into his lungs with each breath of air. 'You are too modest. You underestimate your abilities.' He took her hand and raised it to his lips, inhaling the scent of her skin to the sound of a soft gasp. 'As my duchess, you would be welcome to make whatever changes you wished. I think we would deal well together as husband and wife.'

'You didn't think so when we met first,' she said, sounding a little bit breathless. 'On board ship.'

That husky sound gave him something he hadn't felt in a long time. Hope. She was attracted to him, and he intended using his every advantage, though it seemed he had some lost ground to make up.

'You mistake the matter,' he said, stroking his thumb over her palm and smiling at the way the small hairs on her wrist stood to attention. 'There is this unwritten gentlemanly code of conduct. A man who is not in the market for a wife does not flirt or in any way show an interest in his friend's little sister-in-law. You were barely eighteen when we met. Gabe knew I had no thoughts of marriage. He would have put a bullet in my brain if I had so much as hinted I found you interesting.'

'Did you?'

'Find you interesting? *Bien sûr.*' He kissed the inside of her wrist and inhaled her delicious scent. 'Do you doubt it?'

'You called me a brat.'

'A smokescreen. As I said, there is a rule. I think you might have been throwing off a little smoke yourself at that time.'

She averted her gaze, and he knew he was right. 'What were you hiding?'

She stilled, but the pulse beat in her wrist picked up speed.

'Very well,' he said. 'It is not important. But, Minette, do not hold my past behaviour towards you against me. It will make for an uncomfortable marriage if you do. And we will be married. Make no mistake.'

'Because of your honour. Because of Gabe.' Her words were calm, accepting, but he wasn't idiot enough to step into that sort of trap.

'Because I want you for my wife.'

Her head whipped around. There was disbelief on her face, but was there hope there also? God, he hoped so. Another woman in his life who couldn't abide him was going to make life hell on earth. Not that he deserved anything much better. To be contemplating marriage when he had sworn he would take no benefit from his brother's death and serve simply as custodian. The only defence he'd had to the accusation in his parents' eyes. But he did not expect his Duchess to live on the proceeds of Fools' Paradise, as he had done these past several years. When he married he would have to keep her in proper style. She'd be entitled to wear the family jewels, too. And she ought to have some of her own. Personal items.

He looked at her left hand. Ringless. He should have bought her a ring, a token, something to mark their engagement. To mark her as his. Hell's bells, where had this feeling of possession come from?

He tipped her chin with a fingertip and gazed down into those fascinating eyes. 'Well, brat,' he said softly, 'shall we make the best of it?'

And would she let him seduce her this time?

The heat in his gaze made Minette feel giddy with longing. He almost had her believing he wanted this marriage. Almost. The recollection of his face when he'd realised they'd been caught in a compromising position had faded but not completely disappeared.

'I did not arrange for us to be found in the library,' she said. 'The last thing I wanted was to ruin my reputation.' For Nicky's sake.

'I believe you.'

'You do?' She could not keep the surprise from her voice. It was rare for any man to admit he was wrong.

'I do,' he said firmly. 'While you were reckless in coming to my club to find me, foolhardy in the extreme, you were open and honest about your intentions. At Gosport's ball I let past experiences colour my judgement. I should not have said what I did to you that night. But we can't keep apologising for something that has happened. We have to move on.'

Guilt washed over her. 'To be truthful, I wasn't displeased that it happened. It suited my plans.' He went to speak, and she touched a finger to his lips. 'You must understand.' She stared into her teacup as if it would give her the words she so desperately needed. 'If all else failed, I might have thought trapping you a perfectly acceptable strategy.'

He chuckled softly. 'Honest to a fault. I think my rush to judgement that evening was coloured by your previous partiality for cheating.'

'That I did to annoy you,' she admitted ruefully. 'You seemed so irritated by your role as bear leader. As if you would sooner be anywhere else than playing cards with me.'

'Irritated? So much so I couldn't make out one card from another. All I could think about was kissing you.'

His eyelids dipped a fraction, his gaze dropping to her lips, his mouth softening.

Her breath caught in her throat. The man was positively seductive when he set his mind to it. And his kisses were deliciously tempting, especially as there had been no kissing in her life after coming to England, except for his. There had been no one else she'd wanted to kiss, if she was truthful. Not after Pierre. But there was something else playing on her mind. He was a duke. He had to marry and produce an heir. How would she feel once Moreau was caught and she cried off and he married another?

She would be lying if she said she wouldn't care. She wouldn't like it one little bit. Not now that they had become co-conspirators, friends and perhaps something more.

Yet what right did she have to hold him to his promise of a marriage of convenience, forced upon him by circumstances in which she had played an active part, even if it had been unintentional?

How could she marry him when she'd given away her virtue to a man he considered an enemy of his country? It didn't matter how honourable Freddy was, or how kind; once Moreau was dealt with in a way so that he could never harm Nicky, she must cry off. For his sake. Whether or not the miniature came to light.

Letting him make love to her, as he so obviously wanted to do, might be one way to make sure he didn't object to her ending their betrothal. He'd know for certain she was no innocent miss.

'So you want to kiss me now?' she asked.

'Can't you tell?'

Eyes hot, he lowered his head, and she lifted hers to meet him halfway.

This she would have. This would be accomplished between them, or she would regret it for ever. She wound her arms around his neck and parted her lips to welcome the most sensual of kisses. The strokes of his tongue against hers. The taste of him. The feel of his heart beating against her breasts. Their loud, frenzied breathing.

His hands were large and warm, one on her spine, the other cradling her nape. She felt cherished. Wanted. She stroked his cheek with her fingertips and slowly they broke apart. His eyes were heavy-lidded, his lips curved in a smile, his chest rising and falling in ragged breaths.

Passion personified. Her blood heated, her core fluttered pleasurably, her nipples felt uncomfortable in the confines of her gown. All that with a kiss and a glance. Dark and delicious passion. The man was a wonder.

In a swift, almost negligent move he lifted her onto his lap, one hand casually stroking her shin while the other toyed with a curl that had slipped from its pins. He had a lithe strength that appealed to her femininity in blood-stirring ways. Made her limbs feel languid.

'What if someone comes in?' she said.

A small smile curved his lips. 'One advantage of being a duke. No one enters unless sent for.' He ducked beneath her chin and first kissed and then licked the base of her throat with the sounds of a connoisseur enjoying a fine wine. 'You smell and taste of my favourite things.'

'And what would they be?'

'Aroused woman and jasmine.'

She couldn't help a smile at the sheer devilment in his voice as he drawled the shocking words. She put a hand to her knee to stop his hand wandering above her garter. 'What about your mother?'

'Believe me, that would never happen.'

Utter confidence. And why not? His mother would never arrive unannounced. Not because she was discreet or understanding, she realised with sadness, but because it would never occur to the woman to visit her son.

'Why the worried face?' he murmured, twirling that unruly curl around his finger. He cast her a sidelong glance that glittered in the light of the candles. 'Are you hoping for rescue?'

'Quite the opposite.'

He cracked a short laugh of genuine amusement. 'You are so hard to read. I never have a clue what you are thinking.'

'That is a good thing. A man needs to be kept off kilter.'

'Who told you that?' he asked as he raised his head to look at where his mouth had been. 'Your sister?'

'Something I overheard once.' Minette should not have been listening. But it was how she had learned just what Nicky had endured to keep her safe. She had learned other things, too. Things that had made her feel oddly breathless and hot. Later, she'd understood. She'd also realised what sort of man Nicky's husband had been. His death had not been much of a loss.

He must have heard a note of bitterness in her voice because he gave up teasing her breast to look at her face. 'Unhappy memories?'

'Things best forgotten.' She smiled and pushed up to kiss his cheek, knowing full well the effect of the added pressure on his groin.

He ran his fingers in a light caress down her shin. 'Do you know what attracted me to you the first time I saw you?'

'No.'

His hand closed lightly around her ankle. A gesture of possession that she found very much to her liking. 'This. The prettiest ankles I have ever seen stepped on board that ship. And then, when I looked up at your face, I was done for.'

'I don't believe you.'

'Do you know what the next thing I saw was?' He

nipped at her ear lobe, and a shiver shot through her body. 'Gabe's face. Giving me the fish eye.'

'Fish… What?'

'Glaring murder. Warning me off.'

'And so you were following orders when you were so rude.'

'Mmm.' He dipped his head. Hot lips seared the rise of her breast, his hand curving beneath the swell to plump it up for better access. 'Delicious.'

Delicious indeed. His mouth hot and wet and his tongue teasing at her flesh.

He groaned softly and caught her around the shoulders so he could kiss her with open-mouthed ardour. A kiss of skill and temptation that set her body on fire. She turned into him, her breasts, heavy and sensitive, pressed against his hard chest. He cupped her buttocks and lifted her, adjusting her position on his lap, and she felt the hard ridge of his arousal against her hip.

Once she was settled to his satisfaction, he skimmed a hand up her thigh beneath her skirts and a low sound of approval rumbled through his chest.

Chapter Fourteen

When she'd arrived at his club, he'd done his absolute best to remember she was his best friend's sister-in-law. The woman he'd held in his arms was a passionate, sensual female who appealed to his most primitive of male instincts. Warm and delicious in every way.

An unexpected gift in his life he had no intention of refusing. Not when it would ensure she became his wife. And perhaps, since she wasn't objecting, she wanted the decision taken out of her hands. Please, all the saints above, she didn't say no this time.

The rest of it he'd deal with later. Find a way for them to be together. There were ways a man could make love to his wife and ensure no children resulted. If he was careful.

Her tongue tangled with his, her body melted into him. Her sweet, lush bottom rocked against his rock-hard arousal. Lust clawed at the cage of civility. It was all he could do not to lower her to the floor and take her on the carpet. She deserved more. Better than him, better than this. But it was too late for her to have choices.

She may not have intended their discovery in the library at Gosport's ball, but from that moment on it had been too late to turn back. From that second she'd become his responsibility, no matter what she thought. His to protect.

He stood with her in his arms, found his centre of balance and headed for his bedroom, where he'd closed the curtains and lit the candles after dressing for dinner.

A pang of regret twisted in his chest. Tonight his aim was to make her admit the inevitability of their marriage.

'Oh,' she said softly, as he pushed open his chamber door. 'How unexpected.'

He looked around. Tried to see what she saw. The pile of books on the nightstand. His cricket bat, unused for years in the corner. A bow and arrow next to his shotgun on the wall. The rapiers with which he and Reggie had practised swordplay in the Long Gallery above the mantel. The things he and his brother had collected—birds' eggs, rocks, an old flint arrowhead on the desk in front of the window. It was the bedroom that belonged to the boy, not the man. 'I don't spend much time here to be bothered to change it.' In truth, he had never found the heart.

He lowered her feet to the floor, enjoying the friction of her soft body down the length of his, and nuzzled at her throat, licking and nipping until she turned her head and bit him hard on the jaw and lifted her face, offering her lips.

His body hardened to granite.

He took her mouth softly, wooing her with lips and tongue, nudging her backwards in the direction of his bed. She broke free with an awkward laugh. Had he read her wrong? Had the promise of passion he'd sensed in her, the blatant sensuality of a woman ready for more than play, been driven by hope?

The hunger raking at his body did not want to be denied, but forcing her was not an option.

She turned in a slow circle, her face full of puzzlement. 'You aren't the person I thought.'

A cold hand fisted in his gut. It was the sort of thing Mother would say. 'Your meaning?'

'There is a lot of affection in this room, when you often seem so cold and withdrawn. I like it.'

Not quite the comment he'd expected. Mother always complained about the clutter. He was certainly far from cold at the moment.

She opened her arms.

He stepped into them, gazing into her smiling, welcoming face, and felt something shift deep inside him. A change that was both tender and painful, as if something had broken and been formed anew from the pieces, yet they didn't fit perfectly.

Odd thoughts. Why question what was being offered with such generosity of spirit?

He glanced down at the rise of her breasts, slowly caressed the curve beneath with one hand while the other explored the dip of her waist. The full swell filled his palm and rose in creamy magnificence above the neckline of her gown. Such exquisitely generous flesh and so bounteously exposed to his feasting gaze. So temptingly displayed, yet their full glory hidden from his view. Leisurely, despite the urgings pounding in his veins, he paid them homage with his hands and then his lips and then his tongue. They tasted of honey and cream and delicious woman.

Her fingers threaded through his hair, and his skin sprang to life beneath her touch. His own body ached for the same gentle exploration.

He slid one hand down her leg and drew her skirt upwards, stroking the underside of her knee and the soft silken skin above her garter, sensing her shivers of pleasure in the little catches in her breathing.

She cupped the sides of his face in her small hands and rose up on tiptoe to brush her lips against his, pressing up against him, her hips arching into him. 'Freddy,' she murmured, her hands wandering down to clutch at his shoulders, her breathing increasing until she was panting, her hands fumbling at the buttons of his coat.

The longing in her voice required no explanation.

His heartbeat quickened. Naked. He wanted her naked.

He tore off both his jacket and waistcoat. Spun her round. Her head fell forward. Vulnerable. He pressed a hot open-mouthed kiss to her nape, inhaling the scent of jasmine and summer, then made short work of her fastenings, pressing small kisses to each inch of her back as he worked the gown down her hips until it slid to the floor. The corset went next, leaving her in nothing but her sheer chemise and stockings, the swell of her hips and buttocks so tempting beneath the filmy veil as she lifted one foot, using the bedpost for balance.

He prowled around her, admiring every inch of that sweetly tempting female body, high, full breasts, long, slender legs with the dark triangle at the apex of her thighs.

He went down on one knee, removing first one slipper then the other, the scent of her arousal making him so hard it hurt. Lifting the hem of her slip, he untied a garter, peeling her stockings down over her calf and off before massaging her small, perfectly formed ankle and foot. He kissed her knee and the inside of her thigh above the remaining garter. She gave a soft moan. Pleasure. Longing. Want.

His hands shook as he removed her other stocking while she balanced with her hands on his shoulders. He pressed a quick kiss between her thighs, feeling the heat and the dampness against his lips and shuddering at her gasp of shock.

Slowly. He had to go slowly.

He lurched to his feet, relieved when she didn't react to his clumsiness.

To his surprise and delight, she hopped up the steps, arms held out like a tightrope walker, and leaped into the middle of the bed. The bed creaked as it accommodated her weight. She cast him a look from beneath her lashes that was pure wickedness. 'Care to join me?'

With an answering growl, he leaped from the floor to the bed, kneeling beside her, taking her tempting mouth in a searing kiss.

Her hands fluttered over his chest and shoulders, sending delicious hot chills down his spine.

Slowly, she yielded to his weight and sank back against the pillows. Their lips clung in a long, lingering moment then he lifted his head and looked down at her, so lovely, flushed with desire, lips full and rosy from their kisses, eyes dreamy with sensual longing.

He had never desired a woman as much as he did Minette. The knowledge she also desired him and yet insisted that she would leave him once their quest was over drove him to the edge of madness. Instead of the respect she deserved, he was going to engage in seduction.

A pang of guilt. Easily vanquished.

It was for her own good after all.

Taking his weight on his knees, he gazed down at her and removed his shirt.

Her gaze roamed his upper body then lifted to his face. *'Magnifique.'*

She had always thought of him as lean. Elegant. She hadn't expected his musculature to be so well defined. His lithe figure and grace belied his now clearly revealed strength. The masculinity of the dark patch of crisp hair on his chest, the ridges of muscle across his abdomen awoke her darkest desires, the longing to taste, to bite. She raised herself up on her elbows and licked at the closest nipple. Rough hair rasped across her tongue.

His hiss of indrawn breath tightened a chord deep inside her with a pleasurable pulse.

She suckled at the beaded nub.

A groan vibrated through his chest.

She released the suction and blew across the damp peak.

His hips involuntarily rocked against her core.

Cold on the outside, this man was molten heat within.

Surprise bloomed in his eyes, warning her she'd been too forward, shown too much knowledge for the innocent he'd no doubt expected. She had no wish to scare him away quite yet. He'd discover the truth soon enough.

Next time, if there was one, she would use her powers of seduction to make him writhe and moan and perhaps even beg. She sank back against the pillow and languidly raised her hands above her head, offering him access to her body, handing over the reins, at least this time.

Eyes hooded, his lips curved in a sensual smile, his hot gaze roved the length of her with hunger. The heat of him washed over her body in waves. He pushed up the hem of her chemise until all but the apex of her thighs were exposed to his gaze. 'Lovely.' He stroked her inner thigh with unbearable tenderness, sending sparks of heat all the way to her core. Of their own accord her thighs parted and he shifted one knee between her legs, looking down at her, raking every inch of her with his gaze, his hands following the path in slow, gentle strokes, down her side, over her breasts, traversing the plain of her belly.

He cupped his hand over her mound and pressed its heel against her sensitive bud. So sweetly painful. She arched into his hand, seeking more of the pleasure just out of reach.

He groaned softly and took her mouth, stretching out beside her, one thigh encased in fine wool over hers. The fabric was silky smooth against her skin and his thighs pressed against the juncture of her thigh, while his hand moved to her breast, gently weighing and softly squeezing, his thumb teasing at her nipple. Heat darted along her veins, the muscles in her core tightened until they hurt.

She moaned into his mouth. Writhed beneath his weight, seeking more of the pleasure he gave. He kissed his way from her mouth to her chin to the pulse at the base of her throat. Hot kisses, his tongue laving, his mouth sucking, promising... Ah, yes. He took her nipple in his mouth, toyed with it with his tongue and then suckled.

The arrow of pleasure streaking to her core almost undid her. She arched her back, rocked her hips against his thigh. He broke away, kneeling over her, his breathing ragged.

'I need this off,' he said roughly. He tugged at the hem of her chemise. 'I need to feel every inch of your luscious skin against me.'

She lifted her bottom so he could push it up over her hips, then sat up to help him take it off over her head. 'And these,' she said, pulling at the waistband of his pantaloons.

Never taking his gaze from her face, he leaped down from the bed and snuffed the candles.

The light of a not-quite-full moon filled the room with shadows and patches of soft light. She sensed, rather than saw, him remove his shoes, strip his nether garment down his legs and step out of them. A glimpse of his arousal. The flash of bare flanks as he climbed onto the bed again and his face caught in a stray moonbeam as he leaned over her once more. The shadows sculpted the muscles of his chest into gleaming planes and shadowed curves. He looked otherworldly, dark as sin, handsome as the devil, and unbelievably sensual.

But she had wanted to see him. All of him.

He had quite deliberately made sure she could not. Was it so bad, then? His leg? That he must hide it in the shadows? She wanted to ask but did not quite have the courage. 'Why leave us in the dark?' she said instead.

He stilled. Stroked her hair back from her face in so tender a motion her heart gave a painful twinge. 'I thought you might be more comfortable.'

Protecting her maidenly fears? Or worried about his appearance? She reached up and pulled his head down for a kiss. No sense in hurting his manly pride. The little she had seen of his body had not disappointed, and there would be other occasions on which to see and explore before they finally parted. Hopefully.

He kissed her back, first palming her breasts and then dipping down to kiss and lick and suckle until she thought she might go mad with wanting—no, needing—fulfilment. The evidence of his own arousal pressed against her hip, so hard and so hot she wanted to take him in her hand, but she had already surprised him with her boldness once so she wasn't going to risk shocking him again and having him stop to question what it meant. Instead, she satisfied her need for touch by caressing the solid muscle across his back and the curve of his buttocks, trying not to score his back with her nails as he drove the pitch of her wanting ever higher with his mouth at her breasts.

Unable to bear it any longer, she could not stop from saying his name. 'Freddy,' she pleaded. It had been so long since she'd had a man inside her.

He lifted his head, his gaze searching her face, but she could not make out his expression. Shock? Surprise?

'Impatient, are we?' he said, his voice teasing, his eyes gleaming with amusement.

He was pleased.

He petted her breast, her stomach, and then moved lower, his fingers stroking through her curls. One finger slipped into her. He made a sound of pleasure. 'You are wet for me.'

Her insides were molten heat. 'Freddy, please.'

He worked one finger inside her, gently stroking. Intrusion. Pleasurable friction. But not nearly enough.

'So tight,' he murmured. 'So ready.'

Another finger parted her folds and slowly pushed deeper, while his thumb pressed against her *perle*. She fell apart, shattered into bliss.

He pressed the blunt head of his shaft against her entrance as the sensations rippled through her body.

Mon Dieu, the man knew his way around a woman's body.

'This will hurt,' he murmured, 'but not for long.'

She winced, not in pain but chagrin in anticipation of his disappointment.

He pushed into her swiftly and stilled, staring down at her, and despite the shadows she saw him realise the truth. And then he was moving. Slowly at first, but as she found the counterpoint to his thrust by lifting her hips, he increased the tempo and the depth. He drove into her hard, building the tension, pushing her back up to the crest of desire, watching her face, easing back when she was sure she was going to shatter, holding her there, punishing her with intense, unfulfilled pleasure and need until she clawed at his back to raise herself up, bit his earlobe and thrust her tongue in his ear. He shuddered and rotated his hips to bring pressure to bear against her *perle*. So wickedly sensitive. She toppled over the edge, her vision turned black, pinpricks of light dancing across the dark.

He rode the wave and gave one last powerful thrust, withdrawing from her body at the moment before he, too, reached his climax. A needless protection but a gesture so heartbreakingly sweet it made her want to cry.

Bones melting, limbs useless, heart pounding at the surge of bliss, she lay beneath his hot, heavy weight. Her hard breathing melded with his so precisely she was not sure that he wasn't breathing for her and her heart wasn't beating for his.

Never had *la petite mort* taken her so completely. It really had felt like a moment of death.

With a groan, he rolled off her and pulled her tight to his side, one hand resting on her breast, one thigh pinning her to the bed.

His warmth, his weight made her feel safe. Treasured.

Since when had she started dreaming of such foolishness?

She couldn't hold the thought and drifted into darkness.

Not a virgin. He wasn't surprised. His body was lax, sated, immovable, but his mind, no longer enslaved by lust, calculated and reasoned with swift efficiency. It made perfect sense. Her boldness. Her comfort with her own sensuality. Her lovely kisses. Somewhere in her past there was a lover. And he found he didn't mind. Much. It had made for a very pleasurable, intimate encounter, one that might not have gone so well if she was inexperienced.

Only one question caused him concern. Why would such an intelligent woman allow him to make the discovery prior to their marriage?

Because she didn't still want to marry him. His gut dipped. With the ease of long practice he quelled the pain of loss. There was no emotion in their bargain. It had always been a convenient arrangement, to save her reputation and keep his honour intact. Keep his friend Gabe from repudiating their friendship.

She might well be surprised to discover it changed nothing. They would still marry. And one thing he knew without a doubt, they were compatible where it counted most.

A quiet sense of joy filled him at the thought of a future of such pleasurable intimate encounters. After the knot was tied. Hopefully it would be enough for her, because they would not be having children.

The small fingers, flat on his chest, flexed briefly. A telltale sign she was awake, along with the slight change in her breathing. Awake and pretending.

'Who was he?' he asked.

The fingers tightened into a fist. She pushed away. He refused to let her go, held her firmly, but not to cause hurt. After a second or two she gave up the struggle.

'It is a fair question,' he said.

'*Tiens*. Wasn't it enough that I tell you I do not wish to marry?'

Upset. She sounded upset when he'd expected defiance. Or wheedling. Or excuses. But, no, she was upset, as if it was somehow his fault. Mentally, he sighed. When it came to women, it was always his fault.

'Fine. I don't need to know,' he said evenly. He hoped he didn't. He hoped like hell the man was in her past and not her present.

This time when she pushed away he released his hold.

She sat up and wrapped her arms around her knees beneath the sheets, giving him a glorious view of her delicate back, the dip of her waist, the dimple above each rounded swell of her buttocks. He rolled onto his side and bit lightly on that firm, silky flesh. More to bring her attention back to him than as punishment, though there was an element of that, too, a primal need to mark her as his.

'Ouch.' She turned and gazed down at him, a crease in her brow.

He hoisted himself up, lit the candle on the nightstand and rested his back against the pillows and headboard. He pulled her back to rest against his shoulder. Her body remained rigid, unyielding, but she did not pull away. He nuzzled her neck. 'Does your sister know?'

'No.'

He waited. Sometimes it was better to say nothing.

'He was a mistake. A very stupid mistake.'

The pain in her voice tore at his heart like a serrated blade. Whoever this man was, he had hurt her badly. And was likely the reason she found it difficult to trust. He wanted to call the man out. 'You met him here or in France?'

'France. In Challans.' She sounded ashamed.

His heart wrenched for how young she must have been. Alone, without family. It was hardly surprising she'd sought protection. 'I'm sorry.'

The words sounded trite, and yet she relaxed against him, giving him her full weight.

Trust. More than any she'd given him before. He kissed the point of her shoulder.

'After you escaped the fire the soldiers set at your house,' he murmured. He knew the story of her escape from the house burned to the ground by Napoleon's troops in an attempt to root out loyalists. He knew that the sisters had been separated by the event, Nicky making her way to England and in the process meeting Gabe. Minette had been taken by a group of nuns. She had been little more than a child. He could only imagine how fearful she must have been. How brave.

'A few months later. The nuns were hidden in the house of a merchant. It was dreadful. Locked up day after day in the cellar. Prayers every few hours. I took over obtaining supplies for the kitchen. It got me out of the house. I met Pierre at the market. He was charming, interesting, alive. I left with him.'

His blood chilled at the thought of a gently bred girl alone in a country in the throes of unrest. He threaded his fingers through hers. 'You took a huge risk.'

'It was an adventure. We would join a group harrying the soldiers. When things got too dangerous we would move on, find another group by listening to conversations in the taverns. Quite often they would find me.' She shuddered. 'Such young men. So full of fire and hope.' She shook her head, her face filling with sorrow, and…guilt? 'They didn't stand a chance.'

He put an arm around her shoulders and gave her a small squeeze. 'I am glad you found people who cared for you.' Much as he wanted to hate this Pierre. 'Where did you come across Moreau?'

'He was…' Her expression shuttered. Clearly her trust only went so far. 'He infiltrated the royalists.' Her voice lowered to a whisper. 'He killed them one by one by one.'

'Pierre?'

Bleakness filled her gaze before she buried her face in her hands. 'Moreau fooled us all. He was so very clever.' Anger and desolation rang in her voice. 'Then he used me to get to Nicky.' She lifted her head. Her gaze was bright with unshed tears and the glitter of anger.

'And now you will have your revenge on him.'

'Nicky gave up everything for me. She married to keep me safe. I want to make sure he can never harm her.'

There was something she was not telling him. A part of him wanted to press the issue, the other part wanted only to offer comfort. He decided on comfort.

He put an arm around her shoulders 'We will catch him. Believe me.'

He held his breath, waiting for her answer, hoping that after tonight she would at least trust him that far.

She said nothing.

As he had taught himself so long ago, he absorbed the blow in silence.

But there was more pain in it than he had expected.

The silence stretched and Minette knew he was disappointed with her responses to his questions, though not angry as far as she could tell. Which in itself was a surprise. She wished to tell him all the rest. Desperately. But then he'd no doubt be disgusted. And she didn't want that, not now, when there was a chance to destroy the evidence of her foolishness.

She needed a change of subject before she confessed everything. 'Why do you blame yourself for your brother's death?'

He turned his head sharply, looking at her in surprise and as if trying to decide what to tell her. She kept her expression neutral. If he did not care to talk about it, she was not going to press him. They were both entitled to their secrets.

He stared upwards at the canopy for a long time. He wasn't going to tell her. She startled when he finally spoke.

'My brother and I had been arguing for weeks about who was the better whip. We argued a great deal. Mostly about foolish things. He was two years older and liked to lord it over me. He was, after all, bigger and stronger. But when it came to book learning and logic he didn't stand a chance.'

He smiled softly, his gaze becoming unfocussed as if he saw the past played out before him. 'One thing we were matched in was riding and driving. Our styles were very different. I like precision in a horse. He preferred brute strength. We both had a penchant for speed. I told him I planned to beat his time from the house to the village on a route that involved a couple of turns and one tricky narrow bridge. Naturally, he challenged me to a race. We set it for the following day.

'On the straight his horses pulled ahead, but he took the second turn too wide. He always did. I was expecting it. I feathered by him.' A sad smile curved his lips. 'I can still see the shock on his face as I pulled ahead. He was catching me up as we approached the bridge, though. The rule is that whoever is behind, even by a nose, must drop back to cross that bridge.'

He shook his head slowly and closed his eyes as if in pain. 'Being ahead there was my strategy. But his team was a whole lot faster than I had anticipated.'

He reached for a glass of water beside the bed and offered her a sip. When she declined, he drank. She watched his throat move as he swallowed. This was hard for him. She felt honoured by his confidence and saddened at her own lack of honesty.

He pulled her closer and twined his fingers in a lock of her hair, brought it to his nose and inhaled. 'The last thing I remember was heading for the bridge a nose in front. Then I was on the ground, the carriage on top of me. I was dizzy. Sick from a blow to the head. And then I saw him a short distance off. Watched the light go out of his eyes.'

'Who was ahead at the bridge?'

His fist clenched, bunching up the sheets at his hip. 'I was so sure I could beat him. I had it all mapped out in my mind. All I can recall is the roar of blood in my ears and the sight of the bridge coming closer. My blood was running so hot I felt invincible. I so wanted to beat him, just once.' He closed his eyes. 'And then nothing. I can't remember if he pulled ahead or not. Damn it,' he whispered. 'Why can't I remember?'

The agony in his face caused her chest to squeeze. 'You fear you didn't follow the rules. That the accident was your fault.' She frowned. 'You are not that sort of person.'

She wanted to bite her tongue when his body stiffened. When she glanced up at his face his eyes had gone as dark as midnight, his expression stark. He took a deep, shuddering breath. 'It was my fault. I should never have challenged him. Not when I knew I had a chance to win.'

'And that is why you let your mother treat you so badly. You think she is right to blame you.'

'Yes.'

Chapter Fifteen

God. Had he really said all that? Spoken about that day for the first time since his father had listened to his version of the event? It was certainly the first time he'd expressed his deepest fear.

The possibility that beneath the civilised veneer of a gentleman lay a cold-blooded killer. *A fratricide.* The *ton* whispered it behind his back. His throat dried and he took another swallow of water before putting the glass down. In his heart he was sure he hadn't cheated. In his mind he wasn't certain. He had been so very determined to win.

What the hell had he hoped to gain by talking about those things? Was he really so devious, so deeply committed to his work that he had bared his soul to encourage her to reveal what she was so obviously intent on concealing? Or had he been hoping for sympathy? Neither felt particularly good.

'Was that how your leg was injured?'

Shocked, he could only stare at her. Of course she was likely to think that was the cause. It would be so easy to make it seem as if he, too, had suffered the consequences of that stupid race without exactly lying.

'My foot, not my leg.' He shook his head. 'It's been that

way since birth.' The reason his mother had barely been able to look at him without flinching. And the cause of his vow to never have children. No child of his would suffer the shame of being a cripple.

She cocked her head on one side. 'May I see?'

Bile rose in his throat. There had been others who had wanted to see, when he had been young and had not realised their interest had been ghoulish rather than the concern of friendship. Until they'd grimaced and called him a freak. Schoolboys, so very cruel. And honest. He'd been lucky Gabe and Bane had not been similarly disposed. 'Why would you want to?'

'You saw all of me before you blew out the candles.'

'You are worth looking at.' No, that was not self-pity he heard in his voice. It was a statement of fact, nothing more. 'It is not a pretty sight.' And a woman's sensibilities were delicate.

'Shouldn't I be the judge?' The determined set of her chin said she would not be denied. And, besides, having revealed the worst of it, she may as well satisfy her curiosity now as later. If she found it disconcerting, he could as easily keep it from her sight in future, as he had this evening.

He flung back the sheet. 'Look your fill.' He leaned back against the headboard so he wouldn't have to see her face. He'd seen both pity and disgust, depending on the woman. He didn't need to see either in her face.

When a warm hand skimmed down his calf, his leg jerked with the shock of her touch. He glared down, seeing the ugliness of his foot and ankle next to the white perfection of her hand. He jerked away. 'What are you doing?'

Hand in hovering in mid-air, she looked at him, puzzled. 'Does it hurt?'

'It aches a bit in cold or damp weather.'

A finger traced the place where his foot went awry, turned inwards. 'What did the doctors say?'

'Doctors can do nothing.'

'Are you saying your parents did not have it looked at by a surgeon?'

Anger. On his behalf. Surprising. And very dear. Something inside him warmed. 'If they did, I do not recall. We never speak of it.' They had done nothing, because they had known the outcome. One of his mother's uncles had undergone surgery and had been worse after than before.

A palm smoothed over the crooked bone. The touch a shocking pleasure. His body reacted. He made a grab for the sheet but she was kneeling on it.

'This leg is shorter than the other, yet it barely hinders you.'

Admiration, yes, but also strangely an admonition.

'My boots are specially made. It doesn't hamper me at all.'

'You don't dance or play cricket.'

'I am a duke,' he said. 'I have my dignity.'

She gazed at him aslant, across her lovely shoulder. 'How is that relevant?'

'It would not suit me to go capering and hopping about, though others might find it amusing.'

'Have you ever danced?

'No.'

'Too bad.' Her gaze dropped to his pelvis. A brow arched. 'It is one of life's pleasures.'

His relief at her common-sense practical acceptance, Heaven help him, her touch where he didn't recall anyone ever touching him before was almost more than he could stand. 'Enough about my foot's shortcomings.' He grinned when she got the joke and wasn't the least bit embarrassed. To distract her, he slid his palm over his own arousal and watched her gaze follow the up and down motion of his hand. 'There are many pleasures where it makes no difference at all.'

She smiled brightly. 'So I see, but it is not better alone, surely?'

The purr in her voice, the wicked gleam in her eyes, the flush across her skin caused his body to further harden. She eyed him and licked her lips.

'Tease,' he growled, entranced by her unselfconsciousness and obviously rising passion. What man would want an innocent when he could have this?

She knelt up, straddling his calves, gazing down at him stroking himself.

He let his hands fall away, leaving himself open, wanting her to come to him, to prove that she was not horrified by what she had seen. Not disgusted. Or fearful. Or, worst of all, prurient. All these reactions he had seen from one woman or another. She circled her fingers about him, taking over where he had left off. Without his volition, his hips pushed up, welcoming the heat, the tightness, the sensuality of her touch. He swallowed the urge to plead for more, fisting his hands in the rumpled bedclothes each side of his hips. Gently, she cupped him. He groaned. Eyes alight with mischief, she gazed down at him. 'Too much?'

'Never,' he ground out. He pushed himself up on his elbows, kissed his way across each breast, teasing her nipples with teeth and tongue until she moaned and arched against him. He flipped her over onto her back. The gold in her eyes sparkled. Her lips curved in a welcoming smile. Never had he felt so comfortable with a woman.

'What now?' she asked, her voice teasing.

What came now was pure pleasure. Hers. If she'd allow it. He made his way down her belly to the nest of black curls. He sat back on his heels and parted her delicate rosy pink folds. So achingly beautiful and pearly with her moisture, and perfumed by her arousal.

He licked.

She moaned.

He found her tiny bud already knotted and ready, and licked and flicked with his tongue, learning what had her writhing and what made her so weak she couldn't do any more than cry out her pleasure, and he tormented and teased until he could no longer see for wanting to be inside her.

He lifted her legs over his shoulders, leaving her deliciously open to his gaze. So beautiful. So enticing. He rose up on his knees, pulling her onto him. Pushing into her hard, burying himself deep.

'Yes,' she cried. 'Harder.'

Hard and fast, he pounded into her, their bodies coming together in hard slapping sounds, his grunts of pleasure-pain mingling with her softer cries of approval. Her inner muscles tightened around him, milking him in steady pulls. Seared by flame, he lost control. He heard his name on her lips, felt the flutters of her orgasm around him and pulled out, spilling his seed on the plain of her belly.

In time. Heaven help him, had he been in time?

He collapsed to one side, grabbing for the sheet to wipe her belly and his, and rolled on his side. She rolled to face him, kissed the tip of his nose. 'Next,' she said, breathing hard, 'we will try dancing. At our ball.'

Did that mean she intended to honour their engagement? If so, it was a battle won. Or did she only mean what she had said? If so, it was a battle lost. For he would not dance.

Above all else, right at this moment he needed what was left of his brain to get her back to her room and quickly, before the house began stirring.

* * *

Stiff and sore in a very satisfying way, Minette wended her way down the grand staircase to breakfast. Freddy rose to his feet as she entered and greeted her with a smile, but there was fatigue in his eyes.

The butler hovered over the sideboard. 'Tea, miss?'

'Coffee, please.'

While he poured her a cup and set it on the table, she helped herself to rashers of bacon and a scoop of fluffy scrambled eggs, along with a couple of slices of toast.

She took the seat to Freddy's right, added cream and sugar to her coffee. Her first sip was delicious. Hunger gnawed at her belly, and she attacked her food.

'That will be all, thank you, Patterson,' Freddy said.

The man looked down his nose, but left swiftly.

Minette spread butter on her toast and looked at Freddy in enquiry.

'Barker arrived early this morning.'

'You have seen him already?' No wonder he looked tired.

Freddy gave a terse nod, his face thoughtful. 'Yes. He's setting up camp.'

Minette glanced out of the rain-streaked window at the scudding clouds. 'Poor man. Could he and his men not stay at the farm?'

He shook his head. 'He'll keep an eye on it as well as Falconwood.'

'You think Moreau might take advantage of its vacancy?'

'It would be wonderful if he did. But the man is as slippery as an eel.'

He was right about that. Moreau was also devious, self-serving and conscienceless.

'I'm going to ride out shortly to confer with Barker.'

'I will come with you.'

He raised a brow, looking grave.

She opened her mouth to object to what was clearly going to be a refusal.

He grinned at her. 'I've asked for your horse to be saddled for ten.'

Teasing. He was teasing her. Astonished, she gazed at him and grinned back. *'Très drôle.'*

'I'm glad you are amused.'

There was a softness in his voice. Affection. Did he think last night had changed things between them? While he hadn't said much about her lack of virtue, surely he wouldn't want to marry her now? How did one approach such a question? Inwardly, she winced. One didn't. Besides, there was no need. In this matter she was the one in control. He could not stop her from crying off. Could not force her to the altar.

The regret causing her stomach to squeeze uncomfortably was foolish in the extreme. Appetite gone, she put down her knife and fork. 'I will be ready.'

His expression changed to one of concern. 'Are you well?'

'Of course,' she said lightly, rising to her feet, forcing him to rise also, noticing the way he adjusted his stance for balance. She'd never really noticed that little adjustment before, and now it made her heart ache sweetly. She forced a smile. 'If I am to go riding in the rain, I must change. Please, excuse me.' She left without a backward glance, but she had the very real sense his gaze never left her until she disappeared through the door.

He'd taken them across country, but with the ground wet and heavy their progress was slow. Freddy glanced over at the lady riding beside him, rain dripping from drooping feathers, face set in a determined but cool expression.

She wasn't going to make his wooing easy. Rain hadn't brought on her dark mood. So busy was she with her own thoughts, she barely seemed to notice her surroundings, or him. Whereas last night she had seemed so full of joy.

Perhaps it was the thought of Moreau holding her attention. Or memories of the man he had betrayed. Pierre. Did she still love him? Her first love? And if she did, why would he care? He took a deep breath and enclosed himself within the familiar chill of feeling nothing. It didn't work. Too many fissures ran through his defences, old hurts and new leaking through him like acid.

He glanced up at the sky. 'It's raining harder. Do you want to turn back?' He leaned closer so he did not have to raise his voice and so he could bring the scent of her deep into his lungs. The smell of jasmine and wet summer mornings.

She shot him a brief glance. 'No. Who can tell when it will end?' She lifted her face to look at the sky and lowered it swiftly, using the wide brim of her hat to shield her from the slash of rain.

'Let us hope it lets up before the night of the ball,' he said for something to say, some way to keep the conversation going. Clouds and rain would mean only those who had been invited to stay overnight would attend. 'The locals will be disappointed.'

When Mother had observed the weather this morning, she'd suggested a postponement. He'd vetoed the idea immediately, despite his betrothed's hopeful expression. Something he hadn't anticipated after their intimate relations. Clearly they had not meant as much to her as they had to him. A bitter thought.

'I would have thought you would have preferred a postponement,' she said, as if she had read his thoughts.

The words were delivered in a light tone but they were

edged with wariness. He bared his teeth in a predatory smile. 'Certainly not. The sooner we celebrate our engagement, the sooner we can be married.'

She leaned forward to pat the dripping-wet neck of her mount, hiding her expression. 'Are you sure you want a wedding?'

So they were going to have this conversation now. He stared at the track ahead, taking account of the deeper ruts and higher spots, while he formulated words little more civilised than *You're mine*, which had risen instantly to his tongue. 'There is no reason I know of why I should not.'

Her head whipped around, her eyes wide. 'You don't care, then, that I do not come to you *intacta*?'

He gave her a hard look, because she was right. Under society's rules, lack of virginity was grounds for a man to walk away, and no doubt that had been her plan in giving in to his importunity. He, however, wasn't going to let her use it as a weapon or an excuse. 'Do you care that *I* do not come to you that way?'

'A different thing for a man,' she muttered. Then smiled a little ruefully. 'Though I cannot help feeling it is unfair.'

A chuckle pushed past his reservations. Her ability to surprise him shook him free of dark thoughts. 'It seems we are well matched in our experience. And given a choice between the pleasure of last night and the task of teaching an innocent, I would take last night every time.'

Her eyes showed relief, quickly hidden by a brittle smile. 'All you care about, sir, is winning.' Her expression froze as she realised the import of her words. She winced and gave him a worried look that told him she believed he could well have deliberately forced his brother off the road.

The joy went out of the day. It was back to rainy and chilly and dark and the dull ache deep in his ankle. He held her gaze. 'Never forget it.'

They reached the entrance to the woods and he urged his horse into a trot that made further talk impossible.

Nom d'un nom. She had not intended to imply that she thought he was responsible for his brother's death. She didn't believe it for a moment. Her ill-thought-out words had sounded too much like the doubts he had expressed the previous evening and he had jumped to the conclusion she had doubts, too.

It would be so easy to use his guilt against him. His mother did it all the time. A horrid female trick she would not resort to in order to get her way. It was too cruel. Too destructive.

No. When she cried off, the flaw would be hers. He had never been anything but a gentleman. Even last night, when he had learned she was not pure, he had treated her with respect. As well as given her more pleasure than she had ever experienced in her life.

Pierre had been an expert lover, astonishingly so, and had taught her much. How to be wanton. How to be bold. How to use her femininity to achieve goals she had never dreamed of. His ultimate betrayal. Because she'd thought him her knight in shining armour. Her saviour. When, in truth, he had been the apple in the Garden of Eden.

Freddy led them between large oaks and beech, the ground carpeted with loam and old leaves that muffled the sound of their horses' hooves. When they slowed and entered a clearing, a man appeared from behind a tree, pistol at the ready, an alert expression on his face.

His eyes widened a fraction at the sight of her then twinkled. He bowed. 'Miss Rideau. A pleasure to meet you again.'

'Mr Barker,' she said, inclining her head. 'Good day.'

'Hardly,' he growled, passing a hand down his face as

if to sweep the raindrops away. Then he beamed at her. 'But it does seem brighter for your presence.'

Freddy dismounted, pulled at the strap fastening a saddlebag and a rolled bundle behind his saddle. He tossed them to Barker. 'Do you have all you need?' Freddy said, chill in his voice.

The man opened the packs, sorting quickly through the contents. 'This is everything I asked for.'

'Good. Any sign of anything untoward?'

'Nothing so far.' Barker's gaze returned to Freddy. 'I'll send the lad to you if we see anything out of place.'

'You are letting a small boy sleep out in this weather?' Minette was scandalised. She knew what it was to be cold and wet for hours at a time. She'd seen children die of chills.

Freddy stiffened.

'Now, then, missy,' Barker said, his face glowering. 'Think I don't know how to build a bivouac? Nice and snug we'll be. And the best of oilskins money can buy, too, thanks to His Grace.'

Oh, dear. It seemed she'd insulted their competence. Both of them. 'I should have known the two of you would be prepared for rain,' she said by way of apology. 'It always rains in England.'

Barker bristled. 'We get our share of good days.'

Hopeless.

'Watch your step,' Freddy warned his man. 'When they come, they will no doubt scout the area. They won't want anyone straying onto them by mistake. I'll ride out again after dark to inspect the perimeter around Falconwood that you'll spend today setting up.'

A small figure entered the clearing with a couple of rabbits strung on a stick over his shoulder. 'Guv'nor.' He strode over to his employer with a flash of crooked teeth and displayed his catch.

Barker rolled his eyes. 'I told you no hunting. We can't light a fire. The coves we're after will spot the smoke as quick as a wink. It's cold beef and beer for us for the next couple of days.'

The boy grimaced and held out his catch to Freddy. 'You want them?'

'I can see you want me hanged for poaching,' Freddy said, taking the offering.

'Nah,' the lad said. 'They'll be your rabbits, I'm thinking.'

'Yes. And don't let my gamekeeper catch you snaring them, or you'll find yourself in the local lock-up and that won't suit my purposes at all.'

'Sorry, Guv.'

Freddy whipped off the lad's cap, ruffled his hair. The boy backed up and smoothed his neatly cut hair, looking indignant but secretly pleased.

Freddy tossed him his hat. 'You'll have your chance to catch rabbits when we are done here.'

A grin split the lad's face. 'You mean it?'

'Yes. If you manage to stay out of trouble and do exactly as Barker says for the next day or so.'

'Agreed,' the boy said, and stuck out a grubby paw.

Freddy shook it without a flinch.

He was good with the child. Kind. He would make an excellent father. Surprising when one considered his mother's coldness. He was also an honourable man. A woman would be lucky have his love and his children. Little black-haired imps of Satan if they were anything like their father—or her, if she was honest. A pain speared her heart. They couldn't be hers. Must not be. He would stick to his word and marry her, if she let him. But it wouldn't be right.

She'd lived the wrong sort of a life for a duchess. If any of it ever came to light, it would reflect badly on any man she married. Duke or otherwise.

And it wasn't as if they were in love or anything. Bedding him, finding truly amazing pleasure in his arms, didn't mean love. It certainly didn't mean they had to marry.

No, she was wedded to the idea of being a spinster and an aunt. She just had to convince Nicky it was so once she'd broken off the engagement.

Chapter Sixteen

Jimmy, his tiger, came hours before the time Freddy had set to visit Barker.

One of the grooms brought a message about his horse being in need of shoeing, a prearranged signal, while he and Minette were at dinner. Fortunately, Mother's headache required her to take her dinner on a tray, as it usually did when he was home, so they could exit his apartment with no one being aware. As they crossed the courtyard to the stables, he couldn't stop himself from glancing upwards. To his mother's suite of rooms. Narrow chinks of light indicated she was still awake.

The woman thought she was punishing him by not coming down to dinner. When he'd been young, her withdrawal had hurt. No longer. Her enmity had existed for too many years for him to care. Besides, she was giving him the hours he needed to spend with Minette. What would Mother do if she had any idea she was doing exactly as he wanted? Show up for dinner?

Unlikely. Not even to thwart him would she spend any more time in his company than necessary.

One thing she would not do was stop him from marrying Minette, despite her privately expressed disapproval.

Jimmy jumped up from the table in the saddle room, where he was wolfing down what looked like stew when they walked through the door.

With one eye on the stew and the other on Minette, Jimmy bowed. 'Yer Grace. A man arrived at the farm half an hour before I left to find you.'

'Eat,' Minette said.

Freddy nodded. 'Get something hot inside you while you can.'

'I know one thing, Guv,' the boy said, a spoonful of steaming stew hovering before his lips. 'I ain't cut out to be a soldier. Nor a farmer neither. Sooner we gets back to Lunnon the better I'm goin' to like it.' He shoved the mouthful in, chewed methodically and swallowed. 'Mind you, the vittles is good. I'll give you that.'

'Thank you,' Freddy said. He waited for the boy to clean his dish with the last of his bread. 'Now. The message.'

'Three coves showed up when it was full dark and the moon wasn't up. They's bein' very careful-like, Mr Barker says. They wasn't so leery as Mr Barker didn't see they was carrying barkers and a couple of long pops.'

'Qu'est-ce que c'est?' Minette said. 'Dogs?'

The boy laughed.

'He means pistols and shotguns,' Freddy said. 'Go on.'

'That's it.'

'How did they travel?' Freddy asked. 'Horse? Carriage?'

'One drivin' the carriage and a couple of outriders.' He rubbed at the bridge of his nose. 'One saddle horse, without a rider.'

'So they have enough horses for three of them to ride.' Freddy looked at her. 'It's a small force. The Regent is bound to come with a company of dragoons.'

'Perhaps a member of government isn't the target,' Minette said.

'Then who?'

'Nicky?'

Something in her voice made him look at her hard. 'Why would you think so?'

'He might be angry that she bested him.'

'Revenge, you mean.' Minette wanted revenge on Moreau for the death of her lover. The Frenchman wanted revenge on Nicky because she'd escaped his clutches. 'It all sounds rather Gothic. This is war. He might have been bested by Nicky, but if he wants to rise in Napoleon's favour he needs to do something to grab attention. That was his aim last time. The death or kidnapping of the wife of an earl won't do him a scrap of good. Though I'm sorry to say it, since Nicky's death would be a horrible blow to Gabe and to you, it won't make a ripple as far as the war is concerned.'

She worried her bottom lip with her teeth before speaking. He wanted to be the one to bite that full lip. He folded his arms across his chest to keep himself standing right where he was.

'Only three men to capture or assassinate the Prince or someone in his party?' she said finally, shaking her head. 'Why bother when there are men aplenty to take their places? Yes, that, too, would make a stir but little difference.'

'Honestly, I have no clue. Our best course is to ask them.'

Her gaze rose to meet his face. 'You will arrest them before they have a chance to do anything.'

'No point in shutting the gate after the horse has gone.'

She frowned. '*Certainement*, but I don't see what escaped horses have to do with the matter we are discussing.'

A weird feeling of tenderness he hadn't known for years

lodged in his throat. Heartbreaking in its sweetness. A small chuckle escaped his lips.

Jimmy glanced up at the sound in surprise equalled only by that on Minette's face.

'It's a colloquialism,' he said, smiling. 'We need to nip their plans in the bud. Stop them before find ourselves at *point non plus*.'

'I see. Once captured you think they will tell you their plans?'

'We'll make sure of it.' Once the men were taken, Sceptre would take charge of relieving them of their knowledge. It would be up to him to find the rest of the web of spies. The key would be for no one to learn that Moreau had been arrested. 'As yet, we don't know for certain that Moreau is among these men. I will need you to take a look at first light. In the meantime, we will get some sleep. You, too, young man,' he said to Jimmy. 'You can bed down here for the night. Barker won't expect your return until morning.'

'Aye, Guv. So he said.'

Freddy took Minette's arm and walked her back to the house. Against every instinct and baser urge, he delivered her to her chamber door and stepped back. 'Get some rest. I'll make sure your maid wakes you in time in the morning.'

'What if Moreau is not there?'

'Then we wait and we watch, and hope he comes.'

He opened her door and thrust her inside, catching a glimpse of her waiting maid and walking away quickly before he changed his mind, sent her maid packing and undressed her himself.

He needed to go and consult with Barker. Arrange things for the following day to his satisfaction. Minette would not be put in danger.

* * *

The weather was fair and fine, if a little chilly, the next morning when she and Freddy rode into the clearing. Her heart was beating very fast at the thought of seeing Moreau again. At the thought of retrieving the miniature. A trickle of sweat ran down her spine. Nerves. Because retrieving that little picture under Freddy's nose was not going to be easy. She'd have to find an opportunity to go through Moreau's things without raising suspicion.

A sour-looking Barker rose from a log to greet them.

'What is wrong?' Freddy asked.

'Loped off is what is wrong,' the other man grumbled. 'Some time after you left here last night.'

Minette glared from one to the other. 'You said you would not come here last night. What is this loped off?'

'They've gone,' Freddy said.

Her stomach dropped so fast she felt sick. 'You scared them away?'

'No,' Barker said slowly. 'They'll be back, but as yet I don't know where they went.'

Freddy swung down from the saddle to face his minion eye to eye. 'You have someone following them.'

Barker nodded. 'I do.'

'What makes you think they will be back?' Minette asked.

'They left the carriage and its horses, with enough feed and water for a couple of days.'

Freddy shook his head. 'Damnation.'

'What?' she asked.

'If he's brought a carriage then I assume he means to use it to transport something or someone,' he mused. 'They must have been informed that the place is unoccupied so decided to make use of its nearness to Falconwood.'

Her heart dipped. 'And there is no Moreau conveniently waiting for his arrest.'

'Apparently not.' He turned Barker. 'I need you to send a man to London.' He went to his saddlebag and pulled out a notepad, pencil and a little book. He took a seat on the log where Barker had been sitting and set to work composing a note using the little book as a reference. The note would be in code.

'To whom do you write?' she asked.

He lifted his head and gave her an enigmatic smile. 'No one you know.'

He wasn't going to trust her with that sort of information. Of course he wasn't. The trust between them was a fragile thing and not yet complete. She certainly didn't intend telling him all her secrets. Not unless she had to. She turned to Barker. 'Did you search inside?'

'Top to bottom. Nothing except the horses. They had no intention of staying.'

She wanted to curse. They had been so certain they had their man in their net. 'What do we do now?'

'Wait for my man to report back,' Barker said. 'Keep watch for their return. Guard Falconwood.'

A mocking smile curved Freddy's lips and lit his eyes. 'In the meantime, my guests are due to arrive and I am tied to the house.'

A terrible thought occurred to her, and her hands tightened on the reins. 'You don't think I am part of Moreau's plot?'

He hesitated a fraction too long. 'I don't know.'

At least he was being honest, but it hurt. Deeply. That he would think she would betray him. 'I am not.'

'There are a few too many coincidences for my liking.' He tore a leaf from the notebook and handed it to Barker.

'Get this to our contact right away. Make sure your man is not followed.'

Barker touched his forelock and disappeared into the woods.

Freddy mounted up, his face grim.

'You do think I had something to do with it,' she said.

'I know you are at the centre of what Moreau is plotting. I know there are things you have not told me. That is all I know.'

Heat seared her face at the sound of his anger. She felt as if she had been slapped. She urged her horse up close to him. 'If you think I would do anything to put my sister's life in danger, you really do not know me very well.'

He gave a weary shake of his head. 'You misunderstand my meaning.'

'Then explain.'

'I do not think you are complicit in Moreau's plan, but he is using you.'

A cold hand fisted around her heart. It sounded so like Moreau. 'So what are we going to do?'

'We are going to formally announce our betrothal at our ball tonight. There is nothing else we can do.'

The edge of bitterness in his tone clawed at her heart.

The guests began arriving at noon. First to arrive were Nicky and Gabe. While Nicky and Minette hugged, Freddy shook hands with his best friend, who gave him a hard look. 'Everything all right?' he asked.

'We'll talk later,' Freddy said. When they had a moment alone.

Mother, who had emerged from her rooms looking magnificent in a rose-coloured turban and an imposing gown of green silk, sailed into action. 'The butler will show you to your rooms, my lord. I have, of course, put you beside

Minette, in my wing of the house. You will no doubt require time to recover from your journey. I will have tea sent up to your room.'

'You are very kind, Your Grace,' Nicky said. 'I would indeed like a few minutes to rest. Minette, will you join me? I am longing to hear all about your visit. And since there are others arriving behind us, you may show us the way. Her Grace will need the services of her servants.'

'You are all that is kind, Lady Mooreshead,' Mother said.

Gabe and Nicky followed Minette up the stairs.

The next to arrive was his cousin Arthur and his wife, Liz. The woman looked as if she had bitten into a lemon. Freddy shook his cousin's hand and kissed Liz on the cheek. 'Thank you for coming to celebrate my news at such short notice.'

'Wouldn't have missed it for the world,' Cousin Arthur said. His eyes narrowed. 'Looking a bit pulled, though, what? Shouldn't you be sitting down?'

'You do look rather tired,' Liz said with a sugary-sweet smile. 'Doesn't he, Your Grace?' she appealed to his mother.

Mother sniffed. 'Too much racketing about in the middle of the night.'

Liz gasped.

Cousin Arthur leaned closer. 'Still up to your old tricks? You will have to settle down once you are married, you know.'

Freddy gritted his teeth and passed the couple off to the butler.

And so it went on for three interminable hours. Greeting one overnight guest after another. The rain yesterday had made his leg ache like the devil. The last to arrive in a flurry of gentlemen, dragoons and boon companions was the Prince Regent. His major-domo consulted with the butler and the whole party was led up to the suite of rooms set aside for their royal visitor.

His mother sank onto one of the hall chairs. 'That is everyone, I believe.'

'Yes. Thank you for doing such a sterling job of getting them settled.'

Her shoulders tensed. 'I have never been one to shirk my duty.'

He ignored the implied criticism. 'Indeed not.'

Her face reddened. 'Your father would certainly not have approved of this dreadful misalliance.'

He sighed. 'Mother, I am marrying Miss Rideau, and there is nothing you can say or do to change it.'

'Yes, and I know how it came about. You have made us a laughing stock. My Reginald would never have behaved in such a disgraceful way.'

His fists clenched.

His mother recoiled.

Damn the woman for making him come so close to losing his temper. He sought the coldness of their usual interactions. 'I suggest you repair to your room and ready yourself for this evening.' He limped down the hallway to the library, where the captain of Prinny's guards had been instructed to wait for him.

Captain Stalbridge rose when Freddy entered. 'Your Grace.'

Freddy shook his outstretched hand. The captain was a sensible man, even if he was a Hyde Park soldier. 'Sorry to put you to so much trouble. I have a map of the house and grounds and we can talk about the disposition of your men while the Prince is here.'

'I gather we are expecting trouble.' The man looked eager.

'It is more a case of better to be safe than sorry,' Freddy

said, smiling. No sense getting the man excited. That way led to mistakes. Besides, he much preferred to put his trust in Sceptre's highly trained men.

Chapter Seventeen

The gown Madame Vitesse had sent along with Nicky was the most beautiful creation. A rose-coloured gown, open at the front to reveal its white satin slip, edged in lace and trimmed with pearls and diamonds. The woman really had taken advantage if indeed she had lied to them about Moreau. The gown must have cost Freddy a king's ransom. 'Turn around,' Nicky said, having come to help her dress. 'My word, that is just lovely, and perfect for your colouring.'

A knock came at the door. When Christine opened it, one of the footmen handed her a wooden box with the Duke's compliments. She set it on the dressing table.

'Open it,' Nicky said.

Inside a nest of indigo velvet lay a tiara, along with a matching necklace of pearls and diamonds.

Nicky gasped. 'My goodness. These must have cost a small fortune.'

'According to Her Grace, these are always worn by the bride at her betrothal party,' Minette said. She had been expecting the jewels, but not their opulence. She lifted the necklace, its sparkle almost blinding.

'He must have told Madame Vitesse about them before she made the gown,' Nicky said. 'Clever man.'

That was one of the things she really liked about Freddy. He was exceedingly intelligent. About some things anyway.

Christine artfully worked the tiara into her hair and fastened the necklace around her neck. '*Mademoiselle* looks beautiful,' she said, stepping back.

'You do,' Nicky said, looking quite lovely herself in green taffeta and emeralds. She waved the maid away and once the girl had closed the door behind her came forward to take Minette's hands, searching her face with a worried look. 'You are happy about this marriage?'

'Of course,' she said, hoping she sounded happy, while inside the sadness seemed to be growing. A longing for what might have been. If Freddy had really wanted to marry her, if he hadn't been forced up to the mark, and if her life before she'd met him had been different, she might well have been happy.

An ache set up residence in the region of her heart. He was a good man, even if he was haunted by the demons of the past. He deserved a proper wife. And it was now up to her to make sure he got one. Because, in spite of all her good intentions, she had fallen in love with the man behind the icy mask.

Love. Was that what she thought it was? She'd been mistaken in her feelings before. But she did respect him and want the best for him. She was not what he deserved.

She forced a smile. 'If I look a bit peaky, it is because of Her Grace. She is a difficult woman to please and I have the strong feeling she does not approve of me. She took to her bed almost as soon as I arrived.'

Nicky frowned. 'She was supposed to be acting as your chaperone. It was the only reason I agreed not to come with you.'

'It was only three days. And we are going to be married.' Minette gave her sister a teasing smile. 'You said yourself I needed time to know him better.'

Nicky's eyebrows rose. 'Minette, you surely don't mean—'

The clock on the mantel struck seven.

'Oh, goodness,' Minette said. 'I should have gone down by now. His mother is sure to give me a scold for being late. She was most insistent I be there to greet the guests.'

'As is right.' Nicky frowned. 'You should not let his mother intimidate you. After all, you will be the Duchess very soon. She really should remove to the dower house before you wed.'

'Can we talk about this later?' There wasn't going to be a wedding. She certainly didn't want to worsen the relationship between Freddy and his mother for no good reason.

'Go, then. I'll locate Gabe and see you downstairs.'

Freddy was waiting at the top of the stairs to take her down. 'You look lovely,' he said.

He looked good enough to eat in his black evening coat and satin knee breeches. They went well with his dark looks. So austerely handsome. And ducal. 'Thank you.' She touched the necklace. 'And thank you for sending the jewels. They are *magnifique*.' She would have to return them after the ball, his mother had made very certain to tell her that. 'Any news of you know who?'

'Nothing. And we won't. The cordon around the house is so tight not even a tadpole can wiggle through.'

'Soldiers?'

'They will be of help, too.'

At the bottom of the stairs, his mother waited, wearing a gown of old gold adorned with diamonds and rubies. 'Mother,' Freddy said coolly.

His mother looked both of them up and down. 'Well, at least you won't put me to shame this evening.'

Minette curled her fingers in her palm to stop herself from hitting the critical face, and bit her tongue to prevent the angry words rising up in her throat from issuing forth.

Freddy smiled at her as if he appreciated her struggle, and she stopped herself from rolling her eyes in answer. They were acting like two children caught in mischief.

Then the guests started arriving and they were too busy greeting them to exchange another word for an hour. When they finally entered the ballroom the dancing had already begun and people were laughing and talking.

Lady Priscilla sidled up to her with a wary look at Freddy at her side. 'Everyone is so impressed with the room's decoration,' she murmured. 'I overheard Her Grace say it was all your idea.'

What a surprise. 'Yes. Most of the plants came from the gardens here.'

The other girl looked around her with a smile. 'It is fabulous, despite what Her Grace said. And smells heavenly. Everyone in Town will be copying it for the rest of the season.'

So Her Grace had found a way to be uncomplimentary while giving her the credit. It was almost too bad she was not going to end up marrying Freddy and getting the woman out of his house so he could have a bit of peace from her biting remarks. She just hoped the next wife he chose would manage it.

The set came to a close. 'Oh, I have to go. I promised to dance with Lieutenant Granby.' She gave Minette a worried look. 'You don't mind, do you? I know he was one of your court, but he has been rather at a loss since the announcement of your engagement.' She blushed. 'And I find I like him.'

Minette took her hand. 'That is wonderful. He is a nice young man. I wish you both happy.'

Priscilla gave her a conspiratorial smile. 'I'm going to try to get him to go with me to the library.'

Minette laughed.

'Something amuses you?' Freddy asked.

'Very much.'

'Don't feel you have to keep me company all evening. Go and dance. Enjoy yourself.'

'When are we going to have our dance?'

His eyes gleamed with amusement. 'When hell freezes over.'

'You promised.'

'No. You promised. I'm sorry. No one will be surprised any more than they were surprised that we did not open the dancing.'

'So what will you be doing while I dance the night away?'

'Play cards. Walk the grounds.'

'To make sure all is safe?'

He inclined his head. 'One can never be too careful.'

It wasn't often Freddy bemoaned the things he couldn't do because of his foot. This evening, though, he wished he could have given in to Minette's desire that he dance instead of watch. He loved the way her eyes sparkled, how light she was on her pretty feet as she spun around her partners. He would have given his soul to have partnered her in a dance. If he'd had a soul, that was.

After an hour of standing on the sidelines, talking to guests, accepting congratulations, some of which were actually sincere, and avoiding his cousins, he needed fresh air. He also needed a word with Barker, who, with the men he had brought from London, was patrolling the gardens.

He strolled out of the ballroom, across the terrace to the stairs.

'Frederick. I say, old man.'

Damn, he hadn't notice his cousin had come this way. Too busy watching Minette and trying to look perfectly content as she whirled around the room on other men's arms. 'Arthur.'

'You have chosen a beautiful girl,' his cousin said admiringly.

'I rather think she chose me,' Freddy said.

Arthur coughed behind his hand. 'Does she know about…?' He looked embarrassed.

'About my foot, you mean.'

A wince crossed his cousin's face. 'Too bad you took after your mother's side of the family in that regard.'

His fist clenched. He relaxed his fingers. 'Your point?'

'Well. You know. I was just wondering if…'

The man was a coward and an idiot. 'You were not wondering, Liz was. And it is none of her damned business.' He turned and walked away.

'Freddy,' his cousin said. 'You said…'

By the time he hit the flagstones at the bottom of the steps he could no longer hear his cousin's pleading. Damn it all. Wasn't it bad enough that he couldn't dance with his betrothed? Did he have to have his infirmity thrown up at him at every turn?

The urge to strike at something, someone, was a roar in his ears.

Barker stepped out in front of him, and instinctively Freddy raised his fist.

'Whoa!' Barker said. 'It's me.'

Freddy cursed and dropped his arm. 'Apologies. Let me hear you coming next time. Everything in order?'

'Neat as a pin. A mouse couldn't get near the house without someone seeing.'

Trouble was, the individual they were dealing with was

far more devious than a mouse. 'You checked the guest list?'

'All in order. No one here that should not be.'

'The servants?'

'Not a Frenchie among them.'

'Hmmph.'

'What's wrong, Guv?'

Other than the lies he'd told his betrothed? Lies of omission Arthur had been pleased to remind him of. 'Not a damn thing.'

'You go on now. Enjoy your party. I've got my eye on things out here.'

Barker was right, and besides, he needed to keep watch inside the house, since they had no clue about Moreau's plans. He'd warned Gabe, who would see no harm came to Nicky, but he should be keeping an eye on Minette. Other than Nicky, she was the only person who had ever seen the man, which was a danger all of its own. 'Report to me in my rooms when the ball is over.'

Barker touched his forelock and glanced up at the sky. 'Moon is rising. Pretty soon it will be nigh as clear as day out here.'

'It is the shadows you need to worry about.'

He headed back for the house, crossing the lawn in front of the veranda, the music drifting on the breeze.

The figure of a woman was tripping across the lawn towards him, skirts lifted in one hand, her skin pearly white in the moonlight. Minette.

'Here you are,' she said gaily. She hooked her arm through his and danced along beside him. So much energy. And joy. She was enjoying this party and her joie de vivre lifted his spirits. He'd promised to squire her to balls every night if she would agree to go through with their marriage.

They were halfway across the lawn when the music

stopped. A breeze whispered through the nearby shrubbery like a sigh. She halted, pulling on his arm.

He glanced quickly around them. 'What?'

'Look.' She pointed upwards. 'The moon and the stars. Isn't it beautiful?'

He gazed down into her face. 'Yes. It is.'

She frowned. 'You aren't looking.'

'Because what I am looking at is far more beautiful.' Damn, what had made him say such a thing, even if it was the truth?

A laugh shook her shoulders. 'Flatterer.'

'I never flatter.'

The music began again. Something stately and slow.

She turned to face him, 'Dance with me. Out here where no one can see us.'

'A set of two people?' he scoffed.

'No, there's a dance of two I learned in France. The Ländler. Put your hands on my waist. I dare you.'

Her voice brimmed with mischief. And something else. Affection. And, damn him, he wanted to please her on this night of their betrothal.

'You are anxious to see me fall on my face.' But he was already giving in, holding her as directed, and feeling something fizzing in his veins, something he barely recognised.

She put her hands on his shoulders. 'We step in circles in time to the music. Try it.' She moved her feet. He stumbled. Off balance.

'This is ridiculous.' He let go of her waist.

'Try again,' she said. 'Please. No one can see us.'

'A good thing, too. This is scandalous.' He clasped her once more, this time more firmly.

She laughed. 'Left foot forward, right foot forward, half turn step. Left foot forward, right foot forward, half turn step.' Somehow she adjusted for his limp, which had become more pronounced.

The rhythm came easily. It was like riding a horse. He relaxed and soon they were spinning in slow circles across the lawn in time to the music. It was magical.

'Try going straight for a few steps so we don't get dizzy,' he muttered.

She laughed up at him. 'I'll follow your lead.'

It felt a little awkward at first, but then they were gliding across the lawn, sometimes turning, sometimes not. A rosebush loomed up out of the shadows and, trying to avoid it, he lost his balance. He was going down. Taking her with him.

He twisted, landing on his back, his legs tangling in her skirts, her breasts hard against his chest. 'Damnation,' he said when he felt her shoulders shaking. 'I hurt you.'

A laugh erupted from the woman lying across him. She was laughing. He felt a chill spread out in his chest. He'd made a fool of himself.

'That was so much fun,' she gasped through her laughter. 'It is terribly wicked, you know, in polite society. The common people do it all the time, I am told.'

She wasn't laughing at him, she was enjoying the moment.

He chuckled, then laughed. Out loud. And couldn't stop. He kissed her soundly. 'God, do you have any idea how much I love you?'

He froze. Had he really spoken those words? And meant them? He gazed up at her face, and she looked down at him, her expression clear in the cold moonlight.

She blinked.

He stroked her cheek. 'I love you,' he whispered, knowing it for a truth, and kissed her lips tenderly with his heart so high in his throat it felt like tears.

She inhaled a shaky breath and he held his, hoping, like the idiot he was, that she just might—

'For Heaven's sake!' a voice said in a low whisper. 'What are you doing?'

Shocked back into the present by that hissing tone, he struggled to his feet and helped Minette to hers. He brushed them both off, trying to regain his balance, physically and mentally. 'Mother. What are you doing out here?'

'Me?' she shrilled. She looked over her shoulder. 'Half of our guests are up there, watching you cavort like a fool. Have you no shame?'

Beside him, Minette twitched at her skirts. 'I was teaching His Grace a new dance.'

'I don't know what sort of manners pertain in your family but I can assure you—'

'That's enough,' Freddy bit out.

'It is nowhere near enough. Do you think I do not know what the pair of you were doing the other evening? Dinner in your rooms.' Her voice, though little more than a whisper, shook with rage. 'Have you forgotten the vow you made on your brother's grave?'

His stomach churned. He gripped Minette's arm, intending to walk her away. This was not a conversation they were going to have.

Minette resisted his tug on her arm. 'What vow?'

'Mother,' he warned.

'The vow he swore on his brother's grave to never marry.'

'Why would he do that?' Minette asked, looking at him.

'He got want he wanted,' Mother said, her tone venomous. 'He stole the title from his brother. He doesn't deserve—'

Damn Mother, bringing this out now. 'I will not profit from my brother's death. No child of mine will inherit. My cousin and his son are my heirs.'

'You never spoke of this,' Minette said.

The triumph on his mother's face came as no surprise, but the shock on Minette's face struck him hard. 'I'm sorry.'

'You should have told me.'

Yes, he should have. But she really hadn't given him a lot of options. 'But for your little games, I would not be getting married.' *No, no.* That was not what he'd meant to say.

The hurt on her face paid him back a hundredfold.

Damn it all. He had not meant to be cruel, it was just that… They could not have this conversation now. He glanced up at the veranda. There were only two heads. Those of his cousin and his wife. They must have gone to tell his mother about their foolish dancing. 'It is time to go back inside. We have made enough of an exhibition of ourselves for one night.'

He closed his eyes and took a deep breath. It had been wonderful. He couldn't remember when he'd felt so young or so carefree. Never had he been to a ball where he had actually enjoyed himself. He held out his arm, and she placed her hand upon it. In frigid silence they followed his mother across the lawn to the terrace steps.

The emptiness inside him grew deeper as he recalled her dismay—and that she hadn't said she loved him back.

He felt just as small inside as he had as a child when picked last for every game of cricket, or left behind when his peers had gone off on mischief. No one wanted a cripple along.

Astonishing as it seemed to Minette, Her Grace was in the dining room, playing the charming hostess at breakfast. Perhaps knowing Freddy intended to keep his vow to remain childless had cheered her up. But Freddy was nowhere in evidence. The man had said he loved her and in that shocking, astonishing moment she had realised she loved him, too. Desperately.

And she desperately wished she had said something out there on the lawn, instead of staring at him like a moon calf.

Yes, it was disappointing that he didn't want children. But after a night of tossing and turning she had decided that children were not necessary to her happiness. They would have each other. Now she was searching through the public rooms of the house, trying to find him. To tell him what had been becoming more and more apparent to her over these past few days. His declaration had taken her by surprise, left her momentarily wordless. And if she was honest, fearful that he might regret his declaration in the light of the morning. Still, she'd been cowardly. She should have told him what was in her heart.

And then his horrid mother had arrived and she'd lost her chance.

Both the billiard room and the gun room were empty. She headed for the library, where a footman had told her several gentlemen had gathered. As she approached, male laughter sailed out of the open door. One voice lasting a little longer than the others. A deep, rich chuckle she would know anywhere.

Moreau? She froze. Moreau was in the house? In the library? How was it possible? A footman stationed outside the library door was pretending not to notice her standing as still as a statue in the middle of the corridor. With a quick breath, she set her shoulders and started walking towards the door. He was in library. She would know that laugh anywhere. How was it possible he had entered the house without anyone noticing? She had greeted everyone at the door the previous evening.

The rumble of male voices died out.

Back straight, she entered the room, took in its occupants with a swift glance. There were three men—Freddy's cousin Arthur, a thin young man with a head of cherubic mousy curls and one older man with a large lumpy red nose and a huge belly. None of them were Moreau. All rose to their feet, the fat one creaking loudly as if his corset was about to give way. He must be a friend of the Prince Regent, who also creaked when he moved.

She must have been mistaken about that laugh. Hearing things. 'Good morning, gentlemen.' She dipped a curtsey, hoping it was of the correct depth for while she remembered the other two vaguely from the introductions the previous evening she did not recall names or ranks.

'Good morning, Miss Rideau,' Freddy's cousin said. He had a hearty cheerful voice and a patently false beaming smile. 'I am surprised to see you up so early. Most of the other ladies are still in their chambers after such a rackety evening.'

Was that a sly dig she heard in his voice? Had he seen her dancing with Freddy on the lawn? Seen him fall?

The other men seemed to be waiting for her to say something. They probably wanted her to go so they could get back to their newspapers.

'Have you seen Falconwood this morning?'

'I gather he rode out early,' his cousin said. He smiled genially but there was something oily about his expression. 'You don't have to worry about my cousin, my dear Miss Rideau. He really is an excellent horseman.'

'I am not worried. I simply wanted to speak with him.'

He tugged at his neckcloth. 'I thought you might be concerned for his safety. His foot, you know. Not quite right. But he manages admirably, don't you know.'

Minette wanted to hit him for the insincerity on his face. What with his mother and this idiot, it was no wonder Freddy had withdrawn into himself. And no wonder he risked his life given the future he'd committed himself to. His admission last night of the vow he had made had given her a much greater understanding of the man he was. 'I'm not at all worried. His Grace is one of the most athletic men I know.' She glanced pointedly at the other man's small paunch.

The other two men chuckled and she heard it again. Moreau's voice. Coming from the elderly fat man. It wasn't possible. Could two so very different men have the same laugh?

She wanted to inspect him, walk around him, look at him from every angle, but she had to continue as if she had noticed nothing. She glanced at his face, trying to appear casual. While nothing else about the man looked right, his eyes were Moreau's.

Her heart lurched. With a struggle she maintained her outward calm—at least, she hoped she hadn't given her shock away—and smiled sweetly at Freddy's cousin. 'Thank you for the information. Have you gentlemen had breakfast? It is being served in the dining room.'

'Ate earlier,' the cherub said with a bow. 'Thank you for asking.'

'Feeling a little peckish myself,' Moreau said.

She gave them a vague smile. 'Excellent. Hopefully I will see you this afternoon out on the lawn? Her Grace has planned an *al fresco* tea, provided the weather holds, and we have some games for your entertainment. Shuttlecock. Croquet. Archery.' She accepted their bows with an inclination of her head and strolled out.

That man was Moreau. She was sure of it, though he had disguised everything—his face, his body. He had even managed to look shorter. But that deep, low chuckle was his. The man had ever been bold. But this? What on earth was his purpose? Had he guessed she was onto him? He must certainly recognise her. Her blood ran cold at the thought of the damage the man could do with so many important people inside the house. How could they have missed him last night when the guest list had been checked and rechecked?

Freddy. She had to talk to Freddy. Dash it all, why did he have to choose now to go riding? Perhaps she should talk to Gabe. Nicky would know of his whereabouts. She headed for their chamber on the second floor.

Halfway up the stairs the idea hit her like a bolt of lightning. If Moreau was an overnight guest, why would she not sneak into his room and take back the damning evidence of her past so she and Nicky would no longer have anything to fear?

Freddy would arrest him, and there would be no damage done to anyone.

Blast. Why could she not remember the name he had given when they had been introduced? Mr Patterson, the butler, would know, though she would have to be very careful with her enquiries. It would not do to alert Moreau she'd seen through his disguise.

Chapter Eighteen

Freddy left his horse with a groom and strode into the tap-room of the Bull and Bear, where he found Barker down-ing a tankard of heavy wet. He nodded to the barman to pour him the same. They took their drinks to a table in the corner.

'Well done,' Freddy said. 'What do they have to say for themselves?'

'They know nothing. Not who they were working for or why. They were following orders.'

Freddy finished his drink. 'I think I will have a word.'

Barker signalled to the innkeeper behind the bar. 'We'll be going down to the cellar. No interruptions, mind.'

The man touched his forelock.

'How much did you pay him?' Freddy asked as they made their way down the stone steps.

'Enough for a day or so.'

The underground space reeked of stale beer and damp. Barker lifted a trapdoor in the floor. 'Hidey-hole for con-traband. Luckily there isn't any right now.' He lowered a wooden ladder into the darkness below their feet and grabbed a lantern from the wall. At the bottom there was yet another locked door. When he opened it and shone the light inside, three men blinked like sleepy owls.

'You can't keep us here,' one of the men said, thrusting his chin in their direction. It was the only move he could make as his hands and feet were tied. 'It ain't right. We've done nothing wrong. Report you for kidnapping.'

'That's Herb,' Barker said.

'I am sure the authorities will be delighted to make your acquaintance, Herb,' Freddy said.

'Ho, is that your game?' the same man said, obviously the leader of this little gang. 'We was asked to deliver a carriage to a farm and then to make our way back to Lunnon. Which is just what we were doing.'

'You were asked to act as a decoy for a French spy. In other words, you are traitors.'

The man cursed.

'Tell me about the man who hired you. What did he look like?'

'A proper good 'un,' Herb said. 'Paid half up front. I figured that even if we never got the other half we'd done very well out of the arrangement.'

'Where and when were you to collect the other half?'

'We were to see the cove in charge of the Fools' Paradise. A hell in Whitechapel.'

Barker cracked a laugh. Freddy glowered at him. 'I know it.'

'That's it. In a nutshell.'

'What did he look like? This man who hired you?'

'Not much to look at. Ordinary. Dressed like a cit. Not a nob, but not down at heel. Sat in the shadows so it was hard to see his face.'

'How tall was he?'

'He never stood up. We left first.'

Freddy cursed inwardly. 'And he gave you no hint as to why he wanted you to undertake this delivery?'

'I asked 'im, but he said weren't none of my business if I wanted the money. I got mouths to feed, I 'ave. There ain't no crime in delivering a carriage, now, is there?'

'It is a crime to help a French spy.'

'I didn't know that then, did I? Wouldn't have done it else. I'm as loyal to my country as the next man. He never sounded like a Frenchie.'

'So there is nothing more you can tell us that will help us find him. Listen well. If I find out you lied, that you knew even a smidgeon more of information, I'll have you clapped in irons and off to Newgate quicker than a cat can lick her ear.'

One of his companions squeaked like a mouse and wriggled.

Freddy lifted the lantern to shine on his face. 'Well?'

'I did 'ear somefink,' the fellow said.

Their leader made a growling noise. 'Ratty, I told you not to follow 'em.'

Freddy could quite see why he was called Ratty. His sharp nose and large yellow front teeth gave him a rodent-like appearance.

'I didn't,' Ratty said. 'Honest. I just 'appened upon 'em on my way 'ome.'

The leader made a sound of disgust.

'What did you hear?' Freddy asked.

'Promise you'll let us go?' Ratty pleaded.

Freddy shrugged. 'No promises. But if the information is useful…'

'Tell 'im, you nodcock,' Herb said. 'If you knowed one of 'em was French then you shoulda said.'

Not that Freddy thought it would have made a bit of

difference to Herb, but he would give him the benefit of the doubt. This time.

''E met another cove outside the tavern,' Ratty said. 'Said as how some bird in a forest would never look right under his nose and to have a ship standing ready.' He shook his head. 'Couldn't make any sense of it. Then they started talking foreign like.'

'Who did he meet?' Barker rapped out.

Another shrug. ''E was a Frenchie. Or I think he was. Spoke foreign when he answered. No idea what he was sayin'.'

'*Some bird in a forest* wouldn't happen to be Falconwood, would it?' Freddy asked.

'Yerst. 'Ow did you know?'

'Not your concern, my lad,' Barker said.

A chill slithered down Freddy's spine. 'Right under my nose.' He started for the door, Barker following.

'Hey!' Herb yelled. 'You said—'

Barker locked the door behind them. 'I'll be back for you lot later.'

'What is it?' Barker asked as the climbed the steps to the taproom.

The man had a nose for trouble. 'If I'm right, though I hope to God I'm not, he is in my house.' And everyone he cared about—Nicky, Gabe, Minette—was in there with him.

Heart high in her throat, her pulse racing, Minette stole into the room assigned to the man the butler had identified as a Lord Peckridge. He'd been on the guest list as a distant relation of Freddy's cousin's wife, Liz. The chamber was one of the smaller guests rooms on the third floor in the oldest wing in the house, as far from the public rooms as it was possible to be without entering the servants' quarters. Peckridge was clearly considered one of Falconwood's least important guests.

The room had a bed, a nightstand, a desk, an armchair beside the fire and a wooden chair beside the desk. Against one wall was a clothes press. There was no dressing room for the man's valet—he would be quartered up in the attic with the other servants.

Where to look? She must not linger long. Even though he had expressed the intention of going to breakfast, his servant might return. Or the man himself. Peckridge indeed. Her blood ran cold. But for his laugh she would not have seen through his disguise. And he had been walking among them for hours.

It was not a disguise he had used when she had travelled with him. Then he had usually been a displaced aristocrat or a rebel peasant. It was not important now. Not until she had the portrait in her hands. Then she would reveal him to Freddy.

She started with the desk. There was nothing in its drawers but the obligatory writing paper, pens and ink. The clothes press held linens. The nightstand held a candlestick and a book. Rousseau. Suitable reading material for an English gentleman. Even more suitable for a French revolutionary. The washstand, the usual gentleman's toiletries.

And that was it. Where were his personal papers? Jewellery? Could the valet have them locked away somewhere?

She took a deep breath, tried to calm her rapid breathing. Think. Where would he hide items he wanted no one to find? She slipped a hand under the pillows. Cold metal. She lifted it to reveal a pistol. It wasn't loaded, but the ball and shot were in a small leather pouch alongside. Clearly he was so sure of his disguise he didn't expect to be discovered or it would have been loaded and ready to fire. Useful as it was to know he had a weapon in his room, it wasn't what she had come to find. Carefully she returned the pillow to its original place, smoothing the creases.

She got down on her hands and knees and peered under the bed.

Nothing but a pair of slippers set side by side.

Old memories careened through her mind. Times she'd tried not to remember. She used the pattern on the carpet to establish their exact location, then carefully lifted the slippers clear. With her fingernails she scraped the surface of the carpet around where the slippers had sat until she found an edge. Slowly she lifted a square patch of carpet free and the board beneath it. In a hollow between the floor joists, she discovered a small leather satchel.

Moreau had always been secretive about his hiding places. Though she hadn't ever told him, she had always been able to discover them in the inns where they had stayed. He had liked to hide things under the floorboards, though none of those rooms had been carpeted.

Desperate to lock the door, she didn't dare to in case he or his man came in. She had to hurry. With shaking hands she pulled the bag from its hiding place and set it on the floor beside her. It was locked, of course, but it didn't take her a moment to open it with a hairpin. Inside, she found a notebook and pencil. She flipped the pages. It was full of tiny writing, none of which made any sense. Code others would find of interest.

She pulled out a small leather-covered box. Inside it was a signet ring. A gold fob. A set of collar studs set with emeralds and a matching stick pin.

And beneath a layer of white velvet, the miniature. Just the sight of it made her flush hot then cold. What could she have been thinking to pose in such a lewd manner? But she'd loved him and had thought it a great joke to give him such a gift. Before she'd discovered the truth.

Fear a hard lump in her throat, she slipped it into the valley between her breasts, hiding it between her stays and her chemise.

She packed everything else back exactly as she had found it. Moreau would notice the smallest difference, though hopefully he'd be arrested before he noticed the missing memento. She returned the valise to its hiding place, covering it with the board, the carpet and finally the slippers. She let go a sigh of relief and rose.

A creak as the door opened.

Heart rising in her throat, she took one big step. It brought her up against the desk. She slid the drawer open at the same moment Moreau, in his disguise as Peckridge, stepped in.

Bushy grey eyebrows rose towards his hairline. A smile broke out on his face. It looked more like a leer on that horrible face, but she remembered it well now she was positive of his identity.

'Well, well, my little Netty. What a pleasant surprise. I should have guessed you of all of them would sniff me out.'

'Pierre,' she said, her heart contracting as she forced a smile. To her he would always be Pierre Martin, no matter that he had used the name Paul Moreau in all his dealings in England. 'I certainly never expected to see you at my betrothal ball.'

He opened his arms. 'I have missed you.'

She quelled a shudder and steeled her spine against the trickle of fear creeping through her veins. 'Did you, Pierre, when you abandoned me to my fate?'

He frowned. He shifted, his body growing in height and breadth, though his face remained purely Peckridge. 'You could not possibly believe such a thing of me, my sweet. You break my heart.'

He looked so forlorn, even within his horrid disguise,

she believed him implicitly. That was what made him so very irresistible. His charming sincerity. She also knew he would kill her without a second of thought if she posed the most minute of threats.

His gaze dropped to the desk. 'What are you seeking? You know I would give you all that I have.'

More allusion to their time together sent a shudder through her body. Was he saying he wanted her back? Or was it all a trick to set her at ease before he struck?

She gave him a hesitant smile. 'Your disguise is so good I wanted to make sure I was right. I didn't want to make a mistake in so public a place.'

'Hmm.' He glanced in the mirror, touching his face. 'What gave me away?'

'A small thing. Nothing anyone else would notice.'

'It is good, I admit. I studied the man for weeks. Your Duke should take more care to familiarise himself with his distant family.' His gaze met hers in the glass. He smiled. A quick baring of his perfect white teeth. Another thing she had liked about him. 'Congratulations on your betrothal, by the way. You were always one of the most intelligent females I have ever met.'

'Thank you. So that's what you were doing up north. Establishing a new identity.'

'Indeed. My original plan to capture Falconwood was to use this cousin to get close to him. Your engagement and the invitation to your ball brought things to a head in a much more satisfactory manner. Your Duke has been making a thorough nuisance of himself these past few years. Fouché would be very generous with anyone who could bring him to France for questioning.'

Her heart seemed to stop beating. Of all the people she had assumed Pierre might be here to kill, Freddy had not been among them. Fear was a cold, hard lump in her belly. 'I would have expected you to be more interested in the Prince.'

A burst of the so-familiar laughter filled the room. 'That fat fawn? That tearful, womanising dilettante? You think I'm fool enough to want to replace him with his brother, the Duke of York? A real man and a soldier? The emperor would have my head in a basket and rightly so. No, the loss of your Duke and his secrets will be a setback from which the British will never recover.'

'You plan to kidnap him.'

'Naturally.' He turned away from the mirror, walked over to the bed and retrieved his pistol. He loaded it with methodical ease.

This was not good. She eyed the distance to the door. But he was in between. And the window was closed.

He rammed the shot home and glanced up. 'You haven't yet told anyone of my identity, I presume?' He shook his head. 'Of course not. You were not sure.' He glanced around. 'And there was something you wanted, hmm? A picture perhaps?'

Nausea rose in her throat. He had planned to use it against her somehow. She repressed the urge to press her hand against her bosom, where the miniature suddenly seemed much too large for so small a space, where she was sure he would see it should he happen to look more closely. She had to think of something. Anything. To stop him.

Her heartbeat quickened as she slipped into a version of the games he had taught her when she had thought he was working for the loyalists. When she had handed him their lives, thinking she was saving them. Until she'd discovered his true colours by accident. One day while he'd been out, she'd found a letter from Fouché congratulating him on his success in trapping a leader of a small band of royalists. A heartbreaking shock she'd never revealed and instead had tried to warn his potential victims. And then, with professions of undying devotion, because he'd thought her besotted, he'd used her as bait to trap her sister. It seemed he still thought her besotted. The man's ego knew no bounds at all.

She gave him a winsome smile. 'I am so glad to see you again, safe and whole. I worried about you in Spain, and me stuck here in England with no way to reach you. I thought you had abandoned me entirely.'

He frowned. 'Me, abandon you? You left me completely in the lurch at Boulogne. I was lucky not to lose my head over that debacle. All this time I have been languishing in Madrid, you have been enjoying the delights of English nobility.'

The man had no idea about loyalty or familial love. To him it was all about advancement, power, money.

She widened her eyes as if in shock. 'You think I wanted to come here to live with a sister who left me to my fate in a burning building? You were my only friend in the world.'

A protective friend, she'd thought, and a lover, at least for a time. Until she'd discovered the depths of his betrayal. He had broken her heart, but she had made him pay.

'Why did you leave with your sister?' he asked, his face puzzled. 'You knew I would return.'

'They didn't tell you, did they?'

Doubt filled in his expression. 'What the devil are you talking about?'

'The men who were supposed to be watching over me left me with that boy, David, and went off to the tavern.' She'd gambled with them, deliberately cheated and lost all her money to them, and all the while had teased them with sexual innuendo until the only thing they had been able to think about was swiving. Since they hadn't dared touch Pierre's mistress, they'd gone off to find women of their own.

She certainly wasn't surprised his men hadn't told him the truth. Why would they risk his wrath when they never expected to see her again? 'David will confirm my story if you ask him gently enough and don't make him afraid. The poor lad didn't stand a chance against Mooreshead when he showed up. I had no choice but to go with him.' The lies tripped off her tongue as easily as they had when she had been Pierre's dupe, enticing unsuspecting loyalists into his net. She felt ashamed. She'd told the same lies to Nicky when her sister had asked what had happened to her. Told her she'd spent the entire time hiding with nuns until Moreau had discovered her only weeks before Nicky had. 'Ask David, if you don't believe me.'

His grimaced. 'Dead men don't talk.'

Her heart dipped. David had been sweet. 'You killed him?'

Moreau's jaw dropped. 'Not I. Your brother-in-law.'

She shook her head. 'He was alive when we left. I swear it.'

It was hard to see his real expression through the disguise, but she had the feeling he was beginning to believe her story. 'My men must have killed him,' he said slowly. 'To hide their dereliction.'

'I would never have left, but Mooreshead said you told them where to find me to save your own life. I thought you had betrayed me.' He'd certainly betrayed her, but not then. By then she'd known exactly what Pierre was. And what he had made her into.

'Mooreshead.' He spat the name out. 'He lied, *chérie.*' He put a hand to his heart. 'You should know I would never willingly let you go.'

He'd betray his mother for a *centime*, if it came with

a smidgeon of advancement. She had to get out of here, get rid of the portrait and tell Freddy she'd found Moreau. 'I'm sorry,' she said softly. 'I should have known better. I hate England. Hate their nobility. I thought once I married Falconwood I would have access to all his secrets. I was planning on passing them along. Who would suspect a duke's wife of being a traitor? He has not been easy to catch, however. I missed your help. I missed you.' She didn't have to pretend to sound miserable, she was desperately sorry to be back in his clutches.

Somehow she had to get away and warn Freddy.

'My little brave one,' he cooed at her, as he had so often in the past. He closed in on her, put his arm around her waist and for a moment she thought he would kiss her. She tried not to tense.

He laughed. 'Damn this disguise. I am an unpleasant-looking fellow, am I not?'

Obviously she hadn't succeeded.

'You will return to France with me,' he said. 'Together we will show Falconwood to Fouché, who will extract all his secrets. The Emperor will reward us handsomely, I am sure, when Britain is brought to her knees.'

'I would like that very much.'

'I missed you, *chérie*. It is good to work with you again. This will make things so much easier.

He believed her story. The ego of the man. But then he had always thought she was blinded by his charm. Always. Even when he had left her staked out like a chicken to bait a wolf in Boulogne. Even though it had been so very hard to hide her hatred for him by that point. And he was desperate. 'Was it so very bad in Spain?'

'He put me in the army. As a private. It was hell.'

'How on earth did you get away?'

'I found evidence of a plot against us. Sent the information to Fouché and was forgiven.'

'A real plot?' she asked with a twinkle in her eye.

'Hmm, not so much.'

They laughed as they had laughed together in the old days at their cleverness, only her eyes had been blind to some of that laughter having been directed at her. For believing in him.

'What is your plan? It will be hard to spirit away a duke from his home.'

'Now you are with us it will be very much easier. You will go to the Duke tonight, drug him and let us into his room when the house is asleep.' He tipped her face up to meet his gaze. 'You will do this for me?'

She nodded. 'And we take him to France? Alive.' It was a relief to know he didn't intend to assassinate Freddy out of hand.

'We do. Tonight. There will be a carriage waiting for us.'

The carriage from the farm. Thank God. Even if he did manage somehow to leave Falconwood with Freddy, that carriage was being watched. It would be stopped.

'You have everything arranged.' She filled her voice with admiration. If he would trust her enough to let her go from his room, she could warn Freddy. 'It is perfect. I cannot wait to return to France.'

The door swung open. Freddy stood on the threshold, his pistol levelled at Moreau. 'No one is going anywhere.' His gaze flickered over her, dark, unreadable and so very cold.

Ah, mon Dieu, how much had he heard? Surely he did not believe…

She pressed a hand to her chest, felt the hard lump of the miniature against her sternum. If he found it, would he believe her innocent?

* * *

It hadn't taken a great deal of Freddy's ingenuity to discover which of the gentlemen was the cuckoo in the nest. Peckridge was the only man no one had ever met before and Arthur had been quick to point out that his wife's cousin was known to be a solitary eccentric man, and it had come as a surprise to find him attending a ball, though, of course, he had to be invited.

He was the only one no one could vouch for.

Neither had it taken long to ascertain that the man had gone up to his room after breakfast. With Barker at his back and their men covering all possible exits, Freddy stood with his pistol pointed at the couple embracing by the window. Like old friends. Or lovers. There was no mistaking the familiarity between them or the words he'd heard before he'd opened the door.

Worse was the guilt written across Minette's face. The pain in his chest almost sent him to his knees. He cut himself off from it, keeping his gaze fixed on the Frenchman. Keeping his heartbeat steady. His mind clear. 'Ah, just the man I am looking for.'

A bitter look twisted Moreau's lips as he glanced down at Minette, who remained held close to his side. 'You betrayed me?' He sounded so wounded Freddy's teeth ached with the pressure of his jaw.

'No. I figured it out for myself,' Freddy said. 'We caught the men who brought the carriage.'

Chagrin passed across the other man's face. 'It is a bad workman who blames his tool, but these English peasants, they have no imagination.'

Minette remained in the circle of his arm, so very close to the pistol he held loosely in his hand. One wrong word and the situation might get very nasty. 'You can confirm this is Paul Moreau?' he asked her.

She stared at him wide-eyed and nodded slowly. 'He is.'

Moreau preened. '*Chérie*, you told him about us? That was very brave of you, before the wedding.'

'Not really,' she said softly, regretfully. 'I only told him about Pierre. I never mentioned that my Pierre and Paul Moreau were the same person.'

Pierre. The pieces fell together with an unpleasant little click inside his head. Her Pierre and Paul Moreau were one and the same. She had loved this man. Possibly still did. And now, if he had any sense, he would doubt where her loyalties lay.

Damn it, from the look on her face she was clearly hurting. He couldn't think of that now. He had to make Moreau believe his words. 'It seems you have a penchant for misshapen men, my dear.'

The Frenchman bristled. Used his free hand to remove his bulbous nose and pull off the bushy eyebrows. He spat out wads of padding in his cheeks, becoming a handsome man in his late thirties. '*Voilà*, not misshapen at all.'

Odd bits of glue dripped from his face, making it look as though it was melting. And the damned pistol stayed where it was, firmly grasped in the hand about her waist.

'Step away from the lady,' Freddy said.

Moreau tilted his head. 'You plan to arrest us, I presume? See justice done. Not take us outside and shoot us?'

'I'm a gentleman,' he said coldly. 'What is done with you is not up to me. I will hand you over to the authorities.'

The expression of fear on Minette's face clawed at his vitals.

'Put down your weapon,' Freddy enunciated slowly. 'Miss Rideau, step aside.'

Moreau hesitated.

Freddy cocked his pistol. 'I will shoot you.'

The man swore, glanced down at Minette and back at

Freddy. 'I suppose you would not care which of us got hurt.'

'No.' He prayed like hell the man wouldn't test him on that particular point. 'Why would I?'

Moreau sighed. 'You overheard our conversation.' He tossed the pistol aside.

'Freddy?' Minette said.

'Not now. Barker, see to him.'

Barker and two of his men were across the room in a flash, picking up the Frenchman's weapon, holding him by the arms.

'What the hell is going on?' Gabe said, striding into the room. 'By Jove, you got him. And in the house, too. That was a close-run thing.' He glared at Moreau. 'Mooreshead, *à votre service.*'

'I know who you are,' Moreau ground out, all his smiles and charm gone. 'You stole one of my very best agents.'

Minette sent him a look of appeal. 'Tell Nicky I'm sorry. I never meant to cause her harm. None of this is her fault.'

'Get her out of here, Gabe,' Freddy said, 'while I finish with this one.'

Minette looked startled. Shocked.

Moreau stared at him. 'So she has your *couilles* in her sweet little hands, does she?' His lips twisted in a bitter smile. 'You played me well, Falconwood. But since you care about her, I will make you a trade. Let me go and no one will ever know her part in this.'

The man was a cur. A trapped cur bargaining for his life by saying she was involved in his plan. That not only had she been planning to run off with him, she'd made it possible for Moreau to enter his house. That she'd been involved since the start. Freddy's stomach fell away. The Home Office boys would be very interested to hear it, because it would put him in very bad odour and reflect badly on Sceptre. Something that would please them no end. He could imagine Blazenby taking full advantage of the situation to advance his career. He looked at his friend. 'Get her out of here, Gabe. Now.'

Gabe hustled her out of the room.

God, he hoped he had his temper under control by the time he was ready to talk to her, because right now he wanted to hit something he was so damned angry.

Moreau watched her go, his face puzzled. He straightened his shoulders. 'Doesn't it bother you that she played you for a fool? That she was planning to help me?'

The hollow in his chest widened. 'I doubt she'll want to go where you are going.' He gestured to Barker. 'Tie him up and gag him.'

Once he was sure his prisoner could not possibly escape he went in search of Minette.

Chapter Nineteen

He found her pacing in Gabe and Nicky's drawing room, her eyes sparkling with anger. Why did she think she had the right to be angry?

Seated beside Gabe, Nicky followed her with a worried expression.

The moment Minette saw him she stormed towards him. 'What you heard. I wasn't—'

He cut her off with a chop of his hand. Rude, yes, but he had to know. 'Tell me one thing. Why did you go to his room?'

She gasped, looked indignant, then defiant. 'Why do you think?'

Gabe made as if to stand but subsided at Nicky's murmur of protest, watching them through narrowed eyes.

'I think you are an idiot,' Freddy said.

'Falconwood,' Gabe said with a growl in his voice.

He shot his friend a glare. 'If you wouldn't mind, both of you, I would like to speak to my betrothed alone. We have some matters we need to discuss.'

Looking troubled, Nicky rose. 'I think that is a fair request.'

'Listen to me, Freddy,' Gabe said. 'Hurt one hair of her head and you'll have me to deal with.' The man was barely holding on to his temper. Freddy knew exactly how he felt. His was rapidly slipping from his grasp.

'Gabe,' Nicky urged.

Mooreshead gave him one long last hard look and gently escorted his wife out.

The door closed softly behind them.

'Well?' Freddy bit out. 'Did you think me so incompetent you had to try to capture him yourself?'

Minette stared at him. Took in his fury. Snapped her mouth shut. Was that what he believed? That she thought him incapable, the way his mother did? Thought him less than a man? Not good enough to produce the next heir?

She hurt for him. Badly. And wished and wished she'd spoken of her feelings out there on the lawn.

The weight of the miniature against her heart made itself known when she moved towards him. Brought her up short. If she let him continue in this misapprehension, for which he would no doubt hate her, he would never have to know how careless she'd been with her virtue. Never have to see the picture that would not only have ruined her but destroyed her sister in the eyes of society.

The man had offered her his heart. Told her he loved her. She owed him the truth. He would never expose her folly, not even when he turned away in disgust, glad of a lucky escape. At least she would know she had kept a shred of honour. 'He had something of mine. Something I had to get back before he was arrested. He caught me before I could leave.'

He stilled. 'Did you get it?'

She swallowed and nodded, fumbled in her bodice, and drew forth the miniature. She held it pressed close to her chest for a second or two then held it out, the back towards him, the ugliness of what she was staring her right in the face. She dropped her gaze to the floor, dreading seeing his anger turn to disgust.

'You risked your life for a trinket?'

Her heart ached at the flatness his voice. The distance. 'Not a trinket,' she said, forcing herself to speak what was in her heart. 'It is a portrait of Paul and me in what might be described kindly as *in flagrante delicto*.' Her faced heated. If it was possible to go up in flames and have the ashes of combustion blow away on the wind, now would be the right time. 'It was a jest between lovers. Our faces painted onto a lascivious picture by an artist in the market square. A jest in very poor taste.' When he made no move to take the picture, she let her hand fall.

'When I heard he was back in England I was terrified he might use it as blackmail. To get me back under his control. He would know I could not bear the idea of anyone seeing it, especially you. Worse, though, would be the *ton*'s reaction. Nicky and Gabe sponsored me, introduced me to society. To have it become public knowledge that they'd taken such a woman into their midst would have ruined them socially. Look at the way Sparshott behaved over the matter of a kiss. Moreau would know what would happen. And he would use that knowledge to gain his freedom. Those rivals of yours in the Home Office would be only too glad to see Gabe brought down. I could not let it happen. Surely you can understand?'

Bleak-eyed, he kept his gaze on her face. 'I do understand, though I regret you did not trust me to retrieve it for you.' He strode to the window, staring out as if he could not bear to look at her any longer.

Perhaps knowing that it was Moreau who had been her lover had destroyed his regard, his love. And how could she blame him? She had never been honest with him.

She crossed the room to stand at his shoulder. 'I am sorry, Freddy. My intention was not to cause you pain.'

His fists clenched and then opened. He placed one hand flat on the window frame, as if to stop himself from striking out. But not at her. Never at her.

He gave her a hard glance. 'You have no reason to apologise,' he said in a low, dark voice. 'He might have killed you when you were supposedly under my protection. Seeing you there, so close to that damned pistol… It would have been my fault. My damned fault.'

The pain in his voice squeezed a fist in her chest. 'It was my decision. I thought I had time. I did not mean for him to find me.' She glanced down at the miniature clenched in her hand. 'I had to be sure.'

He glanced her way, shadows deep in his eyes. Sadness. 'If you had trusted me more, you would have waited for my return.' He shook his head. 'But I do not blame you. Not one bit. And I certainly will not hold you to our betrothal,' he added softly. 'I know it is not going to work. Cry off, but give it a week or so. The *ton* will not be pleased at having been dragged out here for nothing.'

Oh, no! How could she tell him she loved him now? He would think it was all about his title and not about him. Oh, why hadn't she spoken of what was in her heart when he had? Now he was giving her what she'd thought she wanted.

Or was she being a fool yet again? Perhaps he hadn't meant what he'd said. Perhaps he was glad he'd found the way out of a marriage he had never wanted. He knew the truth of her relationship with Moreau now. A man of his standing would certainly have trouble explaining a wife who had taken England's enemy to her bed. Something Moreau would no doubt delight in relating to anyone who would listen, even if he no longer had the proof.

'It is likely for the best,' she said, half hoping he would

disagree. And the other half, the honourable half, hoping not.

He nodded.

Impenetrable cold clenched around her heart as he turned and headed for the door.

'Freddy,' she said.

He hesitated. So slightly she almost didn't catch it, but that tiny hesitation provided the courage she needed.

'What if I don't cry off?' she asked. 'What then?'

He stopped, turned back, his expression impenetrable. 'Then you'll be tied to a man you will end up hating because we will never spend another night under the same roof.'

He walked out.

A clock chimed one in the morning. Freddy stared at the note he'd written, but instead he saw Minette's face, her pained expression at his rejection. He hadn't expected it to hurt her. He'd expected relief. Damn it all, what had made him say what he had out there in the darkness on the lawn? The laughter? He couldn't remember laughing like that since his brother had died. No. Hell, no. He was still pretending, lying to himself. His brother hadn't died. He'd killed him. Intentionally or not, the accident had been his fault. Being sorry didn't change what had happened or make it any less his fault.

What if she did insist on going forward with the wedding? Out of pity? For that was all it could possibly be. He could not in all honour walk away.

The pain of longing struck his heart.

And then what? He went cold inside. He'd never resist the temptation of having her under his roof. Past experiences proved he would not. God, he'd made love to her twice already and, despite being careful, she could even now be carrying his child.

They would have to wait to know for certain, before they called off the engagement. Even he wasn't villain enough to abandon a woman carrying his child. Where the hell was his famous cold reserve when it came to Minette? His control. He'd have to talk to her in the morning before she left with Gabe. Make it clear that she must not cry off for a month or two. Just in case. A bubble of hope rose in his chest. What if she was pregnant?

Dear God. He closed his eyes. If she was, it would be a dream come true, and his worst nightmare.

He blinked his thoughts away, forced himself to focus on the task at hand. The resignation Sceptre had insisted upon. He'd been exposed and was no longer useful. Brief and to the point. He signed it. Folded it. Melted wax in the candle, surprised to see that despite his inner turmoil his hand remained steady. One drop. Two. He put the candle and the wax aside and pressed his seal into the blob.

Done.

Over.

What the hell was he to do now?

A whisper of sound behind him. He spun around.

Minette. In her nightgown, her unbound hair a soft fall over her shoulders, her face pale, her eyes wary. God, she look so lovely standing there in a gown so sheer he could see the outline of her form, the thrust of her breasts and hardened nipples, the dark triangle at the apex of her lovely slender legs. He rose to his feet, aware of the pounding of blood in his ears. And farther south. 'What the deuce are you doing here?'

'Don't you want to know what I have decided?'

For a moment he couldn't make sense of her words. He had never been in any doubt what she would decide. No woman would take the kind of rejection he had delivered and think about it. Unless the worst had happened.

His heart leaped as if to greet her, pull her close.

He backed away lest he be tempted to do something they would both regret. 'Tell me in the morning. There is one more thing we needed to discuss.'

'I am here now,' she said softly, with an enquiring tilt of her head.

Damn it all. 'I am asking you to wait awhile before you announced that we do not suit. There is a reason to wait.' His lips felt stiff and awkward. It was hard to form the words, but he could leave nothing to chance. 'Obviously, if you are with child as a result of our... We'll get married.'

She gave him a dark look. 'Are you sure you wouldn't prefer me to pass it off on some other man so you won't have the trouble?'

He flinched. 'No. That would be dishonourable.'

'Honour,' she scoffed, as if she doubted she had a scrap. 'Perhaps you would rather I leave for the country, discreetly abandon it on an orphanage doorstep or give it to some poor family who would be willing to raise it as their own for a large enough sum of money. I am sure you can afford it.'

A way out. She was offering him an escape. A way not to break his vow. His child raised by strangers. And what if that child—? 'No!'

She recoiled.

He'd been too forceful. 'If it is my child, I will do my duty by it.' Too blunt. Too, too blunt. And cold.

A shrug of her shoulders rippled the soft fabric at her feet. 'How very noble.'

'Damn it all. What more do you want of me?'

Her expression softened, she stepped closer. 'I want you.'

He stepped back, maintaining the distance between

them, his body shuddering with the effort to retain the distance when he wanted to ravage her lush mouth, feel her lovely curves pressed against him, bury himself inside her. Ease the pain of his miserable past. Such a coward.

She reached out a hand. He ignored it. 'I'm not expecting your child.'

The faint hope inside him died, though he had not even realised it had existed, not in any rational way. Disappointment swept through him, followed swiftly by relief. Blessed relief. Life would be so much simpler. 'How can you be sure?'

'There are certain herbs a woman can take. Rape was always a risk in France and the nuns taught us how to avoid unwanted children from such an event.'

She sounded so matter-of-fact it shocked him to the core. What must her life have been like in France? 'And you continue to use the herbs?'

'They have other beneficial effects.' She coloured. 'Less painful monthly visits.'

His own face heated. This was not a conversation he should be having with a woman who was not his wife. 'So you are saying, if we married, you could continue taking them?' She would be the one in control. He would have to trust her not to make any mistakes. And he would have his cake and eat it, too.

So very tempting.

And convenient. Keep to the letter of his vow, if not the spirit. The freedom to blame any errors, deliberate or otherwise, on her. He shook his head. 'Too risky.'

'I was looking for you when I recognised Moreau by his laugh,' she said.

'He's gone. There is no more to be said about him.'

Her expression turned stubborn. 'I thought I was hearing things at first. When I saw him in that disguise. But I knew I was right. The opportunity was too good to miss.' She crossed the room to peer at his collection of rocks, picking them up and putting them down as if it would help put her thoughts in order. 'I had to get that miniature for Nicky's sake. He would not have hesitated to find a way use it against us once he realised he was caught.'

'And you have it.' He kept his voice cold and his gaze firmly fixed on a place above her head, but it did not stop him from seeing her beautiful body as she strolled around his room, touching his things so intimately he knew he would never see the items again without thinking of her. 'There is no more to be said.'

'Vilandry was an utter pig. Nicky let him use her in order to protect me.'

She put down a lump of granite and turned to face him. 'She suffered years of that man for my sake. She thought I was too young to realise, but I knew. One of the maids let it fall that he liked very young girls. If Nicky hadn't agreed when our uncle proposed the match, he would have taken me instead. He used the threat of it to keep her in line.'

Bile rose in his throat. 'Then it is a good thing he's dead.'

A painful smile curved her lips. 'It is. I didn't know it until much later but Moreau had visited Vilandry. Saw Nicky and wanted her. When he learned Nicky and I had escaped the fire, he searched for her. It took him a while but he found me. And I led him to Nicky.'

The guilt in her voice pained him greatly. 'It wasn't your fault.'

'I try to tell myself that,' she said.

'No matter how many times you repeat the words, they never quite ring true, do they?' Over and over he'd told himself he wasn't responsible for the death of his brother.

She smiled sadly. 'You understand.' She picked up the

tail feather of a grouse and stroked it across her palm. 'I spent more than a year with Pierre, as he called himself, helping him catch loyalists without realising what I was doing. It was such a grand adventure, spying, reporting back, finding little pockets of resistance, people who needed help. I thought we were fighting for the king. But slowly, slowly, his talk became more revolutionary in tone. And, fool that I was, I followed his lead. For a while. He was handsome and outrageously daring. After a life of trying to be a perfect young lady I had embarked on a grand and courageous adventure. He was my rock in my new strange world. He taught me things. About my body no decent girl should know. He encouraged my wantonness, the results of which you know.' She glanced at him sideways from beneath lowered lashes. 'And that you seemed to like, too, though I thought for certain you would be displeased.'

Displeasure was the furthest thing from what he was feeling right now, with her strolling scantily dressed around his room, her fingers brushing across surfaces he hadn't so much as looked at in years. The thought that she would never do so again was a jagged pain in the emptiness of his chest. 'You loved him.'

'I loved a man who never existed, but I do not believe I was ever in love. I was his pet. I wanted to please him so he would keep me close. I feared being abandoned. It had happened too many times already.'

And Moreau had known it. Used it against her. Did she think he was also abandoning her? The thought tightened his throat.

She drew in a hitching breath. 'He used me, Freddy. And I never suspected a thing. First to trap the local loyalists and then as a lure to force Nicky to do his bidding. By then, of course, I knew the truth of who he worked for and I mitigated the damage as best I could. When we left Boulogne I was happy to be free of him. Happy his plot against Nicky had failed.' She paused in her wandering to look at him.

'It was only later I remembered the gift I had purchased for him months before. Realised the harm it could do if it was made public. I didn't care for myself, but it would have ruined Nicky and Gabe by association. I could not allow it. Not after what she sacrificed for me.'

'The miniature.'

She opened her hand and set it on the desk. 'A portrait of the most salacious sort. They were sold in the market. I had our faces painted in, his and mine, as a joke.' She shrugged.

He glanced down at the scene. A woman sprawled without shame and a man giving her pleasure with his hand, the faces easily recognizable.

He was glad she was telling him her story. It cleared up his lingering questions about Moreau, but he could not let it matter. He deliberately did not glance at the picture again. 'Destroy it and forget it. It is over.'

She wandered to the window, opened the curtains a fraction and stared out into the night. 'I think if two people really love each other there should be no secrets between them.'

His heart gave a lurch. Stuttered, then raced. He pulled her around to face him. 'What are you saying?'

'When you told me you loved me, you caught me by surprise. I was afraid. I'd said it once before to Pierre in a moment of passion, and realised I'd been mistaken in his feelings for me. I thought that by saying nothing I wouldn't give you the power to break my heart.' She huffed out a breath. 'I am such a coward.'

He cupped her cheek with his hand. 'You are the bravest person I know. How you managed to survive alone in France… How you faced Moreau and his damned gun. I was proud of you.'

She gave him a sad smile. 'Not proud enough to go through with our wedding.'

His heart contracted painfully. 'It wouldn't be fair. I can't give you want you want. What every woman wants. I can't take the risk.'

'Children.'

He nodded. 'And I cannot control myself when you are near. I want you too much.'

Her expression lightened a fraction at his admission. 'I can live with not having children as long as we can be together.'

'You think that now, but what if you change your mind? What then?'

'I would forgo them to be with you. But, Freddy, my dearest, not having children cannot bring your brother back. You are punishing yourself for no reason. His death was an accident. You know it was. You would never have cheated. You have far too much pride. Too much honour.'

She was right. In a way. 'I made a vow. I can't go back on my word.'

'Your father was wrong to extract such a dreadful promise.'

'He didn't. He was horrified when I told him. But when I realised Reggie was dead I knew I couldn't do it. Couldn't be the heir. Not and bring another child into the world like me.'

'I don't understand.'

'You saw my foot. It is a hereditary condition, passed down through my mother. My children are likely to be born with it, too.' She didn't react with revulsion, as he'd expected. Her face showed only puzzlement. 'Do you think

I'd let a child go through life with such an impediment?' He gestured downwards.

'You said it didn't hurt.'

'It hurts when your family hates the sight of you, can't bear to watch you limp around so they hide you away in the nursery. Reggie wasn't so bad, most of the time, but Mother couldn't stand the sight of me. I swore to myself I would never put a child of mine through the misery of growing up a cripple.'

'Oh, Freddy.'

There. There was the pity he'd fought to avoid. 'If I don't have children, it can't happen.'

'No child of ours would be treated so poorly.'

Red filmed his eyes, anger along with frustration. 'You don't know that. Can't know.'

'You wouldn't hold a deformity against a child any more than I would. And we would defend them from anyone who tried. Look at you. It makes very little difference to your life. You walk, ride, play cricket occasionally.' She smiled hesitantly. 'You even danced.'

Something inside him cracked open. Warmth and light seemed to fill all the dark places inside him. A grin forced its way to his lip at the memory. 'I did. Not all that well.'

'You would get better if you practised.'

A laugh at her prosaic statement would not be stifled. He sobered. 'Mother would never forgive me for going back on my word.'

She looked at him solemnly. 'Your mother has much to account for, but this is your life, *mon cher.*' She frowned. 'You say this problem comes from your mother's side of the family. Is it possible she blames herself? That she feels guilt?'

The truth hit him like a blow to the head, making his ears ring. Always he had hoped, even if he hadn't fully admitted it, that by doing exactly what his mother wanted, trying to please her, she would find it in her heart to forgive him for not being perfect. For not being his brother. Perhaps even gain her love. But how could she, if she could not forgive herself?

He'd been so heartsick, thinking he might have harmed his brother on purpose, he'd let guilt rule his life. Yet he'd always known, deep inside, he would not have cheated, and had known Reggie would have. He hadn't been the sort of fellow to accept coming in last. Only it wasn't the sort of thing one said about a dead man.

Devil take it, he'd been such a fool.

And he didn't have to be alone—if what Minette was hinting at was true. If.

'I love you,' she said softly, as if sensing his doubt.

A storm raged inside him, hope at war with the dread of being wrong, of once more being rejected by one he held most dear.

'I love you, Freddy.' She opened her arms.

He walked into her embrace. 'I love you,' he said hoarsely, his heart feeling too large in his chest. 'I need you.'

'Yes.' She twined her arms around his neck went up on her toes and kissed his mouth. 'I need you, too.'

For the first time in his life he felt as if he had come home. He had a place where he belonged.

He carried her to the nearest flat surface. His desk. He set her on it. Standing between her thighs, kissing her until he thought he would go mad for wanting to be inside her.

He stroked the silken skin of her calves. The lovely, lovely turn of her ankle.

Chapter Twenty

He wanted her so badly. Not the joys of her body, though, God help him, he wanted that, too, but the radiance of her spirit that had brought light into his increasingly dark world.

If he gave in to this, let himself hope and then lost her, it would finish him.

She cradled his cheek with her fingers. Cool skin. A searing touch. 'Freddy, darling, you don't deserve to be shut out in the cold.'

She understood. What barriers he had left were sundered by the realisation that she really did understand. He caught her wrist before she could draw back, pressed his lips to the centre of her cool little palm. 'I love you. I will always love you.'

'I love you, too.' A small laugh stirred the air across his cheek. He shivered with pleasure. She pulled back to look at him, her eyes full of mischief. 'I thought you were so annoying the first time we met. On that ship. You were so handsome. I wanted you to see me yet you treated me like a child. I wanted to shake you and make you look at me.'

'I saw you,' he croaked, his throat so dry it hurt to speak. 'I was terrified by how much I saw you. I thought the best thing was to keep far away.'

'I missed you.'

The words soothed him like balm on a raw wound. 'You are sure? You really do want to marry me?'

'With all my heart.'

'I will get a special licence.' Urgency filled him. 'Tomorrow. I won't wait any longer to make you mine.'

'I am yours. You don't have to wait.' She twined her arms around his neck and kissed him with all the heat of a passionate woman.

He pulled her tight against his body, feeling her curves and hollows against him, cupping her lush bottom in one hand, a high plump breast with its hard little peak in the other, and tangled his tongue with hers.

It felt right. As if she was the part of him he'd been missing all his life. He'd been broken but hadn't known it. With her he was whole. A new man. A better man.

Her breathing became urgent, ragged, her fingers digging into his back, her hips arching against his now painful arousal.

He broke their kiss on a groan. 'I want you so badly.'

A small smile of satisfaction lit her face. 'Good.'

His body jerked at the erotic note in her voice. He shrugged out of his robe. While she nimbly attacked the buttons of his shirt, he toed off his slippers and shucked off his pantaloons. It was a mess of hard breathing and groping hands and so sexy he couldn't stop his smile. Free of all but his shirt, he gripped her shoulders and kissed her again. Her hands slipped under his shirttails and, no longer cool, stroked his back and his buttocks. He glanced around desperately for a place they could lie down in comfort. She gazed at the jutting evidence of his arousal beneath his shirt. She slid off the desk and lowered herself to her knees, grasping his buttocks in her hands.

'Minette,' he gasped. 'Oh, devil take it...'

She cast him a saucy glance from under her lashes. 'You don't like this?'

The proximity of her mouth so close to his aching flesh, the heat of her breath, left him blind with lust. 'You honour me. You make me so damned happy.' Being this vulnerable with a woman had never been an option.

'It is all I want. You happy.'

Unable to think of a reason to protest, he pulled his shirt up over his head. She leaned back on her heels to look at him. Her gaze travelled from his face and down to his ugly foot, before returning to his face. With any other woman he would have plunged the room in darkness. He stood silent, waiting for her judgement. If she turned away now...

'You are such a beautiful man,' she said softly.

'Hardly that.'

She caressed the backs of his thighs. 'Pure muscle. Like a racehorse.' She licked her lips.

'Please,' he said. Never in his life had he begged for something he wanted. Never had he shown such weakness. But he didn't feel weak. He felt stronger than he'd ever felt before. Because of her he was free to be himself. 'Minette, please.'

She smiled and leaned forward, taking him in her mouth. Heat. Wetness. Suction. Her tongue teasing.

He widened his stance, keeping his balance. She reached up to stroke his belly, and he tunnelled his fingers into her lustrous hair. The sight of her moving rhythmically, the sensation of that movement, sent heat ripping along his veins. She brought him to the brink far too quickly. Blackness and bliss beckoned.

He eased her mouth from his body with a careful hand and brought her to her feet. She smiled knowingly, her mouth rosy and moist. So luscious.

'I need to be inside you.' His voice was barely more than

a hoarse whisper. 'Now.' He swallowed. 'I would please you as you have pleasured me.'

She gave him a tender smile. 'Always so generous.' She touched a finger to his lips. 'I am not sure I deserve you.'

Too full of emotion for words, he swung her up into his arms and carried her to his bedroom. He stumbled a little but he didn't care. He set her down on his bed and kissed her smiling mouth while his hand found her breast, the peak beading beneath his touch. She moaned into his mouth, arching up into his hand. So responsive. He climbed onto the bed and stretched out beside her, admiring the swells and hollows revealed through the sheer fabric of her nightgown, skimming his hand over them, learning her contours with his hands and his gaze. Never would he forget this moment. 'You are so beautiful. And mine.'

'As you are mine.'

Hers. They belonged together. And if they had children she would love them, no matter their faults. He drew her nightgown upwards, above her hips, and slid it off over her head. She didn't hide from him or blush. She lay before him like a banquet prepared only for him, her gaze taking in his state of rigid arousal in a pass down his body. He delicately parted the sweet hot folds of her cleft. So wet. So ready.

'Please, Freddy. I want you. Now.'

A demand he could not resist. He nudged into position and eased himself into her, inch by amazing inch, feeling her delicious heat draw him into her depths. For a moment he couldn't move for the extraordinary gift of the pleasure she gave him. She lifted her legs around his waist, pulling him deep, arching up to meet his thrusts, urging him on with little cries and moans that drove him far too close to the brink when she was nearly there. He must not let her down, not in this.

He nuzzled her throat, curled down to take first one nipple then the other in his mouth, suckling and teasing with his tongue. She cried out her pleasure at his touch. And then she was coming apart around him, so beautifully, so intensely. He followed her into bliss.

The lay in each other's arms, a sated, trusting tangle of limbs. The beauty of it gave him a lump in his throat and a prickling behind his eyes. She sighed and shifted. 'That was...' He waited, breath held. 'Amazing.'

Yes. It was. Truly amazing. Unlike anything he'd ever experienced. Carefully he withdrew from her and held her within the circle of his arms, knowing she was his to protect and he was hers to command. For all time.

He bent and kissed her cheek then her lips.

'No going back after that, my darling,' he said, hearing the sound of his smile in his voice and liking it.

'Oh, indeed not,' she said, smiling up at him. 'From here we go only forward.'

Forward to a future he had never dared imagine.

He kissed her long and lingeringly, wrapped her in his robe and carried her back to her bed.

Epilogue

As Freddy had promised, he obtained a special licence the very next day. Their wedding was held in the drawing room of Falconwood Hall the following morning, with the vicar from the village officiating. The only witnesses were Gabe and Nicky and Barker, who had returned from town to report on the disposition of Moreau earlier that morning, along with the Falconwood servants, who seemed touched at the invitation, if a little intimidated.

Now Minette and Freddy stood on the steps, waving farewell to Nicky and Gabe, who had kindly decided to leave the newlyweds to their own devices. Barker had gone off to the inn in the village.

'Would you care to walk in the grounds with me, Your Grace, since the weather is fair?' Freddy asked.

Suspicious at the note of anticipation she heard in his voice, Minette raised an eyebrow.

He grinned.

The man clearly had something in mind. 'Certainly, Your Grace.' She frowned. 'Is it required that we are so formal in private?'

He gave a shout of laughter. 'Not at all, beloved. I couldn't help it, I feel like I am living in a dream and keep having to remind myself we truly are married.'

'Not a nightmare?'

'Not at all.' He grinned at her, making her toes curl. She had never seen him so carefree, and there was an air of mischief about him. 'A dream come true.'

She pulled him down so she could kiss his cheek. 'You make me so happy, *mon coeur*.' He did. Her heart felt so large it barely fitted behind her ribs, and a feeling of total well-being permeated her.

'I'm sorry Mother refused to attend the ceremony,' he said, his face turning grave. 'But you were right. It is her loss. I assume she is settling into the dower house.'

'I understand so. She has already received calls from some of her cronies.'

'Perhaps she will come round.' In truth, Minette doubted it. The woman had held on to her grief too long to let it go now. Indeed, it seemed to her that Freddy had barely avoided the same fate. Much longer and his heart too would have shrivelled to nothing beneath the weight of guilt and regret.

They walked arm in arm through the formal gardens at the side of the house and onto the lawn at the back. Snatches of music wafted on the breeze. It seemed to be coming through the open French doors leading onto the terrace from the ballroom.

'What is going on up there?' Freddy asked, far too non-chalantly to be innocent.

A wife ought to humour her husband. 'How strange. It sounds like an orchestra.'

'I think we should go and see.'

They crossed the lawn and mounted the steps to the veranda. The music was indeed coming from within. An orchestra had set up in the same place they had been on the night of the betrothal ball, but this time she and Freddy were alone in the vast room. All the decorations had been taken down. Gilt chairs were placed at intervals around the walls, but oddly all the chandeliers were alight. The room glittered.

She frowned. 'Is this your doing, *mon cher mari*?'

'How did you guess?'

'Well, if it was anyone else, I believe it would go hard with them. Such extravagance to light all these candles when there are only a few occupants in the room.'

'I can see you are going to be a fearsome Duchess.'

'I do not like unnecessary waste.'

He was laughing.

She looked around her, and then she realised. 'Your promise. You are keeping your promise.'

'I am.'

He made a gesture to the orchestra, and the music changed. It was the tune they had danced to in the garden. He held out his arms. 'I promised I would dance with you on our wedding day.'

She managed a mock frown. 'Rather clever of you to make sure there was no one here to see us.'

'You are not accusing me of cheating, I hope.' He put a hand on his heart. 'You will give me time to become accustomed to displaying my clumsiness for all to see. And I will, I promise you. I will never let it stand in my way again.'

She couldn't speak for the lump in her throat. The man had so much courage.

He opened his arms, and she stepped into them.

He began to move, gliding her around in circles down the length of the ballroom, a good bit steadier than he had been on the grass in the dark.

'This, *mon cher*,' she said reprovingly, 'is not a dance we can do in public. We would be banished from the *ton*.'

'I have to say, that is quite a relief,' he said, and twirled her under his arm. 'I don't see me mastering the Roger de Coverly in the near future.'

'Oh, I wouldn't be too sure of that.'

'I love you, Your Grace,' he said in a low, dark murmur in her ear.

'I love you, dearest Freddy,' she said, smiling up at him and adjusting her step just a tiny bit to accommodate a slight list to the left.

And then he stopped and pulled her into his arms and kissed her.

The orchestra kept on playing.

* * * * *

RETURN OF
THE PRODIGAL
GILVRY

This book is dedicated to my dad, without whom I would never have had the wonderful adventure of visiting Scotland and thus the desire to return.

My thanks go out to all involved in making this a better book, in particular Joanne Grant, my editor.

Chapter One

Dundee, November 1822

How dare he? The anger inside Rowena MacDonald increased with each oar stroke of the longboat crossing the grey waves between the ship and the quay where she stood. She wrapped her threadbare cloak tighter against the November wind screaming in from the North Sea.

The dark afternoon suited her mood. After two years of absence and no word, how dare her husband demand she welcome him back to Scotland? The rage she had worked so hard at suppressing these past two years lashed her the same way the wind whipped the wave tops into foam.

The letter, forwarded on from her last address, had scarcely arrived at her place of employment in time for her to meet the ship. She'd toyed with the idea of refusing his summons. But he was her husband and had the power to further ruin her life. And now, after she had been sure she was free of him, how easily he'd found her and brought her to heel.

Or so he thought, no doubt. As to that, he was going to hear a few home truths. If nothing else, she would make sure he knew she would never ever forgive him for his lies. Or the heartbreak of realising how pathetic she'd been in thinking that he had actually married her for more than her fortune. That he had some tender feelings towards her.

Not love. She had known it wasn't love, but she had thought he cared, at least a little.

She fought the stab of pain as she recalled his betrayal. She would not show how deeply she'd been hurt. Or how greatly she dreaded their reunion. Calm reason must be the order of the day. She took a deep breath of icy-cold air and steeled herself against any sign of weakness. The moisture trickling from the corner of her eyes was caused by the sting of the salt-laden sea. Nothing else.

The boat drew closer. Close enough to make out its occupants. Six sailors at the oars. Three passengers, all men, muffled in coats and hats and scarves against the wind, arriving on the last merchant ship from America before winter made the Atlantic crossing impossible. And oddly, upright in the stern, a barrel.

An uncomfortable feeling curled in her stomach. None of the passengers looked in the slightest like her husband. Admittedly, she had only been married two months before Samuel had fled like the proverbial thief in the night, but surely she would recognise him from this distance, despite the other people crowded around her at this end of the jetty making it difficult to see, tall though she was? On her side of the barrier, there were longshoremen waiting to unload the ship's cargo. A small family consisting of a mother and two children stirred with excitement at the approach of the boat, no doubt meeting a loved one.

All those waiting were held back by the formalities of landing. The visit to the harbour master, the presenting of passports, paperwork for Customs. And still Rowena could not pick out Samuel amid those mounting the jetty steps to dry land.

Could he have lied to her again? Changed his mind?

Her stomach dipped all the way to the cold stones beneath her feet. Her hand tightened around the strings of her reticule containing his letter. His command to be waiting at Dundee dock.

How could she ever have trusted herself to such a feckless man? Sadly, she knew exactly why. Because she had wanted to believe in him, instead of trusting what she had always known. Handsome gentlemen did not fall in love with her type of female. They just didn't. As he'd made quite clear after the wedding, it was a marriage of convenience, colluded in by a cousin, who ought to have had her interests at heart. But didn't.

Two of the passengers left the quay, one disappearing into the arms of the little family squealing their glee and quickly led off. The second signalled to a waiting carriage and was whisked away.

Finally, the third, a tall man with the carriage of a man in his prime, all lean physique and long stride, prowled along the quay, his coat flying open. He walked as if the ground owed him homage, his by right. Images of the pirate who haunted her dreams with his strong clever fingers and wicked mouth danced across her mind.

Shocked, she squeezed her eyes shut against the flutter of desire low in her belly. Embarrassed, she ignored the salacious sensations. If anyone ever guessed the wicked thoughts that went on in her head in the long reaches of the night, they would never let her near their children.

She forced her attention back to reality. To a sailor pushing a handcart containing the barrel she had noticed on the longboat.

And the fact that there was still no sign of Samuel.

She wasn't sure if the feeling in her chest was more anger or relief. Or was it false hope? She turned her gaze back to the ship standing off from the shore. Could there be a second boat? Had he been delayed on board for some reason?

The last passenger was level with her now, a scarf, so swathed about his head it covered all but his eyes beneath a hat pulled down low. He wore a fashionable greatcoat, a thing with many capes, much like the one Samuel had worn during their whirlwind courtship. It looked too tight. Too short. Perhaps that was why he left it undone. The boots on his feet were scuffed and worn. A man who, for all his appearance of pride, wore second-hand clothes.

'Mrs MacDonald?' The man's voice had the lilt of the Highlands and a raspy disused quality. And he had spoken her name. Her heart followed her stomach to the floor. Samuel had fooled her again.

All she could see of the man's face was a pair of wary

green eyes. They reminded her of dark ocean depths and fierce forest creatures. 'I am Mrs MacDonald,' she said, unable to keep the edge from her voice.

He bowed, hand to heart. 'Andrew Gilvry, at your service.'

She'd been right. Samuel had brought her here for nothing. 'And where, might I ask, is my husband?'

He recoiled slightly at her haughtily delivered question. 'I am sorry...'

She drew herself up to her full height, the way she did with her students. It was the reason they called her the dragon, out of her hearing. Not the younger ones. Or the girls. They didn't need such demonstrations of strength. The two older boys were a different matter. They, she'd learned quickly, would take advantage of any sign she did not have the upper hand.

'So he is not on the ship after all.' The anger she'd been so carefully keeping under control began to bubble hot in her breast.

The man hesitated. 'I gather you didna' get my letter, then?'

What, did he have some excuse to offer for Samuel's absence? 'The only letter I received was from my husband, requesting me to meet him at this ship. And he is not on board after all.'

'He was on board, in a manner of speaking,' the man said gently, the way people did when delivering bad news. He gestured to the sailor with the barrel. 'He charged me with seeing his remains home to his family.'

The air rushed from her lungs. Her heart seemed to stop for a second as if all the blood had drained from her body. The ground beneath her feet felt as if it was spinning. 'His remains?' she whispered.

'Aye.' He reached out and took her by the elbow, clearly fearing she would faint. His coat streamed out behind him, flapping wildly. He wasn't wearing any gloves, she noticed, and the warmth of his hand sent tingles running up beneath her flesh, all the way to her shoulder. Across her breasts. Female awareness. How could that be? Was the pirate now springing forth to plague her days?

She forced her thoughts into proper order. 'Are you saying he is dead?'

He nodded tersely. 'My condolences, ma'am. He was killed by Indians in the mountains of North Carolina. I was with him when he died.'

She stared at the barrel. 'He's in…?' She couldn't finish her question, but received another terse nod.

Staring at the barrel, she took a deep breath. And another. And then a third. 'But why? Why bring him here?'

While she couldn't see his face, she had the feeling he wished he was anywhere else but here. And that he disapproved of her question.

'He wanted to be buried in Scotland.' He released her elbow and stepped back. 'I gave him my word to see him home.' He gestured to the cart. 'And so I have. Or at least I will have, when I have handed him over to an agent of the Duke of Mere.'

'The Duke of Mere? Why on earth would you want to do that?'

The fair brows, just visible beneath his hat brim, lowered in a frown. 'He is executor to your husband's will.'

* * *

In the face of her distress, guilt squirmed in Drew's gut like a live thing. But for him, Samuel MacDonald might have been standing on this quay greeting his wife, instead of him. Mrs MacDonald looked ready to faint, but touching her again was out of the question. She was nothing like the antidote he'd been led to expect. *A veritable harridan of a female.*

He could see why the doughy Samuel MacDonald might have found her physically daunting. She was imposingly tall for a woman, though the top of her head barely reached Drew's eye level, and as lean as a racehorse to the point of boniness.

She was not a pretty woman. The features in her face were too strong and aesthetic for prettiness. Her jaw a little too square for womanly softness, the nose a little too Roman. Her best feature was her dove-grey eyes, clear and bright, and far too intelligent for a man to be comfortable. And yet for some odd reason he found her attractive. Perhaps even alluring.

He fought the stirring of attraction. The effect of too many weeks of male-only company on board ship when he'd been used to— Damn. Why think of that now? A shudder of disgust ran through him. Not only had the woman just discovered she was a widow, but there wasn't a woman alive who would welcome his attentions. Not unless he was paying. Not when they took a look at his face.

The old anger rose in his chest. The desire to wreak vengeance for what had been done to him was always with him, deep inside and like a carefully banked fire.

Once brought back to mind, it blazed like a beacon that would never be doused. Not until he had exacted justice from his brother.

Getting a grip on his anger, he glanced up at the sky. It was three in the afternoon, the sun was already looking to set and no sign of the lawyer who should take charge of the matter at hand. Damnation upon the head of all lawyers.

He glanced along the quay with a frown. 'Where is your carriage, Mrs MacDonald?'

'Carriage?' she asked, looking nonplussed.

No carriage, then. A hackney? Or had she walked the mile from the town to the quay carrying the large bag sitting at her feet? The worn cloak, the practical shoes, the modest undecorated bonnet, things in the old days he would have taken in with one glance, now came into focus. Aye, she would have walked. For a man who bragged of his high connections and incipient wealth, MacDonald had not taken such good care of his wife.

So Drew would have to fill the breach. At least for a day or so.

He gestured for her to walk in the direction of the road at the end of the jetty. 'Do you have a room booked for the night in town?'

She eyed him with a frown. 'Of course not, Mr Gilvry. I must return to my place of employment. I spent last night here, but must leave today.'

Her strength of will in the face of adversity surprised him. A woman who would not submit easily to anyone's command. A burst of heat low in his belly shocked him. He could not be attracted to this domineering woman, as her husband had described her in the most unflattering terms. But there was no denying the surge of lust in his blood. Had his last years among the Indians made him less of a man? His throat dried at the thought. But he knew it wasn't possible.

Unnatural bastard. He'd heard the accusation more than once from the women he'd brought to his bed. But this would not be one of them.

The sooner he delivered her to her husband's family and got on with the business of settling his score with Ian, the better. 'I promised to see you safe in the hands of your husband's family. No doubt the lawyer will be here in the morning. Or I will send him another message. Let us find a carriage to transport us and…' He glanced back at the sailor with the cart, who was shifting from foot to foot with impatience.

She followed his gaze and a small shiver passed through her body. Clearly she was not as unaffected as she made out.

'Very well,' she said. 'I will hear what this lawyer of yours has to say, if he arrives tomorrow. The stage let me down at the Crown. We will go there and I will change my ticket to tomorrow night. I cannot stay a day longer.'

Drew swallowed a sigh of relief at her practical manner. Despite MacDonald's words, he'd expected to suffer through a bout of feminine hysterics. No doubt that would come later, when she got a good look at his face.

'Ye'll find a carriage for hire at the end of the jetty,' the sailor said, who had clearly been listening in to their conversation. The man trundled off with his burden, leaving Drew to escort Mrs MacDonald and carry her bag.

Her spine was so straight, her face so calm, he resisted the temptation to offer his arm for support. She clearly didn't need it or welcome it. So why did he have the feeling that, despite her outward appearance, she might collapse? She didn't look fragile. Anything but. She could have outmarched a general with that straight back of hers. Yet he could not get past the idea that, beneath the outward reserve, she was terrified. The woman was a puzzle and no mistake. But not one he intended to solve.

As the sailor had said, they found a hire carriage at a stand at the end of the quay and reached an agreement on terms to take them into the town centre. Drew helped the widow into the carriage, saw to the disposal of the luggage, then climbed up beside the driver. It would give her time to come to terms with her new circumstance. And allow him to avoid her questions, he admitted grimly.

The Crown Hotel was located in the centre of Dundee, about a mile from the quayside, and when the carriage halted, Drew climbed down and saw to the unloading of the barrel. The driver put his battered valise beside it on the cobbles.

Mrs MacDonald stared at the leather bag for a long moment. She raised her gaze to meet his and his stomach dipped. She must recognise it as her husband's. He had no choice but to answer her silent query.

'You are right. It is your husband's valise,' he said. 'I

have made use of his clothes, since I had to leave mine behind.'

Not that he'd had much to leave, unless you counted a breechclout and a pair of moccasins.

She stiffened slightly. 'And you travelled on his ticket?'

He had not been mistaken in the quick wits behind that high forehead. 'Since he was making the journey in the hold, I saw no reason to purchase another.' He winced at the cold sound of his words. 'And I used what money he had for necessary expenses.' Like the make-shift coffin. And a pair of boots. He could hardly travel barefoot and MacDonald's boots had been far too small. He had bought the cheapest he could find, however.

'How very convenient,' she said.

She suspected him of doing away with her husband and stealing his property. And he had in a manner of speaking. He met her gaze without flinching. 'I gave my word to your husband that he would board that ship, Mrs MacDonald. I kept my promise.' Out of guilt. MacDonald had not really expected to die on the journey back to civilisation. He had been full of talk of a glorious future in his fevered ravings. And of riches beyond any man's dreams. Riches that would no doubt remain untapped now he was dead.

Guilt stabbed Drew anew. But it would not change what had happened, nor his intentions to follow through with his self-imposed duty. He would see MacDonald's remains and his wife delivered safely to the lawyer and that was all he would do.

He picked up the valise and strode into the inn.

'Off the ship, are ye, then?' the innkeeper asked, meeting him just inside the door.

'Yes. The lady needs a room with a private parlour,' Gilvry said. 'I'll bed down in the stables.'

The innkeeper looked him up and down as if trying to decide if he was trying to gull him.

'A chamber is all I require,' Mrs MacDonald said from behind Drew, her reticule clutched at her breast as if she feared its contents would not be enough to pay for her night's lodgings.

He pulled out MacDonald's purse and jingled the few remaining coins. 'The lady's husband charged me with her travel arrangements. A room with a private parlour, if you please, and the use of a maid. Mrs MacDonald will take dinner in her room.'

The innkeeper bowed. 'This way, please, madam.'

'Don't worry about the rest of the luggage, Mrs Mac-Donald,' Drew said as, stiff-backed with indignation, she followed the host up the stairs. 'I will keep it safe.'

She cast him a look of dislike over her shoulder. 'Then I hope you have a good night's rest, Mr Gilvry.'

Ah, irony. He'd missed its edge all these many years. No doubt she was hoping her husband would haunt him. Which he would, because, in a manner of speaking, he had been, ever since he died.

Drew turned and stomped out to the yard.

It was only when Rowena had removed her coat and hat inside her room that she fully absorbed the news. Samuel MacDonald was dead.

She squeezed her eyes closed against the sudden pain

at her temples as her thoughts spiralled out of control. She had to think about this logically.

She was a widow.

A destitute widow, she amended. She had very little hope that anything remained of the money Samuel had realised from the sale of her half of her father's linen factory. Creditors had assailed her from all sides after his sudden departure for America, leaving her no choice but to find work and support herself. Her anger at her foolishness bubbled up all over again. How could she have been so taken in after fending off so many fortune hunters over the years?

But she knew why. After her father died when she was eighteen, she had lived with his partner and cousin. She'd hated it. Not that these family members had been particularly unkind, but whereas her father had respected her mind and listened to her advice, her cousin had insisted she leave all business matters to him. He had not valued her opinions at all.

As far as he was concerned, women were brainless. Only good to decorate a man's arm and attend to his house.

And then she'd proved him right. She'd fallen for the blandishments of an out-and-out scoundrel who had fled almost as soon as he had his hands on her money, leaving her to face the creditors he'd apparently forgotten to pay. Her cousin, who had encouraged the marriage, had washed his hands of her, as well he might, once he owned everything.

She stripped off her thin leather gloves and sat down on the chair beside the hearth, holding her hands out to the flames, revelling in the heat on her frozen fingers. It was a long time since she'd had such a warm fire at her disposal. But creature comforts could not hold her thoughts for long.

Was it possible her cousin had insisted Samuel settle some money on her future when he acted on her behalf in the matter of the marriage?

If so, it was a relief to know that her only family hadn't totally taken advantage of her lapse of good sense in accepting Samuel as a husband. When she'd learned her cousin had bought her half of the family business for a sum vastly below its true worth right after the wedding, she'd suspected her cousin of underhanded dealings.

It seemed she might have been wrong about her cousin. And about Samuel. Partly wrong at any rate, if arrangements had been made for her future.

Samuel was dead.

At least that was what Mr Gilvry had said. But how did she know for certain? She'd be a fool to take any man's word at face value. And she hadn't even seen Mr Gilvry's face. He had raised his hat when he bowed, but not removed his muffler. Nor had he removed it when he entered the inn.

All she had to go on was what she had seen in a pair of piercing green eyes and heard in a deep voice with a lovely Highland lilt. And felt in the flutter deep in her stomach. Attraction. Something she should know better than to trust.

He really hadn't told her what had happened to Samuel. Was there some reason behind his reticence she couldn't fathom?

She got up and rang the bell. It wasn't long before the maid the innkeeper's wife had assigned arrived to do her bidding. 'Be so good as to tell Mr Gilvry I wish to see him at once.' She glanced at the clock. 'Please tell the kitchen I would like dinner for two delivered at half past seven.'

The maid bobbed a curtsy and left.

Now to see if he answered the summons. And if he did not? Then she would know that she definitely should not trust him.

And if he did? Did that mean she should? Likely not. But it would help put an end to the strange feelings she had in his presence. He was just a man, not an enigma she needed to solve. She simply wanted the facts about her husband's death.

She opened her door to the passageway. He was a man who had done her a service, no matter how unpleasant. He should not have to scratch at the door like a servant. She shook her head at this odd sense of the man's pride as she took the chair beside the hearth facing the door.

A few minutes later, he appeared before her, his broad shoulders filling the doorway. How odd that she hadn't heard his footsteps, though she had listened for them. Nor had she realised quite how tall a man he was when they were out on the quay.

She frowned. He was still wearing his scarf, wrapped around his head and draped across his face in the manner of a Turk.

His dark coat, like the greatcoat he'd worn off the ship, fitted him ill, the fabric straining across his shoulders, yet loose at the waist, and the sleeves leaving more cuff visible than was desirable. His pantaloons were tight, too, outlining the musculature of his impressive calves, his long lean thighs and his— She forced her gaze back up to meet his eyes. 'Please come in, Mr Gilvry. Leave the door open, if you please.'

She didn't want the inn servants to gossip about her entertaining a man alone in her room. People were quick to judge and she didn't need a scandal destroying her reputation with her employer.

The man did not so much as walk into the room as he prowled across the space to take her outstretched hand. His steps were silent, light as air, but incredibly manly.

The same walk she'd first noticed on the quay. The walk of a hunter intent on stalking his prey. Or a marauding pirate, or a maiden-stealing sheikh. All man. All danger. A betraying little shiver ran down her spine.

Trying to hide her response to his presence, she gestured coldly to the seat on the other side of the hearth, the way she would direct a recalcitrant student. 'Pray be seated.'

He sat down, folding his long body into the large wing chair with an easy grace. But why hide his face? She'd thought nothing of the muffler out on the quay. She'd tucked her chin into her own scarf in the bitter November wind.

'Please, make yourself comfortable.' She looked pointedly as his headgear.

The wide chest rose and fell on a deep indrawn breath. He straightened his shoulders. 'It is an invitation you might regret.' There was bitter humour in his voice, and something else she could not define. Defiance, perhaps? Bravado?

Turning partly away he unwound the muffler. At first all she could see was the left side of his face and hair of a dark reddish-blonde, thick and surprisingly long. His skin was a warm golden bronze. Side on he looked like an alabaster plaque of a Greek god in profile, only warm and living. Never had she seen a man so handsome.

He turned and faced her full on.

She recoiled with a gasp at the sight of the tributary of scars running down the right side of his face. A jagged, badly healed puckering of skin that sliced a diagonal from cheekbone to chin, pulling the corner of his mouth into a mocking smile. A dreadful mutilation of pure male beauty. She wanted to weep.

'I warned that you'd prefer it covered.' Clearly resigned, he reached for the scarf.

How many people must have turned away in horror at the sight? From a man who would have once drawn eyes because of his unusual beauty.

'Of course not,' she said firmly, deeply regretting her surprised response. 'Would you like a dram of whisky?' She made to rise.

Looking relieved, he rose to his feet. 'I'll help myself.'

He crossed to the table beside the window and poured whisky from the decanter, the good side of his face turned towards her. It made her heart ache to see him so careful. He lifted the glass and tossed off half in one go. He frowned at the remainder. 'I didna' expect to find you alone. Did they no' give you the maid I requested?'

'She has duties in the kitchen, preparing the evening meal.'

He lifted his head, his narrowed gaze meeting hers, the muscles in his jaw jumping, pulling at the scars, making them gleam bone white. Her stomach curled up tight. She could only imagine the pain such an injury must have caused, along with the anguish at the loss of such perfection.

Anger flared in his eyes as if he somehow read her thoughts and resented them.

He did not want her sympathy.

She looked down at her hands and gripped them together in her lap. She had asked him here to answer her questions. She might as well get straight to the point.

'Mr Gilvry, I would like to know exactly what happened to my husband, if you wouldn't mind?' Did she sound too blunt? Too suspicious?

She glanced up to test his reaction to her words. He was gazing out into the darkness, his face partly hidden by his hair. 'Aye. I'll tell you what I can.'

She frowned at the strange choice of words. 'Were you travelling with Samuel, when…when—?'

'No. I found him some time after the Indians had attacked his party. He had managed to crawl away from the camp and hide, but he was badly injured.'

'Why? Why were they attacked?'

He turned his head slightly, watching her from the corner of his eye. 'I don't know.'

Why did she have the sense he was not telling her the truth? What reason would he have to lie? 'So you just happened upon him? Afterwards.'

'I heard shots, but arrived too late to be of help.' His head lowered slightly. 'I'm sorry.'

He sounded sorry. More regretful than she would have expected under the circumstances he described. 'He was alive when you found him?'

He took a deep breath. 'He was. I hoped—' He shook his head. 'I carried him down from the mountains. For a while I thought he would live. The fever took him a few nights later.'

'And he requested that you bring his remains back to me?' She could not help the incredulity in her voice.

He shifted, half turning towards her. 'To Scotland. To his family. That is you, is it not?'

'I doubt he thought of me as family.' She spoke the words without thinking and winced at how bitter she sounded.

'He had regrets, your husband, I think. At the last.' His voice was low and deep and full of sympathy.

An odd lump rose in her throat. The thought that Samuel had cared. Even if it was out of guilt. It had been a long time since anyone had truly cared. She fought the softening emotion. It was too late for her to feel pain. How would it help her now? 'And his executor is to meet us here? In Dundee.'

'Aye. Or at least his lawyer. A Mr Jones. I wrote to him from Wilmington. But if you didna' get my letter…'

'The address you used, it came from Samuel? Naturally it did,' she amended quickly at his frown.

'Aye.'

'I moved. I had no way of letting Samuel know.' She'd also changed her name. She could scarcely have Samuel's creditors coming to her place of employment. 'An old friend forwarded Samuel's note, because I asked him to do so.' Her cousin's butler, once her father's man, would not have forwarded a letter unless he knew the name of the sender. There had been too many odd requests for money and not all of them from tradesmen. 'I doubt your other letter was similarly impeded. Let us hope Mr Jones will arrive tomorrow.'

The sound of footsteps carried along the passageway outside. He turned to look, his fair brows raised in question.

'Our dinner,' she said with a little jolt of her heart, as if she was afraid he would leave.

'Ours?' He looked surprised.

'I thought we could talk while we ate. That is, if you have not already dined?'

'No, I havena',' he said warily. He turned his back on the room, once more looking out into the night as two maids entered, followed by the innkeeper's wife who directed the setting up of the table and the serving of dinner. The plump woman curtsied deeply. 'Will there be anything else, madam?'

'No, thank you,' Rowena said. 'I think we can manage to serve ourselves.'

The woman's gaze rested on Mr Gilvry's back for a moment, her eyes hard. 'Would you like our Emmie to serve you, madam?'

Rowena could see the woman's thoughts about single ladies entertaining a gentleman in her rooms.

She stared at the woman down the nose that had been her plague as a girl, but now had its uses. An arrogant nose, it put people in their place. Her father had used his own bigger version to great effect in his business. 'No, thank you, Mrs Robertson. That will be all.'

The woman huffed out a breath, but stomped out of the room, defeated.

Mr Gilvry turned around as the door closed behind their hostess, his expression dark. 'The woman is right. You should ask the maid to attend you. Or dine alone. You must think of your reputation.' He took an urgent step towards the door.

The vehemence in his voice surprised her. Was he was afraid for her reputation or his? Did he fear she might put him in a compromising position? It hardly seemed likely. 'You honour me with your concern, Mr Gilvry, however, I am not accountable to the wife of an innkeeper.' She lifted her chin as another thought occurred to her. 'Or are you seeing it as an excuse to avoid my questions?'

He glared. 'I have answered all of your questions.'

Had he? Then why did she have the sense he was keeping something back? 'You have,' she said. It would do no good to insult the man. 'But I have more. You must excuse my curiosity. I know little of my husband's activities in America.'

His mouth tightened. His gaze shuttered, hiding his thoughts. 'There is little I can tell you on that score, I am afraid. Perhaps this Mr Jones can tell you more.'

Avoidance. It was as plain as the nose on her face. Her exceedingly plain nose on her exceedingly plain face, as Samuel had made no bones to tell her, once he had control of her money. But it wasn't because she cared whether this man found her attractive or otherwise that she wanted him to stay; she simply wanted to know if she dared trust him. That was all.

For one thing, she had never before heard of this Mr Jones. And she was hoping Mr Gilvry could shed some light on how he fitted into the scheme of things before she faced the man.

She offered a smile. 'I am sorry if I sound over forward, but I find I do not wish to eat alone tonight. My thoughts about the news give me no rest.' And nor did her suspicions.

His shoulders relaxed. 'Aye, I understand it has come as a shock.'

And a welcome relief. Guilt assailed her at the uncharitable thought. He would think her dreadful if he guessed at the direction of her thoughts.

She gestured to the table. 'The food is here. It would be a shame for it to go to waste.'

He swept a red-gold lock back from his forehead. 'To tell the truth, the smell of the food is hard to resist and I doubt they'll feed me in the kitchen, if yon mistress has aught to say in it.'

He glanced at the table with longing and it was only then that she realised how very gaunt was his face. His cheekbones stood out beneath his skin as if he had not eaten well in months. At first one only noticed the scars. And the terrible dichotomy they made of his face.

'Then you will keep me company?' she asked. She wasn't the sort of woman men fell over themselves to be with, but he was not a man who would have much choice in women. Not now. She stilled at the thought.

Was that hope she felt? Surely not. Hope where men were concerned had been stamped out beneath Samuel's careless boots. What man would want her? Especially now, when she was poor.

He shook his head with a rueful expression. 'Aye. It seems I will.'

The gladness she felt at his acceptance was out of all proportion with the circumstances and her reasons for inviting him. A gladness she must not let him see. With a cool nod, she let him seat her at the dining table.

He took the chair opposite. 'May I pour you some wine and carve you a portion of what looks to be an excellent fowl?'

'You may, indeed.'

While she had little appetite herself after the day's events, it was a pleasure to see him eat with obvious enjoyment. And his manners were impeccable. He was a gentleman, no matter his poor clothing.

She cut her slice of chicken into small pieces and tasted a morsel. It was moist and the white sauce was excellent. And she could not help watching him from beneath her lowered lashes as she tasted her food. He might not be handsome any longer, but his youth, his physical strength and powerful male presence were undeniable. Big hands. Wide shoulders. White, even teeth. A formidable man with an energy she could feel from across the table.

She wanted to ask him what it was that drove him. What he cared about. What he planned. It was none of her business. She would do well to remember that.

She held her questions while he satisfied his appetite.

It was her experience, both at home and in the two positions she'd held as a governess, that men became more amenable with a full stomach. She waited until he had cut himself a piece of apple pie before opening a conversation that did not include passing gravy or salt, or the last of the roast pork.

'The locals say that it is likely to be a hard winter,' she said, lifting her wine glass.

'I heard the same,' he replied.

She waited for him to say more, but was not surprised when he did not. He said little unless it was to the point. Idle conversation had a tendency to lead to the baring of souls. He was not that sort of man.

She took a sip of wine and considered her next words. Shock him, perhaps? Get beneath his guard, as her father would have said? Her heart raced a little. 'The coat you are wearing is Samuel's, is it not?'

Eyes wary, he put down his forkful of pie. 'He had no more use for it. My own clothes were ruined on the journey to the coast.'

Defensive. But why? What he said made perfect sense. Perhaps he feared she'd be overcome by her emotions at the thought of him wearing Samuel's clothes? Another woman might be, she supposed.

She kept her voice light and even. 'It must have been a terrible journey?'

'I've had worse.'

She stared, surprised by the edge in his voice. He looked up and caught her gaze. His skin coloured, just a little, as if he realised he'd been brusque.

'But, yes,' he said, his voice a little more gentle, 'it

was no' so easy.' His voice dropped. 'Your husband bore it verra well at the end, if it is of comfort to you.'

It did not sound like the Samuel she had known. He'd been a man who liked an easy life. The reason he had married her money. Could there be some sort of mistake? Her stomach clenched at the idea, but she asked the question anyway. 'You are sure that he is…I mean, he was Samuel MacDonald? My husband?'

Misplaced pity filled his gaze. 'There is no doubt in my mind the man was your husband, Mrs MacDonald. We talked. Of you. Of other things. How else would I know about the lawyer?' He frowned and looked grim. 'But you are right. Someone should identify his remains. To make things legal. I didna' think you…'

Her stomach lurched. She pushed her plate away, stood and moved from the table to the hearth. 'No. You are right. This Mr Jones should do it.'

'If he knew him personally.'

She whirled around. 'You think he did not?'

'Your husband was not always lucid, Mrs MacDonald. He suffered greatly. But he was most insistent on my contacting those in charge of Mere's estate.'

The Duke of Mere. Why did that name sound so familiar? She had heard it spoken of recently, surely? She didn't care for gossip, but now she remembered her employer's remark. She turned to face him. 'The Duke of Mere is dead.'

His jaw dropped. 'But…' He shook his head, got up and took a step towards her. 'One duke dies. Another follows right behind. Like the king.'

He was right. She swallowed. 'Of course.'

He drew closer. Very close, until she could feel the warmth from his body, the sense of male strength held in check, though why that should be she could not imagine. 'Mrs MacDonald,' he said softly, 'dinna fash yourself. Jones will come tomorrow and your husband's family will do their duty by you.'

What family? According to Samuel he was as alone in the world as she was. It was one of the things that had drawn her to him. His need for family. Not that he had needed her, once he had her money. It would be nice to be needed. To be able to lean on a man and have him take care of her in return. She felt herself leaning towards Mr Gilvry, as if his strength could sustain her.

Shocked, she straightened. She moved away, turning to face him with a hard-won smile against the melting sensation in her limbs. 'You are right. It seems that Mr Jones holds the key to everything.' She put a hand to her temple. It was throbbing again. Too much thinking. Too much worrying. Too much hope that she had not been entirely abandoned after all.

'Mr Gilvry, my husband asked much of you.' She looked at his poor ruined face and saw nothing but sympathy in his gaze. She hesitated, her mouth dry, the words stuck fast in her throat. She took a breath. 'Could I trouble you some more? May I request your presence at the interview with Mr Jones?'

If he was surprised, he hid it well. 'If that is your wish,' he said, his voice a little gruff.

Instinctively, she swayed towards all that beautiful male strength, her eyes closing in relief. 'Thank you.'

She felt his hand on her arm, warm and strong and

infinitely gentle. Once more, strange tingles ran up her arm at the strength of his touch. Did he feel them, too? Was that why he released her so quickly?

'Sit down, Mrs MacDonald,' he said in a rasping voice. 'By the hearth. I'll ask our hostess to send up tea. And the maid. It is a good night's sleep you need. Things will be clearer in the morning.'

When she looked up, he was gone. So silently for such a tall man. A man whose absence left a very empty hole in the room. But he had said he would stand by her on the morrow. She clung to that thought as if her life depended on it and wondered at her sudden sensation of weakness.

Chapter Two

Drew paced up and down between the stalls, cursing under his breath. Frustration scoured through his blood. Desire. He struck out at a post and accepted the pain in his knuckles as his just reward.

What the hell did he think he was doing? The woman had just learned of her husband's death and instead of offering platitudes and help, he'd almost pulled her into his arms and kissed her.

He wasn't drawn to respectable women. Ever. He was depraved. And he knew where to find what he wanted. What the hell had he been thinking up there?

How could he possibly consider wanting her, let alone begin envisaging her naked and open and…? He hit the post again, then sucked the copper-tasting blood from his knuckles and remembered her soft, wide mouth.

Damn him. Hadn't his experience with Alice Fulton been lesson enough? If his family hadn't been desperate, he would never have taken her in order to force a wedding. The moment he did it, he'd known it would never work. Not for him. He'd have spent his life in purgatory.

He'd never been so relieved as when she had backed out of their engagement. So why had he almost kissed Rowena MacDonald?

Because he felt sorry for her? Or because he was grateful that, after her first horrified look at his face, she'd acted as if he was normal. As if his appearance didn't make her stomach turn.

Jones had better turn up tomorrow and take charge of this woman, because if he didn't, Drew was just going to walk away. He squeezed his eyes shut. He couldn't. He'd sworn to himself that he would see her safe and secure. He didn't have a choice, not when it was his fault her husband was dead.

A man staggered down the steps from the loft. The old groom in charge of the stables. He glared at Drew, then recoiled as he saw his face in the light from the lantern hanging from a beam.

'Isn't it bad enough that your pounding and cursing knocked me out of my bed,' the old man railed, shaking his fist. 'Do you have to ruin my dreams with that devil's face?'

Drew laughed. He couldn't help it. The old man's reaction was exactly the same as everyone else's, but at least he had the courage to say it.

He bowed. 'I beg your pardon.'

'Aye, well ye might. If ye're wanting to bed down, you best get up that ladder now, because when I'm back from tending to nature I'm bolting the trapdoor from the inside. To keep out Old Nick, you understand.' He staggered to the door at the far end, still muttering under his breath.

Drew wished he had something to keep out the devil he carried around inside him. But he didn't. And while the devil wanted a woman, Drew wanted his revenge on Ian more. And so he would keep the devil caged. He'd done it for the past few years; he would continue.

He had to get Mrs MacDonald off his hands and his conscience. Then he would send Ian to hell, where he belonged.

'A gentleman to see you, Mrs Macdonald,' the maid announced from the doorway to her private parlour the next morning.

She looked up from her struggle to compose a suitable letter to Mrs Preston, her employer, asking for a few more days' absence. For a moment she thought it might be Mr Gilvry and her heart lifted a fraction. But at the same moment she knew it was not. He would not have asked the maid to announce him. 'Did the gentleman give his name?'

Emmie held out a square of white paper. 'His card, ma'am.'

Mr Brian Jones, solicitor, the card stated in bold black letters. On the reverse, a rather crabbed script added cryptically, man of business to the Duke of Mere.

'Show him in, please. And ask Mr Gilvry to come up, if you will.' The girl raised questioning brows, but hurried off without a word.

Rowena moved from the writing desk to the sofa and sat facing the door.

The man who stepped across the threshold a few moments later was surprisingly young for such a responsible position. In his mid-thirties, she thought, and reasonably fair of face, if one ignored the tendency of his long nose to sharpness and the slight weakness of his chin. But his pale blue eyes were sharp and his smile positively charming. He was dressed quite as soberly as one would expect for a lawyer, though his cravat was perhaps a shade flamboyant in its intricacy.

'Mrs MacDonald,' he said with a deeper bow than someone of her station warranted. An odd little slip for such a man.

'Mr Jones. Please, be seated.'

He settled himself into the armchair opposite without a sign of any nervousness. Indeed, if anything, he looked confidently in control. A small smile hovered on his lips as he waited for her to speak. She could wait him out. Her father had taught her the game of negotiation almost before she had learned how to sew a fine seam. But with her future in the balance, she wasn't in the mood.

'You received the message about my husband's death from Mr Gilvry, I assume?'

He arranged his face into an expression of sympathy. 'I did. May I offer you my condolences on your loss,' he said, inclining his head. 'Indians, I understand.'

She nodded. 'So I gather.'

'Most unfortunate.' A touch of colour tinged his cheeks. 'Did you—' He coughed delicately. 'Are you certain he did not survive the attack?'

His eyes were fixed intently on her face. A strange feeling rippled across her shoulders. Her scalp tightened at the shock of it. It was something like the sensation described as a ghost walking over one's grave, only more unpleasant. A premonition of danger. Clearly, she wasn't the only one who had wondered about the truth of Samuel's death. 'If you require confirmation, Mr Jones, you must inspect his remains. They have been returned to Scotland at his wish.'

Distaste twisted his mouth. 'Not me. I never met Mr MacDonald in person.' He coughed behind his hand. 'I have arranged for someone in the duke's household to confirm his identity.'

The duke's household? 'My husband never mentioned the Duke of Mere once to me during our marriage.'

'Ah, dear lady, it is a distant connection. Your husband's branch of the family has long been estranged from its senior branch. He visited Mere shortly before his departure for America. It was Mere's wish that relationships that were broken be mended. The identification is mere formality, you understand, but a necessary one.'

His smile felt just a little too forced. But then it was likely difficult to know what to do with one's face in the presence of a supposedly grieving widow. He drew a notebook from his pocket and a small silver pen. He turned the pages as if looking for something. 'It was a Mr Gilvry who discovered his body. It was his letter we received.'

'Yes. He accompanied my husband's remains from America.' His voice made her wonder if he harboured doubts about Mr Gilvry. She pursed her lips. Where was he? He had promised to attend this meeting. 'He will join us shortly.'

He looked around somewhat disapprovingly as if he expected Mr Gilvry to pop out of her bedroom.

'Nothing can move forward until the circumstances of your husband's death are fully documented and sworn to,' he continued. 'It is this—' he glanced down at his notebook '—Gilvry I need to speak to. As well as verifying the death of your husband and...' He frowned. 'And the validity of your marriage.'

'I beg your pardon?'

'None of the MacDonalds were aware that Mr Samuel MacDonald had taken a wife.'

'You will find it in the records of my parish church.'

Again that delicate cough. 'Or if there are offspring? Our contact with Mr MacDonald was most perfunctory.'

'No.' She raised her chin. 'No offspring.' And she'd been glad of it, too, given how he'd left her in the lurch.

'And Mr Gilvry?'

She glanced towards the door. Where on earth was he?

The call to attend Rowena and Mr Jones came at eleven. Damn it, not Rowena. Mrs MacDonald. All night he'd been thinking about the lovely pale skin glowing in candlelight over dinner, his memories of the challenge her slender curves and hollows presented to his own desires and cursing himself.

He'd made very sure the servants had seen him leave her room. He'd sent the maid up to help her ready for bed, too, so she would know nothing untoward had occurred. He'd done all he could to protect her from gossip. He would have to make sure this lawyer saw only mistress and servant.

Once more he was dressed in her husband's second-best coat, pretending to be what he was not.

The atmosphere when he stepped into the room was tense. Mrs MacDonald sagged at the sight of him. He frowned. What had this lawyer being saying to her that would upset her usual calm?

He bowed. 'You sent for me, Mrs MacDonald.'

'Yes, Mr Gilvry. Mr Jones has some questions for you.'

'Indeed I do,' the dapper young man said. 'On what date did Mr MacDonald meet his end? The day and the month.'

Drew had expected questions about the circumstances of MacDonald's death. Dreaded them. But the date?

He hadn't known at the time. He'd spent too long living by the seasons and the rise and set of the sun to be aware of dates. But he knew it now. The date was carved in his mind by words that chilled him to the bone. *Unbelievable that any man would allow...* 'September fifteenth.' He forced the words out.

The lawyer's eyes flickered with some sort of emotion. Disappointment? He gathered himself so quickly it was hard to be sure. He smiled a prissy smile. 'Are you positive?'

'I am.'

The lawyer looked at him expectantly. When he said nothing, the man shook his head. 'You have proof?'

A deep dark cold entered his gut. 'My word should be enough.'

'Any statement made is subject to being contested without proof.'

The cold expended to fill his chest. He had the proof. But to make his shame public, a byword.... There had to be another way. 'If you dinna have the date, is it a problem?'

The lawyer tapped his chin with a well-manicured nail, making Drew aware of his rough weather-beaten hands. No longer the hands of a gentleman. Jones frowned down at paper before him. 'It is true the date is not so important, once his identity is established. Without proof it is best if we couch it in the most general of terms.' He looked up with a lawyerly smile. 'And remain within the bounds of the law, you understand. Yes. Yes. It will serve very well.'

The man talked in such flowing periods, Drew wanted to hit him.

He picked up his pen and filled in some blank spaces on the document. 'Hmm. Date of death, sometime in late September.'

Drew looked at Rowena. She was pale, worrying at her bottom lip and looking tense. She clearly sensed something was wrong and, damn it, so did he.

The lawyer pushed the paper across the desk. 'Make your mark there,' he said, pointing. 'I'll witness it.'

His younger brother Niall had always wanted to study the law. One of the things he had said when they talked around the dinner table was that it was a foolish man who signed anything he did not understand. And it was clear the lawyer thought he couldn't read. He picked up the pen. 'Why not write the fifteenth as I told you?'

'You cannot put a date if you cannot prove it,' the lawyer said. 'It would not be right.' He moved the paper out of Drew's reach with a frown. 'And as I said, it is not all that important. As long as we have the proof of his death.' He gave a sly little smile. 'As we will do, once the remains are carried to Mere.'

'Then let us omit any mention of the date at all.' Drew replied.

'Will that be sufficient?' Rowena asked, her posture stiff, her expression remote, yet stern. Drew sensed her anxiety.

The lawyer pulled his legal superiority around him like a shield. 'If more is required, we can return to the matter at a later time.'

It seemed reasonable to Drew. Then why did he have this odd sense of worry? He glanced at Rowena. She also looked troubled, but she met his gaze and nodded.

He pulled the paper back across the table, scratched out the line and signed the document.

'Mr Jones,' Mrs MacDonald said sharply, 'there are other matters pressing upon me at the moment with which I require your assistance.'

His gaze sharpened with wariness. 'Matters, madam?'

'Matters such as my husband's will. His estate.'

'My dear Mrs MacDonald,' the man said with a condescension that again made Drew want to hit him, 'probate of a will takes time. There are many formalities to be undertaken, as I have already explained.'

She gazed at him coolly. 'I understand. But you must know something of his affairs. I am a governess. I must return to my position at once.'

His eyes widened. 'Oh, most certainly not. You and Mr Gilvry must travel to Mere.'

Drew stared at him. 'I have no intention of going to Mere. My own affairs take me in quite another direction.'

The lawyer shifted in his seat. 'It was my understanding that you were to accompany Mr MacDonald's remains to his final resting place. That is Mere.'

'I prefer to leave that to you.'

The lawyer shook his head. 'Until a third party has confirmed that the deceased is truly Samuel MacDonald, at which time the court will no doubt accept your information, Mr Gilvry, I cannot release you from your obligations.'

He turned to Rowena and, if anything, his smile became more oily. 'I should not be saying this, but before he left, Mr MacDonald changed his will. Everything is left to Mere's estate. Any settlements will be at the discretion of the new duke. You will not find him ungenerous, I assure you, once your claim is established.'

Drew's hackles rose. The longer he spent in this man's company, the less he trusted him. While at first glance he seemed charming, with that ready smile, his eyes drifted away when met head-on, even taking into account that no one liked to look Drew full in the face.

Rowena visibly wilted as if the stuffing had been knocked out of her. 'He left everything to Mere? He indicated to Mr Gilvry that he made a settlement—'

Jones shook his head. 'It is in Mere's hands now. I am merely his representative. You will have to take your case directly to him.'

Drew glared and the man shifted his gaze to the documents on the table. 'MacDonald told me his wife would be cared for.' The dying man had said it with such bitterness, Drew had been shocked, but he had not doubted his words.

Jones frowned. 'The duke takes his responsibilities seriously, I can assure you.' Again that tight little smile at Rowena. 'As you will discover, Mrs MacDonald, if you will allow yourself to be guided by me.'

Rowena took an unsteady breath. 'It would be enough if I am relieved of his debt.'

The defeat on her face made Drew's chest feel as if it was weighed down with a rock.

'If there are assets, they should be passed on to Mac-Donald's widow,' he said firmly.

The lawyer was tapping his chin again. A sign he was thinking on his feet, perhaps. 'I see you are not satisfied with the word of a duke,' Jones said in an exasperated tone. 'Very well. If your claims are proved—' he inclined his head slightly '—as I am sure they will be, dear lady, there is a house set aside for you, at Mere, and an annuity.'

She perked up. 'The house would be mine? Something I can sell?'

Jones shook his head. 'It is on land that is part of the estate.'

'So the duke will continue to own the house.'

He nodded. 'Indeed. But once your husband's will has gone through probate, there may be more. You did mention debts?'

She looked down her autocratic nose and the lawyer visibly wilted. 'Yes, but none of my making.' She let go a little breath. 'But Mr MacDonald realised a large sum from the sale of my half of McFail's. I cannot believe there is nothing left.'

'Let us hope you are right. In the meantime...'

'In the meantime, it seems I have no choice but to accept the duke's generous offer. I will travel to Mere and learn the outcome of my husband's business affairs.'

Jones turned his gaze to Drew. 'I do hope I can prevail upon you to finish what you set out to accomplish. The return of Mr MacDonald to the bosom of his family. You will, of course, be rewarded for your time.'

'I would prefer to leave it to you,' Drew said. 'I have another engagement.' Ian. His gut clenched painfully.

Jones gathered up his papers. 'My first duty is to ascertain this lady's claim of marriage, which takes me in a different direction, after which I will then make posthaste to Mere. But you must allow it is vital that the poor dear departed be taken swiftly to his final resting place. Who knows what ravages may have occurred during shipment? If it is not possible to prove his identity...'

Rowena paled. Drew felt slightly nauseous, though the undertaker had assured him all would be well.

Rowena looked at him and, while her expression was one of serene indifference, he knew from the pleas deep in those soft grey eyes that she wanted him to say yes. 'Verra well. I will accompany Mrs MacDonald to Mere.'

The lawyer looked far too relieved at his words, but Drew could hardly change his mind, because Rowena had looked equally relieved.

'Excellent,' Jones said. 'You will make your way to Penwood House. No doubt his Grace will be delighted to receive you at the castle once you are established there.'

Drew didn't like the glint of triumph in Jones's eyes. 'And a conveyance?' Drew asked.

'I will arrange for a cart for the transportation of the…luggage.'

Rowena's face shuttered. 'I am to travel on this cart?'

'You may. Unless you prefer to ride. The driver, a man by the name of Pockle, and his wife will serve your needs along the road, which regrettably is a difficult journey this time of year.'

Did the man hope she'd become lost on the way? Drew glared at him, knowing only too well the dangers of cross-country travel. 'How long will it take?' Drew asked.

'Two or three days. Longer if the weather is bad.'

'And where is Mrs MacDonald to spend the nights?' Drew asked. He could not get away from his sense of danger. 'You surely don't expect her to camp out in the hills.'

'Certainly not. There are inns along the way. Please be ready to leave in the morning. I will take care of all the arrangements before I leave later today.' He gathered up his papers and packed them away. 'I look forward to our next meeting at Mere, Mrs MacDonald.'

He bowed and left.

Rowena frowned. 'He was so keen on a date at first. Why do you think he changed his mind so quickly?'

The lass had a very sharp mind.

He shook his head. 'That's a tricky wee fellow, I'm thinking. You are right to seek out the duke.'

'Are you sure you don't mind going, too? While he seemed to want your presence at Mere, I could probably manage with the driver and his wife, since it is not too far distant.'

It was madness to agree to it. To spend more time in her company. To feel the call of her milk-white skin and find himself falling into the depths of her clear grey eyes. Madness and torture for the sake of a promise no one had heard but himself. 'Once I start on something, I have to see it through.'

No matter how long it took.

A soft breath came from her parted lips and he wanted to capture it in his mouth. 'Thank you.'

He turned briskly for the door. 'It seems I must find some sort of nag for the journey.'

His business with Ian could wait. A week. A month. A year. It made no difference; it had waited so long already.

Yet he could not help feeling he might be making the worst mistake of his life. And he'd made some bad ones in the past.

Chapter Three

Why on earth did Mere have to reside in such an inaccessible place in wintertime? Rowena thought, huddling deeper into her cloak. Why couldn't he live in Edinburgh like any civilised person? This was their second day since leaving Dundee and Rowena was already exhausted by the journey. The roads were so abysmal, the cart travelled at less than walking speed and, this afternoon, the sky had turned a lowering grey just skimming the hilltops.

The cold, damp air wormed its way through every fibre of her clothing. Worse was the way Mr Gilvry, riding ahead of the cavalcade, glanced up at the sky from time to time.

She urged her horse forward. 'Is it going to rain?'

She was on his left side and the beauty of his features struck her anew, though she hoped she managed to hide the sudden hitch in her breath.

'Snow,' he said with such assurance, she did not doubt him.

Lovely. She shivered. 'How long before we reach the next inn?' She could just imagine a warm fire and a hot bath.

Mr Gilvry glanced back over his shoulder at the cart, where the driver and his wife sat pressed close together for warmth. 'Our next stopping place is fifteen miles from where we stayed last night. Since we havena' made more than ten miles, I would say we have another five to go.'

'Can we make it by nightfall?'

'Aye.'

He sounded confident, but she wasn't fooled. These one-word answers were meant to disguise his concern. 'You mean, if it doesn't snow and if the cart doesn't get stuck.'

He gave her a quick sideways glance and she could have sworn the corner of his mouth curled up in a smile. The effect was more than charming, it was wickedly se-ductive. Her inner muscles gave a little squeeze. Not the sort of reaction one should be having sitting on a horse. Or at all. But at least a new kind of warmth was now pulsing through her body.

'Aye, that is just what I mean,' he said.

To hide her flush, she also looked over her shoulder at the cart and its occupants. Twice it had become stuck in a muddy rut on the previous day. On both occasions, she'd been impressed with Mr Gilvry's strength and his whipcord leanness when he had removed his coats and heaved with all his might.

'I'm beginning to wonder if I shouldn't have just gone

back to my place of employment and forgotten all about ever being married.'

His amusement faded. 'Would you let that wee mannie Jones have the best of you? I don't know what game Mere is playing, but your husband was telling me the truth. He made some sort of settlement for you.'

'It won't make any difference if I freeze to death out here.'

'I'll be certain that doesna' happen.'

From anyone else she might have taken his words as bravado, but the determination in both his voice and his face gave her a modicum of comfort, even as her heart sank at the sight of the next hill rising before them. The track disappeared up into the clouds. Who knew what lay ahead.

It was the steepest hill they'd encountered so far. 'We'd best walk the horses again,' Mr Gilvry said, dismounting in a swirl of coat. 'They need to rest, but we canna stop if we are to make shelter by nightfall.'

He reached up and lifted her down as he did each time she needed to dismount. Again the heat of his touch warmed her through and through. It was all in her mind, of course, there were layers and layers of clothing between his skin and hers, but it was the only bright spot in a very dreary day.

She smiled her thanks when he set her on her feet and received a nod in reply. A very cool nod, indeed. He was clearly regretting his agreement to escort her to the duke. But he'd given his word and he would keep it. Knowing he at least was a man of his word gave her comfort. A sense of security she had not known in a long time.

And that was a mistake. She'd thought the same about Samuel and look how that had ended. And if this trip to Mere ended the same way, she was going to be in dire straits indeed since Mrs Preston, rather than extending her leave of absence, had terminated her employment.

All her reliance was now on the generosity of the Duke of Mere.

They walked in silence, one behind the other for a while. Rowena turned to look back down the hill. There was no sign of the cart in the mist that had closed in around them.

'Shouldn't we wait for them?' she called out.

'They'll catch us up at the crest,' he replied. 'I'll make tea to warm us and have it ready when they arrive.'

That was the other thing she found strange about him. The way he carried an assortment of objects in his saddlebag, as if he was used to living in the wilds. A handful of oats. A tin kettle to make tea. And of course the leaves. No milk, though. Just a flask of whisky from which he added a splash to the brew. It certainly warmed her from the inside out and she found herself looking forward to their arrival at the top of the hill.

The Pockles also carried supplies in the cart—bread, cheese, some oatcakes—but Mr Gilvry's tea was the best of all of it.

They had plodded upwards for what felt like a good half an hour. At this rate they would be lucky to make the last five miles to the next inn before it was dark.

At the top, catching her breath, Rowena looked around her, but there was nothing to see. Just a rolling blanket of white and a barely visible track disappearing downwards. Disappointing, really. She'd been looking forward to seeing the Highlands in all their glory. But it really was the wrong time of year for travel. She shivered and pulled her cloak tighter around her.

Mr Gilvry set about making a fire from a clump of peat he had picked up somewhere along the way, or perhaps taken from the inn where they stayed the previous night. The inn had only one bedchamber. Everyone else was expected to sleep in the commons. Mr Gilvry had preferred the stables. She didn't really blame him. The driver and his wife were a nice enough couple, if a little dour, but they were not as particular about their cleanliness as they might have been. She would not have wanted to spend a night with them in close quarters.

It didn't take him long to get the fire started and, while the small can heated over the flame, she bent to warm her numb fingers against the heat.

'I wish I understood what game the duke is playing,' she said softly. He crouched beside her on his heels. He looked so comfortable she thought about trying it.

'The only way to find out is to meet him face-to-face,' he said.

'If he will meet with me.'

'I canna see why he would not?'

No, she could not either, but there was something odd about the way Mr Jones had insisted they make this journey. And then there was the issue of the date of Samuel's death. Not just the lawyer's swift change of mind, but the way Mr Gilvry had stiffened at the mention of proof.

The water started to boil and she stepped back from

the fire to give him room to brew his concoction. A few moments later, he held out a small pewter mug. She wrapped her gloved fingers around it and breathed in the steam. Bitter tea and whisky. While she sipped and felt the warmth slide down her throat, she stared into the mist. What sort of house would a duke have set aside for the wife of a distant relative? If she couldn't sell it, and Samuel had not after all left her some money, would she be stuck out here in the Highlands for the rest of her life?

It seemed likely. Unless she married again.

She glanced at Mr Gilvry. He was looking back the way they had come with a frown. And then the jingle of a bridle pierced the muffling mist and the next moment the cart and its occupants came into view.

Mr Gilvry collected the Pockles' mugs and filled them from the kettle. He kicked out the fire and stamped on the embers. 'We'll keep going, aye?' he said to Pockle. 'We don't want to be out here at nightfall.'

'That we don't,' said Pockle, cradling his mug just as Rowena had done and blowing on it to cool it. 'Old McRae willna' open the door to us if we arrive after sunset.'

Mr Gilvry glared at him. 'Why did you say nothing of this before?'

Pockle shrugged. 'We were making good time. Nae need to distress the lady for naught.'

Mrs Pockle took a deep swallow from her mug and made a little sound of satisfaction. Rowena had the feeling she cared more about the whisky than the tea. 'Auld McRae is afraid of the piskies hereabouts,' she announced. 'Locks up tight come the dark.'

Mr Gilvry made no comment, but she could see the irritation in his expression. Not a man to believe in piskies, then.

'We'd best be moving on,' he said. He took her mug, tossed the dregs and wrapped it in a cloth, before throwing her back in the saddle. 'We'll make the best use of the downhill slope to make up a little time.'

'I'll catch ye up,' Pockle said. 'I've a need to empty my bladder.' He handed his empty mug to his wife and jumped down.

'Dinna be taking too long, man,' Mr Gilvry said. 'We'll wait for you at McRae's place and I'll be sure of letting ye in, dark or no.'

Pockle touched a hand to his cap.

'Don't you think it would be better if we all stayed together?' Rowena said. 'What if we get lost? Pockle knows the way.'

'I won't get lost.' Mr Gilvry growled. 'I looked at the map before we left.'

He mounted up and grabbed for Rowena's reins. 'But you might.' He glanced up at the sky. 'The sooner we get going, the sooner we will arrive.'

Normally she would not have considered letting a man lead her along like a child, but the worry in his eyes made such pride a foolish luxury. 'Just be careful, Mr Gilvry,' she said coolly. 'I would not like to follow you off a cliff.'

His sharp stare said the prospect was not out of the realm of possibility and her stomach dipped. So much for trying to strike a lighter note. Something that actually never seemed possible with this particular man, any more than it had been with Samuel.

She sighed. *Say nothing, and then you can't possibly go wrong.*

His horse moved ahead and hers followed at his tug on the bridle. After a few minutes of them heading downhill, big wet flakes drifted down to settle on her shoulders and her horse's neck. They melted almost at once.

Mr Gilvry muttered something under his breath. A curse, no doubt. She felt like cursing herself. Instead, she ducked deeper into her hood.

After a time, the numbness in her fingers and toes spread inwards. She blew on her fingers with little hope it would help and lifted her head to peer ahead, then she wished she hadn't. A gust of windblown snow stung her cheeks. But even that swift glimpse told her night was closing in fast.

Mr Gilvry stopped. Were they lost? Her heart began a sharp staccato in her chest.

She let her horse come up alongside his.

'Lights,' he said, leaning close so she could hear him through the muffling scarf he'd pulled up around his face.

The breath left her body in such a rush, she felt light-headed. 'McRae's?'

He nodded and urged his horse forward at a trot. Her mount followed suit.

He'd been right. He did know the way. She'd have to apologise for her doubts once they were warm and dry.

The inn stood alone, off to one side of the track they'd

been following, a lantern lighting its sign. A golden glow spilled from the windows, making square patches of snow glitter as if dusted with stars.

Mr Gilvry helped her down from her horse. Not only light issued forth from the inn, there was sound, too. The sound of men talking and laughing. She glanced up at Mr Gilvry and, while she could not see his face, she could see his eyes narrow.

'It seems we are not the only company tonight,' she said.

'Aye. Wait here. I'll see the landlord about a room.' He thrust the reins into her hands and ducked as he opened the door.

'Duin an dòras,' someone shouted.

Gaelic. Someone not pleased about the draught from the door being opened. The door slammed shut. Rowena glanced around. The stables must be at the back of the inn, but no one had come to take their horses. Perhaps she should take them herself. She was so cold, the wind biting through her cloak, even the thought of a stable was a lure.

Before she could make a move, Mr Gilvry returned with a man and a woman with a shawl over her head in tow. The man, a spry fellow, regarded her with interest before relieving her of the reins. 'While I help yon lad with the horses, Mrs McRae will see you upstairs.'

The woman gestured for her to follow. 'This way, ma'am. There's a nice warm fire ready and waiting.'

Warmth. What more could she ask? She started to follow.

Mr Gilvry caught her arm, turned her around and

brought her close, grasping her by her elbows and lifting her on her toes so she could see the glitter of the lamp over the door in his eyes. 'The men in there are a dangerous lot,' he murmured close to her ear. 'Do not look their way.'

Then he kissed her. Full on the lips. A warm dry pressure on her mouth. The heat of his breath on her frozen cheek, the thud of his heart beneath her fingertips where they rested on the side of his throat.

He broke away, gazing down at her, his expression dark, his mouth sensuously soft. She must have imagined it, because he set her away from him with a laugh as if it was she who had kissed him.

Stunned, she stared at him and her hand fell to her side.

He swung her around, pushing her forward with a tap on the rump. 'Ye'll be saving that for later, lassie.' He turned away, dragging her horse behind him.

Lassie? Later. What on earth...? She touched her lips still tingling from his unexpected kiss.

The landlady laughed. 'That's one cheeky lad ye have there for a husband.'

Husband? And so the goodwife might think after such a display. Her heart knocking against her ribs, whether out of fear for what she would find inside that he needed to warn her in such an odd way or the effect of that kiss, she didn't quite know.

Right now she didn't care about anything as long as she ended up close to the warmth of a fire. Later, though, when she wasn't too cold to think—cold on the outside, that was—she intended to discover just what sort of game he thought he was playing.

As she entered the inn, she realised he was right about the men in what must be the only barroom in the house. She had a brief impression of three burly males filling the low-beamed room, all looking at her. She kept her gaze firmly fixed on the landlady's back and mounted the stairs to a low rumble of male appreciation.

'Dinna mind them, missus,' the landlady said in comfortable tones, opening the door to a chamber at the end of a short corridor at the top of the stairs. 'McRae won't put up wi' any o' their nonsense.'

She hoped not.

Mrs McRae ushered her into a chamber that barely had room for a bed, a settle by the hearth and a table with two chairs in the corner.

The woman turned down the sheets and gave the bed a pat. 'And that man of yours is more than a match for them, aye?' She chuckled.

Rowena narrowed her eyes at the woman. Now, what should she say to that? Deny that Mr Gilvry was her man, or wait for his explanation? Discretion was no doubt the better part of valour in this circumstance.

'Take off your cloak, my dear,' the landlady urged. 'I'll send up my Sin to help you out of those wet clothes in a minute or two.' And with that she whisked out, shutting the door behind her.

Sin. Well, there was an interesting name. She removed her bonnet and tossed it on the bed, then unfastened her cloak and hung it over the settle where it could dry. She held her hands out to the fire and watched the steam rise off her skirts.

A knock at the door heralded the arrival of Sin, who turned out to be a pretty, blue-eyed, auburn-haired girl of about eighteen. As pretty as sin indeed.

She bobbed a curtsy. 'Mam says I'm to help you undress, mistress.'

'I'm afraid my luggage is still somewhere behind us on the road. I have nothing dry to change into.'

The girl gave her a grin. 'Your man said as how you was to take off your wet things and wrap yourself in the quilt.' She pointed at the bed.

'My man,' Rowena said drily. What on earth were the Pockles going to think when they arrived with the landlady calling Mr Gilvry her man? And what if it came to the duke's ears? She pressed her lips together against the urge to deny that Mr Gilvry was her man. She would let him explain, before she took him to task.

The girl scurried around behind her and began attacking her laces. 'Very positive he was about it, my lady, you being so damp and all. He feared you might take a chill. Said I was to get you out of these wet things, no matter what you said.'

'How very forceful,' Rowena said, wryly imagining Mr Gilvry dishing out orders and feeling a little shiver pass down her spine.

'Oh, yes,' the girl said, coming around to the front to help her unpin her bodice. 'Very forceful he was.' She giggled.

A strong urge to bash the girl over the head with a poker arose in Rowena's breast. Though why that would be, she had no idea. She didn't care in the least if Mr Gilvry made an innkeeper's daughter giggle. She probably hadn't seen his face. Oh, now that was mean.

'Was it a duel?' the girl asked. She sounded breathless. Too breathless for the effort to undo a few tapes on a gown.

'Was what a duel?'

'The scar. Was it a duel over a woman?' She sighed in the most nauseating way.

'I have no idea,' Rowena said repressively and stepped out of the gown. 'I have never asked him.'

'He must have been a right bonnie lad before...' The maid's voice tailed off.

Furious, and not knowing why, Rowena turned her back to give the maid access her stays. 'Do you think so?' She could not keep emotion from colouring her voice.

'I beg your pardon, ma'am. Not that he isn't bonnie now, of course. Lovely wide shoulders and those green eyes of his. They almost make up for the scar. We don't get many handsome young gentlemen passing through these parts.' The girl sighed.

'Are you done?'

The girl dropped the stays on top of the gown and picked up the counterpane. 'If you will just wrap this around you,' she said, 'I'll unpin your hair and gi' it a good brushing.'

Chapter Four

Drew followed the stableman, his head reeling. What the hell had he been thinking, kissing her like that? He'd just wanted to impress on her the importance of his words, and then the way she'd looked up at him, so sinfully tempting and ready to argue, it was all he could think of.

No doubt she'd be having his hide for that piece of foolishness. And for saying he was her husband. But the moment he saw the men inside the inn, he'd known they were trouble. His suspicions were confirmed by what he saw around him. The stables were full to the brim with ponies and stacked with barrels.

The three men in the common room were smugglers, and a rougher-looking lot he hoped never to see. The storm must have brought them in, because if things remained as they had been before he left for America, they would usually avoid any place where the gaugers might visit. There would be no excisemen out on a night like tonight.

It was a damnable nuisance that Pockle had been unable to keep up. It would have evened the odds.

Drew jerked his chin in the direction of the inn. 'Where are the men from?'

The little man's face closed up tighter than a Scotsman's purse. 'You'll find no loose tongues here, sir, but since you are a true Highland gentleman, I can tell you they work for McKenzie out of Edinburgh. A rough lot, I can tell you that. You would do as well to keep an eye on that wife of yours.'

Drew nodded and made a show of pulling his pistol from his saddle holster and tucking it in his belt along with powder and shot.

He glanced up to find the man watching him. 'Aye, well, I'm a man who kens how to look after his own.'

The little man grinned. 'As well to be safe as sorry, they do say.'

The cold feeling in Drew's chest expanded. Pockle should never have suggested they stay at a known smugglers' haunt. They should have stopped earlier in the day.

'You can leave the horses to me,' the groom said. 'I'll look in on them later. You'd best keep an eye on that woman of yours and get yourself warm.' He gave Drew a nudge in the ribs.

Drew gritted his teeth at the thought of the impending chilly reception. He should not have let himself be tempted.

'Is there a back door into the inn?' he asked the groom.

'Aye, straight across. You'll go through the kitchen.' He winked. 'There's but one set of stairs.'

Drew didn't much like the sound of that. It was always good to have more than one way out. He picked up their saddlebags and heaved them over one shoulder, leaving one hand free to use his pistol. He just hoped he wouldn't need it.

He crossed from the stables to the back door of the inn. The goodwife was busy at the hearth, a pot bubbling with stew. It didn't smell too bad and right now he really didn't think he cared what was in it as long as it was hot and filling. She waved her ladle at him. 'I'll be up wi' your dinner in a minute or two.'

He entered the taproom. Only one man seemed to be taking any real interest. His eyes narrowed when they caught sight of Drew's pistol. A grim sense of satisfaction filled him. At least they knew he was not easy pickings. Still, he didn't trust them an inch.

He had nothing against smugglers. He'd dealt with enough of them in the old days. He'd been one. But these men were different. Harder eyed and not Highlanders by their speech.

He sauntered between them to the bar along one wall. 'I'll take a bottle of whisky and two glasses,' he said to the landlord.

'Yes, sir,' the portly, red-faced fellow said, reaching under his counter.

One of the men behind him sniggered. 'Wi' that face you likely have to get her drunk before she'll have ought to do wi' ye.'

Drew turned and faced the room, fists loose but ready. 'If you have something to say, you can say it to my ugly face.'

The oldest man in the room eyed him for a moment, then nodded an acknowledgement. He shoved at a scrawny-looking fellow with a straggling beard. 'Yon Roger's had a wee bitty too much to drink,' he said. 'Haven't you, Roger?'

Roger looked sullen, but at another shove nodded and disappeared into his tankard.

'You'll have your men keep a civil tongue in their heads, man,' the landlord said from behind Drew. 'Or I'll be sending you back out in the snow.'

Drew grinned. 'I wouldn't be asking a dog to go out in that, lads.' He turned back to the innkeeper. 'Give them all a dram on me.'

The mood in the room lightened considerably. Drew picked up the bottle and glasses and raised it in salute, strolling out of the bar as three men rushed forward. Sugar was better than vinegar any day of the week. Not that he'd trust any of them.

He didn't take his eyes off them as he climbed the bottom steps, just to be sure he didn't get a knife in the back. Roger turned and met his gaze. He had the look of a man who was trying to solve a puzzle.

Drew halted. 'Is something else wrong?'

The man shook his head. 'I just had the feeling I've seen you before.'

Drew raised a brow. 'People don't usually forget my face.'

The man grimaced with distaste. 'You never had the scar last time I saw you.'

The hairs on Drew's nape rose. Was it possible he had met this man in his smuggling days? 'You are mistaken, my friend. Sorry.' He continued up the stairs, but from the feeling between his shoulder blades, the man watched him until he was out of sight.

He'd known a lot of people in the trade in the old days. Him and Ian. But he could not think of a reason why any of them would hold a grudge.

He knocked on the door of the chamber assigned to him and Mrs MacDonald.

'Who is it?'

At least she had sense enough not to just open the door without checking. 'Drew.'

'Just a moment.'

A rustle of skirts, the door swung back, opened by a maid, but his gaze went straight to the figure kneeling by the hearth, wrapped in a cotton cover, and his mind ceased working. Her unpinned hair hung down her back, as sleek and as shiny a chestnut as would do a thoroughbred proud.

There was something extraordinarily intimate about seeing a woman with her hair down around her shoulders. And on her knees, too. His body responded as if she'd offered him the most personal of attentions. He almost groaned out loud at the blaze of heat scorching through his blood. At this rate, he wasn't going to need the fire to get warm. Disgusted by his reaction, he dropped the saddlebags off to one side and set the whisky and the glasses on the table.

'Out,' he said to the maid.

Mrs MacDonald rose up on her knees and turned to look at him, surprise on her face.

Drew looked at the maid. 'If you don't mind?' he said as politely as he could manage.

The little lass bustled past him.

Drew closed and locked the door, using the moment to repress the wicked images his mind had conjured up.

'Mrs McRae will be along shortly wi' our supper,' he said, annoyed by the hoarseness in his voice.

She put her hands on her hips. 'Well, well, if it isn't my dear husband.' Her eyes sparkled like water running over pebbles in a brook. Anger or amusement. Whichever it was, it made a breath catch in his throat; she looked so lovely with her hair hanging about her shoulders and her cheeks flushed by the warmth from the fire.

He strode for the window and opened it.

The wind gusted in, bringing with it a whirl of snowflakes and a chill to his overheated blood.

'What on earth are you doing?' she asked, her voice rising in pitch.

'Admiring the view,' he said over his shoulder. And checking for a way out should it be needed. The kitchen roof jutted out a few feet below. An easy climb down to the ground.

He took a deep breath, closed the window and turned back to face her. 'I'm sorry I had to tell them we were wed. I couldna' leave you up here alone with that lot staying below.'

Her lips thinned. 'And I suppose you are sorry you had to kiss me, too.'

Heat travelled up his neck. 'It was necessary, but, aye, I'm sorry.'

The apology didn't seem to mollify her one little bit.

He jerked his chin at her saddlebag. 'Is there something dry in there you can change into?'

She glanced down at the bag and then up at him. 'Only my nightgown. I wasn't expecting to put up at an inn without my luggage, which is now with the Pockles who, by the way, will be surprised to find us calling ourselves man and wife.'

The Pockles were another worry. They could not have been more than a half hour or so behind them, so they should have arrived by now. He didn't see any reason to let her know his concern, though.

He shrugged. 'We'll cross that bridge when we come to it.'

A rap sounded at the door. 'Who is it?' he asked, one hand going to his pistol.

Rowena's eyes widened and he cursed himself for a fool for putting fear in her eyes.

'Mrs McRae, dearie,' the landlady called out. 'With your supper tray.'

'Leave it outside the door. I'll fetch it in when I'm dressed,' Drew said. He moved to the door, listening first to the sound of the tray hitting the floor, then the woman's footsteps moving away. He pulled his pistol and unlocked it with his left hand, ready to leap clear.

Slowly he opened the door. The sound of men's laughter wafted up the stairs.

His instincts told him there was no one there, but still he glanced up and down the hallway before tucking away his pistol and bending to pick up the tray. He set it down on the nearby chest of drawers.

Thank goodness the common room was in the front

of the house and this chamber was at the back or, with that racket, there'd be no chance of sleeping.

Rowena gave him a narrow-eyed look. She nodded at the pistol. 'You really do think we are in danger, then?'

'Aye.' He kicked the door closed and turned the key.

The look on her face said it wasn't enough to make her feel safe. He breathed out through his nose, summoning calm. 'They are smugglers.'

'Oh,' she said. 'Not good.'

'As a general rule, I would no' be concerned. They go about their business and as long as no one interferes...' He shook his head. 'These men have a different look about them.' Not to mention the one who thought he knew him.

'Not your normal run-of-the-mill smugglers, then.'

He couldn't help but smile at the no-nonsense tone of voice, as if she dealt with such criminals on a daily basis. And he had the feeling, if he was truthful, she wouldn't flinch if they did turn up at the door. 'No. Not run-of-the-mill at all. And when I explain why we are sharing a room to the Pockles, they will understand.' He hoped, because if they didn't he was going to find himself with a duke who might feel vengeful. An angry duke might be worse than an inn full of smugglers. And they were quite bad enough.

Another tête-à-tête meal with Mr Gilvry. Rowena felt a rush of warmth in her belly. This time, he rearranged the table so he sat beside her, instead of opposite, presenting his profile. Unlike last time, when she had dressed in her best, she was wrapped in a blanket and he was posing as her husband.

Why?

Was it possible he had deliberately separated her from their escort? After that kiss she might almost believe it, if it wasn't for his mortifying apology.

She was not the sort of woman a man wanted to kiss of his own free will. He'd used it as a pretence to give her instructions. The logical side of the brain applauded his cleverness. Her foolish heart contracted painfully every time she recalled his harsh apology.

Perhaps he wished he could be downstairs, kissing pretty little Sin.

Anger and disappointment rose in her throat, threatening to choke her. Anger at her own stupid thoughts, surely.

But she knew she was lying to herself. She found him attractive.

No matter. There was no use in feeling wounded. It hadn't done any good with Samuel, or her cousin. It would be no different with this man. She just wasn't the sort of woman to engender strong feelings in a man. Instead of worrying about such nonsense, she would use the opportunity to find out more about her escort. Mr Gilvry could hardly walk away, given he had taken it upon himself to remain on guard in her room. And while she didn't dare trust him completely, she trusted the smugglers a whole lot less.

Pulling the counterpane tight around her shoulders, she let him seat her at the table. 'It does smell surprisingly good.'

'Aye.'

'Will you say grace?' It was a habit to ask her pupils to do so, so it came naturally out of her mouth.

Surprise flickered across his face, then something that looked like embarrassment before he bowed his head. 'Thank you, Lord, for this food and for bringing us safe to this place.'

She added a silent prayer that they might leave it in one piece. 'Amen.'

He picked up a bread roll.

'Do you think the duke is aware that one of his tenants entertains smugglers?'

He glanced up, his expression unreadable. 'Probably.'

She huffed out a breath and picked up her own spoon.

'What?' he asked, still looking at her.

There was no point. When a man didn't want to tell you something, asking questions only made him more determined to remain silent. 'Nothing.'

He gave her an irritated look and broke the roll apart with long strong, fingers. 'You asked and I answered.'

'You said *probably* as if you meant *of course.*' Dash it, why was she explaining? Giving him the opportunity to put her in her womanly place?

His sideways glance showed surprise, as if he hadn't expected her to realise he was trying to protect her. 'Smuggling is a matter of survival in the Highlands. A great lord might not admit to it, but he'd be a fool if he didn't know. He probably buys his whisky from them, too.'

The truth. 'But why, if it is such a normal thing, do you think they mean us harm?'

He sighed. 'One of them thinks he knows me. And it is no' a happy reunion.'

'Does he know you?'

'No.'

This time she believed him. She glanced at the door he had locked so carefully and recalled the pistol he had to hand in his waistband. 'Do you have another gun?'

His eyebrows shot up. 'Can you use a pistol?'

'No. Surely it can't be so very difficult?' Even the stupidest men seemed to manage it.

He gave a short laugh, but there was no humour in it. 'I have no wish to be shot by mistake, thank you verra much.'

'But you are worried about their intentions.'

'Persistent wee thing, aren't you?'

She should have been a bit more persistent in her refusal to accept Samuel's suit. If she hadn't been so unhappy in her cousin's house… Not true. After her first refusal Samuel had made it his mission to gain her hand. She'd never had a chance. The lure of marriage and what she took for love had been far too tempting. But she had learned her lesson. Hadn't she?

'Do you think they will attack us?'

'Honestly, I dinna ken.'

Her jaw dropped. What a surprise. A man admitting he was unsure about something?

He touched his cheek and shook his head. 'I canna understand why this man thinks he knows me.'

'What happened to your face? Were you attacked by some sort of animal?'

His face shuttered.

She winced. 'I beg your pardon. It is none of my business. It is not so bad, when one becomes accustomed—'

'I am in no need of soothing words, ma'am. I see how I look every time I shave.'

'Then we are both accustomed,' she flashed back.

He gave her a look that was neither irritated nor friendly and resumed eating. He ate quickly, something she had noticed before, as if it might be his last meal.

Taking a chance on his apparent lack of ire, she decided to plunge on with her questions, albeit in a different direction.

'Mr Gilvry, you never really said what it was that you were doing in the mountains of North Carolina when you met my husband.'

His expression darkened as if the question was unwelcome, yet not unexpected. He glanced at her face and then her bowl of untouched stew. 'Eat first and I will tell you.'

Or would he find yet another excuse to avoid her questions? 'I find I am not all that hungry.' Her stomach growled, giving her the lie.

He gave her an I-told-you-so look. He was very good at looks that spoke volumes. She tasted the stew. It was as good as it smelled. Thick rich gravy. Tender meat and plenty of vegetables. 'The inn must be doing well to provide such an excellent meal.'

'Likely it's a regular stop for those in the trade. They pay well for silence.'

'You know a great deal about the smuggling trade.'

She was surprised when he answered, 'Aye. I used to be one. Before I went to America.'

She closed her mouth on a gasp. 'I am surprised you admit to it so freely,' she said as calmly as she could manage. 'Were you… I mean, is that why you went to America?'

'Was I transported there, you mean?'

So much for being tactful. 'That is precisely what I mean.'

He leaned back. 'I wasna' transported for any crime by the government.' His tone was bitter. 'I had no choice but to go, however.'

'Oh.' His tone did not encourage further questions. But that didn't mean she wasn't going to ask. Not at all.

He pushed his chair back from the table. His roll had disappeared and so had his stew, whereas she had eaten only a few mouthfuls.

'Well?'

'Eat your meal, Mrs MacDonald.' He got up and went to the hearth, crouching down and poking at the fire as if it had gone out, instead of being the merry blaze it was.

He was no doubt regretting saying as much as he had. And it really was none of her business. She ate the rest of her stew and finally sat back, completely sated.

'That was good.'

He glanced at her plate. 'Will you no' eat your bread?'

'I couldn't eat another bite. You can have it if you wish.'

He picked up the bread, but did not eat it. He tucked it into his saddlebag. 'Would you care for a dram?'

A splash of *usquebaugh* in tea to keep out the cold was one thing, but it was a long time since she'd enjoyed a glass for its own sake. Her father had never drunk anything else and had often invited Rowena to join him in a wee glass after dinner. As a governess, she never drank.

'I would love a dram.' She got up, drew the counterpane carefully around her and went to join him at the fire, taking up residence on the settle. She couldn't help thinking of those evenings with her father. He had been such a kindly man and had never belittled her abilities. While he was ill, he had come to trust her with his business. All that had changed when he died. She'd become nothing but a spinster relative to be accommodated under her cousin's roof.

If she had known what Samuel would do with her half of the factory, she would have run a mile. She should have listened to her head instead of her heart. Well, she certainly wasn't going to make that mistake again.

He poured them both a drink and lifted his glass in a toast. *'Sláinte.'*

'Good health.'

They sipped their drinks in silence.

Steam was rising from his trousers below his knees, just as it had risen from her skirts. 'You are still wet,' she said.

He glanced down and shrugged. 'Looks like I'll be dry soon enough. My change of clothes is also in the wagon.'

Now mist was curling up from his coat. It would take for ever to dry. 'Perhaps the landlord could loan you his shirt.'

He shook his head.

'What if you take a chill? You can't sit there soaking wet.'

'Surely you aren't suggesting I strip down to my

skin?' There was a mocking note in his voice, but the very thought of it made her insides melt. How infuriating that he would plant such a picture in her mind.

'At least take your coat off and get nearer to the fire,' she said crossly.

He huffed out a breath, stripped out of his coat and went to fetch one of the dining chairs, which he set on the other side of the hearth. He hung the coat over the back. 'Will this do?'

'And the waistcoat.'

He took that off, too, hung it up and came back to sit beside her.

'Satisfied?'

She eyed his trousers. 'You really should…'

He put up a hand. 'No, I really should not.'

'Stubborn man.'

'Aye, that may be so.' He breathed deeply through his nose. 'I thought you wanted to hear my story?'

She stilled. 'I do.'

'Then cease your fashing and I'll tell you. Though there is little to tell, Mrs MacDonald.'

'Would you very much mind calling me Rowena? It is dreadfully hard hearing Samuel's name every time someone speaks.'

He looked…guilty. What reason did he have for guilt?

He turned his face away, staring into the fire, his sculpted jaw softened by its glow, and flames flickering in the depths of his eye as if he was peering into hell.

'Verra well. Rowena,' he murmured.

It sounded beautiful the way he said it. Softly. As if he was tasting the syllables on his tongue. Her insides clenched, sending a wave of desire rippling through her body. And now he was looking at her with something akin to horror. Self-disgust washed through her and she looked down at her hands. What on earth was wrong with her? She'd never had trouble containing her desires before now.

She clasped her fingers to keep her hands steady.

In the ensuing silence she glanced up at him and saw that his gaze was very far away. He seemed to be gathering his thoughts. His expression said they were painful. It was hard to imagine such a hard man feeling emotional pain.

She held her breath and waited for him to speak.

'I had been living in the mountains for some time. I made up my mind it was time to leave. To take control of my life.' His voice sounded a little strained. As if the memories were painful.

At her look of puzzlement, he shrugged. 'When an opportunity presented itself, I headed for the coast. Then I heard sounds of the Indians attacking your husband's camp. By the time I got there only your husband was alive. He told me he was on his way back to Scotland when he'd heard that this group of Indians had gold and knew where to find it.'

He looked her straight in the eye. 'As I understand it, he thought to trade brandy for information.'

At her blank look, he shook his head. 'Even a dolt knows that Indians have no head for strong liquor. They become wild and aggressive.'

'So they attacked him?'

'Not at first. They were too drunk to do more than

pass out. But the next day, when they saw he had left, taking the rest of the drink with him, they were no' verra pleased.'

An understatement if ever she heard one. 'They followed him?'

'Aye. I arrived too late to be of any assistance. I'm verra sorry.'

'His foolish actions were hardly your fault.'

Her words, intended to absolve, seemed only to add to the pain in his eyes.

'If I had arrived sooner—'

'They might have killed you, too,' she said.

He blinked and looked as if he thought that might have been preferable.

A pain stabbed at her heart. 'I won't hear another word of you taking the blame for my husband's stupidity.'

He turned his head away and looked into the fire as if he could see the events playing out before his eyes. 'By the time I got to the camp, the Indians had taken what they came for and left everyone for dead.'

'The brandy,' she whispered.

'That they drank as soon as they found it. They took the horses, clothes, money, trinkets. Anything that took their fancy. They are a bit like children in that regard. They left some things. Mostly papers. They were crazy with drink again by then. Everyone in the camp was dead, I thought.' He shook his head. 'I was leaving when I heard a noise from the bushes. Somehow, they'd missed him. I pulled him clear. The wound was in his belly.' He glanced at her. 'There was nothing I could do. I thought if I could get him to a white…to a doctor… Charlotte was closest. I carried him. It was slow going. I could hardly believe he was still alive when I made camp that first night.'

She sighed. 'Go on.'

'We talked. He was in a lot of pain. Mostly he talked and I listened. He spoke about his wife.' He gave her a sideways look.

'What did he say?' She steeled herself.

'Your name. That he had some regrets.'

She gave a small laugh at that statement. Samuel had suffered regrets from the moment the knot was tied.

'He was determined to get back to Scotland. To make amends, he said. I swore I would see that he did.'

It was hard to believe that Samuel would have cared one way or the other about her. And in his last moments, too. The thought brought tears to her eyes. Tears of regret that she hadn't been the kind of wife he had wanted.

'The rest you know,' he said.

Looking at his expressionless face, she was certain he was holding something back, telling her only what he thought she needed to know.

Out of kindness? Or was there something more to his reticence? And did she really need to know all the gory details? It couldn't possibly impact on her current predicament.

He pushed slowly to his feet, as if he carried a heavy weight. 'I am thinking it is time to sleep. Tomorrow will be another hard day.'

Suddenly suspicious, she frowned. 'Where will you sleep?'

'In here. As your husband, I can hardly bed down in the common room or outside your door. And besides, I've no intention of leaving you alone, even with the door locked.'

Her gaze strayed to the bed and her heart started to race. What would it be like to lie beside a strong virile man like him? Would he let her see him naked? Touch him. She put a hand to her throat.

'I'll be sleeping on the floor,' he said harshly as if guessing her thoughts and being repulsed.

He bent and picked up her saddlebag and tossed it beside the screen. 'Change behind there.'

'Yes,' she said, breathless. 'Yes, of course.' Flustered by the heat generated by her wayward thoughts, she ducked behind the screen and changed. When she came out, face washed, teeth cleaned, dressed in her night-gown and wrapped in the counterpane, he was standing at the window, staring into the dark.

It was almost as if he'd forgotten her presence.

She hopped into bed and drew the covers up to her chin. 'I left some clean water in the jug,' she said. 'And you might as well have the counterpane as a cover.' She hesitated. 'If you would like.'

'Thank you.' His voice was grim. He must really be regretting agreeing to this journey, she thought dismally. She tossed the cover on to the floor and pulled the sheet up over her head. The least she could do was give him some privacy.

And she didn't dare let him catch her peeking.

Chapter Five

Lying on the hard floor beside the bed in the dark, Drew didn't know which was worse, listening to her get ready for bed and imagining her baring the slim body that he'd felt pressed against him for one brief instant out in the yard or glimpsing her chestnut locks spread out over a white pillow before she disappeared beneath the sheets.

And now there was the sound of her breathing inches from his head. His body ached at the thought of those sweetly curved lips and the image of soft little breasts rising and falling beneath the covers.

He couldn't believe how much his body wanted more of those swells and hollows. The sparks prickling along his skin every time he came within just a few feet of her were one thing. This more intimate sensual knowledge had added a new and higher pitch to his lust.

He clenched the counterpane tight in his fists and rolled on his side, facing away from her. He didn't want to find her attractive. He was his own man now, with no fetters or ties. That was how he wanted his life, and the sooner he left her with the duke, the better.

If he hadn't said he was her husband, he could have spent the night in the common room, drinking with the other men. And fighting if he had to, though he had no recollection of the man who had looked at him with such rancour. It might be a case of mistaken identity. He rubbed his fingers over his scar, feeling the raised and twisted welts. Hardly likely.

No matter what, their kind of trouble was far more welcome than what he risked in this room. But if he was busy defending himself, there would be no one looking after Rowena. He didn't dare take the chance of leaving her alone with a gang of cut-throats nearby.

He huffed out a breath. No doubt he'd have some explaining to do when he left her with the duke. There was no way around it, given that the innkeeper was the duke's tenant, not to mention what the Pockles would hear when they arrived.

Thank goodness she was a widow. At least he wouldn't be facing down an angry husband. Or worse yet, the father of an unmarried lass with a wedding on his mind. But the knowledge that she was a widow, an experienced woman, was a temptation he didn't need. Disgust at his weakness writhed like a monster in his gut.

He forced himself to breathe deeply. To listen to the sounds of the night, the way he had done so often in the vast forests. The sounds of the men below filtered through the floorboards. The carousing seemed to have tapered off. There was only the occasional mutter or shout of laughter. No doubt they would slip beneath the tables as drink overcame them. It was why he had ordered the whisky. The inn's comforting warmth would also do its work, since this sort of man usually slept out of doors. He could remember his own nights travelling the Highlands with contraband. He and Ian had thought it such an adventure, they hadn't cared about the cold and the damp. But they'd been young then, and carefree.

Was Ian still smuggling brandy for Carrick? The men downstairs would likely know. McKenzie's men from Edinburgh, the stableman had said. He wasn't familiar with the name, but no doubt the people involved had changed over the years. What they did was the same as it had always been.

He had been tempted to go back downstairs and ask after his brothers, but it seemed he'd already aroused suspicions enough. And besides, what was the point of torturing himself with thoughts of a family who had banished him out of their lives? Aye, or with recollections of an older brother who had arranged for his death? He gritted his teeth as the old pain of it squeezed the air out of his lungs.

No, he'd find out soon enough what was happening with his family when he had delivered Rowena and her husband's remains to Mere.

He forced himself to relax, to let the dark enter his mind, to welcome the oblivion of sleep.

A soft sound brought him upright, hand on the pistol he had primed and placed at his side before lying down. A whimper. From the bed. She was dreaming. No doubt she was seeing his face in her dreams. It would be enough to make anyone cry out.

She turned over.

He could see only her outline in the light from the candle, a lock of hair hanging over the side of the bed. His fingers itched to stroke its silky length.

She screamed.

He leaped to his feet and leaned over her. She was panting and fighting the bed sheets.

'Rowena,' he said, his mouth close to her ear, his nose filling with the scent of soap and warm woman. Lust surged. He bit back a curse. 'Rowena.' He shook her shoulder.

She opened her mouth. He cut off the scream with his palm. Her head thrashed back and forth, her fingers clawed at his hand. Scratching at his wrist.

'Rowena,' he said in an urgent whisper. 'Stop. It's me. Drew.'

Her eyes opened, dazed, confused. Her breathing rapid, her body trembling with fear.

Slowly he lifted his hand.

'It is you,' she murmured. Her voice cracked on the last word, tears welling.

'Yes,' he said, 'You were having a bad dream.'

Staring at him, she took a few deep breaths and sat up. 'You were trying to smother me.'

He reared back at the accusation in her voice. 'You screamed. Another one and we'd have had that lot from downstairs knocking on the door offering assistance.' Or asking to participate. 'You didn't want that, did you?'

'Oh.' Her eyes cleared as if she was only now coming fully awake and conscious. 'No. Of course not.'

He let go a breath he didn't know he'd been holding. For a moment, when she'd looked at him in terror, it had given him an unpleasant, sickening sensation in the pit of his stomach. It receded and left a very fine appreciation for the way her breasts created two snowy mounds beneath her flimsy nightgown. Under his gaze, the peaks pearled, little hard nubs at the crest of high firm breasts the size of peaches.

She followed the direction of his gaze and her face flushed bright red.

He bit down hard on a string of curses and moved away from her, going to the hearth to rake at a perfectly smoored fire. After such violent treatment, he'd be lucky if it lasted until morning. He set to work putting it right, banking it so it would once more give off enough heat to keep the chill off the air, but not use all the fuel before it was time to rise.

'I'm sorry I woke you,' she said softly from the other side of the room.

'It must have been a pretty bad dream,' he said, standing up, satisfied with his efforts. He glanced her way and was surprised to see she had not pulled the sheets up, but instead was sitting with her arms around her knees, watching him with those cool grey eyes.

Blood stirred in his veins. His shaft responded to the quickening throb of his pulse. How did a woman who looked as stern as an angel of retribution able to see a man's sins rouse his passions so easily?

Because he was little better than an animal, he

thought bitterly. *She* had roused him, too. Made him a slave to her desires. It had been the only way to survive.

He turned away, running a hand over the beard forming on his chin. *She*'d hated those bristles almost as much as he had hated her. But if he'd stayed with her, Samuel MacDonald would still be alive and his wife wouldn't be having nightmares likely brought on by all the details he'd revealed. And by hours of seeing nothing but his ugly face.

'I think you'll sleep better alone.' He picked up the cotton cover and headed for the door. 'I'll be right outside the door.'

'Drew,' she said, and while she spoke quietly there was a note of panic in her voice. 'Please. Don't go.'

Stunned at the sound of his name on her lips, he stared at her. She looked away, twisting the sheet in her fingers. 'I don't want to be alone right at this moment.' She lifted her gaze. 'Talk to me. I've slept enough.'

She'd slept all of four hours. But she was still upset. Those restless hands were trembling.

She gave a small self-mocking laugh. 'I'm sorry to make such a fuss about a dream. You need your rest. Please take no notice of my foolishness. And please don't go sleeping in a draughty corridor on my account. Indeed, take the bed. I will be quite happy to sit in the chair.'

She was babbling like a nervous child, but she was smiling at him. A smile that made him think of kindness and courage. A smile that pushed back at the shadows he saw in her eyes.

'I'll no' be putting you out of your bed,' he said. 'But I'll stay, if that is your wish.'

'You are very kind, Mr Gilvry.'

So they were back on formal terms. As they should be, but he couldn't help liking the way his name sounded on her lips. It was a long time since anyone had called him Drew.

She had always called him her yellow dog. The others in the band had followed suit, when they called him anything at all.

Sometimes, in his head, he'd begun to think of himself that way, too.

He brought a chair from the table and set it near the bed. 'Do you want to tell me about your dream?'

She frowned. 'Something or someone was chasing me. That is all I remember.'

A common enough dream. A shaman might have read something into it, but Drew didn't believe in their heathen superstitions. Or not much anyway.

'What would you like to talk about?' He prayed it wouldn't be more questions about her husband. He'd revealed far more than he intended over dinner. The lingering death. Their conversations. The man had been utterly callous with respect to his wife, only caring about the prospect of wealth. Nor did he want to reveal how he had slipped away from the band who had held him prisoner for two long years. It was their drunkenness that had given him the chance to escape. But he should have known that *she*'d want him back. They must have thought he'd try to join up with MacDonald. He'd known better, but it hadn't made any difference.

'Tell me more about you,' she said. 'Where you grew up. Your family.'

His blood ran cold. 'I'm no' a very interesting topic of conversation, I'm afraid.'

He slouched in the chair, trying to look at ease. It wasn't easy when he was still as hard as granite. 'Where to start?'

'Where in Scotland did you grow up?'

As topics went it was fairly neutral. 'My family is from Dunross, a small village north of Inverness. My father was the laird. And my brother after him.'

She straightened. 'You have a brother? I had the impression you were alone in the world.'

Curse intelligent females who listened to what you said. 'I have family, but they are not looking for me to return.'

'Why?'

Well, here was his chance to confess just what sort of man she'd been trusting. A way to serve up a bit of reality to keep her at a distance. Yet something held him back. Pride. He did not want her to think worse of him than she already did. And a measure of lingering shame. He had hurt Alice badly. He couldn't think about it without a nasty lurch in his stomach. He'd deserved his punishment. But he had not deserved to die for his mistake.

He shrugged. 'Let us say it was better for all that I left.'

'How long ago did you leave?' she asked softly.

Hell, if it was the year 1822 now, then it had to be… 'Six years.'

'And you haven't seen your family since?'

Hadn't seen them or heard from them. There had been no way to get in touch even if he had wanted to. And he hadn't. And when he did, it wasn't going to be pleasant.

He shook his head.

'And your parents?'

He winced inwardly. 'My father died years before I left. My ma—' It was hard to say it. He forced the words out. 'Ma was alive when I left.'

'She must be terribly worried.'

That was females for you. Straight for the kill. Rip out your throat or your heart. 'I doubt it.'

A lie. His mother had been devastated when he had told her he was leaving. Had begged him to write. He hadn't sent one letter. Ian had made sure of that.

They must all assume he was dead. He steeled his heart against a surge of longing. He'd made his decision. He'd see Carrick first. Confirm exactly what favour Ian had asked of him. And then he'd send Ian to the same kind of hell as he had endured.

Her face softened. 'And your injury?' She touched her own cheek. 'If it is not too difficult a topic.'

He inhaled a breath though his nose. He could slough her off, but it would come up again. It wasn't as though he could hide it, not really. And every time she looked at him, she would wonder. A deep longing filled him. The need to tell someone. To tell her. Something about this woman made him want to be rid of the weight of his past. To unburden himself. But he couldn't. The shame of her knowing would finish off what was left of his soul. But he must tell her something.

'I had been in America less than a week. I went hunting. It seemed like a grand adventure, ye ken.' He paused to gather his thoughts. 'There was an accident.'

It wasn't until his fingers encountered the welted, knotted skin that he realised he had touched the scar. He grimaced, then smoothed out his expression. Any sort of emotion only made him look worse.

'What sort of accident?' she asked.

'A stray bullet.' It had strayed off its target. Either his brain or his heart, he didn't know. His foot had slipped at the same moment the shot had been fired. 'It knocked me off my feet and I fell into a river. An Indian band found me downstream in verra poor shape.'

At her wide-eyed gasp, he shook his head. 'Nae those who killed your husband. A small, peaceful family. They did what they could. Fed me and cared for me. And when I was well…I just stayed.'

He'd been unable to face going back as he was. Scarred. Angry, yes, but also hurt that Ian had wanted to be rid of him in such a final way. He'd decided to try to forget the words he'd heard before the shot was fired. To let his brother think he had won. Then anyway.

'You lived among them for six years?'

Not for the last two. But she didn't need to know that. 'It was a simple life. Almost spiritual. They are verra close to the natural world. It reminded me of the Highlands.'

He winced at how stupid that sounded, but her expression held only interest.

'How fascinating,' she said. 'But you decided to leave? You weren't satisfied with such a simple life?'

That life had changed. Later. When they were attacked

by a band of renegades. The warriors had wanted to kill him, but their *woman of magic* had been fascinated by his yellow hair. She stopped them. And because she'd saved his life she considered him her property. He froze out the images that seared though his brain.

'It was time to leave.' Hundreds of miles from where he'd first been taken, when her husband had showed up with the firewater and given him the chance he needed. And her husband had paid the price.

'What about you?' he asked, changing the subject, hoping she wouldn't delve any deeper. He didn't want to lie to her, but he would not tell her the worst of it. 'Where is your family?'

'I was an only child. My mother and father are dead.' Sorrow coloured her voice. 'There is a cousin, of my father's, but we are not close.'

He frowned. 'The duke—'

She shook her head. 'That is what I don't understand. Samuel never mentioned Mere. He told me he was alone in the world apart from very distant relatives who would not approve of him marrying into the *bourgeoisie*.' She lifted her chin. 'It didn't matter that Mother's grandfather was an earl, of course, since she'd married into trade.' She sighed. 'I really thought he cared for me. But it turned out he just needed my money.'

What she was saying accorded pretty well with what her husband had said, and part of him was glad the man had died. Another part felt guilty, that he'd been the one to cause his death. She'd be a great deal better off if MacDonald had lived. 'I'm sorry.'

She sighed. 'It was my own stupid fault. I thought

he was my one chance for happiness. It turned out that it only made things worse.' She gave a small laugh and buried her face against her upraised knees. 'Pride comes before a fall, doesn't it?'

The pain in her voice was like a blade of steel pressing into his temple. It was as if her vulnerability called out to him. He couldn't help himself, he leaned forward and touched her shoulder, felt the bone smooth, round and cool to his palm through the fine linen. 'Any man would be proud to have you for a wife.'

Her short laugh was hard edged. 'Mr Gilvry, please do not insult my intelligence. If he could have had the money without me, he would have been the happiest man alive. He couldn't wait to escape, once he had my fortune in his pocket.'

He could hear tears in her voice and for some reason he couldn't bear to think of her crying. He moved to sit on the edge of the bed. 'Hush now. You've had a bad dream. It's the blackest part of the night. Things will seem better in daylight.'

She sniffed, a small sound that made his chest clench painfully. He wanted to hold her in his arms, protect her, but he didn't dare—even sitting this close had him hard with wanting. Something he could and would control. Besides, she would never consent to give him what he needed.

'You must think me a fool.'

'Not at all. I think you should sleep now, though. With the snow and all, it will be a long, hard day tomorrow.'

A small laugh shook her frame. 'And the sooner we get there the sooner you can be about your own affairs.'

She looked at him, her grey eyes misty, but a brave smile pinned to her lips. Lips he wanted to kiss. He pushed the thought aside.

That was her, though, he thought. Brave. Full of courage. And no matter what she said about her marriage, she would be worse off as a widow if the duke did not treat her right. For a moment he considered confessing the whole of it. Unburdening his soul. What then? Likely she'd scream bloody murder and he'd find himself behind bars. Imprisoned yet again.

He stood up. 'Try to get some sleep.' He picked up the candle and blew it out. With the glow from the fire and the moonlight from the window now the storm had blown over, there was more than enough light for him to see his way to his blanket.

The bed ropes creaked as she lay down with a sigh. 'Thank you, Mr Gilvry,' she said softly.

'For what?'

'For listening to a foolish woman.'

If there was anything she was, it was not foolish. Anyone would be troubled with nightmares after the story he'd told her of what the savages had done to her husband and his party. He wrapped himself in the counterpane and settled into his spot on the floor. He put his hands behind his head and stared up where the ceiling would be, if it wasn't hidden in the dark.

Tomorrow they'd reach the duke's estate where he'd be questioned very closely. The thing was, would he tell the duke all of it? For her sake? Would it help? The lawyer had said since there was no proof, the date wasna' important. His eyes said he was lying.

Drew listened to the sounds of a house breathing as his mind grappled with the question. The soft sounds of a dwelling at rest.

A creak. Outside the door. Heavy weight pressing down on wood. Metal against metal. He sat up. So did Rowena. Silently he rose, pistol in hand, leaning over her, once again pressing his palm to her lovely mouth. 'Hush,' he breathed softly in her ear.

She nodded. Not only brave, but trusting. Of him. Too trusting.

The thought was a sickening lurch in his stomach he could not afford to acknowledge. He crept to the door, careful to avoid the loose board in the middle of the room and another in front of the door.

The latch lifted, the door moved in the frame, just a wee bit. As far as the lock would allow. Now, who would be trying the door in the middle of the night? And what sort of idiot would expect it would not be locked?

He glanced over his shoulder. Rowena was watching him, her profile outlined by the glow of the fire, her body rigid.

The pressure against the door ceased and it returned to its former position in the frame, but he could hear the sound of quiet breathing on the other side. A sound of metal against metal. Whoever was out there was determined to get in and, if he wasn't mistaken, they had another key.

All Rowena could see was the dark bulk of Drew's shape in the shadows near the door where the moonbeams streaming through the window did not reach.

Breath held, she watched, her stomach clenched tight, her throat aching with the urge to say something to break the tension she felt in the room.

Was someone really trying to break in?

A sharp sound. Something dropping to the floor. Drew picked it up. In a flash, she realised it must be the key from their side of the door. Startled, she threw back the covers.

At the same moment, Drew flung open the door to reveal two burly men, one holding a lantern. Rowena, half out of bed, covered her eyes against the sudden glare.

Someone—one of them, she thought—cursed.

When she looked again, she could see why. Drew was holding them at bay at pistol point. The man with the lantern was backing up, struggling to free his pistol from his belt, the other one had what looked like a lump of wood in his hand.

'Leave that where it is,' Drew said calmly to the man with the lantern. The man held still.

Drew narrowed his eyes. 'Planning on robbing us while we slept? Who gave you the key?'

'We just wanted to ask a few questions,' the man with the cudgel said, his voice hoarse. He looked at the pistol and licked his lips.

Drew glared at him. 'You could have asked me in the morning.'

'We won't be here come morning,' the man with the lantern said. 'I do know you. I've seen you afore.'

Drew stiffened. 'I have never met you in my life.'

He frowned. 'Gilvry your name is. Not MacDonald.

Led us a pretty chase in Edinburgh last summer, didn't he, Morris?'

'Aye,' the man called Morris said. 'Caused our boss a load of trouble.'

An expression of shock passed across Drew's face. He masked it quickly, but Rowena knew the man's words had hit home for some reason. But how could he have been in Edinburgh last summer? It didn't make sense.

'You are mistaken,' he said. 'I am Samuel MacDonald. And this is my wife.'

The man with the cudgel, the one who seemed to be in charge, shook his head. 'No, laddie. You might have fooled us poor folks, what ne'er meet with the nobs, but you can't fool McRae. He's met Samuel MacDonald. You're a Gilvry. A spy. You ruined McKenzie's business once—he'll no' be very happy if you ruin more of it. So what I wants to know is, what game are ye playing?'

Comprehension dawned on Drew's face. 'Whisky,' he said. 'You think I'm here because of the whisky. Well, I'm not.'

The man shook his head. 'Not good enough, laddie. You'll need to explain to McKenzie. We'll be takin' you to Edinburgh.'

Rowena gasped.

Drew smiled tightly. 'I see. Well, if we are going on a journey, I hope you won't mind if my wife gets dressed.'

The man with the lantern leered. 'She is more than welcome to come as she is.'

'Rowena,' Drew said.

The word was a command. Legs shaking, she scurried behind the screen. Stays were impossible, but she could manage her shirt and riding habit. With a bit of a struggle she got dressed. If only her hands would stop shaking. And her throat was so dry, she couldn't swallow.

She pulled on her boots and sidled around the screen.

'Are you ready?' Drew asked.

'Yes,' she croaked and tried swallowing again.

Drew smiled and cocked his weapon. 'This pistol says I am no' going anywhere with you.'

The men at the door gaped at him.

Then there was a noise beyond the window. A sort of scraping sound. From the cocking of his head, she knew Drew heard it, too. He jerked his head in that direction and she ran to look out.

And screamed, leaping back. There was a bearded face on the other side of the glass, grinning at her.

In that second, all hell seemed to break loose. The door slammed shut. The room went dark. A pistol fired with a blinding flash and deafening bang. Glass shattered. The smell of black powder hit the back of her throat. She threw herself to the floor.

'Get up,' Drew said, his voice cold, his hand gripping hard on her arm as he pulled her to her feet. 'Get your cloak.'

As ordered she grabbed her cloak from the settle and wrapped it around her. Still damp, but warm from the fire.

Shouts and bangs came from beyond the door. Then the sound of someone running downstairs.

'Come here,' he said. He flung something out of the window and then knelt by the bed, tying something to the leg. A rope.

Then he picked up their saddlebags and threw them out. 'What are you doing?' she cried.

'We're leaving.' He picked her up, flung her over his shoulder and climbed out of the window.

It was a short drop to a roof just below the window. And another to the ground. He landed in a shower of snow. Another bang and a flash. She ducked. Someone was firing at them from the window they had just left. A scream lodged in her throat.

'Run,' Drew said. 'This way.' He grabbed her hand, snatching up the saddlebags on the way past. They charged into the stables.

The horses stirred.

'No time for saddles,' Drew said hastily untying the horses. 'Can you ride astride?'

She had no idea, but, too breathless to speak, her heart thundering too loud, she nodded.

He threw her up on her horse. 'Tuck your skirts between your legs, aye.'

Her jaw dropped, but he'd left her to mount his own horse at a leap. Assuming he knew whereof he spoke, she did as he suggested. He grabbed her horse's reins and they charged out of the stable door at a gallop.

A shape holding a lantern darted towards them, but when he realised they were not going to stop, he dived out of the way.

A gun fired. She half expected to feel a searing pain in her back. But no, it seemed whoever was shooting had missed. And then they were fleeing into the night, leaving behind them the sound of curses.

They rode uphill, sometimes walking the horses to

give them a brief rest, sometimes breaking into a bone-jarring trot. Moonlight reflecting on snow made the landscape featureless and ghostly.

Ahead of her, Drew kept looking over his shoulder. She looked back once, but almost lost her seat, so contented herself with clinging on desperately and praying that they were not going to stumble off a cliff or fall into a burn. The cold bit into the bare flesh of her legs above her boots and stockings and the rough horse blanket rubbed against the insides of her lower legs. She could not deny she was glad of the fabric of her skirts between the blankets and her thighs, but even so she did not know how long she could ride without a saddle.

Soon it was clear the horses were blown and about the time she was going to suggest they stop for a rest, he halted. Once more he looked back.

Her heart tripped and stumbled. 'Are they coming?'

'No.'

The hoof prints in the snow would be hard to miss. 'Do you think they will follow?'

'Lucky for us, they only have ponies. The wee beasties canna follow us through the drifts.'

'Well, that's a relief.'

He looked at her, then laughed.

'What is so funny?'

'Nothing. I'm just relieved you are no' having a fit of the hysterics.'

'Do you think it would help?'

'Not at all.' He looked up at the stars. 'North-west is where we need to go if I remember right from the map.'

She looked up. 'You can tell where we are from the stars?'

'Aye. Something I learned from the Indians. It works the same on land as it does on the ocean.'

He turned away.

She grabbed his arm. 'Wait. What on earth was going on back there? Why did they attack us?'

Even with only moonbeams to light his face, she could see his jaw harden. He touched a hand to his scars. 'It seems they mistook me for one of my brothers.'

'I don't understand.'

'My brothers smuggle whisky for a living. I assume they are competitors.'

His brothers were criminals. Like those men at the inn. Her heart raced. An overwhelming sense of danger flowed through her. The same feeling that had woken her earlier in the night.

'Come along,' he said, pushing ahead.

What choice did she have?

Chapter Six

It had been getting colder as they climbed upwards, as Drew had expected. It might not be snowing, but the wind was raw and biting. Neither of them were dressed for it. It didn't matter to him. He was used to being cold and hungry, but Rowena was a whole different matter.

They had to find shelter, and soon. He was just hoping that by climbing, he would make it harder for the smugglers to follow. Hoping they wouldn't bother.

Damn Ian and his bloody smuggling.

What the hell had he been up to in the years Drew had been gone? Starting a war, by the sound of it. And then there was the Pockles. They were bound to reach McRae's some time the next day and their ears would be filled with the account of him and Rowena posing as husband and wife. He just hoped he could speak to them and explain before they reached the duke.

Right now, though, that didn't matter. What mattered was finding somewhere to shelter until it was light, which wouldn't be until around nine in the morning these short winter days.

He glanced back at Rowena hunched into her cloak, her horse struggling through the snow. The lass was as valiant as a soldier. She hadn't offered one word of blame for what had happened back at the inn, but she had been very quiet. Withdrawn.

Likely in fear for her life.

And it was his fault. His lack of judgement about those men at the inn. He'd not trusted them, but he had not really expected an attack. He turned and looked ahead, keeping his gaze fixed on a small break in the vegetation, almost disguised by snow. He was sure it was a track and plunged ahead. The horses were beginning to flag. If they didn't find shelter soon, they'd be forced to dismount.

He'd done a lot of walking in snow in the winter these past few years. After spending a good few days floundering along behind the rest of the band, much to their amusement, he'd learned to fashion the snowshoes they used. This snow was nowhere near as deep and difficult. Not yet anyway.

A dark shadow loomed out of the hillside. He halted. Pleased could hardly describe his emotion at that moment.

'What is it?' Rowena called out from behind him. 'Is something wrong?'

Was that an edge of panic he heard in her voice?

'Nothing's wrong. We have shelter.' A lowly building to be sure, with a low-pitched peat-covered roof, no windows, no outbuildings. And there was no doubt it was deserted.

Rowena brought her horse up alongside him. 'What is it?'

He pointed. 'A bothy. We'll stay here for the rest of the night and continue on in the morning.'

She looked puzzled. 'Will they mind if we get them out of bed at such a late hour?'

He almost laughed. 'There is no they. No one lives here. It's used in the summer by shepherds. We'll be lucky if I can make us a fire.'

She glanced around. 'Do you think the smugglers know about this place?'

'They might, which is why we will need to be away early. And if we are lucky, we'll have a wee bit more snow and they won't be able to follow our tracks.' He got down and helped her off her horse.

Luck didn't seem to be something he had much of, but he saw that his words had cheered her up. A little.

He tried the door. As he expected, it swung open. Bare stone walls, a dirt floor, an open hearth, a flat lump of granite balanced on rocks for a low table. It was better than he had expected, worse than he'd hoped. He'd hoped for a cot or two. Some blankets to keep out the cold.

'Oh, dear,' she said as he ushered her into the small stone chamber.

At least they'd be out of the wind. And against the wall was a small pile of peat. They would have a fire after all. And hot tea. He fumbled around the walls until he found what he was seeking. Tallow candles. He lit one, dripped wax on the table and it stood there, a small warm glow.

'I'll see to the horses, then light the fire,' he said.

She rubbed her hands together, the candlelight showing her face, calm and accepting. No anger. Not even worry as she looked around at the bareness of the place, which made him feel somehow worse. He'd been an idiot for not following up with the fellow who had stared at him so hard at the inn. A sensible word with the man might have prevented what had happened tonight.

Angry at his failure to protect the woman in his charge, he stomped out to see to the horses, who were standing patiently outside. He hobbled them, rubbed them down with one of the blankets and hoped for the best. They'd already been fed, so they should be fine outdoors for a few hours.

He removed the saddlebags and blankets and took them inside. It was little enough to offer comfort, but at least the blankets wouldn't take long to dry.

He was surprised to find Rowena piling peat in the central open hearth. She looked up at his entry. 'I thought I would help get it started, although I am not sure I have laid it correctly.'

'Is there kindling?'

She shook her head.

Without kindling it would be difficult to make it catch. He tried not to let his concern show. No sense in worrying her about something until it was a real problem. He cast his gaze around the room for something to get the peat started. 'I expect they use gorse or heather in the summer.'

Rowena held up a small book. 'My journal,' she said at his glance of enquiry. She ripped out the small sheets of paper and twisted them into spills. 'They will light very nicely, I think.'

Smart as paint, this woman. He had a journal, too, buried deep in his saddlebag. Not his, though, and he was loath to dig it out, fearing she might recognise it. It had been one of the few personal things the Indians hadn't taken or destroyed when they attacked MacDonald's camp.

What he had read of its contents on his way down from the hills had revealed it to be a document he would never want another living soul to see, but since MacDonald had written his authority to use his money and property to get him to Scotland on one of the pages, he'd had no choice but to keep it, in case anyone asked. Not that MacDonald had expected he would be transported in a barrel. The man had had no idea of the extent of his injuries.

And as soon as Drew was free of this duty of his, he would burn the journal. But not to keep out the cold.

'Will it be enough, do you think?' Her hands were trembling with cold as she worked and her teeth chattered every now and then.

They had to have heat.

He arranged the blankets close to the hearth. 'It will do very well,' he said and let her hear his admiration.

She glanced up at him and their eyes met and lingered. There was warmth in her gaze.

It sparked a fire inside him. His throat dried. 'I'll see if I can find some brush, as well. To make it burn better.'

Cold air was what he needed right now. Or better yet, a dip in the nearest loch and the more ice, the better.

* * *

Rowena poked the few twists of paper deeper into the overlapping slabs of peat. They had never used peat in her father's house in Edinburgh. Coal had been plentiful, but it seemed to her that fuel was fuel, and the maids had used paper spills to light the fires.

She stood up, rubbing her hands together trying to get some feeling back in her fingertips, then strode to the slab of rock that served as a table, cupping them around the candle flame for a moment before slipping her gloves back on.

Even frozen as she was, she could still feel the warmth of Drew's intense gaze in her belly. It had been better than a shot of whisky. Not that he seemed to notice. To him she was just a responsibility. There had to be something wrong with her, being attracted to such a man. He was no different from Samuel, using her for his own gain. No doubt he expected the duke to reward him handsomely for delivering his relative's remains. And her.

The duke might not feel so generous when he learned he was naught but a smuggler. She sighed. Not that she would tell him, but it would be hard to keep it a secret. The Pockles were bound to arrive at the inn and hear the whole story.

Drew brought in a rush of cold air. And she'd thought the air in the bothy was freezing before. She clenched her jaw to prevent her teeth from chattering while he, with his arms full of brush, stamped the snow off his feet in the doorway. Without a word he crouched before her peat pile, rearranging the earthy slabs, lifting them, inserting clumps of heather. She was pleased to see that he also took care with the placement of her little bits of paper in the heart of the pile.

She freed the candle from its wax blob and held it ready. He looked up and met her eyes. Her heart tumbled over. Her hand shook, splattering hot wax on her glove. She could feel the heat of it through the leather, but it was nowhere near as hot as the flare of heat blazing a path through her veins.

She had no business feeling such things. Even if he had kissed her, it had meant nothing. His shoulders tensed, as if he sensed her dismay. Then he took the candle and touched it to each twist of paper.

Pinpricks of flame. He dropped cross-legged to the floor and nurtured each little lick of bright light, breathing on each tiny flicker, protecting them from the draughts that eddied around them.

'Ah,' he said softly as little curls of smoke rose up.

The peat caught. At first just a glow of tiny embers, like hair caught in a candle, then real flames. She breathed a sigh of relief. They were not going to freeze to death after all.

He pulled his little pot from his saddlebag and the tea and the whisky and she bit back a laugh. 'Too bad you don't have a loaf of bread tucked in there, too.'

'I have your roll left from dinner and something better,' he said. He pulled out the small muslin pouch of oats and dangled it in the air. 'Porridge, ye ken. We'll no' set out on an empty belly in the morning.'

'Porridge. The Scotsman's answer to everything.' She could not help but smile.

His face tightened as if with a painful memory. 'A Highlander never leaves home without one night's food in his sporran. Something my grandfather taught me.'

'Well, my thanks to your grandfather, where e'er he may be.'

'Aye.' He glanced up at the roof where the smoke was curling around in the low rafters. 'I'll open the chimney or we'll be kippered by morning.'

Smoked like fish. She couldn't help a smile at the vision.

He climbed up a series of larger stones set like steps in one of the walls and then up to balance on one of the beams supporting the thatched roof. He found what looked like a long piece of metal, hooked at one end, and used it to push at a trapdoor let into the thatch. It opened an inch or two. The smoke disappeared through the gap and into the night.

While he climbed down, she sank onto the nearest blanket, glad of the warmth of the fire. 'What do you think we should do about the Pockles?'

He dropped to sit beside her. 'Nothing we can do. We'll either meet them on the road or at our destination.'

'You think they will look for us?'

'They might.' His mouth tightened, one corner curling up as if to mock his words. 'I'd sooner they didn't.'

'You are thinking of those men.'

'Aye.'

'Did you know them, as they said?'

'No, but I have no doubt they know my youngest brother, Logan. As wild a wee scamp as there ever was. He was a fair way to looking like me when I left.'

Two like him. It seemed hard to imagine. 'They don't seem to like him very much.'

'I can't imagine why,' he said drily, as if he knew very well.

Under that sullen demeanour she sometimes suspected he had a wry sense of humour. 'Business, I suppose.'

He raised his gaze to hers and she was right, there was amusement glinting there, hidden unless you cared to look. Not that she thought he'd be pleased that she'd noticed. He'd likely deny any kind of warm feelings.

But right now there was one rather urgent problem she needed to deal with. 'I don't suppose there is a privy out there?'

He winced. 'No.'

'But there are bushes.' She nodded at the few bits of brush he'd kept back from the fire.

'Aye, but you canna go out there alone. It's too dark. Too easy to lose your way. I'm afraid you will have to suffer my escort.'

So much for modesty. But there was no sense to being missish. She rose to her feet and he stood with her. 'I am sure you will not mind turning your back.'

Outside, she couldn't see an inch in front of her face, once he shut the door. She looked up at the sky. The moon had either set or disappeared behind clouds. She would have been afraid to take one step farther if it had not been for his strong hand beneath her elbow.

They went around the side of the house where the wind was less fierce. 'This will have to do, I'm afraid.'

He stood with one hand against the wall, his back

towards her. She followed the length of the wall to the furthest corner, putting the width of the house between them, and took care of her needs. It was at times like these that she found differences in rank more than ridiculous. People were people, no matter what they were called, and if they were above the animals in the fields, it was not by much. She stood, straightened her skirts and followed the wall back to Mr Gilvry.

'Thank you.'

He grunted, then put a hand on her shoulder. 'You're not like any lady I ever met.'

She couldn't see his face in the dark, but she heard something odd in his tone. Criticism? The kind she'd endured from her husband.

'I'm sorry if you find me a disappointment, Mr Gilvry.' Head high, she stalked back to the front door and inside.

It seemed he'd unintentionally touched a nerve when he'd intended his words as a compliment. Apparently, he was out of practice in the charming of women. Not that he'd had to practise when he was last in Scotland. Or in London, for that matter. All he'd ever needed was a smile. A smile wouldn't do him a bit of good anymore, since it made him look like a gargoyle, the kind that terrified small children in the night. More than one had run away in terror after seeing his face.

As he'd do well to remember. So did he say he was sorry, or let it go?

Given their circumstances, their close quarters and his visceral responses to her presence, it was probably best if she was annoyed. It would keep them both at a distance.

While she seated herself cross-legged on her blanket beside the fire, he proceeded to heat the snow he had collected while waiting for her outside. A bothy usually came equipped with a couple of cooking pots and a trivet. Either someone had stolen them or the landlord was discouraging the bothy's use by itinerants. Lots of people had been cleared off their ancestral lands these past years, many roaming the hills looking for somewhere to settle. No landlord worth his salt wanted squatters on his land.

He balanced his tin pot on the peat and turned his attention to his pistol. He did not want to be caught unawares and unready if the men at McRae's had followed them. Her gaze followed his every movement as he primed the pan and loaded the ball.

'It is warming up in here already,' she said with determined cheerfulness.

An olive branch. A courageous attempt to be brave. Damp chill clung to the stone walls, making the room as cold as the grave. Still, he wasn't going to negate her courage, not when he could not help but admire it. But nor did he want to meet that clear steady gaze of hers. Every time he did, he found himself drowning in their cool depths, wanting more that he should, saying far more than he intended.

He'd already revealed more than he should about his past. Perhaps because it was the first time in a long time that anyone had shown the slightest interest.

He kept his gaze fixed on what he was doing. 'If we

can keep the fire going, we shouldn't freeze to death. There's enough peat for a night or two.'

'A night or two?' She sounded horrified.

'Aye. If it snows again and we canna get out.'

'Oh, dear.'

He set the pistol aside, close to hand, pulled his knife from his boot and stirred the melting snow. 'It might not come to that.'

'I hope not.'

And so did he. Given the growing attraction he felt towards this woman, and not just to her physical being, but to her as a person, the next several hours would not be easy, no matter whether they stayed here or continued their journey.

The water in the pot began to steam. He tossed in some tea leaves. It would warm them through and perhaps she'd sleep for a while. And he could pretend he felt nothing.

He watched the water, waiting for it to come to a full boil, but could not help but feel her gaze upon him, or stop recalling to mind the shape of her body beneath her nightgown. There was no doubt about it. The sooner he was rid of her the better he would like it. She was too much of a temptation. No matter what his body thought, she was not the kind of woman he needed.

His mind went back to their discussions with the lawyer. 'I have the sense yon Jones didna' like the date of your husband's death. Do you think he had a date he preferred? A date later in the month?' he asked as a distraction from his carnal thoughts. 'I could make it whatever date he wanted if you thought it would help with the duke. I canna see that a few days here or there would make any great difference.'

She stripped off her gloves and held her hands out to the fire. They were capable-looking hands, he noticed. Hands that looked as if they knew their way around a man's body.

A wave of heat rolled through his blood. Hell and damnation, had his time in captivity made him naught but a beast? Even there, he'd had more control over his thoughts than he seemed to have now.

'I thought he said he didn't care about the date,' she mused, seemingly unaware of his inner struggle.

'His tongue said he didn't care. His face said otherwise.'

Her eyes sharpened. 'Are you sure?'

'It's hard to be sure of anything. But he definitely winced at the mention of the date, then went to a deal of trouble to deny its importance.' He shook his head. 'It makes no sense to care about such a thing. Unless there's money in it.'

'A loan? Something in Samuel's will?' She blew on the tips of those long slender fingers. 'I can't make any scenario work that would tie to the date of his death.'

Nor could he. 'But there is something.'

'Perhaps the duke will be more forthcoming when I see him.'

A sound outside the door brought him to his feet and the pistol into his hand. He pulled Rowena to her feet and pushed her behind him.

'What is it?' she asked in a whisper.

'I heard something.'

'It's them. They've found us.'

Inside, he went still, cold, listening with his body as well as his ears, becoming at one with the air to feel any small disturbance. He lifted a finger to his lips and to his relief she nodded and remained utterly silent. There were only two smugglers left, if he was right about the one he'd shot, and the night was dark. He blew out the candle. He didn't want the light behind him, making him a perfect target. Too bad he didn't have the moon to help him see whoever was outside.

He moved slowly towards the door. Reached for the latch.

A bang. The door rattled in its frame.

Rowena gasped and clutched at his coat. She'd crept along right behind him, using him for a shield. He was glad of it.

But…

Another bang. Metal on wood. Low on the door. Heavy breathing on the other side. And another metallic sound like…

What the hell? He whipped the door open, pistol cocked.

Her horse huffed out a breath and made to come in.

Air rushed from his lungs. 'Yon beastie wants in.' He crouched and felt for her hobble. Still there. He gave her a push. 'Sorry, lassie. People only in here.' He shut the door in the animal's face.

Rowena, behind him, was making odd little noises. Crying? She must have been terrified. He found the candle and lit it from the ashes and held it aloft.

She was leaning against the wall, doubled over, her

face covered by her hands and her shoulders shaking. Sobbing.

His stomach dipped. His heart lurched. He crossed the room and put an arm around her shoulders. 'It's all right,' he soothed, horribly aware of her body against his and the loud beating of his heart.

'It's all right. It was only your horse.'

Her shoulders shook harder.

Heavens, after all she'd gone through tonight so bravely, and now she was falling apart. He turned her in his arms, pressed her face to his shoulder, held her close, felt her soft curves and sweet hollows down the length of his body, felt her warm breath on his neck and wanted to groan with frustration.

'Please, *mo cridhe*, don't cry.'

'Oh,' she gasped, looking up. 'I'm not...crying.'

He looked down into her face. Her eyes had tears and her face was bright pink, but her mouth was...laughing. She was laughing?

'It was just your...expression. When you saw the h-horse.' She dissolved into giggles.

A laugh rose in his chest, bubbling up where no laugh should be. 'She was cold,' he said.

'She wanted a cup of tea.'

And then he did laugh. And laugh. Holding her fast, grinning like a fool. And laughing until they were both breathless.

'Oh, Drew, I thought we were done for.' She flung her arms around his neck and kissed him full on the mouth, still laughing.

He pulled her arms down from around his neck, holding her hands fast at her sides, intending to set her away, but as he gazed into eyes dancing with merriment, he found himself entranced.

And he moved his grip to her back and kissed her in return. And kissed her. Savouring the softness of her lips and the sweet way she opened her mouth and her tongue tangled with his. Nothing, not even the best *usquebaugh*, had ever tasted so good as her passion or warmed the coldness inside him so deeply.

Her hands strayed under his coat, caressing his back, while her hips arched into him in open invitation.

Deep in his bones he felt a shudder so strong he could have sworn the ground was shaking. And he didn't care if the stone walls crumbled around them, as long as she held him and stroked his chest, her thumbs teasing his nipples, her sweet soft belly grinding against his swollen shaft.

His mind was a hot dark pit of lust and torment. Yet her kiss, the dark slide of her tongue against his brought warmth to the deepest reaches of his heart, to the shivering creature that craved her heat.

The pain of it was too hard to bear.

Because somewhere at the edges of his consciousness he knew this was wrong, though he wanted her badly. He should not be doing this, taking advantage of a woman far too good for him.

On a wild groan he could not contain, he let her go and stepped back, panting and shaken. 'Rowena,' he rasped in a voice that sounded as if it was broken.

'Drew,' she said. 'I want this. I want you.'

He heard the demand in her voice. An order from the past he'd been forced to obey.

Resentment flared to life. 'I'm no' yours to command.' Not anymore. Never again. 'If you want what I have, you'll beg for it.'

Eyes hazed by desire, she drew in a hiss of breathy pleasure. 'Please,' she whispered. 'Oh, please, Drew.'

Heat blazed in his veins even as he stared at her, caught up by lust and shock as her words brought his every fantasy to the fore. Had she somehow guessed at the flaw in his nature and thought to mock him? He suffered a pang of shame.

Or could she...? No, it was impossible. She did not know what she was saying, what it did to him. It was the shock of the events of the night making her ask for comfort. And heaven help him, he wasn't sure he could resist that quietly spoken plea.

She dropped her gaze. 'Please,' she said again.

Heat blazed a trail across his skin. Desire ran rampant. 'You'll do exactly as I say.'

'Yes,' she murmured. 'Anything.'

The battle was lost.

He teased the seam of her lips with his tongue and they parted on a sigh. He stroked the inside of her mouth and she moaned, arching into him, responsive to each little flick of his tongue, her hands coming up to rest on his shoulders for support as she melted in his arms.

'No touching,' he muttered. She let her hands fall away.

He slid his fingers around her nape, angling her head to deepen the kiss, and felt the thunder of her pulse at her throat. He let the other hand drop to her shoulder, glide over her back, caress the dip of her waist.

Their lips clung and their tongues tasted, and their breath mingled until he was the white heat in the centre of the flame. And the demands of his body blazed into life.

Doubts assailed him. He broke their kiss. 'Are you sure?'

Heavy lidded, her liquid silver eyes gazed back at him. 'Positive,' she whispered.

God help him, those words undid him. He scanned the room, the cold dirt floor, the blankets, and he wanted to howl with frustration. Then his gaze took in the table behind her. He swallowed and backed her up to its edge.

She shivered.

Cold stone. He couldn't... 'Blanket,' he muttered, releasing her shoulders. He folded both blankets and arranged them on the table. Then he set his hands to her narrow waist and lifted her to perch on the rough wool. He kissed her again, his hips pushing between her legs, one hand pushing up under the full fabric of her skirt until it found the soft silken skin above her stocking. As his fingers stroked the delicate flesh of her inner thigh, she sighed into his mouth and shifted closer to the table's edge.

Lust hit his groin in a hot river of pulsing blood. He took her mouth in a brutal ravaging kiss, forcing her head back with his assault, and she tangled her tongue with his and made little sounds of encouragement. Urging him on with her fingers in his hair, then stroking his jaw, his scars with a feathery sweeps of her fingers. Trying to gentle him. To control him.

A feral growl ripped at his throat. The need for possession, a beast on the rampage. 'You must do only what I tell you. Do you understand?'

She nodded.

'Do not touch me, unless I say you may.'

She licked her lips and opened her mouth to speak.

'Say nothing,' he warned.

Eyes wide, she gazed at him and said nothing.

One arm around her back, he lifted her, sweeping her skirts up and away until they were bunched at her waist. He gazed down at the wickedly delicious sight of her long slim thighs parted to embrace his hips and the soft dark curls at their juncture. A low groan broke free.

He fell to his knees, and she gasped. Surprise? Shock. He looked up to see her staring down at him, her lips rosy and swollen from his brutal assault on her mouth. But instead of fear in her eyes there was the heat of molten metal. And puzzlement.

Triumph settled deep in the pit of his stomach. He was not her first, but he would be the first to teach her this pleasure. He lifted her legs and hooked them over his shoulders. Her eyes widened.

Holding her gaze, he parted the soft folds of her feminine flesh with his thumbs and stroked a finger over the already swollen bud hiding deep within. Her eyelids fluttered, then drifted closed, and she moaned sweetly.

He leaned forward and pressed a kiss to the hot centre, inhaling the deep rich scent of aroused woman, feeling the dampness on his lips.

She hissed in a breath, her fingers gripping the edge of the table as if afraid she might fall. He nuzzled deeper, using his lips and his tongue to sweep the sweet cleft of her body.

'Oh,' she cried out as his tongue flickered over the hot little bud deep in her folds.

Oh, yes, the beast inside him said. *Yes.*

Chapter Seven

The delicious wickedness of his mouth made Rowena's limbs feel boneless. The quick, light flicks of his tongue against her flesh were a constant torment. The sight of that dark chestnut hair between her thighs made her insides clench tighter.

The most salacious hedonism she could have imagined held her in its thrall. How had he guessed at her secret fantasy? Her dreams of ravaging pirates and marauding sheikhs who bound her and made her submit to their every whim. Who dominated and forced her into submission. She shuddered with the power of his masculine strength.

At any moment, it would happen. The waves of pleasure, followed by a rush of heat that she'd discovered as a girl and that were so shamefully addictive.

She loved the sensations storming her body. Never had she created any so powerful from her mental images as he created with his lips and tongue.

The end hovered just out of reach. She wove her fingers in the silky waves of his hair, opening herself wider, lifting her hips, pressing into him, seeking to break the mounting tension.

He jerked away, those incredible green eyes blazing up at her, his face a mask of agony.

'Lean back,' he ordered, his voice a low, feral growl. 'Palms on the table. Do. Not. Move.'

The command, the threat, lashed her with hot pulses at her core. Languorous with desire, she complied, leaning back, legs spread, completely at his mercy.

With a grunt of satisfaction, he renewed his assault, licking the little tiny nub that was the source of the pleasure she sought. Such a small thing to turn her limbs to butter, she'd thought when she peeked in a mirror. Hardly impressive compared to the male of the species.

He suckled.

Her hips shot off the table. That she had not expected. She moaned her pleasure. The ache inside her increased tenfold, making her tremble. 'Please,' she begged, seeking the tipping point just out of reach, which loomed in every dark, hot corner of her body.

'Silence,' he ordered, 'or I will walk away.'

She melted. Thrills chased down her spine at the power of command in the deep growl of his voice. This was her pirate. The man who prowled through her dreams, taking control of her body and soul. She closed her eyes in submission.

He eased one finger inside her and her inner walls clamped tight as he stroked within and without with his thumb. The ache intensified. Tears of joy leaked from the corners of her eyes as she let him do with her as he would.

And he lowered her legs to hang over the edge. Stepped back and left her, cold and bereft.

'No,' she moaned. She sat up, reached for him.

His gaze dropped to the place his mouth had so recently vacated, so raw and aching, the look on his face dark and sensual. 'Palms on the table,' he said roughly. 'Do as I bid or I'll end this now.'

The words made her quiver and shiver as if he was still touching her with his mouth.

She gasped. Lolling back, too weak and melting to do anything else. A jerk of a nod signified his approval.

His hand went to his breeches. He unbuttoned his falls. She wanted to offer to help. To touch him as he had touched her, but the darkness in his expression kept her hands glued to the table and her breath coming in little soft pants.

He dropped his coat to the floor and dragged off his boots and stockings while she watched, fascinated. No man had ever undressed in her presence before. She hadn't even seen her husband naked. The few times he'd coupled with her, he'd always blown out the candles before he removed his banyan.

Breathless with anticipation, she watched. She licked her lips as he peeled the pantaloons down his legs, but saw only a glimpse of his thighs as his shirt, released from its confines, fell to his knees.

She made a sound of disappointment.

He went still and her gaze drifted up to his face.

'Did you speak?' he asked in rough, hoarse tones.

She quickly shook her head.

His eyes narrowed, but his hands got busy with his shirt buttons. The placket opened to reveal a narrow strip of chest with a dusting of crisp reddish-gold hair. What would it feel like, that hair, against her skin? Her palms tingled with the desire to touch. She kept them pressed against the cold stone while he pulled the shirt off over his head.

The breath left her body in a long sigh. A Greek statue had never looked so beautiful. Arms that she had known were strong were gilded by the sun and warmed by the light of the candle and the fire. They were beautifully formed. Lovely. And she longed to touch the smooth planes, the curve of muscle. She itched to curl her fingers in the crisp hair sprinkling gold dust across his chest, to trace the hard ridges of muscle beneath his ribs.

Fear held her back. The certain knowledge that if she did, he would not be pleased, and she desperately wanted to please him. To feel desirable.

And right now, he did want her. He was aroused. His male member standing erect from a nest of crisp reddish curls, its head dark and glistening.

It stirred under her gaze and she sucked in a breath, her gaze shooting up to his face.

His eyes were hooded, his mouth sultry, yet mocking her with its slight upward tilt at one corner. Her body trembled with anticipation. Ached for what he might bring her.

He stepped between her knees and she looked down

to see their hips were in perfect alignment, his shaft brushing hot against her inner thigh.

'Wider,' he ground out through a jaw that was clenched as if he felt pain.

She inhaled a shaky breath and complied.

He clasped her hips and pulled her closer. He placed his knuckle beneath her chin, lifting her face with gentle but firm pressure. There was something in his expression she didn't quite understand. Shame?

'Are you sure?' There was no mistaking the desire in his hard-edged voice—it sent wild shivers all the way to her core, hot little pulses of wicked pleasure. An ache tightened inside her. The need for release from the tension of longing.

She swallowed. 'Yes,' she whispered. A shudder of anticipation rippled through her at the power he exuded. He made her feel feminine, desired and strangely— protected.

He reached between them, gazing deep into her eyes as if to gauge her response, and guided his hot hard flesh to her core, pressing against her most private place, a hot, deliciously tempting pressure as he rocked his hips.

He stilled, looking down at her, watching her as if testing her resolve.

She panted, wanting to move, to arch into him, to make him… No. He was like a wild animal—one wrong move and he would walk away and leave her with nothing but the shame of being undeserving of what most women took for granted: male desire for an attractive woman.

She shook with the effort of remaining utterly still.

He leaned forward, his body coming over her, his hands unfastening her gown then trapping hers to the table, pressing her back onto her elbows, her breasts exposed to his mouth. She let her head fall back, eyes closed, exposing her throat. Offering her surrender to his will.

A deep dark sound rose up from low in his chest, a feral sound of possession, and his hot breath scorched her cheek, before he took her mouth in a soul-searing kiss. She melted beneath his assault, her thoughts giving way to the sensation of his lips on hers, his tongue exploring her mouth, the feel of his hard body against her naked breasts and the tantalising feel of him between her thighs.

How could she not have guessed how wonderful it could be? Why had she never known?

He raised his head, leaving behind her lips to trail hot kisses down her throat and then first on one breast, then the other. Sensations chased across her skin in rapid succession. The peaks ached and tightened as he licked and nuzzled the sensitive tips. It felt wicked and wildly exciting. Though she tried, she could not stop the sounds of encouragement coming from the back of her throat.

He teased at her nipples with his tongue, with his teeth, and then he suckled.

Inside and out, her body convulsed at the painfully sharp pleasure that arrowed straight to her womb. She cried out with the shock of it.

He raised his head and the chill air across her wet breast made shivers ripple across her skin to settle low in her belly. Then he suckled at the other breast and the delicious torture started all over again.

It was perfect, wonderful, his mouth was wonderful, an instrument of pleasure that worshipped her body. She lifted her head to look at him. Sensing her movement, he glanced up. For a brief moment she thought she saw a flare of heat in his eyes, of desire. But his expression was cold, remote, as if he was only doing this to please her and sought nothing for himself. Felt nothing.

Her arms trembled with the strain of holding herself in place, but before she collapsed, one hand left hers to support her nape, while the other went between them, stroking her centre in strong, slick motions that made her gasp and cry out. Gently he parted those folds and guided himself to the entrance of her body until she felt herself opening and flesh give way. She felt his flesh enter her a fraction, intrusive, hot and delicious.

He shuddered as if under some great strain. A warm hand stroked her thigh behind her knee, lifting it, and he pressed deeper inside, stroking her inner flesh with small rocks of his hips.

She wanted more. She lifted the other leg, wrapped both of them around his hips, opening herself fully, bringing him closer to her sweetly aching centre.

Without warning, he drove forward, hard, to the hilt. Uncontrollable pleasure washed through her in a searing surge. She cried out.

A growl of warning rumbled up from his throat, a feral sound laced with torment. He nuzzled at her neck first nipping, then soothing with his tongue. He nibbled at her ear all the while driving into her. He filled her and left no room for anything but raw sensation: the rhythm of their panting breaths loud in her ears; the sound of their bodies joining; the sensations of one hand on her breast, the other holding her up so his mouth could feast on her lips, her tongue; and the slapping of his hips against her inner thighs.

Then he swirled his tongue in her ear. His hand left her breast and went to the tiny straining numb buried in the soft folds of her female flesh, expertly rubbing and pressing and...

She shattered in a fountain of heat forced up from her core that blazed along her veins like a forest fire caught by the wind. Her body went limp and she collapsed backwards on to the table.

He groaned softly and withdrew from her body. He hung over her, his hands either side of her, his breath coming in harsh, raw gasps hot against her breasts and his head hanging low. He looked like a man in the throes of terrible agony.

Because... Because he had not found his release. Her heart slowed. Where there had been heat, there was ice.

He had been unable to... She had not been enough for him. She wanted to weep.

Instead, she took a deep breath and sat up. With unsteady fingers, she eased her gown up her arms and over her shoulders, covering her breasts.

He moved away, turning his back while he hastily pulled on his trousers and fastened them over his arousal with a wince.

She pulled her skirts down over her legs. Before she could jump down from the table, he turned back and helped her, holding her up when her legs threatened to buckle.

Never had she felt so languid, so wonderfully relaxed… or so inadequate.

He brushed her hair back from her face and peered into her eyes. 'Satisfied?' he asked in a mocking voice.

'Yes,' she admitted, but wishing she'd been enough of a woman to bring him to completion. For breathless minutes, she had felt like a siren. Now she knew her husband had spoken the truth. As a woman, she really was a failure.

In silence, he finished dressing, picked up his coat and walked out into the night, leaving her to shiver in a blast of cold air.

What on earth had just happened? Clearly she was not the woman he wanted. He'd found her inadequate. Undesirable.

Why would she feel surprised? Or hurt? Deeply hurt. No man, not even her husband, wanted her in that way. She just wasn't the kind of woman men found appealing and she'd pushed him into doing something he hadn't wanted.

And now he was gone. Out into the night. Leaving her feeling sickened by shame.

She stared at the door.

Her heart stopped still in her chest. What if he never came back?

No. She wouldn't believe he would abandon her out here in the wilderness. He'd been angry. He'd gone to cool off. To settle his temper. To take care of his needs. Mortification washed through her that she wasn't enough.

He would come back.

He had to.

The hours of waiting passed interminably slowly, and while she had lain down beside the fire and huddled under her cloak, she didn't sleep. It was fear making the time crawl.

Finally, she gave up pretending and rose and folded the blankets. She put more peat on the fire, coaxing it into a blaze. Lit the candle, wishing there were windows that would spill light out into the night and welcome him back.

Inside she trembled.

What if he didn't come back?

He had looked so disgusted. So appalled. Even in the little light given off by the fire, and the single candle, she had seen his revulsion. As if what had happened was her fault.

She should have fought him the moment he touched her. Fought him? That was a lie. She should have fought herself. While she could still not believe the strength of her climax, something she would never forget, her heart ached for the loss of their growing friendship. He'd laughed with her. And she'd spoiled it all by throwing herself at him like some frustrated spinster.

No wonder he'd walked out with that look of disgust on his face.

She let go a shuddering breath and paced around the small room. Walking to keep warm and to dispel the fear inside her, the burgeoning panic. And as she walked she could not help looking at that door. Waiting for him to return.

But he didn't.

And when she couldn't bear it anymore, she peeked out. The sky had lightened. It was morning. And he hadn't returned. Had he taken his horse?

The idea robbed her of breath.

If he had ridden away, did that mean he wouldn't return? Her heart pounded hard in her chest. She picked up her cloak and pulled it around her.

His horse would be there. He would not have taken it unless he planned to go far away. He wouldn't do that. He had promised to see her safe to the duke. Swallowing the dryness in her throat, she opened the door wide and peered outside. The wind tugged at her cloak, trying to rip it from her clutching hand as she took in the view. The clouds still lowered over the hills, obscuring their tops. And it had snowed again during the night. There were no tracks.

She walked around to the back of the bothy. Her horse raised its head and pawed at the ground. Drew's mount was nowhere to be seen.

If his horse was gone, then he had left. And she was now on her own. Alone in the Highlands and no idea where to go for safety. Her knees weakened. Threatened to give way.

She forced herself to stand straight, took a deep breath and glanced around at the white landscape. If only she had looked at the map before they left. She had left it all to him. Trusted him to see her there safely. There was nothing to tell her which way to go.

Should she go and risk getting hopelessly lost? Or stay and freeze once the peat for the fire ran out?

Quite the conundrum. The sort of problem she sometimes set for her pupils as an exercise in logic for their young minds. In the warm comfort of their schoolroom it hadn't seemed quite so terrifying.

But whereas she might want to be mastered in her fantasies, in real life she needed to be strong. She'd sooner die trying to rescue herself than simply wait for the end. And that meant she'd have to gather up her belongings and try to find her way to a village. Or back to McRae's inn.

The inn would be closest, if she could only remember the way.

Downhill. She would head downhill away from the bothy. She strode back inside. The heat inside the little house felt blissful on her chilled face. She went to the fire and stood over it, revelling in the warmth percolating through her clothes. It would be hard to leave such lovely heat and head out into the unknown with only hope and a vague sense of direction as her guide. She looked at the pile of peat against the wall. It might last another day. Perhaps she should wait. Trust he would come back.

And set out if he did not.

Her stomach growled.

If she was hungry now, she would be worse later. She crouched down and ransacked his saddlebag. There was the handful of oats, the bread roll, a tinder box, a handkerchief and a pouch of coins. In the bottom she found the little bag of tea leaves. And beneath that she felt a small book. Not her business.

She frowned as the thought occurred that he'd taken nothing with him. He must have meant to come back.

Perhaps something had happened to him? Her stomach roiled. Could he have run into the smugglers and come to some harm? Were they even now on their way here? If so, she'd be a fool to remain.

Whatever those men wanted, they had meant nothing good.

She looked at the tiny hoard of victuals spread out on the blanket, wishing she had also thought to bring food. She broke a piece of the crust and chewed it slowly. And then another piece. And then half of it was gone and her stomach ached for more, urging her to finish it all. She forced herself to put it back in the saddlebag, stuffing everything back inside. She might need the rest of it later. Although a few tea leaves in hot water would help with her hunger. And warm her, too.

She would make tea, and then she would leave.

The door opened. Cold air filled the cabin.

Surprised, she sat down on her rump with a bump and stared at the tall figure in the doorway.

Drew. He'd come back. He stared at the saddlebag and then up to her face.

Relief flooded through her, chasing away the fear. Followed swiftly by anger. 'Where have you been?'

He dropped a bundle of fur on the floor. Rabbits. 'I went hunting.'

'How dare you leave without a word?'

Anger blazed in his eyes, like the rage of a cornered beast.

She'd said too much. She turned away, her hands clenched together, searching for words that wouldn't have him disappearing again. 'I thought you'd left for good.'

There was a long silence. And then the door opened. She swung around, heart in her throat.

He paused in the doorway, looking back. 'I'm going to clean these wee beasties so we can cook them.' His voice was harsh and raw. He went out with a slam of the door.

She closed her eyes. He had come back.

Outside, behind the bothy, Drew skinned and eviscerated the rabbits. Even that act of violence wasn't enough for the rage deep inside him. He wanted to hit something.

He was rock hard. Again. He'd thought he'd dealt with that problem. He'd walked away to distance himself. To get himself back under control. Then he'd come back and done exactly what he said he would never do again.

Let himself be seduced by a woman. Her frightened face had left him wanting to hold her. And to use her again.

Guilt swirled in his gut. He'd used her as if he was some sort of animal. He could see from the pain in her face that he'd hurt her. He'd shamed her. Forced her to submit to his disgusting fantasy. As if she was *her*.

And she wasn't. She was a strong, brave woman who deserved so much better.

At least she wouldn't trouble him anymore with her

sweet smiles and soft eyes and the temptations of her sweet body. It would not happen again.

He quartered the rabbits, then sliced the meat thin. It was little enough, but it would fill their stomachs before they set out. He walked a little distance off from the bothy and hid the remains under a few rocks. Foxes or other scavengers would no doubt find it, but it wouldn't be obvious to any casual observer that it was human killed. He'd retraced their flight from the previous evening for a good long way and, as far as he could tell, the smugglers had not followed them, which didn't mean they wouldn't, but it did mean they had time to eat before they set out.

Steeling himself for more of her anger, he went back inside to discover that she had put water in the pot and it was already beginning to steam.

'Good thinking,' he said gruffly.

He was not surprised that her smile was small and painful, as though it hurt. She gestured to the bit of bread he had brought from the inn. 'I ate my half while you were gone.'

He heard the guilt in her voice and looked into her smoke-grey eyes.

'I really thought you weren't coming back,' she added softly.

He wanted to say she should have known he would. But how would she? He'd behaved like the worst cur imaginable. He shrugged. 'It took longer than I expected.'

She took a deep breath. 'Did you see anything of them? Those men?'

'No.' Her face said she didn't believe him. She was too clever for such an offhand assurance.

'Not that I'm thinking we've seen the last of them,' he continued. 'But they'd be here by now if they'd followed us last night, and I saw no sign of them on the track. And if they've waited for morning's light, as I believe they have, then it will be a while before they make their way here. By then we'll be gone.' He pulled a thin, flat rock from his pocket and set it on top of the fire. As a skillet, it wasn't much, but it would serve a turn.

Soon the little stone room was filled with the aroma of roasting meat and they were taking turns at sipping from the mug containing the last of his tea. He broke the remains of the roll in half and offered her one.

She shook her head. 'You need it more than I.'

He raised a brow.

'There's more of you,' she said, her smile tentative.

A soft feeling invaded his chest at the kindness of her words. He'd forgotten that women could be kind. *She* had always eaten first and thrown him whatever scraps were left. And if he had angered her, she'd given him nothing but punishment. It still shamed him that he'd let her treat him that way. Let her use him, at first out of gratitude and then out of weakness.

But he couldn't let Rowena's kindness sway him into being soft. It would make it too difficult to keep his distance. He grunted. 'Your choice.' He turned the meat on the stone. It looked ready. He cut into a piece with his knife to ensure it was cooked through.

'How did you catch them?' she asked.

Surprised by her interest, he looked up. 'With a snare.' He pulled a piece of looped string from his pocket. 'I learned a great deal from the Indians. They are clever hunters.'

He skewered one of the strips and held it out to her.

She pulled out her handkerchief and took it from him, blowing on it to cool it, then took a small hesitant bite. A smile spread across her stern face, making her look younger and almost pretty, more like the woman he'd pleasured in the night. He hardened. The devil confound him, why would his mind keep going back to that?

'Oh, my,' she said. 'That's delicious.'

Warm pleasure at her compliment spread through him. Warmth he should not be feeling. 'Because you're hungry,' he said curtly.

She flinched. And he ground his teeth at the look of hurt in her eyes. He preferred her anger.

He divided the strips between them and they tucked in. He ate his with the bread. It didn't take very long and he wished there was more, but he was used to an empty belly. She wasn't. He could see it in her face.

'Let us be on the road, then,' he said. 'If we are lucky we will reach our journey's end in time for supper.'

The look of longing on her face filled him with guilt. He couldn't even feed her properly. He was supposed to be protecting her, not putting her in danger. She'd come to him for comfort and he'd treated her like some low class of woman. But it was too late to put the beast back in the cage. All he could do was go forward so she would not have to suffer his presence for very much longer. Soon she would not be his responsibility.

The thought caused him to suffer a pang in his chest. Bloody indigestion, that was all.

He rose and began tidying up. 'We'll leave it just as we found it. For the next traveller.'

In silence, they began packing up.

Chapter Eight

After an hour or so of slow riding through the drifts, the sun came out. The glistening snow made it hard to see, but despite the cool wind, Rowena felt the warmth of the sun on her shoulders. She watched with interest at the way Drew had looked up at the sky, then adjusted their course.

'Do you know where we are?' she asked during one of their stops to rest the horses.

'Roughly.' He pointed ahead. 'That way is north-west. The map I saw showed that mountain due north of where we are headed.' He pointed at a distant jagged peak.

'How do you know that is the mountain you saw on the map?'

'I've been here before.'

'You have?'

'A long time ago. I was on my way to London.' He urged his horse into motion and she followed suit, catching him up.

'You've been to London?'

'For my sins.'

She had the feeling he didn't want to say any more about it, but she could not hold back her questions. 'Is it as large as they say? As grand?'

'It is much bigger than Edinburgh, certainly. And crowded and dirty. Except for the small area occupied by the very rich. Mayfair and St James's. That is grand enough, I suppose.'

She digested this in silence. 'You don't sound very impressed. Why did you go?'

'Family business.'

And that was all he was going to say on the matter, she realised from the finality in his voice. A stab of hurt twisted in her chest. She forced herself to ignore it. Men did not like women poking their noses into their business, private or personal. She meant nothing to him. She couldn't even bring him the most basic of pleasures.

Heat rippled across her skin at the memory of the pleasure she had found in his arms. And the disgust she had seen on his face. Perhaps if she could make him understand that she had been true to her husband until that very moment, he wouldn't think her quite so wanton. And perhaps if he understood she planned never to marry again, he wouldn't fear he'd be trapped. She was a widow and she could do as she pleased, provided she was discreet, if that was what had bothered him so.

Clearly what had happened had been a mistake. For both of them. It would not happen again. Because he didn't want it to. The hollowness inside her grew.

They mounted up again and as the path narrowed she let her horse fall back, content to follow, and only glanced back over her shoulder occasionally, when she heard the sound of a bird or some other small noise.

Just in case it was those horrible men.

When they arrived, late that afternoon, the house was nothing like Drew expected. It was a mean and ill-appointed stone two-storey dwelling, lying ten miles from the duke's residence and five from the nearest village. It stood at the edge of a small forest of pines with a burn wandering through an overgrown patch of snow-covered garden. Why send her to a place so far from anywhere? As if he didn't want her talking to anyone.

It wasn't as bad as the bothy they'd so recently left, but not far off.

Rowena looked about her calmly, though also clearly disappointed. He could not help but admire her calm manner when dealing with adversity.

She had not been so calm when she thought he had abandoned her, he acknowledged wryly, but who could blame her? He had walked out on her without a word, shamed by knowing he should have stopped what had happened. He still could not believe he had treated a lady so roughly. He'd expected recriminations. When they hadn't come, he'd felt worse, realising she feared he would abandon her to her fate.

But there was little he could say to explain.

He leaped from his horse. 'The place looks deserted.' He helped her down.

'It does,' she said, glancing up at a chimney absent of smoke.

He tied the horses to a fence post and tossed the saddlebags over his shoulder. 'Let us take a look inside.'

She handed him the key the Pockles had passed on from Jones the morning they had left. The front door opened with a painful shriek of rusted metal. He wanted to curse the duke. Instead, he stepped over the threshold. Inside it smelled musty and dusty and damp. He grimaced at the smell. 'I think you might have to take rooms at an inn until the place has been aired out.'

She stepped around him and peered into the first room leading off the hallway. A parlour, of sorts, furnished with a sofa and a chair and table for eating. The room at the end of the hallway was a small kitchen with a door out to the garden, the path leading to a shed at the end, which might be assumed to serve as a stable. There were holes in its thatch and boards missing from the walls.

'You can't stay here,' he said as she turned back.

The glance she gave him caused him to close his mouth with a snap.

He followed her up the stairs. Two bedrooms. The one at the front a decent size. He trailed her into the one at the back. It overlooked the untidy garden.

'Is there an attic?' she asked. 'For servants?'

He went out to the landing to check. 'Not that I can see.'

'You'll stay in this room, then.'

He shook his head. 'I'll stay with the horses.' He didn't trust himself to sleep so close to her. 'We have enough explaining to do.'

Was that disappointment he saw in her face as she turned away to look out of the window? Surely not?

'You can't sleep out there,' she said.

He huffed out a breath. 'Well, I canna sleep in the house. There is no excuse for it. And Mrs Pockle will need the room when she arrives.'

'What if the smugglers come after us?'

'They willna'.' He huffed out a breath. 'But if they do, I'll hear them long before they get close. Dinna fash about that.' He gave her a mischievous grin to take the force out of his words. 'And Pockle will ha' to sleep out there, too, since there's no separate quarters for servants.' It wasn't right for married servants to cohabit with a single mistress. What could Jones have been thinking?

'Poor Mr Pockle.' Her eyes were large and sad, her smile tight. 'As you wish.'

Dammit, it was nothing to do with what he wished. It was what was right. 'It won't take me long to repair the worst of the holes and we'll be as snug as bugs for a night or two. Then you will send a message to the duke and tell him that this really won't do.'

'I can't afford to stay at the inn.'

'But the duke—'

'Mr Jones was very clear. This is all the duke is prepared to give until my claims are settled. I am to stay here and await his pleasure.'

'It isna' right.'

She turned to face him. 'I know. And that is what makes me think there is something underhanded going on. I intend to get to the bottom of it.'

The determination on her face made him want to smile. 'I can't argue with your sense of unease. I have it, too.'

She frowned. 'I am to wait here until the duke sees fit to receive me. In the meantime, I have only sufficient funds either to hire a maid or to buy food.'

'I have what is left of your husband's money,' he said.

'But he gave that to you.'

'He gave it to me to see you safe home to his relatives.' He winced. 'There isna' verra much left.'

She sighed. 'Samuel was not blessed with the ability to hang on to his coin.'

'Or yours.'

Her smile was brief and pained. 'And what about you? Do you not need the money to continue your journey? It seems once you have answered the duke's questions you will have more than met your obligation. Indeed, the money is yours by right. You must keep it as payment for your service.'

He stiffened. 'I didna' do it for pay.' It was guilt that drove him. But that was something she did not need to know and so he lied. 'The money is yours.' He pulled the pouch from his pocket and held it out to her.

She looked at it for a long moment. 'My honour tells me I should refuse. My need tells me I do not have the luxury of honour.'

The bitterness in her voice struck a painful chord deep in his chest. He knew that feeling only too well. 'You can pay me back, then. When things are settled.'

'I will.' Determination filled her voice. She turned

away, but not before he saw her cheeks flush with embarrassment. At being in debt to him, no doubt.

'I'll light a fire in the kitchen and take care of the horses, then see if I can snare some fresh meat,' he said, as if he had not noticed. 'The Pockles are sure to be here in the morning with our luggage.'

She turned away from the window with a sigh. 'I had hoped they might have arrived before us. I do hope they are not lost.'

Or attacked by the smugglers. He tried to look confident. 'Pockle's travelled the route many times before, winter and summer, he told me so.'

'Let us hope he was telling the truth. The duke might not be pleased if we have somehow mislaid his cousin.'

Drew narrowed his eyes at the thought. Hell, it might even give the duke the excuse he needed to refuse to acknowledge her at all. It seemed nothing about this affair was straightforward. 'If that time comes, I will see to it that he is found.'

'It seems I do nothing but accept your help, Mr Gilvry.' She pressed her lips together for a moment, then released a breath. 'Would you leave if I told you to go?'

'No.'

'Then it seems I have no choice but to accept your assistance. Thank you.'

Feeling very much like an intruder, he turned and clattered down the stairs. 'I'll be back with something for supper.'

What was she going to do? Rowena turned in a circle at the bottom of the stairs, looking at the little house in which she was supposed to live. A house that was hers, yet belonged to the duke. In the middle of nowhere.

She loved the Scottish countryside. The grandeur. The wildness. From a distance. She'd been raised in Edinburgh and lived there all her life. A city full of culture and education. How could she live in a place like this?

She could not. Not for very long, at least. Somehow she would have to find a way to see this reclusive duke and either convince him to honour the settlement left by her husband, if any, or seek another position.

Having come to a decision of how to proceed, she set about dealing with her circumstances. When the Pockles arrived, she would have a change of clothes. In the meantime, if Drew was going to hunt, she was at least going to make the place habitable.

She turned up her sleeves and went into the kitchen, the only warm room in the house, and gazed in disgust at the dust and the dirt. First things first. Water.

She trudged through the snow in the garden to fetch water from the little stream to fill the kettle. Hands on hips, she surveyed the shed, now containing the horses. It was worse close up than it had been from a distance. It was barely good enough for a horse, let alone a man. And so she would tell him. Her heart sank. Perhaps he preferred to be out here, rather than inside with her. Perhaps he feared she would attack him while he slept.

She wouldn't. She wasn't that bold. Not now that she knew he found her unattractive. An antidote. Bad enough to make a husband run off to America.

She sighed. No, he wouldn't stay in the house, even if she begged him. She struggled back to the house.

Very well. She was on her own. An independent woman. Not even the duke could take that away. And if there was some money owed to her from Samuel's will, perhaps she could start her own little school. For girls. Teach them to think for themselves. She blinked. Could she?

A sound at the front door sent her heart leaping in her throat. She ran to the window in the parlour that overlooked the front door.

A short middle-aged man stood on the step, knocking the snow off his boots and looking perfectly respectable. And behind him, at the gate, stood a cart. The man knocked.

Smugglers wouldn't knock. But still her heart raced painfully. The man knocked again and stepped back, looking up at the second storey as if he thought she might be still abed. He must know someone was here given the smoke no doubt issuing from the chimney.

Taking a deep breath, she left the room and hurried to the front door. She pulled it open and stepped back warily. Whoever he was, he might think she had no right to be here.

'Yes?' she said.

The man doffed his hat. His gaze took in the kerchief on her head and the rag in her left hand. 'I am here to see Mrs MacDonald.'

Startled by the use of her name, she stared at him. 'Who are you?'

'Jeffrey Weir. Duke of Mere's steward. To see your mistress, if you please.' She took the card he handed over. The duke's steward. Just the man she wanted to see. And since it seemed unlikely he posed a threat, she gestured for him to enter. 'Come in.'

She led him into the parlour.

He sat down. She followed suit. He frowned as if puzzled.

'I am Mrs MacDonald,' she said.

He popped up from his seat, looking thoroughly discomposed. 'I beg your pardon, madam.'

She raised a brow. 'Who else did you expect to answer the door?'

He swallowed and tugged at his neckcloth. 'Your servant?'

With a theatrical sigh, she glanced around. 'This house hasn't seen a servant in months, if ever. As the duke's steward, you must be aware of that fact.' She really shouldn't be so cruel to the poor man, whose face was now as red as a carnation, but she could not help it. If he was the duke's steward, then it was his responsibility to ensure the house was habitable, surely?

'A couple by the name of Pockle,' he managed to gasp. 'They were to accompany you, I understand.'

'Ah, yes, the Pockles,' she said with a lift of one brow. 'Unfortunately, they became separated from me on the road, where I was subsequently attacked by smugglers and forced to flee in the middle of the night. By the good offices of Mr Gilvry did I escape with my life. Only to arrive at a derelict house.'

'I beg your pardon, ma'am. I had intended to be here several days ago. The duke sent me with supplies, but with the snowstorm…' He gestured vaguely at the window. 'The Pockles…'

'At this moment, I have no clue what has happened to the Pockles.'

He swallowed. 'Mr Samuel—'

'His remains are with them.'

'Yes,' he said hurriedly. 'Yes, of course. But the duke is most anxious to see his cousin appropriately interred, you understand. Most anxious.' He gave her a look askance. 'If it is his cousin.'

She stared at him and narrowed her eyes in a sudden suspicion. Was this what they planned? To find a way to deny that Samuel was really dead? 'Of course it is.'

'The body must be properly identified. To the duke's satisfaction.' He pulled a handkerchief from his pocket and wiped his brow. The man was sweating despite the room being as cold as charity. 'And the date of death properly established.'

The date? Aha. Now they were back to the date. 'Then the sooner I and Mr Gilvry, who knows the date, meet with the duke, the better.'

Sounds emanated from the kitchen. Loud sounds. Drew returning. The steward sent her a questioning look.

Rowena smiled calmly, folding her hands in her lap.

The next moment Drew appeared in the doorway, glowering at her guest. 'Who is this, then?'

'This is the duke's steward, Mr Weir,' she said, 'sent to see if I am pleased with my new accommodations.'

Weir, who had been staring at Drew's face with a kind of fascinated horror, rose to his feet and held out his hand. 'You must be Gilvry.'

Drew looked him up and down with a dismissive expression. 'I hope you have apologised to Mrs MacDonald for the dreadful state of this property. Not a stick of wood or a bite of food in the place. Not to mention the dirt.'

'I...I have indeed begged her pardon,' Weir said in a choking voice. 'I have brought supplies.'

'How long will it take to get to Mere from here?' Drew asked.

'It is a day's journey, on a good day, the roads being what they are. I set out yesterday, but was delayed by the storm.'

'As were we,' Gilvry said in a voice as dry as dust. 'Come on, then, man, let us see what you have. You can give me a hand to unload.'

The steward stiffened. 'I...'

Drew glared at him. Only by dint of will did Rowena stop herself from grinning when the little man seemed to deflate as Drew ushered him out.

Chapter Nine

Something was wrong. Drew could feel it deep in his bones. And in the bitter taste on his tongue.

He stomped out of the front door and made his way to the back of the cart. When he'd heard about the house set aside for her on the ducal estate, he'd assumed it meant a dower house in the grounds, near the duke's abode, not some cottage in the middle of nowhere.

It was almost as if the duke had decided to isolate her from the world. As if she was some sort of dirty secret.

He threw back the tarpaulin. A cage full of chickens fluttered and squawked in panic. His gut fell away as he stared at the rest of the contents. Flour. Salt beef. Ham. A barrel of apples. Winter supplies. And those were the things he could make out at a glance.

He swung around to face Weir, grabbing the man's lapels, bringing him close to his face with a snarl. 'What the hell is going on?'

The steward leaned back, ineffectually batting at Drew's hands. 'How dare you, sir? Release me at once.'

Drew shoved him away. 'Well? Answer my question.'

'I do not take your meaning, Gilvry.'

'I mean,' he said, holding on to his anger, just barely, 'she is the widow of the duke's cousin, damn it. Why is she being treated like some sort of pariah?'

The little man's moustache's bristled. He tugged his coat straight. 'She was Mr MacDonald's responsibility. Not the duke's. She has no official status in the family. He is being more than generous.' He gestured to the house and the cart.

Drew's fingers trembled with the strain of not closing around the other man's throat and squeezing. Hard. 'She's a lady. Is she supposed to raise chickens? Keep a cow? Cook and clean?'

Weir retreated a step. 'The Pockles were hired—'

He snorted his disgust. 'The Pockles. A lazy good-for-naught and his slatternly wife and nowhere to house them decently. I demand that Mrs MacDonald be taken to the duke immediately, as is fitting.'

The little man stiffened. 'Demand, sir? Demand? You are in no position to demand anything. Were you not the man who was present at Mr MacDonald's death? And now the man who sticks like a burr to his widow?' His lip curled. 'And the pair of you giving the Pockles the slip? How many nights is it since the lady had any sort of chaperon?'

Drew's hands curled into fists. Every muscle in his body tensed. 'Are you accusing me of some sort of dishonourable conduct with respect to the lady?'

Weir hesitated, his beady eyes clearly calculating the odds of his escaping with his life. He must have realised they were not good. 'No. Of course not,' he muttered. 'But you must see this from the duke's perspective. A woman who the duke has never heard of arrives, announcing his cousin's demise with the man who said he witnessed the death, and demanding settlement of her affairs. The duke is bound to be cautious. As are his advisors.'

Drew forced his hands to relax. 'The duke owes her the courtesy of speaking to her in person.'

'Perhaps if you and the lady could provide a little more definitive information.' His smile was ingratiating.

'Will her husband's body be definitive enough?'

'Once it is identified it will go part way to easing the duke's concerns.'

Drew smiled, or at least bared his teeth in what might be interpreted as a smile, but clearly was not by Weir, who backed up hard against the cartwheel. 'It can be identified. I ha' made sure of it, if the damned Pockles have not lost the body along the way. Perhaps the duke should be sending out a search party. Does he know there are smugglers using his land for convenient passage?'

'Smugglers?'

'Oh, aye, you know, all right. I can see it in your face. They set upon us at McRae's inn last evening, which is why we have now arrived without the damned Pockles.' A thought occurred to him. His gut clenched. 'We can only hope the Pockles did not encounter them on the road.'

'I doubt smugglers would have any reason to bother a coffin,' the man said a little stiffly.

'Unless that coffin is also a cask full of the best brandy to be found in North Carolina.'

Mr Weir turned green.

Drew glared at him. 'Well, let us get this cart unloaded. We can continue our conversation while we work.'

Rowena watched as Drew piled two sacks onto the steward's outstretched arms. The little man's knees buckled, but he bravely staggered around the back of the house with his burden.

She stared open-mouthed at the crate of chickens Drew pulled off next. Live chickens? Was she supposed to keep them, or eat them? Her only experience of chickens was with a roast or a fricassee presented on a plate on the table. Or paying the butcher's bill.

But without any servants, or money to pay them, she had the horrid feeling she might be learning a whole new way of dealing with them. She glanced down the lane in front of the house, hoping to see the Pockles riding to the rescue.

No. She couldn't rely on anyone else to help her out of this peculiar situation. She must attack the problem head-on. Take on the duke. She ran upstairs and dug around in her saddlebag. Yes, here it was. The tattered remains of her journal and a pencil Samuel had purchased for her as a bride gift. He had one just like it, only his was bound in blue morocco leather, while hers was red.

What had happened to his journal? It might have shed some light on just what her husband had been doing out there in the wilds. It was completely out of character for a man like Samuel, who liked his comforts, to stray from the pleasures offered in town.

She ripped a blank page from the back and looked at the tip of her pencil. A bit blunt, but not completely useless. She sat at the dresser and began to write.

Your Grace,
While we have as yet to meet, I find myself compelled to introduce myself. I am, as you are aware, your cousin by marriage to Samuel MacDonald. It is most important that you grant me an interview at your earliest convenience, to discuss matters that I believe we will find of mutual benefit. I look forward to hearing from you as to when such a meeting will be convenient. If you have not come to see me before the week is out, I shall call on you at your residence.
Respectfully yours...

Once more she raked through the saddlebag and this time located a stub of sealing wax and Samuel's ring.

She took her letter downstairs, heated the wax over the fire until she managed to get a few drops to fall on the fold then pressed the ring into it.

She spun around as Mr Weir entered the kitchen with an arm full of logs, followed by a glowering Drew.

'That's everything,' he said.

'Are there candles?' she asked.

'Aye. I put them in the dresser,' Drew said.

'Excellent.' She turned to Weir. 'I have a letter for you to take back to the duke, if you would be so good.'

The man glanced at Drew and shifted from foot to foot. 'It would be my pleasure, ma'am.'

'If I do not hear back from the duke within a week, do tell him to expect my call,' she said sweetly. 'I am sure Mr Gilvry would be happy to accompany me to the castle.'

A look of panic crossed Weir's face.

She frowned. 'Would that be a problem?'

But the man had already pulled himself together and his face was once more without expression. 'I will give his Grace your message.'

He turned, then realised Drew was standing right behind him. He tried to dodge, but both men stepped in the same direction. Once, twice and a third time. Drew finally took pity on him and stepped aside to let him pass.

'One week, mind,' he said as the man scurried out of the kitchen door.

When she was sure he was out of the house and turning his cart around in the lane, she took a deep breath. 'I don't care what the duke answers. I will not stay here for more than one week.' She paced across the floor to gaze out of the window. Weir and his cart had disappeared. She spun around. 'He queried Sam's date of death.'

'What? Why?'

'It was a passing mention. It is very strange. If only there was something to prove your recollection.'

A shadow passed across his face. 'I'm sorry,' he said.

Her stomach dipped. His expression was wooden. He had thought of something, but it did not suit him to tell her.

He must have seen the doubt in her face because he

grimaced, the movement pulling at the scar on his cheek and making his lip curl more than usual. 'Perhaps the duke will take a man's word without cavilling.'

'I don't think they mean to impugn your honour,' she said. 'It seems to be more a matter of legalities.'

'It is some sort of bureaucratic nonsense, if you want my opinion.' His fingers flexed, then he let out a short breath. 'I know for certain he died on September fifteenth and so I will swear before God and the courts.'

'Then we have to hope it will suffice.'

'Aye.'

Such a wealth of meaning in that one word. Distrust. Regret. Anger. Drew Gilvry was a complex man who had secrets. And he wasn't going to part with them for a mere duke. Or for her. Not unless it suited him. But if he did have some sort of proof of the date, what possible reason could he have for keeping such a thing a secret?

No, her suspicions were groundless. It was wishful thinking that something good could come from all this. She sighed. 'In the meantime, I suppose we must kick our heels until we hear back from the duke.'

'Indeed.'

'Then it is a good thing I gave him an ultimatum.'

'Aye. I suppose it is.' He sounded amused.

She shot him a hard stare. 'Then let us see if we can turn some of those supplies into a decent meal.'

'Oh, I think that can be done, Mrs MacDonald.'

The next afternoon, the Pockles arrived.

Sans the barrel.

'Where is it?' Drew barked at Pockle, looking into the back of the cart.

'That is what I would like to know,' Rowena said, marching down the path. 'I am glad to see you have not lost my luggage, but what have you done with my husband?'

Pockle touched a finger to his forelock. 'We broke a wheel when we were setting out from McRae's. We were only hours behind you, but had to stay until it was repaired.'

She looked down her haughty nose, like a queen observing the lowest of her subjects, and Pockle seemed to shrivel. Drew held his tongue. She didn't need any help from him. Pockle was most definitely cowed.

Mrs Pockle gave her a look of dislike. 'One of the duke's men met us on the road. Mr Weir. He took charge of his Grace's cousin. And glad of it I am.' She shuddered.

Rowena's eyes widened. She glanced at Drew, worry clouding her gaze.

'Why did he do that?' Drew asked.

'He said the duke was anxious to see his cousin's remains decently cared for.'

And if the duke saw fit not to identify them as his cousin? He could see the same thought flickering over Rowena's face.

'I think we should not wait for his Grace to agree to a meeting,' Drew said.

Pockle stared at him. 'What? No. You are to stay here until the duke sends for you. Weir said so.'

'I don't answer to Mr Weir,' Rowena said. 'Or the duke, actually.'

'Och, now, listen here,' Pockle said. 'His Grace is to send his lawyer to visit you. In a day or so.'

Weir had said nothing about sending the lawyer. It was something Weir must have made up on his way to meet the Pockles. Now, why would he do that?

'You mean Mr Jones, I assume,' Rowena said sweetly.

Pockle scratched at his shoulder. 'That's it. That's the name he gave.'

'I already met Mr Jones. The person I have not yet met is his Grace.'

'We will set out first thing in the morning,' Drew said.

Mrs Pockle gave a sort of a wail. 'But we only just got here.'

'You don't have to come with us,' Rowena said.

Pockle glowered. Drew tried to hide a smile as she lifted her chin and the man seemed to crumble.

'There is one thing I wanted to ask you,' Drew said. 'Did you run into a gang of smugglers at McRae's?'

'No,' Pockle said. 'But I heard they attacked the inn. You were lucky you escaped with your lives.'

'Attacked the inn, did they?' Drew said his voice dry. He could imagine McRae covering his own arse in case he or Rowena went to the duke, demanding justice.

'And the one I shot?' Drew asked.

'Dead.'

Drew swallowed a curse, not wanting to worry Rowena, but he had the feeling that he wouldn't have heard the last of the smugglers if he'd killed one of their number. Something else to lay at his brother's door.

'Did McRae say anything else?' he asked. Such as he'd slept in Rowena's chamber?

'He said he was sorry it happened under his roof,' Pockle said, his eyes innocent of any slyness. 'He asked me to apologise. To say he would not have had the lady so inconvenienced for the world and so he would tell the duke if need be.'

And if Rowena didn't blame him for what happened, no doubt he would say nothing about their pretence to be a married couple.

He noticed Rowena eyeing her bag with eagerness. He could imagine why. The poor lass hadn't had a change of clothes in days. He lifted it down and carried it into the house.

'Don't bother carrying it upstairs,' she said, following him in, 'since we will be carrying it out again tomorrow.'

'It is no trouble, madam,' he said, and marched upstairs.

'And where do I sleep?' he could hear Mrs Pockle asking Rowena.

'There is another bedroom at the back,' she replied. 'Pockle will join Mr Gilvry in the stables until we can make a better arrangement. It is something I mean to take up with the duke.'

He grinned at the sound of Pockle's groan of displeasure. But it made a point: that he had not been sleeping in the same house as a woman on her own. Whether the Pockles would believe it was another matter, but since he had made his bed out there last night and the evidence was quite plain to be seen, there was no reason for them not to believe it.

And having Pockle for company, much as he despised the man, would keep him from succumbing to the temptation he'd barely resisted the previous night. Not that he expected Rowena would welcome his company.

He dropped the bag on the floor and could not help from glancing at the bed, the covers neatly straightened as if no one had slept there.

All last night he had kept envisaging the way she had surrendered to his uncouth demands. How she had submitted to his rampant lust. His blood ran hot. And then he remembered the shame on her face. The embarrassment. His blood chilled as if he had stepped neck deep into the stream in the garden.

Thank goodness they were leaving tomorrow. Once under the duke's roof there would be no further opportunities for temptation.

If he felt disappointment at the thought, it was because his inner beast had no conscience. But he did. And the weight of it was a heavy burden. He made his way downstairs.

Rowena, with a grumpy-looking Mrs Pockle, met him at the bottom. He gave the servant a hard look. 'Mrs MacDonald will be needing hot water to bathe and a change of clothes.'

He bowed to Rowena. 'If it is all right with you, I will go and see if my traps have resulted in fresh meat. Hopefully, Mrs Pockle can make stew for dinner. Or perhaps a nice rabbit pie.'

'That would be wonderful,' Rowena said.

Mrs Pockle looked as if she wanted to hit Drew over the head. He made good his escape before she found a rolling pin.

Pockle drained his tankard of small beer and leaned back in his chair, folding his hands over his belly. 'Very nice, Mrs Pockle,' he said.

Drew's traps had yielded up some game and, with the supplies Weir had dropped off and the surprisingly excellent cooking skills of Mrs Pockle, he had to admit dinner was excellent.

Rowena was dining in solitary state in the parlour, while he and the Pockles ate in the warm, if somewhat overcrowded, kitchen.

'Yes,' Drew said. 'Excellent meal. My compliments, Mrs Pockle.' He drained his own tankard and pushed his chair back.

'A moment afore you go, Mr Gilvry,' Pockle said.

'Yes?'

'You and Mrs MacDonald seem to have a pretty good understanding.'

Drew stiffened. 'What do you imply?'

Pockle blinked. 'Why, naught but to say that she seems to take your advice. Can I suggest that you advise her to wait here at the duke's pleasure? It is not a good thing to go upsetting a duke, ye ken.'

It was definitely a warning. Likely something cooked up between the Pockles while he was out in the woods, no doubt. 'You think he will turn her away from his door?'

Pockle leaned forward. 'He's a duke. Who knows

what he will do? But Mr Weir's instructions were very clear. It won't do her any good to set his Grace against her, now will it?'

'Do you know why he would not want to receive a visit from Mrs MacDonald?'

Pockle rolled his eyes. 'Dukes don't confide in the likes of me.' He picked up his tankard and looked into the bottom of it, clearly hoping it wasn't empty. He put it down again with a sigh when he was wrong. 'All I'm sayin' is that Mr Weir made his orders very clear.'

'And you want me to speak to Mrs MacDonald about it.'

Mrs Pockle nodded her head vigorously. 'She won't listen to us, but she might listen to you.'

'Not if her mind is made up.' Still, it would be an opportunity to talk over their strategy for the morrow in private. 'Verra well. I'll talk to her.'

'You do that, lad,' Pockle said.

Ignoring the urge to shove the word *lad* down the other man's throat, Drew got up from the table. He closed the kitchen door behind him and strode into the parlour.

Rowena had made little of the meal he saw and was now seated beside the hearth.

'You should eat more,' he said.

When she looked up, her gaze was bleak. 'I'm worried about tomorrow.'

And there wasn't much he could say to ease her concern. 'Do you think we should wait? You did give the duke a week to respond.'

'Is that your advice?'

He shook his head. 'There is something havey-cavey

going on.' He raised a hand. 'I know. I am not being completely helpful. Still, it seems odd to me that Weir did not inform you that Jones was to pay you a visit. It was almost as if he thought it up on the way to find Pockle.'

Some of the worry left her face. 'You thought that, too?'

'I did.' He went to the door and looked down the hall-way. The kitchen door remained closed. 'I think attack is the best form of defence. And surprise will give you an advantage.'

'Then it's settled.' She rose to her feet. She was wear-ing the same gown she'd been wearing the first time he saw her. She'd looked so calm that evening. So con-trolled. So much in command. It was hard to put that side of her together with the woman who had subjugated herself to his dark desires.

He wanted to apologise. Beg forgiveness. To do so would be a lie. Because if he had the chance, he would do it all over again.

Chapter Ten

Castle was a complete misnomer, Rowena thought as the cart rocked its way up the long drive. Yes, off to the right there were some ruins that might have been a castle once, long ago. The ducal residence was in fact a grand mansion built some time in the late seventeenth century that had somehow survived the wars between England and Scotland.

Its walls were grim and grey, as was the statuary decorating the corners and niches across its face. It had a slightly shabby look about it. Imposing, yes, but here and there brickwork showed through the stuccoed facade. And some of the statues were missing an arm or a bit of their drapery.

A place like this would be enormously expensive to keep up.

'Have you been here before?' she asked Mrs Pockle seated beside her on the cart. Drew and Pockle rode either side of them, like an honour guard.

The woman nodded. 'My family lived on the estate. So did Pockle's, but ne'er did I expect to go inside the house.'

She might not enter upon this occasion either, if the duke turned them away at the door. Rowena glanced down at her clothing. She'd worn her second-best gown and spencer. Fortunately, a governess wore subdued practical colours and dark grey was very nearly appropriate for mourning. They halted outside the front door. Drew helped her down from the cart. She eyed the imposing entrance askance. No sense in hesitating. She squared her shoulders and walked towards the front door.

Drew kept pace. As usual he wore Samuel's coats and linen as well as snug-fitting doeskin breeches, and his boots were polished to a high shine that did not hide that they were neither new nor in the first stare of fashion.

But for all that the greatcoat was too tight across his shoulders and chest, he looked remarkably handsome. And to his surprise, she had told him so before they left.

He'd touched his cheek and she'd shaken her head. 'I hardly notice it, you know,' she had said. An odd look had softened his usually harsh expression, but he had turned away before she could interpret it.

Now he strode at her side, looking grimly purposeful, as if preparing to fight a dragon on her behalf. How could she not feel safe with such a strong, commanding man at her side? Yet it would not do to rely on him too much. He had made it quite clear he intended to hand off his responsibility for her at the earliest opportunity.

He rapped on the monstrous wooden door.

It creaked open, loudly proclaiming it needed oil. Something a good housekeeper would never allow.

An elderly footman looked at them with enquiry.

'Mrs MacDonald to see the duke,' Drew proclaimed and handed him her calling card. Or rather the card she had created from a flyleaf at the back of her woebegone journal.

With a muttered, 'Wait here,' the man shut the door in their faces.

Rowena raised a brow and looked at Drew.

He shrugged. 'He didna' say go away.'

So they waited. After five minutes, Rowena wondered if she should ask Drew to knock again.

She opened her mouth to do so, but the door once more protested on its hinges and swung inwards. This time, a butler stood at attention, wearing a black frock coat and a severe expression.

'You are to come in,' he said, and gestured for her to enter.

Relief slid down her spine in a whisper. It seemed the duke was not as unreasonable as his minions seemed to indicate. She stepped over the threshold and Drew followed her in. The butler, a man well into his sixties, with a few grey hairs pasted to his bald pate, took their coats. He looked at Drew and then at her. 'Who else shall I say is calling, madam?'

'This is Mr Gilvry, my man of business. Mr Jones is acquainted with him.'

'Will you send someone to see to the horses?' Drew requested. 'And Mrs MacDonald's driver and maid.'

The butler bowed. 'Yes, sir.' He walked to one of the doors leading off the great hall and opened it. 'If you would wait here? I will inform her ladyship.'

'Are you speaking of the duchess?' Rowena asked.

'Lady Cragg, madam.'

'We wish to see the duke,' Drew said.

'The duke is indisposed.' He whisked away before they could ask more questions.

'I have no idea who Lady Cragg might be,' she said to Drew.

'Nor I. It is not a name I have heard on anyone's lips before now.'

'It seems odd that the duke would send someone who is not a family member to receive me.'

'She could be a cousin. Or a companion to the duchess.'

Rowena frowned. 'Is there a duchess? I wish I had been able to look him up in *Debrett's*. Indeed, I should have thought to do so before we left Dundee. It just didn't occur to me.'

The sound of quick, sharp footsteps on marble echoed in the great hall on the other side of the door. 'I suspect all is about to be revealed,' Drew said.

'Dear Mrs MacDonald, it is my pleasure to welcome to you to Mere, despite the sadness of the times.'

The woman who entered, holding out her hands and offering a gentle smile to Rowena, was in her sixties, with crimped grey hair beneath a black lace cap. She was wearing deep mourning. For the recently departed duke? She was followed in by Jones, the lawyer. He must have set out for Mere at the same time they had. Why had he lied about going to Edinburgh?

'Thank you,' Rowena said, clearly taken aback by the effusive welcome as she let the woman take both her hands in hers, but her frowning gaze had fixed upon Mr Jones, who bowed and smirked.

'I am Lady Cragg,' the other woman said. 'Also a distant relation to your poor husband. You know Mr Jones, of course. Please, do sit down.'

Rowena sank into the offered chair. The woman looked pointedly at Drew and then recoiled as she took in his face. He should have worn his scarf. Her gaze wandered over his too-small coats and shabby boots, and her lip curled in a sneer. He met her gaze with a glower. 'Andrew Gilvry, my lady. At your service.' He bowed.

'Please, do be seated, Mr Gilvry.'

This was a woman very much used to obedience and a woman very much in command of the situation. A strange prickle ran across the back of his neck.

Drew sat to the right and a little behind Rowena, offering his support, but making it clear she was in charge. After pulling the bell rope, Mr Jones sat on a gilt chair a few feet from Drew.

'I wish to speak to his Grace,' Rowena said, gathering herself once more.

'Sadly, he is indisposed,' Lady Cragg said calmly. 'He was laid low by the death of the late duke, and I, as his only living relative, am charged with looking after his affairs until his doctor indicates he is well enough to face the world.'

Rowena frowned. 'I understood that there was no direct heir to the dukedom. That there were some doubts—'

'All doubts have been resolved,' Mr Jones said. 'Even now the late duke's will is in probate.'

'That is the reason I wish to see the duke. I understand that my husband, Mr Samuel MacDonald, left the duke as executor to his will. So far, Mr Jones has been able to give me very little information about my husband's financial affairs. While the duke is kind to provide me with a house, I really prefer my independence. So I have come to sort out my affairs.'

Nothing like attacking a problem head-on, Drew thought with admiration.

'I understand your anxiety, Mrs MacDonald. Indeed I do. You must understand there have been many petitioners coming forward seeking financial redress of the duke. A most distressing time for all. Clearly as family, you have more claim than most, hence the offer of a house until matters could be resolved. Am I to understand that you are rejecting the duke's largesse?'

Drew looked to see how Rowena would receive what was obviously a reprimand. Her face was pale and her expression worried. His anger pushed to the fore. 'Mrs MacDonald has no wish to discommode anyone, Lady Cragg,' he said. 'But the house is most unsuitable for a widow of her standing. Not only is it in the middle of nowhere, but it is practically in ruins.'

It was pushing it a bit, but he could not sit by and see her bullied.

Lady Cragg turned her gaze on Drew. While her smile was pleasant enough the brown eyes were shrewd and calculating. 'Ah, yes. I understand from Mr Jones that you are the man who brought Mr Samuel back to Scotland and that you are acting as Mrs MacDonald's man of affairs.'

She made it sound sordid. Had the Pockles said something to Weir about them spending a night together alone after all? He glared at her. 'I am. And it seems to me, that as a member of Mere's family—'

'Your defence of your client is commendable, Mr Gilvry,' Lady Cragg said. 'And I wholeheartedly agree with your sentiments. I don't know what Mr Weir was thinking when he suggested that cottage. Likely it was the only vacant property available. I was appalled at Weir's description when he returned yesterday. You must understand that our lives have been at sixes and sevens here at Mere for some weeks now.' She bowed her head slightly. 'I apologise for his mistake.' Her smile was tight and a little forced. 'Please, Mrs MacDonald, do forgive us, and may I welcome you to reside at Mere Castle until the duke is able to meet with you. You may be sure that appropriate arrangements will be made for your future. The duke is not one to avoid his obligations.'

That took the wind out of their sails to be sure and the worry out of Rowena's face. 'You are very kind,' she said.

It was just too easy. 'What sort of arrangements?' Drew asked.

The gimlet eyes returned to his face and she visibly repressed a shudder of distaste. 'I do not believe Mrs MacDonald will require your services any longer, Mr Gilvry. The remains have been identified as Mr Samuel MacDonald's. Mr Jones is undertaking the probate of his will along with that of the duke's...' She frowned. 'You are not a lawyer, I understand?'

'No, I am no' a lawyer,' he said. 'I stand as a friend and an advisor—'

'I am sure Mrs MacDonald will be more than happy to leave legal matters in Mr Jones's capable hands?' She looked at Rowena, who in turn looked at Drew.

'What about the matter of the date of Mr MacDonald's death? There has been some importance placed on this issue in our conversation with Mr Jones. And with Mr Weir.'

Lady Cragg waved a dismissive hand. 'Mr Jones was following my instructions, I am afraid. Our concern was the interment, the carving of the stone. A date is required.'

He glanced at Rowena, who was looking at her open-mouthed. 'I gave Mr Jones the date. He said he needed proof.'

Lady Cragg raised her iron-grey brows at Mr Jones, who gave a little cough behind his hand. 'A misunderstanding, I'm afraid. I was confusing the date with that of the duke. A most unfortunate lapse. I do apologise. Your word is not being questioned.'

He gaped at the smarmy young man, who shrugged.

'May I have a moment alone with Mrs MacDonald?' Drew asked.

'Certainly,' Lady Cragg said. 'I will arrange for tea to be served in the parlour, Mrs MacDonald. Ring for a footman to show you the way when you are done here. Mr Gilvry, you have been of great service to our family. You will attend Mr Jones in his office when you are ready to leave and you will be recompensed as is only right.'

She got up and swept out.

Jones bowed to Rowena. He looked at Drew. 'I will wait outside in the hall.' He also withdrew.

Drew frowned. 'They seem very…accommodating.'

Rowena rose to her feet and paced around the room. 'Almost a complete about-face.' She looked at him. 'Do you think I should trust them? Lady Cragg seems very nice. Very open. The date is no longer an issue and they are my husband's family…'

Did being family make Lady Cragg worthy of trust? He wouldn't trust his own family. Not anymore. But his responsibility ended here. He had done what he set out to do and they were accepting his verbal account. 'If you feel comfortable, then it seems my presence is no longer required.'

She took a deep breath and gave him a smile that was gentle and quite endearing. 'I do thank you for your help. And your patience.' She coloured and looked away. 'Perhaps, once this is settled and I have returned to Edinburgh, you might wish to call.'

Stunned, he stared at her. He had not expected her to wish to continue their acquaintance, not after the way he had treated her. His heart gave an odd little lurch. A pang of longing. Desire heated his blood.

But when he left here, he was going to seek out Ian. And once he found him, he wouldn't have a future. 'I don't think—'

'No. No, of course not. You have your own affairs to consider. It was foolish of me to ask.'

Now, why the hell did she sound so embarrassed? And even a little distraught.

She held out her hand. 'Then I must wish you good-bye, Mr Gilvry. And thank you for all your help.'

He bowed over her hand. 'My pleasure, Mrs Mac-Donald.'

An empty space filled his chest and, with a sense that he was leaving something very precious, he strode out quickly, in case he did what he really wanted to and disgraced her before her family by taking her lovely mouth in a punishing kiss.

Feeling strangely hollow, he found Jones waiting in the corridor outside the drawing room, too far away for him to have been listening to the conversation inside the room, yet he looked relieved when Drew appeared, as if he had not been sure of the outcome of his discussions with Rowena.

Was there some meaning to that worry?

'This way,' Jones said. 'We'll go to my office in the east wing.'

He followed the lawyer along a series of passages and down a flight of stairs. The office he entered was small, with a window overlooking the stables. Its shelves were lined with law books and ledgers.

Jones pulled out a metal box from the bottom drawer of a plain wooden desk and unlocked it with a key from the chain attached to his fob. He drew out of it a leather pouch that landed on the table with a heavy thump. 'For your trouble. There's enough gold here to carry you far from here. Back to America if you wish.'

Drew's jaw dropped. 'What the devil is this for?'

'Your reward for bringing Mr Samuel home.'

Guilt was a sour taste in his mouth. 'I need no payment for doing my duty.'

'Then take it as payment for your discretion.'

If Drew had been uneasy before, something in his head was sending messages of alarm. 'Mrs MacDonald—'

'She is no longer your concern. You can hardly expect Mere's relative to acknowledge any sort of connection with the Gilvrys of Dunross.' Jones gave him a narrow-eyed stare. 'Any sort of connection.'

A warning. That Rowena was above his touch. Weir or Pockle must have given voice to suspicions. Jones was buying him off. 'Stuff it,' he said crudely.

Jones looked startled, then shrugged. 'As you wish.' He swept up the pouch and locked it away again. 'I'll have a footman see you out.' He reached out and pulled at the bell on the wall behind him. The liveried footman had clearly been waiting nearby, since he appeared almost immediately. 'Good day, Mr Gilvry. Jeremiah, please escort Mr Gilvry to the stables.' He gave Drew a look that contained an element of triumph. 'You will find your horse ready and waiting.'

He walked out.

Outside in the corridor, another footman was also waiting. He fell in behind Drew as he followed Jeremiah out of the house and across the stable yard. They weren't taking any chances. What, did they think he would steal the silver?

Not that a couple of pampered footman could stop him if he decided he wanted the silver. But he didn't. He just wanted to be on his way. To be rid of the sickening emptiness in his gut that accompanied the understanding he would never see Rowena again. He recognised the feeling. Loss.

He'd had the same one when he'd said goodbye to his family six years before. And again when he'd realised just how permanent Ian had intended that parting to be. Well, Ian was in for a shock. And it would give Drew a good deal of satisfaction to see it in his brother's face when he met his end.

He mounted up and his escort saw him out of the gate.

He focused his mind on the form that shock would take and not on the distance he was putting between himself and Mere Castle.

The suite of rooms assigned to Rowena were at the far end of the west wing. They were sumptuous indeed. A sitting room adjoined the bedchamber to which was also attached a dressing room with a truckle bed for her maid.

Luxury, indeed. She had not lived in such fine surroundings since she'd left her father's house after his death.

'I hope you have found Pockle to your satisfaction,' Lady Cragg enquired after showing her around her apartments. 'She is the only maid I have available at the moment. We keep minimal staff here at Mere.'

'I can't say I have had much of an opportunity to judge,' Rowena replied. 'We were separated from the Pockles after the first night of our journey.'

'Separated?' Lady Cragg's voice rose in shock. 'You were left alone?'

'No. Mr Gilvry was with me.' She blushed at the sight of the other woman's horrified countenance.

'Oh, my dear.' Lady Cragg's voice faded. 'Think of your reputation. Of Mere's good name. Never speak of it again.'

'Very well,' Rowena said. 'But—'

Lady Cragg raised a hand. 'Pockle tells me you do not have attire suitable for mourning. It must be attended to at once. We should not wish to show any lack of respect, either for your husband, or the duke, should we?'

'Certainly not,' Rowena said, as expected.

'In the meantime, you will keep to your rooms if you do not mind. We have guests at Mere who would be shocked if... Well, you do understand, do you not?'

The question was purely rhetorical.

Lady Cragg smiled. 'In the meantime, do, my dear Mrs MacDonald, make yourself comfortable. I am sure you need to rest after your journey. I will have supper sent up to you later.'

'When will I meet the duke?'

The woman paused, her expression altering into lines of sorrow. 'The duke is much affected by all the bad news. Prostrate upon his bed. Perhaps when you are appropriately gowned? Believe me, you will see him at the earliest opportunity.'

She bustled out.

Rowena sat down in the armchair beside the window that looked out over the formal grounds. To her surprise, a small boy of about five, bundled against the chilly air, was skipping along one of the walkways trailed by what she could only assume was a nurse. The duke's child? Or perhaps he belonged to one of the visitors. The nurse caught him and swung him around before carrying him out of sight.

Rowena stared at the long drive leading out to the gate. No sign of Drew. He would be long gone by now. She would have liked to have discussed in more detail his impressions of Lady Cragg and the duke's household. For example, why was Lady Cragg so evasive? So set on her having gowns made before she saw the duke? Still, it was no secret that the grandest families set a great deal of store by the proprieties and she certainly didn't want to do anything that would set up the duke's back. Not before she had a chance to air her concerns.

But she was going to miss Drew. Both his company and, if she was honest, the unbelievable pleasure she had experienced only once.

She closed her eyes to ward off the pain she felt around her heart. Because it was nonsense.

Someone was watching him. He could feel their gaze like a knife piercing a layer of skin between his shoulder blades.

It wasn't the first time he had been hunted.

And his discomfort had nothing to do with the regret he'd felt at leaving Rowena; that was a hollow ache in his chest. It would fade. Eventually. And besides, he wouldn't have to suffer it long, once he carried out his intent.

But this other sensation was annoying. The sensation of being watched by a predator. And since there were neither bears nor wolves nor large cats in Scotland, there was only one other alternative. Men.

He rose up in his saddle and looked about. Hills and rocks, scattered pine trees, clumps of gorse rising from the snow. All could serve to hide a man who did not wish to be seen. Footpads? One look at his nag and mean dress and no self-respecting thief would be interested in such poor pickings.

Though there were a great many in poorer case than he was. He'd seen that in the streets of Dundee. But his size and obvious strength should act as a deterrent. And if it did not, he had his pistol.

Something rustled in the gorse off to his right.

He brought his horse's head around to face the danger as his right hand went for the pistol in the holster on his saddle. His heart hammered a warning in his chest. His gaze narrowed, inspecting the gorse for signs of movement, then wandered up the hillside to the line of trees not far distant. Holding the horse steady with his knees, he slowly undid his coat buttons for ease of access to his knife.

Nothing.

He turned to continue down the road. A man stood in the road five yards ahead, a rifle levelled.

A man he recognised. One of McRae's smuggler friends, the one he had thought of as their leader, Morris.

The rifle barrel jerked. 'Get off the horse,' the smuggler called out.

Drew weighed the odds of riding away without taking a bullet. Not good. Not with a rifle, if the man knew how to use it. He swung down out of the saddle and put his hands up.

More men rose up from behind the gorse and heather

on each side of him, their pistols cocked and levelled. It seemed he'd made the right choice.

Drew cursed as the men closed in on him.

Morris wagged the rifle and grinned. 'Now, there's blasphemy for you.'

'I've verra little coin,' Drew said. 'And only the clothes on my back and the horse. It's no' a verra good horse, but you are welcome to it.'

'It's not what you have that McKenzie cares about. It's what you Gilvrys already cost him.'

Drew gave him a level stare. 'You've got the wrong man.'

'Edinburgh. O'Banyon,' the man said, as if those two words held all the information he needed.

Ian. It had to be some underhanded dealing his brother was involved in. 'I've not been in Edinburgh in six years. I have never heard of O'Banyon.' He started lowering his hands.

'Hands up,' the man said. 'Take his pistol,' he ordered.

One of the other men sidled up to him and took his gun. Drew dropped his hands and let them hang loose at his sides, aware of the knife nestled against his spine beneath his shirt.

'There's also the matter of Geordie.'

At Drew's blank look, he grinned, revealing two missing teeth. 'The man you killed at McRae's.'

'You don't blame a man for defending his lady, surely?'

'Your lady, is she? Then, where is she now?'

He gritted his teeth. Of course, Rowena wasn't his in

the sense the smuggler meant. 'She employed me to see her safe to her destination. And I have.'

'Sandy, take charge of that there sad-looking beastie. You—' he grinned at Drew '—start walking. That way.' He pointed up the steep valley side. 'It seems there's more than McKenzie who wants a slice of your hide. And is willing to pay handsomely for it, too.'

'More than one? Who would the other be, then?'

The man shook his head. 'Not your business, my lad. On ye go.'

Could Ian have heard about his return? It was possible. Did that mean his brother intended to finish the job he had started six years ago?

The next morning the skies over Mere were clear. Having nothing to do while she waited for her new clothes, and needing some fresh air, Rowena slipped down the servants' stairs and out into the gardens. As long as she avoided any guests, who were unlikely to be abroad at so early an hour, she couldn't see how a walk in the grounds could cause any problem. Since her cloak was black, she wouldn't be offending anyone's sensibilities even if she was to encounter someone.

And if she just happened to run into the duke, that would not be such a bad thing. If only she knew what he looked like.

According to Pockle, the park stretched for miles, but since it was covered in snow, Rowena confined herself to the formal gardens she had seen from her window.

She toured the rose garden, laid out with fine gravel walks between the beds. Not that there were any flowers or leaves to be seen. It was simply a matter of stretching her legs and getting some fresh air into her lungs. It was something she always insisted on for her pupils, winter and summer.

As she turned a corner of the leafless hedges that formed a maze, she saw two men deep in discussion in the parterre. Mr Jones and someone she did not recognise. The duke? If she could be sure it was he, then she might consider approaching him, but if it was not the duke, it would be highly embarrassing. And Mr Jones would have no hesitation in reporting her to Lady Cragg.

The men were deep in conversation and had not noticed her. It would be rude to interrupt, so she slipped into the maze where she found a stone bench. She would sit here until they were gone and then return to her room.

The sound of footsteps crunching on the gravel on the other side of the hedge brought her to her feet.

'He seemed a decent enough man,' Mr Jones's voice said.

She should not be listening. It was extremely rude. She started to move deeper into the maze, away from the men.

'A pity about the scar, though.'

They were talking about Drew. She couldn't help it; she stopped to listen.

'His face won't matter where he's going,' another voice said. A deep voice with a strong Highland burr. 'You are sure McKenzie's men have him?'

'They do, my lord,' Jones said. 'I spoke to their leader this morning.'

'They know they are to take him to Edinburgh and

put him on the convict ship leaving for Botany Bay next week? He survived my efforts to be rid of him once. He won't do so again. They are to let McKenzie know he's to leave the rest of them to me.'

Who did he mean by the rest of them?

'And Mrs MacDonald?' Mr Jones asked.

Rowena stifled a gasp with her gloved hand. She tip-toed closer to the hedge, which despite its lack of leaves was tangled and woven and so wide she could not see either man with any clarity.

'I've already advised Lady Cragg on the matter. Get her married off to a relative of Mere's and furnish him with a nice competence. I'll provide the land in America. There can be no possible objection to such generosity.'

Really? No objection?

The sound of gloved hands rubbing together filtered through the hedge. 'With all legal concerns put to rest, I'll expect those who owe allegiance to Mere to support me against Gordon, when he speaks in the House in the new year.'

'Have no fear of that, my lord.'

What legal concerns was he talking about? What possible harm could she do to a duke? The footsteps crunched away. Rowena sat down to wait until she was sure they had gone.

Marry her off? Send her to America? Why on earth would they think they needed to do that? All she was asking for was what was rightfully hers, so she could go about her business. Indeed, she wasn't even sure there was anything left from her husband's estate. Who was this other man who had spoken with such authority, dishing out orders as if he was in charge? At first she'd thought he must be the duke. But Mr Jones had called him my lord, not your Grace.

But she could not worry about that now, not when she knew the smugglers had captured Drew. She had to find him before they put him on board a ship bound for Australia.

Chapter Eleven

When she got upstairs to her room there was no sign of Pockle. Just as well given her plan for immediate departure. She picked up her reticule with its few coins and changed into a pair of sturdy shoes. She looked regretfully at her valise. Anyone seeing her with that would guess at what she was doing and she had the feeling that letting them know she was leaving might be a bad idea.

Reluctantly, she removed her cloak and hoped she'd be warm enough in her riding habit. When she opened the door a footman was standing outside.

'Can I help you?' he asked.

Shocked, she stared at him. 'I…er… Yes, do you think you could direct me to the library?'

'Certainly, madam.'

She ignored his unspoken question. It was none of his business if she was bored and wanted a book to read. 'Please, lead the way.'

He set off down the hallway and she followed along. They went down one flight of stairs, which brought them to the first-floor landing. He opened a set of double doors. 'The library, madam.'

She stepped inside. 'Thank you. That will be all.'

'I'll have Arthur let Mrs Pockle know where you are, shall I, madam? She was in a bit of a taking when she discovered you were not in your room. Luckily one of the gardeners saw you taking the air and was able to set her mind at rest.'

So that was why they had posted a footman outside her door. 'Thank you. Have him tell her I will expect at least one of the gowns to be ready by noon.' Hopefully that would keep her plying her needle instead of checking up on Rowena's whereabouts.

The footman went out and she heard him conversing with one of his fellows in the hallway. Was it normal for ducal footmen to follow guests around? Or was it something they were doing especially for her? It would make slipping away far more difficult, but then she supposed that was their purpose.

She went to the door and, as she suspected, her footman was standing just outside. 'Can I help you, madam?' he asked politely.

'Oh, no, thank you. I am just going to close the door to keep out the draught.' She swung the door shut and eyed the key. Should she lock it? He would hear her do so and that might make him suspicious.

She hurried over to the window and looked out. The library overlooked the back of the house. Beyond the balcony and down a set of stone steps was a large expanse of lawn. Off to the right she could make out the gardens where she had walked earlier. And to the left the stables.

There was no one in sight.

She ran to the shelves and pulled a book at random. If anyone came in she wanted to be ready with her excuse. Then she went to one of the French windows leading out to the balcony. After a bit of a struggle with the latch, she managed to get it open. She shivered in the cold blast of air. She waited to see if the footman noticed anything and decided to take a look.

Nothing.

Drawing a deep breath, she stepped outside on the balcony, and, preferring not to know if anyone was watching from the windows, she walked briskly to the stables as if she had every right. With each step, she expected to hear a cry of alarm, until finally she entered the building.

The smell of sweet hay, manure and warm horse filled the air. Now to find the beast she brought with her. To her surprise, there was a horse saddled and waiting. Not her horse, though. A big chestnut gelding. The groom must have readied it for one of the guests and then gone off on another errand.

Hanging on a peg nearby was a rather ratty-looking frieze coat and an old battered hat. Belonging to one of the grooms, she supposed. Just what she needed to keep her warm. She slipped the coat on and after a moment's hesitation put the hat on, too.

'Caleb,' a rough voice shouted down the length of the stables, 'get a move on. Her ladyship won't be best pleased if she's ready to go riding and that horse be misbehavin' for want of a run.'

Lady Cragg's horse, then. She touched a hand to

her hat, hopped up on the mounting block and climbed aboard. Would the groom giving the orders notice her skirt? She glanced his way, but he had already disappeared back into one of the stalls.

Praying her luck would hold, she rode out of the stables and headed for the gates at a canter. She didn't dare look back to see if she was pursued, but she couldn't help straining her ears for a shout. It wouldn't be long before Caleb returned and discovered the horse missing.

Wind whipping her cheeks, her breath rising in front of her face, she dashed through the gates and out into the road, where she turned the horse in a circle. Which way?

Well, she'd come from Dundee and it lay to the right. Ergo, Edinburgh lay in the opposite direction.

She put her heels to the horse and set off.

As a lad, Drew had spent many nights outdoors in the Highlands and thought nothing of it. But it wasn't the cold that had his nerves stretched to their limit. It was his anger at being hog-tied for the second night in a row.

Last night their leader had left him in a small cave in the hillside while he went off to confer with someone he called the chief. He'd come back and announced they were headed for Edinburgh. Away from Dunross. Completely the wrong direction as far as Drew was concerned. But he'd said not a word. All day, as they'd walked parallel to the road, he'd done his best to allay any fear they might have that he'd run, and they'd still tied him hand and foot.

One of the men got up from the fire and kicked him in the ribs.

Drew grunted at the pain and cursed him foully.

The man grinned, his teeth gleaming red in the light of a fire too far away for Drew to feel much of its warmth.

'Tha's for the merry chase you led us in Edinburgh.'

'I told you. You've got the wrong man. I haven't been to Edinburgh in six years.'

'I'd know that face anywhere. It cost us a lot of money, even if it did get all scarred up.'

'The scar is old, you fool. The man you met was my brother Logan.'

'Brother, is it? Well, one Gilvry is just as good as another.' He drew his foot back.

Morris, the leader of the ruffians looked up. 'Leave him be, Sandy. Break his ribs and you'll be carrying him tomorrow.'

'Why don't we just kill him and leave him here?' his tormentor asked.

'Because that's not what we are being paid to do,' the leader said, getting up from the fire and pulling a brand from the flames.

He sauntered the few feet to where Drew was lying on a blanket on top of hard-packed snow. He held the brand high. The warmth of it on Drew's face was welcome even if it destroyed his vision for the moment.

'It's not the same Gilvry,' he pronounced. 'He's older. Darker skinned. And the scar has been there a very long time. Now get back to the fire, Sandy, and leave him be.'

Sandy stomped off.

Morris crouched down. 'So what is your name, Gilvry?'

Surprised, Drew looked at his unshaven face and dark eyes and saw pity. He forced himself not to react. 'Andrew. They call me Drew.'

'Never heard mention of you. I thought there was only three Gilvry brothers.'

A pang twisted in his chest. Dead and forgotten, then. His rage against Ian sparked to life. But that was no one's business but his own. 'I've had naught to do with any of them of six years. I've no love for my brothers and mean no harm to you or McKenzie.'

'I suppose you think I should let you go?'

'There is no reason you should not.'

'Sorry, laddie. That's not what I've been told. But even though you shot one of my men back at the inn, I've no quarrel with you. We both did what we were paid to do.' He bent down and cut the rope around Drew's ankles. 'Come closer to the fire. There's no sense in having you frozen by morning.' He untied his hands from behind him and tied them loosely in front.

'You mean you want to ride the horse, rather than have it carry my lifeless body,' Drew said.

The man chuckled. 'Smart lad.' He helped Drew to his feet, picked up the blanket and rolled it, before setting it down near the fire. 'Sit there and Sandy will give you some bread and cheese to fill your belly and a mug of tea to warm you.'

'Thank you,' Drew said. He'd have preferred to hit him over the head, but that wasn't going to get him anywhere. Having his bonds a little less tight did, however, give him a huge advantage for when it was time to leave.

The tin mug warmed his palms and he let the heat

steep into his skin before putting it down to eat the bread and cheese that Sandy had tossed into his lap. It had been a long day of walking, but he was used to rough going. He picked up the mug to take a drink and Morris leaned forward and splashed a drop of whisky into it from a flask. 'That'll help keep you warm.'

'Thanks,' Drew said and meant it. 'I'm sorry about what happened to your friend.'

'He was an idiot. He could have killed you or the woman, and that was against our orders.'

They'd been lying in wait for them? Drew tried not to show his shock. Or his fear for Rowena. 'Whose orders?'

Morris chuckled wryly. 'Everyone's.'

'My, I am a popular fellow.'

Damn it all. He thought he'd left Rowena safe with her family. This didn't sound good. He and this group of ruffians would have to part company, and soon. Thank goodness for the knife he had hidden away in his boot when they were sleeping.

The other man jerked his chin. 'How did you come by such a nasty scar, lad? Properly put paid to those good looks of yours.' Drew felt an echo of the old pain he'd felt when he first saw the results of the near miss. It hadn't been a physical pain, but something much deeper and more permanent. And it had been nowhere near as bad as it was now. Just to torment him, *she*'d made it much, much worse.

'A woman,' he said.

'Cheated on her, did you?'

He'd refused to cooperate. To be *her* idea of a good slave. To his shame he'd given in when he realised she meant to have his eye on the point of her knife if he gave her any more trouble. His gut roiled at the recollection of the nights of service he'd given in exchange for his sight. 'She thought so,' he said.

Ian was going to pay for that, too. He swigged his tea and welcomed the heat of the whisky sliding into his belly. He wiped his mouth on his sleeve. 'What do you hear of my oldest brother, Ian?'

'The Laird of Dunross, is it?'

'Aye.'

Morris grimaced. 'Got himself a rich wife and a castle in the bargain, I'm hearing.'

Drew stiffened. 'What rich wife?'

Morris shrugged. 'Albritten?' He shook his head. 'Something like that.'

'Albright?'

'Aye, that's it.'

The image of a tiny blonde girl sitting beside Ian on the sand in Balnaen Cove flashed into his mind. 'Lady Selina,' he breathed.

'Aye, that's her. Got a babe, too, they say.'

The slow-burning anger inside Drew quickened, flaring hot. His fists clenched. 'The bloody hypocrite.'

Morris looked at him curiously. 'Not to your liking, then?'

'Not much.' Ian had apparently married the daughter of his family's enemy. And Alice's friend. It was she who had betrayed him to Ian before he could carry out his plan. And Ian had married her, curse him.

His body shook with the effort of containing the blistering rage consuming his thoughts. 'Is it a son? The child?'

'I dinna ken, man. Does it matter?'

'No.' Son or daughter, it would soon lack a father. Great heavens, if it was a son, a half-*Sassenach* Albright brat would be the heir to the Gilvry name. But that didn't mean the clan would choose the child as laird. They wouldn't. Drew would make sure of it. His father and grandfather would never rest in their graves if such a thing came to pass. He couldn't believe that Niall and Logan had gone along with such a travesty.

'Do you hear aught of my brother Niall?'

'The lawyer? Doing well for himself. Got an office in Old Town and a house in New Town. Got himself a title.' Morris offered him the flask. 'More whisky? I've plenty more where that came from.'

Stunned, he reached for the flask. Heaven help him, he needed it after such news. But not too much. He needed his wits sharp and ready.

Frozen to the bone, Rowena looked longingly at the flicker of the fire farther up the hillside. She'd ridden hard all day, terrified of pursuit, worried that she wouldn't find Drew on the road. But if she didn't, she knew where they intended he should end up. She stroked the gelding's sweating neck. 'Do you think that is them?'

She glanced up at the sky, at the twinkle of stars that disappeared behind the occasional scudding cloud. She'd been lucky with her departure from Mere Castle; the gelding was fast and full of spirit, and she'd been lucky with the weather. But could she really have been lucky enough to catch up to Drew? Or rather, Drew and a dangerous gang of smugglers. She winced.

But she couldn't afford to wait. At any moment, Mere's men might arrive. She climbed down from the horse and led it clear of the road. She patted its rump. 'If we come out of this safely, I promise you'll have the best bucket of oats money can buy,' she whispered. The horse started cropping at the bushes.

As quietly as possible, feeling her way over the rough terrain, she approached the fire. She could see shadowy figures, but was one of them Drew? Something deep in her bones told her he was there. A feeling she'd never had before. Dare she trust it? Heart thundering in her ears, terrified of tripping and attracting attention, she crept closer. Starlight did little more than make some shadows stand out more than others. She could only hope she wouldn't fall over a smuggler standing guard.

She inched forward at a crouch. After what felt like a very long time, she ducked behind a clump of gorse. She was close enough to see not only that there were four men seated around the fire, but that one of them was blonde.

A horse whickered from somewhere nearby. Drew's horse. Had it somehow recognised her?

Drew straightened, looking in the direction of the sound, and then out into the darkness. Could he see her? She froze.

He said something to the man sitting beside him. The men chuckled and the man closest slapped him on the back. Drew rose and walked directly to her gorse bush.

'Who's there?' he whispered so quietly she could

barely hear him. He opened his coat and undid his falls, turning half away from her. Then came the sound of a man answering the call of nature.

'Me. Rowena,' she whispered.

The sound stopped and then started again. 'Good God,' he murmured. He glanced over his shoulder, then adjusted his falls. 'Wait here.'

He turned and walked back to the fire and sat down with the men. He accepted a metal container from the man beside him. It glinted as it caught the light of the fire.

One of the others was sipping at a steaming brew. Hot tea? She would give her soul for a cup of something hot. She huffed on her freezing fingers and hunched closer to the gorse bush, curling in on herself for warmth.

Fortunately, while the old coat she'd grabbed in the stable was coarse to the touch, it was surprisingly warm. She stuffed her hands into its pockets.

A hand on Rowena's shoulder and another clamped over her mouth to silence her cry of alarm brought her awake.

She stared at the shadow looming over her.

'It's me,' Drew said.

She collapsed in relief. He took her hand and led her away from the camp. While she struggled not to trip, he seemed to walk as if it was daylight. Finally he stopped and pulled her around to face him.

'Gracious, lass. What are you doing here?'

'I thought you were in some sort of trouble. Have you taken up with the smugglers, then?'

A breath hissed through his teeth. Anger? Worry? She wasn't sure.

'I thought I left you safe in the bosom of your family.'

Anger, then. 'I decided I would prefer to go to Edinburgh.'

'The devil you did.'

'Besides, I heard someone say you were going to be transported to Australia. I thought you might not like the idea.'

'What?'

'I overheard someone speaking to Mr Jones.'

'What someone?'

'I don't know his name. I wasn't introduced.'

She could hear him breathing hard.

'How did you manage to get free of them?' she asked.

'I waited until they fell asleep and cut the rope,' he said almost mechanically. 'Your horse?'

'Near the road.'

'Good.' He gave a soft whistle. His horse loomed up out of the dark with a small whuffling sound.

'How—?'

'Shh. It is no' important right now. Come on, we'll need to be far from here before they wake.'

'Where are we going?'

'Where they will least expect us to go.'

'And where is that?' she said as he helped her to walk down the hillside.

'Edinburgh.'

When they reached her horse, he threw her up. 'You'd already planned to escape from them, hadn't you?' she asked.

'Yes.'

Of course he had. He hadn't needed her help at all.

After two nights and two days on the road, Drew was glad to see the lights of Edinburgh gleaming in the distance. It had taken longer than it would have by road and they'd slept rough, sharing body heat since they hadn't dared risk a fire.

The beast inside him had wanted to do more than sleep beside her, but he wasn't prepared to risk letting it out of its cage. She was just too tempting and he had no illusion that he could keep things normal.

He'd pushed hard, through snow and wind, and kept them both too exhausted for anything but sleep. Which didn't mean he'd slept o'er much.

But here they were, at their destination. He pushed on until they reached the entrance to Old Town. It looked pretty much the way it had before he left. The castle crouched on the mountain, the palace at its foot and the tenements of Old Town sprawled between the two.

Their horses walked wearily up High Street. 'What now?' Rowena asked.

'We can do nothing tonight but find lodgings. In the morning we will get ourselves a lawyer and find out what the hell is going on.'

She frowned. 'I have very little money, I'm afraid.'

'That's more than I have.' He'd left a fortune on Jones's table back at Mere Castle, but even if he had accepted it, it would not have done him any good. Morris would have taken the lot, just as he had taken the few coins in his purse. 'But I may have a contact who might be able to offer some help.'

Niall. Would he be willing to come to their aid? Niall had always been the most reasonable of his brothers. Had always listened to all sides of a story before deciding whose side to take. He could only hope he hadn't changed. Hadn't been influenced too much by Ian.

'We could try the Whitehorse Inn, near Holyrood Palace,' Rowena said doubtfully. 'I might just have enough to pay for one room.'

'With no luggage, and us as dirty as a couple of gypsies?' He shook his head. 'One look and they'll turn us away.' They also needed somewhere safe. Somewhere no one would could possibly find them.

'I don't think my cousin would take us in,' she said. There was pain in her voice. 'Do you think your family—?'

'No.'

Her shoulders slumped.

If he'd been by himself, he'd have gone to a tavern and nursed a drink all night, or slept on the floor in a stable. But he wasn't alone. The only other place he could think of was little better. But it was better. And Belle could be relied on to keep a still tongue in her head.

'I have a friend. She's not exactly respectable, but if she can, she'll give us a room.'

Rowena perked up. 'Then let's go there.'

And he'd tell her just what Belle was, when they knew whether or not she could put them up for the night. No sense in causing a fuss before it was necessary.

He turned into one of the narrow wynds behind the

grass market and dismounted outside the back door of a six-storey-high tenement. He helped Rowena down and knocked on the door.

It was opened by a burly individual with a much-broken nose and a cauliflower ear. 'We're closed.' He started to shut the door.

Drew thrust his foot in the back. 'Bobbie. Dinna ye ken me, man?'

The man peered at his face, blinked and opened the door wide. 'Gilvry. It's a long time since we saw you here. What happened to your face?'

'I ran into a knife.'

'Careless of you, man.'

'Aye. Is Belle in?'

Bobbie gazed over his shoulder at Rowena. 'She's no looking for any lasses just now.'

'Full house, is it? She must be doing well.'

'Well enough since the king came to visit.'

'The king came here?'

'To Edinburgh. Where have you been?'

'Abroad.'

'Och, aye.'

'I need to see Belle, Bobbie.'

The man looked up and down the alley and then seemed to make up his mind. 'Always had a soft spot for you. You'd best come in, then.'

He stood back and Drew ushered a very puzzled-looking Rowena in. She had set her face in stern lines and her back was straight. She looked very disapproving, but knowing her as he did, he could tell she was scared. 'It's all right. I have friends here.'

'Wait here,' Bobbie said. 'I'll fetch Madam Belle.'

'What is this place?' she whispered.

'You ken verra well what it is,' he said.

She gazed at the lurid red walls and the badly done *trompe l'oeil* images of cupids. 'A brothel.'

He nodded. 'Leave the talking to me.'

A few seconds later the rustle of skirts announced the arrival of the establishment's owner.

'Drew,' Belle said, her faded fair face beaming with pleasure.

She stopped with a gasp. 'Oh, your poor face.'

Drew touched the scar with his fingertips. 'I thought it made me a touch out of the common.'

'Oh, Drew,' she said softly. 'Still not one to let down your guard. Welcome back. Some of the lasses you know are still here and will be glad to see you.'

He'd always paid well for what he needed. The lasses had liked that part of it, at least.

She turned to Rowena with a guarded expression. 'And who is this, then?'

Rowena drew herself up to her full height and looked down her nose.

Belle recoiled.

'Belle, this is my wife, Rowena.'

Belle swung back to him with a horrified look on her face. 'Your wife! What are you doing, man, bringing her here?'

'I need your help,' he said simply. 'Or I wouldn't have come. Will you turn me away?'

She stared at him for a moment, then reached her palm to his face. He flinched.

Rowena quickly stepped forward and forestalled the touch. She smiled and her face transformed from stern to young and vulnerable.

'We would be very grateful if you would permit us to stay the night. We find ourselves at a standstill, you see. No one must know we are in town.'

Belle narrowed her pale blue eyes, finally smiling back. 'Then step this way. You can wait in my private parlour while I have the maid prepare a room. My stock in trade is discretion, so you need not fear loose tongues here.'

'Thank you,' Rowena said with genuine warmth.

'This way,' Belle said. 'I'll have a bite of supper sent up while you are waiting. And a dram of whisky.'

'Tea for me, please,' Rowena said. 'If you don't mind?'

'Not at all. It will be a pleasure.' She looked at Drew. 'You are a fortunate man. I didn't think you'd find one.'

She left them in a small parlour at the back of the house and bustled away.

'What did she mean?' Rowena asked.

Drew knew. She was talking about his preferences. Not something he wished to discuss. It was bad enough that she'd endured a small part of what he liked. 'I suppose she never thought I'd be married.'

Rowena nodded, shrugged out of her disreputable-looking coat and went to the fire blazing in the hearth to warm her hands while she looked around the room.

'It could be anyone's parlour,' she said.

'Aye. They're just lasses, you know.'

Her face softened. 'Yes, I suppose they are.'

Belle returned with a smile. 'Your room will soon be ready.' She looked at Rowena. 'Eva will be glad to help with your dressing and such. She does it for all the girls.'

'You are very kind,' Rowena said.

Bobbie entered with a tray. Tea for Rowena and whisky for Belle and Drew. Rowena poured her tea, while Drew did the honours for him and Belle.

'I havena' seen Niall or Ian for ages. Both married well. I was sorry to lose their business.' She trilled a knowing laugh. 'But glad to see them happily settled.'

They weren't going to be so happy when they realised he was back and why. 'What about Logan? He must be up-and-coming.'

Belle shook her head in mock sorrow. 'He never came here. Nor anywhere else as far as I know and him as beautiful as you were in the old days.'

Drew raised a brow. Not about his brother's good looks, but about what Belle's words implied. 'Too bad,' he said non-committally.

'He's married.'

He swallowed his surprise and adjusted his thoughts. 'Logan? He's still wet behind the ears.'

'Married a widow, I hear. I have never seen her. They are rarely in town. Well, if you are ready I should be able to show you up to your room.' She looked at Rowena. 'Drew will have to play ladies' maid tonight, I'm afraid. Eva will be busy getting the girls ready for this evening.'

Drew clamped his mouth shut on the urge to say it would be a pleasure. It would be. But that didn't make it right.

Rowena blushed. 'I'm sure I can manage.'

They followed Belle past a downstairs drawing room where some of the girls were gathered waiting for their customers, up the stairs and along a corridor on the third floor. She stopped by a door at the end. 'It's probably not what you are used to, Mrs Gilvry,' she said, 'but I hope it will do. You'll find it clean and tidy. The young lady who used to be here found herself a protector a month ago and I have been waiting to see if she would come back or no'.' She flung open the door to reveal blood-red walls, curtains and bedcovers. 'A bath is waiting.'

He ushered Rowena inside. 'I'll owe you a debt for this, Belle,' he said, turning back to her.

She shook her head. 'You were always good to my girls, Drew. I am glad to return the favour.'

She turned and headed back down the hallway. Drew closed the door. The perfume of roses filled the air, clearly coming from the hip bath in the corner.

Rowena was standing in the middle of the room, look-ing about her with an odd sort of expression. One he couldn't interpret. He winced. 'I'm sorry.'

She shook her head and gave him a hesitant smile. 'I find it…interesting.' She coloured.

She was embarrassed. He looked at the bath. Of course she was embarrassed, if she thought he would stay.

'I'll leave you to bathe in peace,' he said. 'There are public baths nearby for me.'

'Oh,' she said. Was that disappointment he heard in her voice, or simply wishful thinking? More likely the latter. But then she turned her back before he could be sure.

'Would you unlace my stays before you go, since the maid is busy?'

'Aye,' he said hoarsely. He put down his hat and undid the strings of her gown and then the tapes of her stays. The temptation to kiss the silky skin of her shoulders tingled on his lips, but when he glanced up he realised she was watching him in one of several mirrors strategically placed around the room. He bit back a curse and stepped away. 'I'll be back. Lock the door behind me.'

He paused outside the door until he heard the key turn.

Chapter Twelve

E rotic. It was the only word Rowena could think of to described the chamber as she soaked in the tub, with the scent of roses filling the air and the warm water making her feel sleepy.

She hadn't been at all surprised when Drew had declined to play lady's maid. She'd seen his expression of distaste when he undid her gown and stays. She wasn't the sort of woman a man liked to look at. Too tall. Too angular. Not enough meat on her bones, Samuel had said. It wouldn't surprise her one little bit if he decided to spend the night with one of the buxom creatures she'd spotted below.

The thought sent a piercing pain through her chest. Tears blurred her vision. She squeezed her eyes shut. Forced the hot moisture back where it belonged. Unacknowledged.

What had happened in that cold little bothy had been the result of the terrible events of that night. They'd sought comfort from each other. It meant nothing. Not to him, certainly, since he'd found no relief in her body. Or to her. Not really. She'd revelled in the shattering bliss he'd given her and the brief sense that she could let him shoulder her worries. But in the cold light of day, she didn't want a man ruling her life. She certainly wasn't going to give another one the opportunity to break her heart.

Not that Samuel had, she acknowledged. With him it was more her pride that had been hurt. But with Drew it would be different. If she gave him her heart and he threw it away, she would want to die.

No, what she had was the memory of his touch. The way he made her feel. Dreamily she stroked her feminine flesh, recalling the way his fingers had felt. And his tongue.

Languorous pleasure blossomed low in her belly. Good. But nowhere near as delicious as his touch had been, or as arousing as his harsh commands. A flush travelled over her skin at the memory.

A knock sounded at the door. Hot with arousal and embarrassment, she jerked upright in the tub, water sloshing on to the floor.

'Who is it?'

'Eva, *madame*. Belle sent me up to ask if you are done with the tub and to send up a bit to eat to tide you over until dinner.'

'Thank you. Wait a moment and I'll open the door.'

'No need, ma'am. I'll leave the tray outside. Bobbie'll be up in a minute or two to take the tub and bring your clothes down to be washed.'

'But I have nothing else to wear.'

'You'll find a robe in the cupboard,' the girl said cheerfully. 'Help yourself.'

Afraid Bobbie might arrive at any moment, Rowena stepped out of the bath and dried herself off. The porter, she suspected, wouldn't raise an eyebrow at finding her unclothed, given the place he worked, but she wouldn't feel at all comfortable. The offered robe she discovered was a little diaphanous for her taste, but beggars could not be choosers. She opened the door and carried the tray in and set it on the table.

A bite to eat consisted of a round of cheese and a heel of bread, with a pat of fresh butter, cake and a pot of tea.

Whatever one might think about her profession, Madam Belle was clearly a very kind woman.

A few minutes later, Bobbie and a young lad came for the tub. Rowena wrapped herself in the red quilt before she let them in and watched with interest as, working together, they lifted the tub and tipped the water out of the window after a shout of 'Gardy loo!' to anyone unfortunate enough to be walking in the alley below.

'Will there be anything else, ma'am?' Bobbie asked, his gaze fixed at a point above her head.

'No, thank you.'

He and his lad trundled out with the tub and she locked the door behind them. She went to the bed, intending to rest until Drew returned. Her foot hit something beneath the bed. Thinking it might be a book, she bent to take a peek. Beside the chamber pot was a wooden box. Intrigued, she picked it up and set it on the bed.

She opened the lid.

And her eyes nearly popped out of her head.

* * *

Drew nodded to Bobbie when he let him in the back door.

'The missus is finished with her bath,' the bruiser said with a wink.

An image of Rowena naked flashed through his mind, doing away with all the good effects of the cold plunge. His shaft gave a happy little twitch. He gave Bobbie a hard-eyed glare and headed upstairs, rubbing his close-shaven chin with his thumb and wondering if she might welcome him in her bed a second time. If he kept things on an even keel.

Behaved like a gentleman.

As if. And nor did he want her to. He still couldn't believe her courage. She'd actually risked her own safety to rescue him from McKenzie's men. He owed her more than he could ever repay. He was not going to take advantage of the kind gentle woman who hid behind the facade of stern reserve. Samuel MacDonald had been a fool not to realise the treasure he had in his wife.

He tapped on the door.

'Who is it?' Her voice was husky, almost breathless. Had something happened? 'Drew. Let me in.'

There was a scuffling sound, then the door opened. Her face was bright pink. He took in the see-through robe she was wearing. It clung to every swell and hollow, revealing more than it hid: the small, high bosom, the curve of her waist and swell of her hips. He jerked his gaze up to her face. Far from trying to avoid his gaze, she seemed to be trying to block his view of the bed.

A sharp blade of something ugly twisted in his chest. 'What's going on?'

'Nothing.'

Guilt filled her voice. He stepped around her. His gaze swept the four-poster bed and... His stomach lurched. Cold as ice, he turned to face her. 'Where did that come from?'

She gave an awkward laugh and unsuccessfully tried to look severe. 'I found it under the bed.'

Had Belle brought it up, thinking he would want it? His mouth dried. His heart pounded hard. His shaft hardened to rock.

He brought his gaze up to her face and saw excitement in the flush of her skin and the sparkle in her silvery eyes.

He had to be imagining it. If she had opened it, she would be horrified.

Her gaze slid away. She gestured to the table. 'Belle sent up tea for me and whisky for you, if you would care for some. Supper will be sent up later, I understand.'

Whisky might dull the terrible ache in his groin. He strode to the table against the wall and with a shaking hand poured some into the glass. He swallowed the liquid in one swallow. Felt it burn all the way to his belly and poured another glass, glad to see his hand had steadied.

He nodded at the bed. 'It must have been left by the previous occupant.' He looked into his glass. 'This whisky is excellent.' Much better than the gut-rot he'd shared with McKenzie's men.

'Eva said it comes from Dunross. The...er...mistress

of the house orders it for her special clients, though Eva says she never tells them where it comes from.'

He rolled another sip around in his mouth and she was right—it tasted of home. A wave of longing surged through him. He ruthlessly crushed it. 'I thought it tasted familiar. Did Eva say why they keep it a secret?'

She gave a little shrug. The filmy fabric skimmed over her nipples, making them pearl. His breath caught in his throat.

'Something about McKenzie not liking the competition,' she said. 'Apparently, it's all right to tell me because I'm a Gilvry. I didn't disabuse her of the notion.'

He finished his drink and turned to pour another, then put the glass down. Too much whisky and he'd lose what little control he had.

Again his gaze strayed to the bed. Rowena moved away from it with a look of embarrassment. As she would, given that they were alone in a room in which the bed was the focus. She wasn't an innocent. She would know what went on in a bawdy house, if not in detail, then in general terms at least.

He just wished she hadn't found that box. Its contents were all too familiar. Too damned tempting and she was too good for him and his needs.

How awkward that Eva had not delivered her clothes before Drew arrived. More awkward yet, he had returned before she'd had a chance to put the box and its strange contents back under the bed. Just looking at what it contained had sent her blood pounding through her veins, which in turn had made her feel hot all over. The slide of the silky robe on her sensitised skin had only made the strange feelings grow worse.

Her imagination had run riot as she'd picked each item out of the box. Her body had tingled and burned. She'd wanted to stroke her breasts, touch her— She blocked out the wicked thoughts. Only Drew's arrival had stopped her from behaving in the most shameful way.

And now he was looking at the box with a dark expression. Not anger. It held too much sensuality for that, but not interest either. A kind of dread.

'I stubbed my toe on the box,' she said, her voice sounding a little breathless. As if she'd been running. Was it her imagination or had the chamber become warm and close? She swallowed and looked away from the piercing look he shot her from under his brows. 'It's…um…things. For use by the girls who work here, I assume.'

'Are you saying you looked inside?' he asked, his voice low and gruff and incredulous.

She gave a small laugh that sounded forced. 'I was curious.'

He turned away, staring down at the decanter, his face rigid. He must think she was dreadful. Wanton.

But she couldn't seem to stop herself from asking the question that had been on her mind since she opened the box. 'Do you think they use all those things?'

'Things?'

A shiver rolled down her back. 'Chains. Ropes. Blindfolds. A schoolmaster's leather strap.' Her inner muscles tightened with a pleasurable little pulse and she swallowed a gasp.

He made a sound of disgust. 'I'll have them come and fetch it away.'

'Yes.' She looked down her nose at the polished wood. 'Of course. But Eva told me she would be busy downstairs for the next little while.'

When she looked back at him, he was watching her with hooded eyes, but even so she could feel the heat of his gaze on her skin.

Oh, how she wished she had never opened that box. She moved to the chair by the fireplace and looked up at him. 'Were the baths to your satisfaction?' she asked as a mean of distraction.

'Aye. Yours?'

'Oh, yes. Eva took my clothes to be washed. You might want to give her your shirt if we are to visit your brother tomorrow.'

He moved to the window and looked down into the street. 'I'll take it down later.'

With the box. *Stop thinking about it.* She clasped her hands together in her lap. 'I expect you are looking forward to meeting him.' Oh, heaven help her, she was babbling.

'Yes.'

His monosyllabic answers were unravelling her nerves, but she couldn't seem to stop asking questions. 'Do you know where to find him?'

He turned back from the window, his face expressionless. 'The attendant at the bathhouse gave me the address. I went round to take a look at the building. He's in a wynd just off Princes Street. The office opens at half past nine in the morning.'

'Oh,' she said, mollified by the fullness of his answer. 'So we know where we are to go.'

'Aye.'

'He will be surprised to see you after all this time.'

'Surprised, aye.'

'And pleased,' she hazarded.

He shook his head. 'Doubtful. But he's not one to turn his back on his own.' His jaw flickered. 'Not the Niall I knew anyway. Things may have changed since...' He let his voice trail away. He seemed to be looking into the past. He shook his head. 'There's no sense in guessing.' His hands opened and closed.

He was worried. And not only his tension gave him away. She could see concern in the shadows darkening his eyes from their usual emerald to the colour of pine forests.

'I saved you a piece of cake,' she said, pointing to the tea tray. 'To tide you over until dinner. Unless you ate while you were out?'

'No. I didna' realise dinner would be late, so I didna' give it a thought.' He picked up the slice of cake and it disappeared in one bite.

'I should have saved more of it.'

'I'll be fine. I'm more used to an empty belly than you are.'

She wasn't so sure of that. Governesses did get fed, but they often had to wait until after their charges were looked after.

'I should write to my employer again,' she said with a sigh. 'Tell her where to send my wages.'

She frowned. 'And if in the end there is no money set

aside, I fear it will be difficult to find another position without a letter of reference.'

His face looked grimmer than ever.

'Please, Drew, don't blame yourself. I should have known better than to think Samuel would have done anything so sensible as provide for me.' She tidied up the tray. 'Eva said to put this outside the door. One of the footman will pass by and pick it up.' She glanced at the bed. 'We could leave that outside, too, if you wish.'

He gave the box a look of dislike. 'Aye. It would be best.'

She hurried to the bed and picked up the chest. For some unaccountable reason her hands were shaking. The heavy weight slipped through fingers that seemed to have lost all of their strength and it crashed to the floor, scattering its contents across the carpet.

Drew let out a curse. In one long stride he had reached the site of the disaster and crouched at her feet.

She dropped to her knees beside him as he righted the box. She picked up a pair of manacles. They were heavy and lined with velvet. She glanced up and found his gaze fixed on her hands. She rubbed at the velvet with her fingers, her breasts tightening. His gaze drifted from her hands up her body to her nipples, which she was sure he must be able to see through the fabric of the robe, and then continued up to her face.

His breathing sounded harsh in the silence as their gazes met.

She licked her lips and swallowed the dryness in her throat. Her heart was rattling in her chest, making it hard to form words. 'Have you ever...?' she whispered. 'I mean, do you know...?'

'What?' he said his voice harsh. 'Do I know what?'

'How they are used?'

He stilled. Something changed in his expression; it lightened, and though he frowned, the glint in his eyes was curiosity, not anger. And yes—at least, she was almost sure—hope.

'Do you like the idea of being shackled?' His voice deepened and became silky and dark and mesmerising as his eyes seemed to look right into her soul. 'Of being held in chains. Helpless to defend your honour against a man who will do with you just as he will.'

Her insides melted. She gasped, helpless against the deliciously wicked sensations rippling through her body. Afraid to breathe. Afraid to speak. Afraid of what she might reveal. Fearing he would turn away in disgust. Then she nodded and waited for his revulsion.

'And would you submit to such a man, obey his every dark demand?'

Her eyes fluttered closed on a little moan of helpless pleasure.

'Rowena,' he said, his voice a rough whisper. 'Look at me.'

She opened her eyes. His mouth was so close to hers. His breath warm on her lips.

'Rowena,' he murmured, 'would you submit like that to me? Let me do as I willed? Give way to my every wish?' He drew in a harsh breath. 'If I promise I wouldna' hurt you? Not really?'

All her life she had longed for a man who would want her badly enough to take command of her body and soul. Could she humble herself enough to ask for what she wanted? 'I have dreamed of a man who…' He would find her disgusting.

'Of a man who what?' he asked hoarsely. 'Who what, Rowena? Answer me.'

'Who would be my master and I his slave.' She blushed and bowed her head in shame. 'It is a foolish fancy.'

She started to rise.

He put a heavy hand on her shoulder. 'Do not move.' He picked up the box and set it on the table beside the bed.

She looked up at his face, the face of half devil, half angel. 'I—'

'You do not have my permission to speak.'

She shuddered with pleasure.

Drew stared down at her bowed head. Had he understood? He thought he had. Or had he simply wished to hear what he wanted? Or had she agreed because she was afraid?

'Look at me, Rowena.'

She raised her gaze to meet his and he saw excitement and breathless anticipation in her expression.

'You don't have to do this,' he said. 'Not if you don't want to.'

'I do,' she said. 'If you think you would like it.'

Like it? He had a feeling it would kill him if she changed her mind. 'If anything I do, we do, makes you afraid, you can always stop me. Cry "uncle" and I'll stop at once. I swear it. Do you understand?'

'Uncle,' she said, nodding.

'So you want to stop?'

'No. Not now. Not yet.'

He looked down at her, saw the courage in her eyes and the melting softness. Had he actually found a woman who liked this game as much as he did? She always seemed so strong, so self-contained. But as she knelt before him, he could see that this was something she wanted and he let the beast inside him out of its cage. Not loose—never did he let it go entirely free—but he would let it play a while. Just for a moment or two.

'Stand up, girl, and face me.'

She did as he bid. He could see she was trembling, the sheer fabric of her robe shivering at the hem.

'Do you know who I am?'

She shook her head.

'I have captured the ship on which you travelled and will sell you in the slave markets of Algeria if you do not please me.'

Her soft mouth parted on a gasp and her breathing quickened. His blood pounded in answer to that betraying little sign of pleasure.

'Let your hair down. I want to see it free around your shoulders.'

She pulled the pins free and it tumbled down. It reminded him of the way he'd seen it at McRae's. It was long and straight and a pretty shade of chestnut brown.

'Untie your belt, girl. Quickly now.'

Her lovely long fingers hastened to do as he bid and the robe fell open.

Just as he recalled from the night in the bothy, her breasts were small and high and beautifully firm. The curls at the juncture of her thighs were a lovely dark chestnut, darker than the hair on her head.

A desperate urge to touch her with hands and mouth almost overwhelmed him, but she was not yet ready. 'Let the robe fall.'

'Must I?' she asked, raising her gaze to his.

Ah, a little bit of defiance. He let his mouth curl in a mocking smile. 'You must if you don't want me to hand you over to my men.'

A shiver racked her body. She let the robe fall from her shoulders and slide to pool at her feet.

'Up on the bed with you.'

She glanced over her shoulder and then shook her head. 'Sir, would you steal my innocence?'

His shaft hardened inside his trousers at the words and the sound of her breathy voice. 'Everything belongs to me now.' He selected the whip from the box, a light riding crop, and ran it through his palm suggestively.

She licked her lips, staring at the whip, then looked into his face.

She would tell him no. He knew she would. Rowena wasn't that kind of woman. His kind of woman.

She turned, walked to the bed and climbed up.

He let a breath go and stalked after her, standing at the side of the bed as she watched him approach, her arms and hands covering her body.

'None of that now,' he said with a scowl, tapping her fingers with the tip of the whip. 'I want to see my prize. Lie back and put your hands at your sides.'

After a moment's hesitation she lay back on the pillows and placed her hands flat on the bed, her grey eyes fixed on his face, her breasts rising and falling with little breaths. Slowly her milk-white skin flushed and the air filled with the scent of arousal. Hers. And his.

Damn, she was lovely. And she wanted him. Like this.

Slowly, lightly he ran the whip down her body, over her breasts, watched the peaks tighten to hard rosy little nubs and heard a little whimper from deep in her throat.

Not fear.

She was too brave to be afraid. Too courageous.

He couldn't believe how aroused he was. It was a long time since he had played his little games with a woman. And he didn't remember one who had entered into it with such abandon. He stroked the leather across the flat plane of her belly. Lord, but she was slender. Almost thin, as if she'd not been well fed.

A surge of anger at her husband rippled through him. And guilt that he hadn't noticed. He circled her navel with the tip of the crop and her flesh quivered beneath the touch. He traced the jut of her hip bones and the sensitive hollow.

She flinched. Just as he knew she would.

He shook his head. 'Lie still, I said. Now you must be punished. Roll over.'

She hesitated.

'Now,' he said harshly, giving her the tiniest flick with the crop. Not enough to leave a mark. Not enough to cause anything but a lick of pleasure-pain. And she moaned and rolled over, burying her face in the pillows, her hands on each side of her head.

Her back was long and lovely, every bone of her spine visible through the skin. Her bottom was beautiful. Womanly. Round, high and firm, with its dark shadow below her tail bone. It really was the most delectable sight he had viewed in a long time.

He hardened to rock and revelled in the agony of denial. For only when he was sure she was satisfied could he take what he wanted.

He stripped out of his breeches and shirt, knowing she could hear what he was doing, and, seeing her hands curl into the sheet, he knew she wanted to look at him the way he was looking at her. Somehow she knew better than to take a peek.

'It's too late to be good,' he said. 'You deserve all you get.'

Her buttocks tightened in anticipation. He bit back a groan at the sight of that little twitch. He wanted to bite each cheek until she cried for mercy.

He knelt on the bed beside her and raised his hand. He slapped that lovely, sumptuous flesh, not hard enough to hurt—to hurt her would kill him—just enough to cause it to tingle and warm.

She gave a little squeak of surprise.

'That earns you five more,' he said. And waited.

She tensed.

So he waited.

Slowly she relaxed and he slapped her again, carefully, just enough to feel the weight of his hand, his strength. And he counted out loud until he reached five.

Her bottom was a delicious pink, and warm beneath his hand.

He swept her pretty brown hair aside and leaned over to breath in her ear, to flick his tongue around the tender little curls, then kissed the leaping pulse below her ear. 'Will you disobey again?'

She made no sound and his heart tumbled over. 'You may answer.'

'No,' she said. 'I'll not disobey again.' The laugher in her voice said she probably would. And something warm and very tender filled his chest, soothing the ugliness inside him.

'Turn over and face me.'

She flipped on to her back. Her gaze raked his body, her eyelids drooped sensually, a smile curved her wide mouth, making her look beautiful and lascivious as she took in his rampant arousal.

'So,' he said, jerking his chin, 'you like what you see.'

She raised her gaze to his face. 'I like it very much.'

'Speaking again, unbidden?'

She bit her lip.

'Another punishment is in order.'

She eyed the whip warily.

He set it down alongside her and rummaged in the box. 'Ah,' he said, like a gloating pirate who had just found buried treasure. 'Close your eyes.'

When he turned back to her, her eyes were squeezed shut. He quickly tied the blindfold around her head. Now the real fun would begin.

Darkness. Not a scrap of light penetrated the silk binding her eyes. All she could hear was the thunder of her heart and her rapid breathing. And all she seemed to feel was the slight sting of her buttocks. It seemed so much more intense now she couldn't see.

Panic surged. The word *uncle* forced its way up into her throat.

A firm warm hand gave her shoulder a gentle squeeze. 'Give me your hands, little one,' his dark voice murmured.

Little one? She choked back a laugh, more hysterical than amused. No one had ever called her little. Not since she was a child. But this was Drew. Humouring her with the game she'd wanted to play. Not some terrible stranger wanting to do her harm.

Her fears dissipated. Her body relaxed and she lifted her hands.

He caught them in his and she heard the clink of metal and felt the grip of something solid around her wrists. Solid, but soft. The manacles lined with velvet. She remembered how she'd held them in her hands. They snicked closed.

Slowly, infinitely carefully, her hands were drawn upwards and another click above her head made her test the bonds that held her fast.

'You'll not be escaping from there,' he said gruffly.

But she could. She just had to say the word and he would let her go. But she didn't want him to, not yet. The shivers of fear had turned to trembling excitement. What would he do next?

Something stroked across her breasts. She gasped at the way her skin tightened at the unexpected touch.

What was it? Not the riding crop. It had been nowhere near as light a sensation. It swirled around first one nipple, then the other. Her breasts seemed to become heavy and full. Her nipples hardened. She could feel them puckering and pulling tight. It felt wickedly delicious. Unbearable.

She almost cried out when it stopped. Almost begged for more. And then it touched her lips, a delicate whisper of touch. The feather. It had to be the feather. Who would ever have thought such a soft delicate thing could create such torment?

She moaned.

'Ah, my little beauty,' he said. 'If you think this is bad, just wait.'

The feather, for she was certain that was what it was, trailed a path across her cheek and swirled in her ear. She shivered and twitched.

'Be still,' he ordered, without a smidgeon of mercy for her predicament.

She was trying, but it was hard in the face of such delicate torture. She gulped in a breath of air and tried to control her body's reactions.

He chuckled softly as she lay still.

'Oh, my brave beauty,' he said softly.

The touch of the feather left her. Silence surrounded her. Every nerve in her body awaited what he would do next.

The feather ticked her inner thigh.

She gasped. Shocked. Surprised.

'Open,' he said in a rough command.

A shudder of pleasure hit her hard. She complied instantly.

He continued his torment, stroking each inner thigh in turn, then gently brushing her woman's flesh, which sprang to life, hot and wanting.

Did he want her, too?

She didn't know, couldn't tell in her dark world, though she could hear his harsh breathing somewhere beside her. Above her. All around her. Her fingers twitched in their bindings with the longing to touch him, to feel the hard mass of his arms and the deep chest she had glimpsed so briefly.

But she couldn't. He had her held fast. His captive.

Her insides seemed to melt. Her body flushed with the heat of desire.

The feather returned to her breasts, stroking all the places that loved to be touched: behind her knee, the rise of her breasts and the hollow of her throat.

And tormenting all the places that jumped and flickered: the hollow of her hip, the soles of her feet, the place below her ear.

And never did she know where he would touch her next. She was panting and breathless and almost out of her mind with longing and pleasure and exquisite pain from her sensitised skin. Almost ready to cry *uncle*.

The bed dipped. Him, shifting his weight. Then the warmth of him beside her hip. A knee pressed between her legs. 'Wider,' he said.

And then he was between her thighs, the rough hair on his legs just as tormenting as the feather.

Then she felt his fingers at her entrance, parting her folds, and the blunt tip of his shaft pressing against her.

'You will take me,' he said. 'All of me.'

And he drove home to the hilt and she dissolved into bliss.

And he continued to drive into her, bringing her to

the peak and beyond twice more, before he withdrew and spilled his seed on her belly.

He collapsed beside her, his hands reaching up to untie the blindfold.

She blinked at the sudden light as she regained her vision. He was up on one elbow, working the lock of the manacles. She was rewarded by seeing a look of sensual bliss and contentment on his face. He looked younger. Less careworn.

He freed her wrists and looked down at her face. She couldn't stop herself. She stretched up and kissed his mouth.

He gazed at her with what was clearly astonishment. 'Are you all right?' he murmured softly.

'Oh, yes,' she whispered, smiling. 'Thank you.'

If anything his expression of astonishment grew more intense. He shook his head. 'Rowena, rest now.'

He must think her exceedingly strange, but there was a slight smile on his lips as he lay down beside her and pulled her into the crook of his arm, positioning her so her head rested against his shoulder. Gently, he stroked her hair where it fell over her breast.

'Little one,' he said. His eyelids drooped and his breathing deepened.

'Mr Gilvry.'

Rapping. On a door. And a weight on his shoulder. Drew jerked awake. The warmth at his side was a woman. Rowena. The knocking on the door?

Careful not to wake his sleeping companion, he slid out of bed to another round of knocks.

'Who is it?'

'Eva, with your supper.'

Right. No food since earlier in the day. No wonder his belly felt empty. He glanced over at Rowena. She pulled the sheet up over her head with a mutter about the racket.

He scooped his shirt from the floor, pulled it over his head and unlocked the door.

Eva trotted in. She glanced at the tangled sheets on the bed with a knowing grin. 'Madam Belle thought as how you might be in need of a bit of sustenance.' She set a tray on the table.

'Thank her for me.'

The girl gave him a saucy smile. 'She's lucky, your lady is, having such a well set-up fellow as you, even with that face. You should see some of the flawns and dodderers the girls have to put up with.'

'I'll take that as a compliment.' Drew fished sixpence from his coat pocket and slipped it into the girl's palm. 'I'll leave the tray outside when we're done. No need to come back until morning.'

'Thank you kindly, sir.' She dipped a little bob and scuttled out.

Drew locked the door behind her.

Rowena threw back the sheet and gazed at him, her expression puzzled and her eyes misty with sleep. 'What is happening?'

'Eva with supper.'

'Oh.' She sat up, careful to keep herself wrapped in the sheet. As if he hadn't seen her a few minutes before in nothing but her skin. And a beautiful skin it was. Very responsive. And silky soft.

His blood thickened and his thoughts must have shown on his face, because hers turned red.

Dammit. He hadn't wanted to make her embarrassed. Not after she'd given him the most pleasurable interlude in his life.

He still couldn't quite believe that he had found a woman who had participated in his deepest, darkest fantasies. Had her enjoyment been real or out of gratitude?

Even as the thought flittered through his mind, he knew it wasn't true. The blush on her face was not embarrassment. It was desire. For some unfathomable reason, the fates had sent him a woman who liked the opposite of what he liked.

He hardened. And inwardly cursed the thrum of hot blood in his veins. Even if it had been a long time since he'd been able to indulge in his particular vices and even if she was willing, he'd tormented her enough for one night.

They had important matters to see to tomorrow and they would both need their wits about them. 'Come, sweetling. You need to eat.'

She blinked and then smiled. 'I can't believe how hungry I feel.'

'It's not surprising,' he said, raising a brow. He picked up her robe from the floor and handed it to her, turning his back so she could slip out of bed and put it on.

He didn't do it because he didn't want to see her. He did it because he knew if he caught so much as a glimpse, she would never get as far as the table.

He pulled out a chair and she gave him a smile and sat down. 'What have they sent up?'

It was a cold supper of the sort of plain fare Belle would have available to her customers downstairs. He'd partaken of it often enough in the past. Cold meats and haggis, fruit tart, bread and cheese and a flagon of small beer. They tucked in. He was glad to see that she ate heartily, though nowhere near as much as he, and when she was done she watched him finish his meal.

'Do you really think your brother will help us?' she asked when he, too, sat back with a sigh.

Of all of his brothers, Niall was the most likely not to toss him out on his ear. But if he did? What then? 'Dinna worry. We'll find someone else, if he cannot.' There was something else troubling him. 'I still do not see why Lady Cragg was so set against me.'

Rowena frowned. 'I never heard her say any such thing.'

'Did you no' say that she told Mr Jones she would be glad to see me deported? That was why she had McKenzie's men lying in wait for me when I left.'

'Oh.' Her eyes widened. 'It wasn't Lady Cragg talking to Mr Jones. It was a gentleman.'

'The duke?'

She frowned, as if trying to recall something. 'It could not have been the duke. Mr Jones called him my lord. Not your Grace.'

'It might have been a slip of the tongue.'

'Mr Jones does not seem the sort of man who would make such a mistake.'

'Aye, but if it was no' Lady Cragg or the duke, who the devil was it? What did he look like?'

'I couldn't see him very well, he was the other side

of a very thick hedge. I had the sense he was an older gentleman, by his voice.'

'If you heard that voice again, would you ken it?'

'I believe so. The air was clear and their voices carried, farther than they might have guessed, I think.'

'It is too bad I didn't know this when I was a guest of McKenzie's men,' he mused. 'Morris liked to talk. He might have told me.' He frowned. 'He did say something about me giving them the slip once before. I assumed he was talking about Logan.'

It couldn't be Ian. Not if it was an older man. But someone working with Ian? Someone like...Carrick?

Not possible, surely?

But the men who had delivered Ian's message had been Carrick's men. And it was Carrick who had offered him a place in his American business.

'What is it?' Rowena asked. 'You look worried.'

It surprised him that she could make out any expression at all on his face. It was as if she saw right past the ruined flesh and only saw the man behind it.

His heart gave an odd little lurch.

Now she was looking worried and he did not want her bothered by his musings, which had nothing to do with her problems. 'No, not worried. Just thinking. Don't be concerned about Niall. We'll know very quickly if he will help us or no'. We have a great deal to do in the morning, I think it is time you went to bed.'

She looked down her nose at him. 'I'll decide for myself when I'm ready for bed.'

He let his glance slide to the chest standing on the table.

Her breath gave a little hitch. 'Oh.'

He shook his head. 'Much as I'd like to play some more, I need my sleep, even if you don't.'

She went bright pink. 'Oh, I'm sorry. I didn't wish to be disobliging, I just didn't want you to think you could order me around.' Her colour went brighter. 'As a general rule, I mean. In the daytime.'

Heavens, she really was an absolute treasure. It was a shame he didn't deserve her. 'I understand,' he said. 'You take the bed. I'll take the floor.'

'Oh, no. I wouldn't hear of it. We will share.'

'So you intend to boss me around, do you?' he said with a teasing note in his voice.

'Certainly not. I am just being sensible.'

'Sensible. Aye. Then I'll accept your kind offer.'

His hands were unsteady as he laced her stays. Eva had returned her clothes along with the water for washing. He was glad Rowena had her back to him right at that moment and could not see his reaction to touching her.

He wanted her again. And she had given him so much already. In his heart he knew he would never get enough of her, and it wasn't right. Not when his future was so unsure.

'Your brother is going to be very surprised to meet us, I think.'

Us.

His fingers stilled. He'd been alone for so long, fighting for his own survival, it came as a shock to think of himself as something more. He pulled at the laces and tied off the bow. 'Aye. He'll be surprised.'

She seemed satisfied with his answer.

He went to the mirror and tied his cravat while she put on her stockings. Such lovely long legs she had. He glanced at the tumbled bedclothes and then at the clock and wondered if there might be time…

A knock sounded at the door. 'Who is it?'

'Eva with your breakfast.'

'I'm ravenous,' Rowena said.

So was he. And not only for food. With a regretful sigh he went to the door and opened it. The young maid bustled in with a tray.

'Madam Belle wants to know if you'll be wanting this room tonight, as well?'

He glanced at Rowena and discovered she was looking towards the bed with what he could only describe as a hopeful expression. His groin tightened at the thought that she was actually looking forward to another night with him. It seemed so improbable that he would meet a woman, who on the outside seemed so self-assured, and yet who craved what gave him pleasure.

How wrong her husband had been to call her cold and reserved. She was a passionate delight who had somehow filled a very empty place in the deepest reaches of his soul.

'Tell Belle, yes, if she can spare us the room.'

The maid whisked off. He seated Rowena and as she lowered herself on to the chair she looked up at him with a pink wash of colour. How could he ever have thought she was plain, seeing that blush over her pale-as-milk skin that covered every inch of her body?

She spread butter and jam on her toast. 'We will go

together to your brother's office,' she said in the decided
way that she had. She used it to hide her uncertainty, he
realised. Her fear of rejection.

Such a small insight into her vulnerability, but it made
him feel suddenly protective.

'We will,' he agreed, selecting bread and slicing off
a lump of cheese. 'After all, this is your business. Not
mine.' His business was with Ian. The urgency to face
his brother seemed to have faded. Because it would mean
leaving Rowena and likely never seeing her again? He
pushed the thought aside, unready to deal with that part
of his future.

He had sworn to give her his aid and he would see it
through to the end.

Breakfast over, they dressed for the chill of a winter
morning in Edinburgh. He wrapped his muffler around
his face. 'No sense in setting the dogs to barking,' he
joked when he saw her watching him.

She shook her head. 'I hardly notice the scar any longer. It's your expressions I see. Your kindness.'

As he had suspected the previous evening, but to
hear her say it made something hard and uncomfortable rise in his throat. He swallowed it down without
examining the emotion at its source, though he had a
feeling it was gratitude. He was grateful to her for so
many things, it seemed. Would it give her some sort
of power over him? Make him weak? He pushed the
thought aside. 'Let us go.'

They hurried down the back stairs and out the side
door. He gestured for her to stay in the shadows while

he took a quick look to see who was about on the street. There were the usual hawkers—the baker, the milkmaid, a girl with a basket of turnips—crying their wares. A dustcart rumbled by. No sign of the smugglers. 'Gardy loo!' He dodged back into the alley to avoid a stream of night soil from a front room of the brothel.

'All seems well,' he said, holding out his arm.

She took it. They walked briskly. Rapidly enough to show they had purpose, without looking hurried or anxious. At the corner of the street where Niall's office was located, Drew stopped. 'Let me make sure it is safe.' He'd been both hunter and prey. He knew better than to be caught out in the open.

She nodded. He peered around the corner.

Drew had no trouble identifying the man standing on the opposite side of the street against the apothecary's window. His friend from two nights ago. Morris. Cursing, Drew came back to Rowena.

'What is it?' she asked.

'The smugglers are watching Niall's office.' And they could be watching the nearby streets, too.

He grabbed her hand and they ran, ducking into alleyways and doubling back. He didn't stop moving until he was sure they weren't being pursued.

Out of breath and panting, Rowena leaned against the wall. 'Did they see you?' she gasped.

He shook his head. 'No.' He was almost sure they had not.

'What now?'

'We could try his house…'

'But they might be waiting there, too,' she finished.

'Aye. Likely. If they know of his office, they would easily discover where he is living.'

'And we wouldn't want to put his family in danger.'

How did she know what he was thinking at the same moment he thought it? He grinned at her, then realised that beneath his muffler she wouldn't be able to see his expression. Probably just as well. Right now he was feeling a little too besotted for comfort.

'Do you think we could ask him to visit us at the brothel?' she said. 'Send a note.'

'We will send a note, but we'll not meet him at Belle's. We need to find somewhere we can be sure *he* isna' followed.'

'What about Waterloo Place at Regent Bridge?'

'They finished it, then?' It reminded him just how long he had been away. A painful reminder full of resentment that made his fists clench as he thought about Ian and his treachery.

'There is a clear view in both directions,' she said.

'It sounds ideal.'

'Is something wrong?'

Clearly the bitterness in his heart showed in his voice. 'No. Nothing wrong. Let us go back to Belle's and write the note.'

Despite Drew's assurance that nothing was wrong, he'd left her at Madam Belle's the moment his note to his brother had been dispatched. He had wanted to look at the place they had set for the meeting. And he'd wanted to go alone, leaving Rowena sitting on tenterhooks fearing he'd be caught.

The lad they had sent to his brother's office was to wait for a reply. Given their fear of interception, Drew had kept the note very brief. It had talked about there being no need to climb the bridge to collect the eggs. It would, he had said, let his brother know who was seeking the meeting, but would mean nothing to anyone else.

A rap sounded on the door. 'Who is it?' she asked, having been warned by Drew not to open it to anyone unless she recognised the voice.

'Me, ma'am. Nat.' The errand boy.

She opened the door. The boy grinned and waved a piece of paper.

'You saw him? Lord Aleyne?'

'Not me. His clerk. He'd not be letting the likes of me near his lordship. But he did send a reply.'

Too bad Drew wasn't here to receive it. Heavy footsteps on the stairs made her look up. It was Drew. 'We have a reply,' she said.

He took the note from the boy, gave him a coin and came inside and closed the door, tapping the note against his gloved palm.

'Open it,' she said. 'If he says no, then we will find someone else to help us. My father had a lawyer. Mr Murchison. He might be willing to talk to us.'

Drew set the note on the table, removed his gloves, coat, hat and scarf. She wanted to shout at him, he was so deliberately slow. But she did not blame him. This was his brother from whom he was estranged. She sensed that if the note was a rejection he would take it hard.

He sat down on the bed and patted the place beside him. She joined him on the bed. Breath held, she watched him open the note. He handed it over without a glance at the contents.

'Read it.'

So commanding. Pleasure unfurled low in her belly. She took it from him.

The hand was bold and black and the words brief.

'"Logan, what game are you playing? If you are in trouble with the law or with McKenzie, I will have your head on a plate. Niall."'

She wrinkled her nose and looked at Drew. 'He didn't know it was you.'

The muscles in his jaw flickered. 'Perhaps it is just as well. If he had guessed it was me, he might not have replied.'

'Oh, Drew,' she said, feeling the hurt in his voice as a pang in her chest.

He squared his shoulders. 'But he will come for Logan. So perhaps it is just as well he did not recognise my writing.'

'He mentions McKenzie, too.'

'Aye. God knows what Logan is about. He always was a wild scamp.' He looked at the small clock on the mantel. 'It is but a half hour to the time I set for the meeting. We had best get going.'

The clouds had rolled in over the city, grey and heavy with the threat of snow. People in the streets scurried head down about their business. To Rowena, everyone looked suspicious, but after a circuitous route, Drew stopped for a second.

'No one is following. Unless they are very, very clever.'

She breathed a sigh of relief, trusting him to know and happy to leave such matters in his hands.

Finally, they were in sight of the bridge. Standing right at the centre was a young man in a dark coat and hat, pacing up and down and slapping his arms across his chest.

'That's him,' Drew said, at the place where the bridge began to cross the old Calton Road. 'Niall.'

She took his hand, as much for his comfort as for hers. He tucked it into the crook of his arm and patted it lightly.

Niall stopped his pacing and looked towards them. He was dark, not blonde like Drew. He took a step in their direction and then stopped, frowning, but he wasn't looking at Drew, he was looking at her, and as they came closer his frown deepened.

'What the devil is going on?' he said as they came within earshot. His gaze dropped to where their arms linked. 'Who is this?'

'Is that a proper greeting for a brother you haven't seen in six years?'

There was a careless drawl in his voice. A devil-may-care note she hadn't heard before. His arm beneath her fingers had tensed. It was as rigid as a board. He was ready for his brother to turn away. Steeled against it.

Rowena could only watch as the other man peered into Drew's eyes uncertainly.

Drew pulled down the muffler.

Niall reared back. 'What? Who? My God, Drew!' he whispered. 'Can it really be you?'

Drew nodded stiffly. 'It is.'

Niall lunged forward, clutching his brother to his chest, then leaning back to look at his face. 'We heard you were dead.'

'Not yet,' Drew said drily.

'Hell's teeth,' he said, his eyes taking in the scar. 'What happened? Why didn't you come to the house? Why the strange message? I have been standing here for the past half hour, thinking Logan was in some sort of trouble. Just wait until Ian knows you have returned. And Mother.'

'Mother is… She's well?' His voice sounded strained.

'She'll be all the better for seeing you.'

If Drew noticed the evasion, he didn't mention it. He glanced around. 'To tell you the truth, Niall, I am in a wee spot of trouble. Is there somewhere we can talk? Somewhere we won't be seen?'

Niall stared at him, smiling, seemingly lost in some sort of reverie. 'You have to meet my wife. And Ian's Selina. And—'

'Niall, we don't have time. There are dangerous men—' He looked over his shoulder. 'Damnation.'

Rowena followed the direction of his stare. Her heart sunk. Walking towards them was the man whose narrowed gaze focused only on them.

'You were followed,' Drew said. 'My note said to take care no one followed you.'

'Damn it, Drew. I bloody well did.'

'There's no time for this,' Rowena said. 'We can't risk—'

The smuggler must have realised he had been spotted because he started to run, one hand tucked under his coat. Probably holding a pistol. Drew looked the other way and groaned. Another one was coming from the other direction.

'There's only one thing to do,' Niall said. 'Rush the man coming from the far side of the bridge.'

'Come on, then,' Drew said grimly. He took Rowena's hand and she hoiked up her skirts in the other and they ran straight at the smuggler.

He must have thought they hadn't seen him because he started to grin and unbuttoned his coat. Rowena could see the grip of a pistol sticking up from his waistband.

'He's got a gun,' she gasped.

'I see it,' Drew said.

'He's not the only one,' Niall said. He reached under his coat and pulled out an ornate duelling pistol. He cocked and fired. The smuggler hit the ground with a howl.

And then they were over the bridge and running alongside a building.

Rowena glanced over her shoulder. The man they'd seen first was catching them up and he had drawn his pistol. She tried to run faster.

'Stop them,' the smuggler behind them yelled at passers-by. 'Stop, thief.'

A burly man on the pavement in front of them put his arms out to block them.

Chapter Thirteen

'Let them pass,' Niall shouted at the man standing in their path. To Rowena's surprise he stepped aside.

'Guard the door,' Niall said to him. 'Don't let anyone in.' He dived through the building's nearest door.

Drew thrust Rowena ahead of him, lifting her off her feet in his rush to get her inside.

Niall slammed the door and locked it.

'What the devil?' Drew said, staring at his brother. 'Who was that outside? I thought we were done for.'

'Bodyguard,' Niall said. 'I'll explain in a moment.' He led the way down a narrow corridor that opened out into the great hall of a sumptuous office building. A porter hurried forward to greet him with a bow. 'My lord?'

Drew made a snorting noise through his nose.

Niall ignored him. 'We need a room where we can be private, and brandy.' He glanced at Rowena.

'Tea, please,' she said, still gasping from their wild run. How they had managed to cross the bridge ahead of their pursuer she wasn't quite sure. It seemed that with

Drew holding her hand, her feet had barely touched the ground.

The servant opened the door to a small sitting room tucked away behind some columns. 'Will this do, my lord?'

'Excellent,' Niall Gilvry said. No, he was Lord Aleyne, Rowena reminded herself.

She sank down on to the nearest sofa and perched on its edge, watching Drew eye his beaming younger brother warily.

Aleyne stepped towards Drew as if he would offer an embrace, but Drew stiffened and took a half step back. Aleyne shook his head, but his grin remained. 'I can't believe you are here.'

'Believe it.'

'We heard you were killed in a hunting accident.'

'Heard from whom?'

'Carrick. By way of the hunting party.'

'Is that so? Well, whether you like it or no', I am still alive.' His voice was hard and grim.

'Good heavens, Drew! Are you saying you think I would be glad if you were not?'

The muscle in Drew's face flickered as he fought some emotion he did not let show in his eyes. Rowena had the feeling it was pain. But it could just as easily have been anger.

'You've been missed,' Aleyne said. 'By Mother, especially. You were always her favourite after Logan. She refused to accept you were gone. Not without proof. And, by Jove, she was right.'

At that last, Drew turned away and paced to the window.

Aleyne stared at him, a puzzled frown on his face. 'Dammit, Drew, so much has happened since you left, I have no idea where to start. All of us are married. Even Logan, and to the unlikeliest of women. Though she has been good for him. Settled him down no end.' He shook his head. 'And you? What happened to you? Why didn't you let us know you were alive until now?'

'It is a long story,' Drew said. 'And not relevant to our current situation. What is all this I hear about you being a lord? And why the bodyguard?'

Aleyne's handsome face hardened. 'Also long stories. But since you ask, my title came through my wife.'

Drew curled his lip. 'Married an heiress, did you? Ian thought it was all right for you, then.'

'Ian had no knowledge of it until it was done. Ours is a love match.' His tone held disapproval.

Drew winced. 'And he married the Albright woman.'

'Lady Selina is a grand lass and has been very good for our Ian.'

'Not to mention good for the family coffers. She brought him Dunross, I understand.' Drew's voice and eyes were as cold as ice. 'Whereas I was banished for trying to save the family fortunes.'

Aleyne shook his head. 'You have no idea how much he regretted… But I should let him tell you himself. He will be here tomorrow to meet with Lord Gordon.'

'I'll be here then, too,' Drew said. To Rowena it sounded like a threat.

'Good. He's bringing Mother, too, to see a specialist for her lungs.'

'Why the bodyguard?' Drew asked abruptly.

'Ian's idea,' Niall said. 'There are some unsavoury elements who have caused us problems recently.'

'Do they work for a man named McKenzie? They mistook me for Logan, at first.'

Now, why was he not telling his brother everything with respect to the smugglers? Didn't he trust him? Were there things about his family Drew hadn't told her?

'He does look like you, Drew,' Niall said. 'His hair is lighter and he doesna'…' He winced.

'His face isna' scarred,' Drew said. 'It was what finally convinced the blackguards I wasna' him. It seems like young Logan has been creating quite a stir.'

'Aye. McKenzie is our competitor. Logan runs rings around him. The man would like nothing better than to see an end to him. You were lucky to escape with your life.'

Drew looked at Rowena. 'I had help.'

That look warmed her through.

Niall looked shocked. 'You want to be careful. They are dangerous.'

'So we discovered,' Drew said.

Rowena expected him to say more. To speak of his capture. He didn't. He looked at her. 'I should introduce you to my companion. Mrs Samuel MacDonald, this is Niall Gilvry, my brother, Lord Aleyne.'

Aleyne stared at her open-mouthed and then looked from her to his brother. 'Hell's teeth! You have the missing MacDonalds?' He turned to Rowena. 'Is your husband with you?'

Rowena gaped at him. 'My husband is dead.'

'What do you mean?' Drew asked at the same moment. 'The missing MacDonalds?'

Niall looked from one to the other. 'Haven't you heard? Mere died some weeks ago, in a boating accident. The lawyers for the estate have been trying to contact surviving family members.'

'I have indeed been in contact with the Duke of Mere's lawyers. The duke was named executor of my husband's will,' Rowena said.

An odd expression crossed Aleyne's face. 'And how do you come to be involved in the case, Drew?'

'Case?' Drew said. 'I was there when Samuel MacDonald met his end. I was tasked with bringing his remains home to his family.'

'I see,' Aleyne said thoughtfully.

Drew narrowed his eyes. 'Just what is it that you see?'

'The matter was in all the papers. The search for the heir. The estate is in a state of limbo until all the relevant relations have been contacted.'

Rowena stared at him. 'No one mentioned any word of this. Indeed, I understood that the new duke was already in place. I never met him when I visited Mere Castle. I was told he was indisposed.'

'It is all verra odd,' Aleyne said. 'To whom did you speak?'

'Mr Jones, the duke's lawyer,' Rowena said.

'Jones? Never heard of him. He certainly wasn't the old duke's lawyer,' Aleyne said. 'Carstairs and Raglin have served the Dukes of Mere for three generations. And I can tell you that there is no lawyer or clerk named Jones in their office. I deal with other clients of theirs on a regular basis.'

'But he met us at Mere,' Rowena said.

Drew nodded in confirmation.

Aleyne looked at her with consternation.

'And then there was Lady Cragg,' Rowena said.

'And who might she be?'

She looked helplessly at Drew. 'I don't know. I thought she must be the duke's hostess. A member of his family. She was in charge of the servants.'

'A distant cousin of the old duke, perhaps,' Aleyne said. 'There is no new duke confirmed as yet. Though there have, as I understand it, been a few claimants to the title.'

'Surely a duke would know the identity of his heir,' Rowena protested.

'You would think so,' Aleyne said. 'But though we are calling him the old duke, he was younger than I am by a good bit and he was about to be married. I doubt he expected to cut his stick quite yet.'

'Are you saying that you think that perhaps my husband might have been his heir?' Rowena finally said. She'd kept trying not to think that this was what all this meant, but logically what else could it be?

'Only someone from Carstairs and Raglan could say for certain. But he was one of those mentioned in the papers as being sought. Another is a small lad barely out of petticoats.'

'I saw a small boy,' Rowena said. 'At Mere. He was playing in the gardens.'

'Why didn't they tell Rowena all of this?' Drew asked.

Rowena stiffened as Lord Aleyne's sharp gaze went to her face at Drew's use of her first name. She looked down her nose at Drew's brother. 'That is a question I would like answered,' she said tersely. 'Lady Cragg did mention the need for legal matters to be ironed out.'

Lord Aleyne went to the hearth and leaned an elbow on the mantel, looking at them both with a frown. 'I will speak to Will Carstairs. He's a friend of mine. Of course, he won't give away any confidences, but there are things he might be able to tell me. I will need the answer to a few questions before I see him.'

'What would you like to know?' Rowena asked.

'First, is there proof of your husband's death?' Aleyne said.

'There is,' Drew replied. 'We delivered his remains to Mere Castle on our way to Edinburgh.'

Aleyne's frown deepened.

'There is something else I should mention,' Drew said, leaning back. 'This man Jones, who said he was the duke's lawyer, seemed very insistent on establishing the exact date of Mr MacDonald's death. Or at least, he was for a while. When I told him I didn't have proof, he suddenly didn't seem to care.'

'Do you know the date of death?' Aleyne asked in a strange tone of voice.

Drew shot him a hard look. 'Tell me why it is so important.'

'The date, Drew,' Aleyne said.

'September fifteenth,' Drew growled.

'By all that's holy,' Aleyne whispered. 'Are you sure?'

Drew bristled. 'I wouldna' say it if I wasna'. I suppose now you will be asking me for proof.'

Aleyne turned his gaze on Rowena. 'If you have it, you are a very wealthy woman, your Grace.'

Drew felt the same as he had below decks on the ship. As if he was suffocating. Rowena stared open-mouthed at his brother.

'What are you talking about?' she asked.

'If your husband died on the fifteenth of September, he died as the duke,' Niall pronounced.

'It doesn't make him any less dead,' she said.

'But it makes you the dowager duchess.'

Rowena's eyes widened. 'An empty title, Lord Aleyne.'

Drew had a strange sense about where this was leading. He kept his face impassive and waited to see what his brother would say.

'And there will be settlements and privileges that attain.'

Drew felt his chest squeeze. 'It all hinges on the date of MacDonald's death, then.'

'Do you have proof?' Niall asked.

An image of the page from MacDonald's journal leaped to his mind. 'Is my word not good enough for you either?'

Niall cocked his head to one side. 'Not when large sums of money are concerned. You would have to be proved a witness without any interest in the outcome.'

'I have none,' Drew said.

'You are travelling together,' Niall mused. 'Which might not be a problem. I assume you have not—' he hesitated and gave a grimace of distaste '—been indiscreet? Your past reputation for dalliance…'

'That was years ago.'

'A clever lawyer would not hesitate to use it if it suited him.'

Drew bit back a curse at all lawyers.

Niall looked at Rowena. 'I assume you are travelling with a companion? Or a maid?'

Rowena blushed fiery red and Drew wanted to hit Niall for making her look so embarrassed. 'Mrs Mac-Donald's private life is no one else's business.'

Rowena gave him a smile of gratitude, then shook her head. 'Lord Aleyne is right. Innocent or guilty, facts will be twisted by others who have an axe to grind.' She looked down her long nose at Drew. 'We have spent more than one night alone together.' Her blush deepened. She was, of course, embarrassed by what they had done.

'It will be an expensive fight, Mrs MacDonald,' Niall said regretfully. 'And a difficult one without any proof.'

She bowed her head. 'It is your advice that we not make the attempt and I accept whatever they feel inclined to offer, then?'

Niall sighed. 'It might be. Let me consult with Carstairs before we come to a decision.'

Bile rose in Drew's throat. He didn't want to deprive Rowena of what should be hers by right. A dowager duchess! Who would ever have guessed such an outcome?

But if Drew offered the proof he had of the date, circumstantial evidence at best, and it was not accepted, the shameful revelations in the journal would have been made for nothing.

No. They must take his word. The journal was a last resort. 'We will hear what these friends of yours have to say before proceeding further.' He looked at Rowena. She nodded.

Niall bowed his head. 'That is also my advice. Where are you staying?'

Drew tensed. He didn't want anyone to know where they were staying. He took a deep breath. This was Niall. Not a stranger. Not a renegade. Or a smuggler. 'At Madam Belle's.'

Niall's jaw dropped. He swallowed. 'Interesting choice.'

Rowena's expression became remote. Drew glowered. 'It's where no one would think to look for us.'

'McKenzie's men,' Niall said. 'I'd almost forgotten. What the deuce is going on?'

'Something to do with Logan.'

'But they must know you are not Logan.'

Rowena leaned forward. 'Someone else means Drew harm. A man visiting Mere Castle. I heard him talking.'

'Let it go, Mrs MacDonald. It's not important,' Drew said. It was something he would solve on his own.

'Someone else?' Niall's eyes narrowed. 'Who?'

'I have no idea.' He couldn't keep the bitterness from his voice as he kept his suspicions firmly behind his teeth. Niall would never hear a word against Ian without proof, and that he didn't have. Yet. 'How long will it take for you to get the information from Carstairs?'

'I should have something by noon. Come home with me and wait. I know Jenna would be thrilled to meet you. She's heard so much about you. Us. Our antics as boys.'

Had she heard about how he was banished from the family and why? 'These men are trouble. You don't need them at your house.'

Niall nodded. 'As I know only too well.'

There was something in his face Drew didn't quite understand, but he thought better of asking. He didn't want to get too close to his brother. Not given what the future held.

'I don't want them showing up at Belle's either,' he said.

'Where shall we meet, then?' Niall asked.

'In a private parlour at the Whitehorse Inn.' It was public enough and had entrances and exits to make it a place of safety.

Niall nodded. 'When Logan arrives tonight, I'll ask him if he has any idea of what McKenzie is about.'

'He'll be in the city, too?'

'He and Charity are visiting for a few days. Ian called a meeting.'

His gut lurched at the sound of his older brother's name. He forced himself to remain impassive. 'I suppose there's no harm in asking Logan about McKenzie. What I need right now is a back door out of here.'

'That I can do.'

Drew brought Rowena to her feet and escorted her to the door. He opened it. Niall caught his arm as she passed through the door. 'Drew,' he said in a low voice. 'Man, we've missed you.' Drew shook off his hand.

'What's wrong?' Niall said. 'Aren't you glad to be home?'

A lump of something hot seemed to stick in the back of his throat. 'It's complicated,' he said and was horrified at the thick sound in his voice.

Drew paced back and forth across the private parlour in the Whitehorse Inn like a caged animal. And every time Rowena opened her mouth she closed it again, because she sensed that whatever was going on in his head, he would not welcome an interruption.

Finally, he stopped and stared out of the window into the courtyard below, his body stiff and rigid.

Unable to bear the tension in the room any longer, she took a deep breath. 'Were we followed here, do you think?'

He shook his head slowly and turned back to face her. There was resolution in his expression. 'No.'

'Then what is wrong, Drew?' she said softly, treading warily.

He reached inside his coat and pulled out a small book bound in blue leather. 'Your husband's journal.'

'Oh,' she said and frowned, a cold sensation rippling through her stomach. 'It must contain some pretty damning things if you have kept it hidden all this time.' Her husband must have said the same vile things about her in there as he had said to her face. How like Drew to want to protect her from Sam's wicked tongue.

His eyes widened. His mouth twisted in a wry grimace. 'Damning. Aye.' He held it out to her.

'I don't want to see it.'

He hesitated, then thrust it towards her as if it was hot and he wanted to be rid of it. 'You need it,' he said. 'It proves he was still alive two days after the duke died.'

For a moment she couldn't assimilate the words. 'Proves?' She rose to her feet and took the book. 'You have had this all along and you said nothing?' She shook her head, staring at the book he held out to her. 'Of course. You had not yet read it. When did you discover…? Why say nothing to Lord Aleyne?' She raised her gaze to his face and was shocked by the pain in his eyes and the cruel twist to his mouth. 'Drew?' she said.

'I've known it all along,' he ground out through a jaw clenched hard.

'But—'

'It didn't suit me to hand it over.'

An odd sensation ran down her spine. Her scalp prickled and tightened. What was he not telling her?

Again he thrust it towards her and this time she took it, running her palm over butter-soft leather, still warm with the heat of his body. She started to open the cover.

'Wait,' he commanded. The usual shiver ran down her spine, but this was not the game they played at night. He was not in charge of what she did or did not do.

She lifted the cover and moved to the window for more light.

'Please, Rowena,' he said.

The agony in his voice halted her, made her look at him. She'd been wrong—he wasn't angry, he was suffering from some sort of dread.

'What is it?' she asked.

'There are some things I must tell you. Before you read what is there. Before you learn them from others.'

She'd always known he was a man with secrets. That he would want to share them with her made her feel warm inside. She glanced down at the book, and then nodded. 'Very well.'

'It might be better if you sat down.' The wry humour was back in his voice. 'If you would.' And he wasn't telling her, he was asking. She returned to her seat by the hearth, the book clasped in both hands.

He looked as if he wanted to continue his pacing, but instead he took the chair opposite and leaned forward, hands clasped between his knees, his gaze fixed on them. 'I told you that I left Scotland in disgrace.'

'Yes.'

'I didn't tell you why I left Scotland. My brother Ian banished me from these shores.'

'Does it matter? Your younger brother seemed delighted—'

He cut her off with a quick shake of his head. 'Likely Niall doesn't know the full story.' He raised his gaze to meet hers and there was sorrow and regret in the shadows of his eyes. 'I seduced a woman and ruined her in the eyes of London society.'

Shock stole her breath and she gasped. 'Why?'

His laugh was short and bitter. 'She was an heiress. We needed money at Dunross. It was the quickest way to fill our coffers.'

Her heart stilled. 'Are you married, then?'

'No. I picked her because she seemed such a practical wee lass. Not one to engage in flights of fancy. Or want to live in my pocket. I was wrong. It turned out she fell head over ears in love and then discovered I was just marrying her for her money.'

'Oh.' Just like Samuel. A pain seemed to grow around her heart.

'Aye, oh. But it was too late by then. Everyone knew she'd been in my bed.'

Shocked, she stared at him. 'And you didn't marry her?'

'She wouldna' have me. Not even to save her reputation. Ian got to learn of what I'd done. He was verra angry. Said he was ashamed of me. I'd dishonoured the family name. You would never have known he was only a year older than me, he gave me such a bear-garden jaw. He said it was best if I left the country and arranged with our clan chief for work in America.'

She waited, terrified of what he might say next.

He huffed out a breath. 'Ian arranged that I would never come back.'

She blinked. 'He said you could never come home again?'

'He arranged to have me killed. And I should have been, if I hadna' stumbled right at the moment his henchman made his shot.' He touched his cheek. 'He was aiming for my heart. Not my head. My head is a lot harder.'

'Oh, Drew.' She reached out a hand.

He shook his head, refusing her sympathy. 'The thing is, I have come back. And Ian is going to pay for what he did.'

'What do you mean, pay?'

'With his life.'

The words were spoken flatly. The sound of it made her heart stand still. Then race. 'Drew, no. You can't mean that. I understand your anger, but he's your brother. How can you be sure of his intentions?'

'His man told me, right before he took his shot.'

She felt sick. 'But what does this have to do with the journal?'

'It has the proof of the date of Samuel's death. I've always known it.'

'And you never said.'

'No. I never said.'

'But why?' She looked down at the little book.

'You'll know, when you read it.'

Her stomach fell away. Her heart began to ache as she realised what he was telling her. 'You knew he was the duke's heir? You seduced me to...to...' Wealth? Position? Was that his motive?

He was staring at her. For a moment, she thought he would deny the charge. He got up and took a short, jerky pace away from her. Then turned back. 'Aye. He told me. He told me he never expected to inherit, though. But I guessed the family would pay handsomely to know what had happened to him. And then there was you. A woman I guessed was about to become a very wealthy widow.'

Anger bubbled hot through her veins. 'You guessed? And never said a word? What, did you think I would marry you?'

'Would you no'? Had I asked you?'

Oh, heavens above. She would have. She had fallen for him, hard. Made the same mistake again.

He smiled cruelly, yet she could almost imagine his eyes told a different story. One of regret.

'Aye, you would have,' he said in harsh tones. 'Any fool would grasp that it would serve my purpose, do you see? With that much money in my pocket, I'd be well able to deal with my brother and no one the wiser.'

'Then why are you telling me this now? Why not just carry on with your foul scheme of ruining another woman's reputation and forcing her to wed you?' The bitterness in her words shocked her, but the hurt in her heart was far worse. She felt as if a knife had pierced right to her soul and she wanted to hurt him, too.

He flinched, then straightened his shoulders and looked down at the journal. 'Because they will no' accept my word about the date. And I find I canna rightfully deprive you of what should be yours.' He gave a bitter laugh. 'And once they see the journal, they will know what sort of man I am. Rowena, if I thought an apology would make a difference, I would make one. You'll be fine, lass. The journal will prove your claim. You'll be set up for the rest of your life.'

He headed towards the door.

'Where are you going?' she demanded.

'To hell.' He opened the door, then turned to look back at her, his face a mask of beauty and destruction. 'I'm going to do what I set out to do when I boarded that ship with your husband's body. I'm going to see justice done.' There was a wealth of agony in his voice.

He walked out.

He was going to kill his brother. And if he did, there

was no doubt Niall would seek his own justice. Through the mighty arm of the law.

The pain in her heart at the way he had used her for his own ends was nothing to her fear for him. He might not have fallen for her, the way she had fallen for him, but that didn't mean she wanted to see him die on the gallows. She had to stop him.

And the only way she could do that was to tell his brother Niall of his plan. She glanced down at the journal and opened it at the length of silk between its pages.

Chapter Fourteen

Yellow Dog melted into the shadows. Watching. Waiting. Patient, the way only a predator could be. Unfeeling as stone.

Yet he wasn't unfeeling. There was a cursed pain behind his ribs like the ache of a festering sore. A wound that would never heal. It was the recollection of the way she had looked at him. Her. Rowena. Of the devastation in her expression. The realisation of betrayal.

Betrayal hurt.

Yellow Dog snarled at the fates that had made him cause that look on her face. Made him say the lie about caring only for the money, for her sake. So afterwards she could live with herself. And forget him. But he would never forget her. Not if he lived to be a hundred. Which he wouldn't. He would be lucky if he lasted the night.

He didn't care. He had nothing left. Except his revenge.

A pedestrian strolled along the street, sauntering with no idea death lurked in the shadows of New Town.

Yellow Dog became one with the darkness as the Indians had shown him.

No. Not Yellow Dog. Damn it. Where the hell had that come from after all these months? He was Drew Gilvry. And he was standing opposite his brother Niall's house for a just purpose. He was waiting for Ian. He was waiting with his loaded pistol and the knife in his boot, because they would not let him in the house with his pistol.

She would have told Niall his intentions.

He had no reservations or doubts on that score. Once the hurt had worn off, anger would have set in. And she would have betrayed him, just as he had betrayed her. And he could not but feel glad of it. For her sake. Tonight, they would both have their justice. And he would love her for it.

Love. Hell. He had never believed in love. Not for him. Not for the way he was. And yet he'd found the one woman who did not revile his disgusting needs and habits. She almost made them seem...acceptable. Despite that his first woman had told him that his proclivities were unnatural. Perverted. Only when need drove him hard had he let them get the better of him.

Until Rowena.

With Rowena, it was like being transported to a different world. He'd felt clean. And he had thought he never would again, after what *she* had forced him to do.

They would all know the truth of it now. Know what he'd been called. And how he'd been used. The slavery. The obedience. It was all in MacDonald's journal. Not quite all. The worst of it, even MacDonald hadn't known. But enough that they would guess.

And so tonight Ian would finally have his way. Drew would die. But so would Ian. And they'd both go to hell.

It didn't matter to him. He'd been in a living hell for the past two years. Death would be a welcome relief.

If it wasn't for Rowena.

Perhaps she wouldn't be there.

He'd seen Logan arrive. So tall. And broad shouldered. He knew him by his yellow hair, which had caught in the lamplight as he removed his hat to enter the house. His wife had been bundled in fur and he'd seen nothing of her but her height. She was tall for a woman. For a moment, he'd thought it might be Rowena, but he'd known it was not.

The north wind tugged at his cloak, but he didn't feel its bite. He was dressed warmer than he ever had been with the Indians. He'd been lucky they'd given him anything to wear at all.

A carriage rolled down the street.

He let his breath go and remained perfectly still. Not a puff of misty air through the muffling scarf would betray his presence to his prey, because instinct told him this was Ian.

A large man stepped down swiftly and waved off the footman who, instead of letting down the steps, hurried up to the front door to knock. A carriage and a footman. It appeared Ian's fortunes had improved considerably. Anger rose in his throat. He unclenched his fists. Time enough for anger when he faced the man with his crime.

Ian bent to let down the steps. Drew could see him, a moving shadow on the other side of the coach, which was lit by a street lamp. Not one, but two others alighted. Two ladies.

His heart lurched. One was short and the other tall. Rowena. Without doubt. How the hell? This he had not expected.

Niall must have somehow got word to Ian earlier in the day. After his meeting with Rowena, when she would have revealed all. It didn't matter. He'd expected her to be there. To be at Niall's house, awaiting his arrival. He'd assumed Niall would smuggle her in through a back door from the mews behind the house. Ian was taking the threat pretty calmly, then, if he was strolling in through the front door.

Drew eyed the distance between him and his target. And then saw through Ian's plan. If Drew tried to kill him on the doorstep, he might miss and hurt one of the women. He put his hand on the pistol in his pocket. He could make the shot. Rowena was ahead of Ian, her head rising above him as she mounted the steps. In the lamplight, he easily recognised her bonnet. But as he knew only too well, even a clear shot could go awry. He touched his cheek, reminding himself why he was here. Why he could not make any mistake. A man didn't take kindly to being shot at. A near miss would only prolong matters.

The door was already open when Rowena reached the top step. She stepped inside. The others followed.

Drew couldn't help but feel a spark of admiration for his older brother. Not once did he look around him. Nowhere in his bearing did he show any worry. Yet he must know Drew was out here. Watching. Waiting.

The door closed.

Now to enter the house.

The tension in the drawing room was palpable. Rowena had been introduced to the Gilvry men and their wives, the vivacious little Lady Aleyne sitting beside the hearth, the tall, beautiful and coolly sophisticated Mrs Logan Gilvry on the couch beside Lady Selina, who was as tiny as she was fair. Gorgeous women.

And her. In her shabby governess clothes.

Even dressed as fine as five pence she would have been nowhere near as elegant or lovely as these women. They must wonder at Drew. What he'd seen in her. But of course they didn't. They knew he'd seen money. Nothing else.

The pain of it stabbed her heart anew.

'Are you sure your men will see him if he should arrive?' the Laird of Dunross said, his stern face set in harsh lines as he addressed the golden youngest brother, Logan.

He was what Drew would have been without the scar. Stunningly handsome. His wife had an aura of hardness about her, until she looked at her husband as she did now, with a smile. 'You don't have to worry about Logan's men doing their duty,' she said.

English. Like Lady Selina.

'I have them on all the roofs,' Logan added. 'Not even a wee mouse can creep by without them seeing.'

Ian Gilvry grunted. 'I don't want him hurt, ye ken. Just immobilised and brought in.'

Some of the tension went out of Rowena at the knowledge they wouldn't hurt him. Some. But not enough to make her neck stop aching. 'He's very skilled,' she said and, aware of all the eyes in the room swivelling her way, lifted her chin, giving them her best governess stare. 'He learned from the Indians.'

'One Highlander is better than ten savages, I can assure you, Mrs MacDonald,' Logan asserted with his charming grin. He walked to the window and made as if to part the curtains to look out.

'Logan. Keep back,' the laird ordered.

'If he's out there, he'll ken I'm not you by the hair,' Logan replied, but he let his hand fall.

'Why take the chance?' Niall said. 'If he's been waiting all these years, he'll be ruthless. And desperate to bring it to a close.'

'Then it is a good thing we took your mother and the children to stay with the Carstairs,' Jenna said, her voice a little wobbly.

'He would never harm Ma or the children,' Ian said. 'Not Drew.'

'He's changed,' Niall said. 'I—'

The door swung back slowly. A man in a black greatcoat, head swathed in a scarf, slipped silently into the room and stood with his back against the wall, a pistol in each hand, both cocked, one pointed at Ian's heart.

Someone, perhaps Lady Selina, gave a little scream.

'Your men should be watching the basement windows,' Drew said.

Logan cursed and stepped forward.

'Stay out of it,' Drew said, lining the other pistol up on him. 'I've nae quarrel with you, lad. This is between me and Ian.' He moved the pistol slightly, so it was pointed at Lady Jenna.

Logan halted, looking at Ian, whose face was grim. 'This is nonsense, Drew.'

'Nonsense, is it? That's why you have your men lying in wait for me. No doubt with orders to kill on sight. They failed last time. And they have failed again.'

Ian let out an exasperated sigh. 'They are there to prevent you from doing anything stupid.'

'Why not just admit the truth, Ian?' Drew said, his voice cold and hard. 'Tell them what you did.'

'I did nothing but send you away,' Ian said. He took a step towards Drew, who straightened, his eyes narrowing a fraction.

She couldn't bear it. He was just so damned angry. He wasn't going to listen to reason. Not from his brother. But would he listen to reason from her?

She rose from her chair and stepped between Ian and Drew. 'Don't do this. Please, Drew.'

'Damn you, Rowena. Stay out of this. You have everything you want.'

'Everything except you.'

He flinched. Then shook his head. 'You don't want me. Not now.'

The journal. Her heart ached. Feeling helpless against the barrier he had thrown up, she pressed on. 'Drew, I won't let you do this. It isn't right. He's your brother.'

'A brother who wanted me dead. Well, he'll have his way after tonight. But he'll no' be around to know it.'

Trembling deep inside, she took a step closer. She

knew he wouldn't shoot her. But he could so easily sweep her aside. 'He says it isn't true.'

'And you'll take his word over mine.' The hurt in his voice shattered her heart.

'Please, Drew.' She held out a hand. 'I love you.'

His gaze flew to her face. 'No,' he said. 'You're with them.'

The denial pierced her soul. Hot tears welled at the back of her nose. She reached for the pistol. 'Drew—'

'Rowena,' he said, his voice cracking. 'Don't make me choose. You know I need this.'

'No, Drew.'

The pistol wavered. Logan and Niall launched themselves at Drew and threw him to the floor. His hat fell off, his scarf came unravelled as he fought like a wild man to keep his pistols.

Ian stepped in and wrenched one away. Niall took the other and tossed it aside.

In sick horror, Rowena could only watch as he slowly came to the realisation he was outmatched. Niall and Logan heaved him to his feet.

Lady Selina gasped and turned away as she saw his face. Jenna took her hands and said something in a low voice. The other woman, Logan's wife, narrowed her eyes, her mouth set in a straight line.

Logan pulled a rope from his pocket and began binding Drew's hands behind his back. 'So we can talk, aye?'

Drew struggled against the ropes, crashing Logan into the wall, almost breaking free of the two men.

'Stop,' Rowena said. 'Don't...don't tie him. He'll give you his parole.'

Drew lifted his head to look at her and the hurt of betrayal was in his face. 'Will I, now?' he said, his chest rising and falling from the effort. He already had the start of a bruise around his one eye and another on his chin.

'You will,' she said in a voice that had cowed more than one recalcitrant lad.

'Give me your word you'll do nothing until we get to the bottom of what happened,' Ian said.

Drew sneered, 'So you can pull the wool over everyone's eyes, you mean.' His gaze flicked to the Lady Selina. 'You were always very good at that.'

Logan began binding his wrists.

'Drew,' Rowena said.

He glared at her. 'All right. My parole. For now.' He shrugged off the hands that were holding him.

She became aware of Ian staring at him, at the ruined flesh, and of the regret in his face. 'Drew,' he said. 'I am so bloody sorry.'

Drew touched his cheek and turned his face side on, a gesture she hadn't seen from him for a while. It struck a blow to her chest far harder than the mistrust in his eyes. 'I don't care about sorry,' Drew said to his brother harshly. 'I care about justice.'

'Are we all done with the brawling you Highlanders seem to enjoy so much?' a cynical cultured voice said from the doorway.

A tall man with fair hair, handsome in a refined sort of way, sauntered in with an expression of weary distaste.

'Jaimie,' Logan said. 'Any luck?'

The dandy brushed an imaginary speck of lint from his sleeve. 'It is not about luck, dear boy.' He looked up and gave an especially sweet smile to the occupants of the room, his blue eyes twinkling. 'It is about knowing where to look and having the means to do so.' He turned back to the door. 'Bring him in.'

A couple of burly rough-looking men dragged a woebegone figure through the door and pushed down on his shoulders until he sat slumped in a chair. He was conscious, barely.

'Morris,' Drew exclaimed.

'Oh, have you two met already? Allow me to introduce him to the others.'

'I know him,' Logan said. 'Tab Morris. One of McKenzie's bully boys.'

One of the toughs holding him, a man who looked like a bruiser, touched his forelock. 'Ye'll not be having any trouble with him now, milord,' he said in a gravelly voice. He glanced over at Logan's wife and inclined his head. 'Ma'am.'

She smiled at him. 'Growler. Your sister is well?'

'Yes, ma'am. In the pink.'

Both men left the room, leaving their victim behind clutching one of his arms.

Drew was glaring at the man they had called Jaimie. 'Who the hell are you?'

'Lord Sanford,' Ian said. 'Drew Gilvry. Another of my brothers. Mrs MacDonald you met earlier at the Whitehorse Inn.'

Sanford bowed with languid grace, but Drew wasn't watching the lordling, he was looking at her, frowning, guessing that she'd been instrumental in his capture, no doubt.

'He's a friend of my wife's friend, Alice Fulton, now Lady Hawkhurst.' Ian's face hardened to granite. 'You remember Alice, Drew?'

Drew's expression twisted as his gaze went back to his brother. 'How could I forget?'

Lady Selina made a small sound of protest.

'Well, now that the niceties are dealt with,' Lord Sanford said, 'shall we see what this disreputable chap has to say?'

She'd said she loved him. The force of those words were still battering against his brain even as he tried to make sense of what was going on.

She couldn't have read the journal.

She didna' know yet what he was. What he'd been. Or she had. And she'd decided he was better off out of the way. Because it didn't matter what Ian said, or how many paroles he gave, he was not going to give up. Not as long as he lived.

He forced himself to focus on what the dandified English lordling was saying to Morris.

'Who do you work for?'

'McKenzie,' that man said, wiping a bloody nose on his sleeve.

'There's nothing new in that,' Drew said.

'And what were your orders?'

Morris gave him a resentful look. 'I already told you.'

'Then tell Mr Gilvry…if you wouldn't mind?'

The soft menace in the quiet voice sent a shiver down

Drew's back. There was more steel in that pleasant request than in any threat he'd ever heard. Perhaps he was
mistaken in thinking him a dandy after all.

'I was to bring yon laddie—' he nodded at Drew
'—to Edinburgh and put him in irons on a ship bound
for Botany Bay.' He grinned at Drew with an echo of his
old defiance. 'It leaves the day after tomorrow. There's
still time.'

Drew bared his teeth at him. 'No, thanks.'

Sanford shook his head wearily and Morris hunched
his shoulders.

'At whose request?' Sanford asked.

Morris snuffled. 'I wasn't supposed to know that, ye
ken, but McKenzie was taking his orders from a lord.'
He glowered at Sanford. 'A proper Scottish lord.'

Or did he mean laird? Drew glanced at Ian, who was
leaning forward. 'Do you have a name for us?'

'Carrick.'

A collective sigh rippled around the room. His brothers and their wives looked at each other in shock.

'Never,' Drew said. 'That is rubbish. Carrick has no
reason to do away wi' me.' He turned back to his brother.
'Do you know what he said? Your man, right before he
pulled the trigger? No! Well, you should then. You'd
like it, Ian. He said I have a message for you from your
brother.'

'It wasna' my message,' Ian said.

'Drew,' Rowena said. 'He swore to me—'

Drew gave Rowena a hard stare. 'And you believed
him over me?'

She stiffened against his assault. 'This is the first I

have heard about Carrick. But—' she looked at Morris '—was he visiting Mere Castle when we were there?'

Morris nodded. 'It was him who set us on when the laddie left the house.'

'I remember now,' she said, her voice rising as if she was terrified. 'The man I overheard. He said he'd failed to do away with you once, but this time he would personally make sure of it.'

'And it was Carrick who was in deep conversation with Jack O'Banyon before he tried to kill me,' Logan said bitterly, shaking his head, 'just this past summer. Or so Growler thinks.'

'And it was Carrick's steward who tried to kill Selina,' Ian said with deceptive softness.

'It makes no sense,' Drew said, staring at each one in turn. 'He is chief of our clan. He's sworn to protect us.'

'I know,' Ian said. 'I'm having trouble believing it myself.'

'Who shot you, Drew?' Niall asked.

'The men I was travelling with to Boston.'

'Men sent by Carrick, no doubt,' Logan said with a sound of disgust.

Drew frowned. 'I met up with them at the inn near the docks. I had a room there waiting.'

'A room booked by Carrick.'

'Gordon,' Logan said. 'Remember, he said he heard Carrick's men laughing about losing Drew while out hunting? It has to be Carrick.'

'Damn it all,' Niall said. 'He's cousin to my wife. I would never have believed it if I had not heard it with my own ears.'

Drew's head was spinning. He felt sick. He felt the way he had that time he tumbled over the bank and into the river. Dark water closing over his head. The roar of white water. Drowning. He put a hand to his temple and took a deep breath.

'Drew?' Rowena said.

He brushed her concern aside and looked at Ian, tried to hold on to his anger, but found it slipping away. 'Why?' he said hoarsely. Then he knew. 'The land. He wants the land. But it was the Lady Selina's.'

She nodded. 'Yes. And I was to marry one of his kin. Perhaps he was worried you would seduce me next.'

He winced. 'I would ha', if the thought had come to me.'

Ian shifted, his hands balling into fists.

Drew held up a hand. 'A jest.'

Ian relaxed, somewhat. 'A bad one.'

'Aye.' Drew huffed out a breath. 'I was just trying to help, ye ken.' He looked at Rowena's tight expression. 'We were in trouble. I thought an heiress was the answer.'

'Do you think I don't know that, Drew?' Ian said. 'But it was Carrick who advised me to send you off to America. To let the scandal die down. He kindly offered work. I thought it might help the clan down the road if we had someone over there. I feared we might all have to go. It was getting harder and harder to sustain our people.'

He'd known that. He'd wanted to help his brother. And what he'd done to Alice had been inexcusable. He'd seen it as soon as he'd seen the pain he'd caused. He closed his eyes. 'Carrick,' he murmured. He opened his eyes to meet Ian's straightforward gaze. 'I should ha' known you would never—'

'Yes,' Ian said. 'You should have.' He nodded at Morris. 'Take him away.'

Sanford poked his head out of the door and in short order his two henchmen were back for their prisoner.

Morris gave a look of appeal at Drew.

'He's no' such a bad man for a smuggler,' Drew said.

Logan cracked a laugh. 'Want to join the Gilvrys?' he offered.

Morris nodded his head vigorously.

'You can talk about that later,' Sanford said. 'I have need of more information from you, my lad, and if you want to join Logan there, you'll tell me everything.'

Morris groaned and shuffled out with his gaolers, followed by the sauntering Lord Sanford, who departed after making an exquisite bow.

'That's it, then,' Niall said, when the door closed behind Sanford and his odd little crew. He gave Drew a sharp look. 'We are all agreed. Carrick is the man behind all of our troubles.'

Everyone nodded agreement with sombre faces.

And Drew found himself nodding, too.

And the anger inside him was gone in the same instant. The rage. The hatred that had sustained him for a great many months dissipated. And he couldn't summon the same measure of feeling against Carrick.

The knowledge left nothing but an empty shell.

He had no purpose. No reason to stay. Not when they all knew how low he had sunk. 'I'll be on my way, then.'

* * *

Drew looked Rowena's way, though he did not meet her eyes. He bowed. 'It has been a pleasure, your Grace.'

Rowena's heart sank at his wooden expression. She desperately wanted to ask him to stay, but this was the first time he'd glanced her way in the past fifteen minutes. He probably hated her blatant defiance and for taking sides with his brothers. Even if it was for his sake.

And when she'd told him she loved him, he'd stared at her as if she was mad. Well, telling him had been a bit of a forlorn hope. She hadn't really expected that what was between them was more than bedsport. But she had thought he cared a little.

Apparently not, if he was leaving. When he picked up his scarf and hat and turned towards the door, in her trembling sad little heart, she found just enough courage to risk another rejection. She opened her mouth to speak.

'Wait, Drew,' Niall said. 'Where are you going?'

Drew looked at him. 'It's over. I was wrong. I have no reason to stay.'

'But we haven't yet solved the problem of Mrs Mac-Donald's claim. You haven't heard what Carstairs told me. If the courts accept your testimony, she'll not only be dowager duchess, she'll be guardian to the new duke. He's six, poor little lad, and in charge of his grand-mother, Lady Cragg.' He grimaced. 'A good friend of Carrick's, so I'm told. Carstairs thinks your oath before a judge might well be accepted with the proper character witnesses. Certainly Lady Cragg's involvement in plotting Drew's deportation with Carrick will work against her claim to keep her guardianship.'

Drew frowned. 'What the devil are you talking about? You don't need me to swear to anything. I gave Mrs MacDonald irrefutable proof that her husband was still alive on September fifteenth. Nothing more is needed. You don't need to parade me in front of a judge like some sort of freak.'

Rowena winced at the anger and the lacerated pride in his voice.

She shook her head when he gave her a look askance. 'I didn't give them the....the proof.'

How could she? What Samuel had described was horrible. A man chained naked like a cur and fed from some old woman's hand like a wild pet. Samuel said he only knew the creature was white by his tangled gold-coloured hair and matted beard. And when Sam had looked closer, he'd seen a face horribly scarred.

The Indians had said their yellow dog brought them luck. Even his own guide had warned against noticing, let alone protesting, his treatment, because he feared this particular band would not take kindly to any inter-ference with their prisoner.

Samuel, ever a coward, had decided the prisoner, who had turned his back to them, seemed quite content and had parted company with the Indians after an exchange of whisky for gold and a description of where it had been found. All Samuel had been thinking of was gold in the hills of North Carolina and convincing the duke to fund another expedition.

The moment she read those few words from Sep-tember thirteenth, she'd known why Drew had held the journal back. And she didn't blame him. She could only wish he had trusted her enough to tell her. No one would ever see the journal.

'It was very kind of you, *mo cridhe*,' she said softly. 'But I don't care about the money. I care—'

Drew's face had grown more and more thunderous as she spoke, the scarred side of his face becoming more and more devilish looking. 'Give them the journal.'

'You can't possibly want me to,' she pleaded.

In one stride he was standing before her, towering in his anger. 'Will you no' let me have a shred of my pride, then? If I had not escaped and led those savages to your husband, he'd still be alive and you'd be a duchess now. Am I to have not even a morsel of redemption from my guilt?'

'What the deuce are you talking about?' Ian asked. 'What journal?'

Drew kept his gaze fixed on her face. 'Her husband's journal. He wrote in it every day. Including the day he died. Where is it?'

Instinctively, she clutched her reticule tight to her chest. 'You can't have it. You gave it to me. It is my decision.'

He wrenched the reticule from her hands, tore open the strings and pulled it out. 'This shows the last date that Samuel MacDonald wrote in his diary. Two days after Mere inhaled his last breath.' He handed it to Niall. 'There's your damned proof.'

He was so angry, he had lost all vestiges of civility.

'Easy, man,' Ian said.

'Easy? I'm not some dog to be soothed with soft words, damn you.'

Rowena backed away as everyone started shouting at everyone else. She nipped the little book from Niall's hand, the way she had nipped illicit material from more than one pupil in her recent past, and with two quick steps tossed it into the flames.

Not quick enough. Drew had seen what she was about. He lunged for it, pulling it clear of the flames. His sleeve began to smoke. Logan whipped off his coat and swatted at the smouldering cuff. The smell of singeing wool filled the air.

They were all breathing hard.

Ian held up a hand. 'It seems to me that you two need to sort out whatever it is between you.' He took the journal. 'I don't know what is in here, but if it is as bad as Mrs—I mean, her Grace seems to think, then you both must agree, before anyone reads it.'

Drew gave a snort of disgust. 'When did you start putting words before action?'

A small smile softened the laird's hard mouth. 'When I got married. I have the wee book, Drew. I'll keep it safe in my pocket and you'll tell me when you come to a decision. Come on, everyone. Out.'

Another man who liked to dish out orders. But she felt nothing. No shiver. No pleasure. Not even a whisper of a fantasy.

Even so, there was power behind the words, and the room cleared quickly.

Drew stood in the middle of the room, glowering like a fiend. 'There is nothing you can do to change my mind,' he said the moment the door closed and they were left alone.

'I love you,' she said, throwing caution and pride to the wind.

He groaned. 'And I love you too well to saddle you with a man who is little more than an animal. You know now what I was. I would see it in your eyes every day. And I canna bear it.'

She gave a short bitter laugh. 'If you loved me, you'd want to do everything you could to stay. So we could be together.'

He muttered something under his breath.

She raised a schoolteacher brow.

He just stared back at her, immobile, immovable, his eyes full of pain. Pride. It wasn't going to let them be together. And how could she ask him to forgo his pride? It was who he was. It must have been what had kept him alive under the most cruel of conditions. That and his need for revenge. And she'd been the instrument in taking both from him.

There really was nothing more to say. Tears forced their way into her throat and she did her best to swallow them.

'I am such a fool, aren't I?' she said, scrabbling in her reticule for her handkerchief. 'I thought I had actually found a man who would be so much more than my fantasies. A man who would actually understand these strange thoughts in my head.' She tried to laugh, and it sounded pathetic and broken. 'You were just being kind. Pandering to my nonsense. How ridiculous you must have thought me, a dried-up, ageing governess with such dreams.'

'Rowena, no.' He stepped towards her and the heartbreak in his voice gave her leave to hope. A small hope, still lingering. But she was going to have her say, now she had started.

She waved him back with her handkerchief. 'It's kind of you to pretend that you care. I shall always remember your kindness.' She hiccuped. 'Among other things. Please, don't let me keep you from your plans.'

'Dammit, woman. I don't have any plans.'

'Then you must make some, I suppose. But, Drew, I will not have the contents of that journal bandied about. I just won't, and I believe your brothers will agree with me on that score. It would be an unpardonable crime against a man who has suffered as you have. No amount of money in the world would ever change my mind.'

'So you will go back to the drudgery of the school-room, no matter what I say,' he said.

'Yes. Now go, before you have me in tears again.' She turned her back. If he was going to leave, she did not want to watch. It would be like stepping on a heart that was already broken.

Warm hands grasped her shoulders. 'Rowena,' he said. 'Beloved. Lord, how I love you. Please, I can't bear to see you cry over me.'

She sniffed. 'I'm not.'

He spun her about to face him, his strength far too much for her to attempt to resist. She gazed up at his face and cupped the ruined flesh of his cheek. 'Oh, Drew, how can I live without you?'

'My dear little love.'

He drew her close and kissed her with ruthlessness and passion. It was just as magical as it had been that very first time. Perhaps more so because they knew each other so much better that they fit together like two halves of a whole.

When they finally came up for breath, he gave her an unsteady smile. 'I see how it is, ma'am. While you may be a gentle modest maid who will obey my every wish in the bedroom, in daylight you are nothing but a demanding witch of a woman.'

'Yes,' she said, smiling.

'Oh, saints in heaven preserve me,' he said and kissed her again.

Epilogue

At Dunross Keep

The family had gathered to welcome Drew and Rowena home from their delayed honeymoon on the Isle of Skye. It had taken weeks to sort things out in the courts without the journal for evidence. It was almost midnight and Drew sat beside Rowena on one side of the hearth, listening to Lady Selina playing the piano.

One of the nurses brought the children for their goodnight courtesies. Ian's daughter and Niall's little boy. Such lovely children. And with them the dark-haired, serious-eyed, six-year-old Duke of Mere, who had been thrilled to leave his grandmama to visit with his new guardians and meet the children of their family.

Mrs Gilvry, Drew's mother, followed them across the flagstones, leaning heavily on her stick.

Drew leaped to his feet. 'Ma.' He kissed her hands.

His mother patted his arm as if she still couldn't believe he had returned to her. 'I'm awa' to my bed.

It's been lovely welcoming you and your bride home, dearest boy.'

Rowena got up and kissed her cheek. 'Can I help you upstairs?'

'No, lass. Enjoy the music. Ian will see me up.'

Rowena had heard how her mother-in-law had blamed Ian for her second son's death. But now that Drew had returned all was forgiven. Frail, but indomitable, she had even forgiven the laird his *Sassenach* wife, as she had much more quickly forgiven Logan for the same transgression. The old lady started down the length of the room. Ian met her before she had taken more than a few steps and with her hand on his strong right arm, he escorted her to the stairs at the end of the vast chamber.

Happy to watch the other couples who were now dancing a waltz, she and Drew returned to their seats.

Drew gazed down at her and she could only marvel at the love in his eyes. Hidden in the folds of her skirts, he threaded his fingers through hers. His brothers were still teasing him about how besotted he was and it was taking him time to become used to their careless jesting.

'Happy, *mo cridhe*?' he asked in a low murmur.

'I have never been so happy in my life.'

'No' too tired? You dinna have to wait up, you ken.'

His concern stemmed from the news the doctor had given her a week ago. She was expecting a happy event at the end of the summer. 'I'm not the least bit tired.' She gave him a haughty look. 'I'm not an invalid.'

He looked at her belly, though there was little to see. 'The doctor said lots of rest.'

'I'll rest when I'm tired.'

He gave her a look that said she'd pay in delicious punishment for that remark and she laughed.

A stir at the door brought his head up.

'Who is it?' she asked. 'Surely we are not expecting more company?'

'A messenger in the Duke of Gordon's livery.'

'Your brother never ceases to surprise me with his friends in high places,' she whispered in his ear.

'It is probably about Carrick,' he said grimly. 'Gordon has insisted he step down as clan chief and retire to the Hebrides where he can cause no more trouble. His oldest son will make a grand chieftain.'

When faced with his crimes, Lord Carrick had confessed the whole to the duke. He had seen the Gilvrys as an impediment to protecting his family and gaining all the land he wanted for his sheep. His first act in his plan had been to rid the family of Drew, who he knew to be Ian's right-hand man. And once he had started down his path of destruction, he'd had no choice but to continue.

But the stir around the door seemed to contain more excitement than such old news would engender. The babble around at that end of the room grew louder.

'Quiet,' Ian said, pushing through into the middle of the room, waving a letter.

Drew helped Rowena to her feet. Not that she wasn't perfectly capable of rising unassisted, but she adored his tender solicitation. Each little thing he did for her made her heart tumble over with a love that grew stronger day by day.

'What is it, man?' Drew said, his voice louder than anyone's. 'Have they put yon Carrick in the Tower?'

Ian's face when he turned to look at his brother held triumph.

'Better than that,' Niall said, striding to stand beside Ian.

'He's done it,' Ian said. 'Gordon has convinced Parliament to pass a new Excise Act. We will soon be a legal business.'

Selina left the pianoforte and came and planted a kiss on his cheek. 'Well done. You have been working very hard to convince the poor man to speak out.'

'Ah,' Ian said. 'It is not entirely for our sakes. I believe he has more than a couple of illegal stills operating on his land.'

'No more smuggling,' Logan said, looking comically dismayed.

Charity wagged a finger. 'You are sure to find some new adventure.'

Ian looked at his brother. 'Dinna worry, I've plenty for you to be doing.' He looked down at the note in his hand. 'There's a postscript from Sanford. He said Gordon's speech was a work of art and it carried the lords along with him.'

'I expect Sanford wrote the speech,' Logan quipped, to much laughter.

'Well, I for one am glad my family is about to become legal,' Niall said with a saintly expression and a twinkle in his eye. 'I have judicial ambitions, you know.'

His brothers drowned him with jeers and cheers.

Rowena looked up at Drew. He was watching his brothers with an extraordinarily fond expression. He had missed them and was only slowly coming to realise he was with them again.

'So it's over,' she said softly.

He looked down at her with his devilish smile. 'No, my little beauty, it's just the beginning.'

* * * * *